THE MAROUF QUARTER

Hakeem's hash den was particularly well situated relative to all the other dens in the Marouf Quarter, which is just behind Talat Harb (formerly, Suliman Pasha) Street. The main drag in the neighborhood, Marouf Street, runs parallel to Talat Harb, beginning at Tahrir Square and cutting across Antikkhana Street—now Mahmud Bassiouni—where the Library and Museum of Modern Art used to be. Back when we were the masters of our own time, we used to spend countless hours in the library and museum, listening to music, reading expensive books, and admiring the paintings. Marouf Street ends where 26th of July and Tharwat streets meet, in front of the High Court building, which looks out onto 26th of July and Ramses streets. There are a few similarly styled buildings attached to its solemn edifice: the Judges' Club and the Lawyers' Syndicate, which look out over Tharwat Street toward the Church of the Sacred Heart and the Railway Hospital on the other side. Marouf Street and Talat Harb Street are completely different though they're only a few steps apart. Taking a shortcut or two, we could get from Café Riche in Talat Harb Square—where intellectuals, celebrities, and the cream of the tourist crop hung out—to the clump of hash dens in Marouf in less than three minutes, but we'd arrive feeling as if we'd been magically transported to another life in another

1

city inhabited by another people. The entire length of the street was packed full of countless people and objects: donkey- and horse-carts; handcarts; vegetables, fruit, and fish for sale; plastic and aluminum tableware in all shapes and sizes spread over blankets on the ground, to say nothing of the knickknacks, the refrigerators stocked with soft drinks, and the stores all alongside: grocers', fuul and falafel stands, kushari stands, auto parts stores, bike shops, spray-painting, mechanics', and electricians' workshops, and coffeehouses. And on top of all that, little bits from all of the above being carried around in roving vendors' display cases. To say nothing of the tiny corner stores where they fixed locks and car doors and primus stoves, and where you could find cobblers who were pros at fixing worn-out shoes and getting them to shine again. These stores all had scores of customers who came by car and on foot and the most amazing thing was that they actually managed to squeeze their cars into whatever empty spots they could find, calmly parking amid a storm of noise and shouting, and the kind of relentless honking that could drive you mad. And yet, because Egyptians are so generous—and because of that alone—everything had to be allowed to reach its destination. Cars passed through the eye of a needle but no headlights were smashed, no fenders dented, no merchandise upset, no pedestrians injured. The traffic only ever stopped for a second or two before starting up again. If for some reason there were a backup, several passersby would take it upon themselves to start directing traffic and others would push a stalled car out of the way; even the mechanic might haul himself down to the car when called for. And then there were all the people who came to shop for vegetables, fruit, meat, fish, and bread: most of the customers were women of various social classes armed with baskets and palm-leaf bags. Some of them were housewives who looked like foreigners—or else even blonder, paler versions of foreigners—while some others were scrawny, dimwitted, fish-out-of-water maids who never stopped jabbering. Still others came barefoot and dressed in black on black from who knows where to sit out in the street and sell white cheese, butter, mish cheese, and pigeon chicks out of huge pans. Everyone who lived downtown came to do their shopping on that market street, which buzzed all day and all night and made anyone caught up in its throng feel like it was the earth itself that was moving. Yet all the same, the street was a fun place to hang out day or night. Life there was also as cheap as could be: instead of costing you the equivalent of a humble government clerk's monthly salary like a meal on Talat Harb Street would, on Marouf Street you could stuff your belly for two piasters. For one piaster, you could probably even get a sandwich stuffed with fuul, falafel, and fixin's, or a chunk of delicious and filling roast sweet potato. You could sit at one of the street's many coffeehouses or snack bars and have a cup of tea with milk and smoke a water pipe for just two and a half piasters. As an added bonus, your eyes could delight in the sight of a stupendous crowd of women of all different ages, shapes, and colors; it was as if every house in the city had dumped its fair ladies out onto the street. They were dressed in simple house-clothes that showed off all their curves, especially those parts that were supposed to be covered up. The women walked along naturally, without any cares, without even the slightest sense that they were being ogled, as freely as if they were walking around in their own homes. Their chests spilled over the cages, their breasts mingling with the pigeons and rabbits lying there with appallingly calm resignation; their cheeks blending in with the pomegranates and apples and peaches; their armpits, white and flushed and depilated, with legs of lamb and veal hanging from large hooks. Nile perch, whitefish, and catfish shuddered in the air above fishmongers' baskets at the touch of lady-Nile perches. Nights on Marouf Street had their own special magic. Traffic would die down after sunset and the muddy street would be washed down, foul water flowing between the revolting pavement tiles. The air would fill with a heavy stench, like the smell of all the sweat that had fallen to the ground that day, and then be freshened by the smell of meat grilling over coals and of liver and brain being fried up in pans on clean, white pushcarts decorated with colorful glass and lights. The clamoring, fragrant fruits on display looked like a grandstand of flowers, a festival of natural colors. The sound of bottles of beer and soft drinks being opened grew louder; as did the sound of pieces slamming down onto backgammon boards and tongs clanging on marble countertops in coffeehouses. Umm Kulthum's voice rose up out of the radio and spread in every direction, only to echo back from every corner of the street. Life there seemed as easy, as calm, as pleasant, as perfectly gratifying as could be. The screeching neon lights created a canopy of happy serenity that gave infinite space to imaginations intoxicated by philanthropic emotions that felt moist and green and warm all at once; especially when you were just stepping out of one of the hash dens hidden in the depths of that great big carnival.

CLEAR PATH

There were several ways to get to Hakeem's den. You could get there from Ramses Street, in which case you'd have to pass by Galal's den. This was actually mildly embarrassing because Galal competed with our favorite den, which was no more than a coffeehouse built of wood and reeds in the middle of a large bank of ruins. All the houses around it—down Marouf Street and Ramses Street—were, according to official government records, at risk of collapse. Their expected lifespan had run out more than half a century ago and many stern orders to evacuate the buildings had been handed down; yet despite their age, they had maintained the charm of their inventive design. Each house was a priceless architectural treasure, but they'd ended up looking like big-shots who'd seen better days and were reduced to trying—albeit in vain—to get some bastard somewhere to take pity on them. The residents hadn't been able to find anywhere else to live so they just stayed put, accepting responsibility for themselves, and, as far as the government records were concerned, the houses were simply condemned and abandoned. This, despite the fact that everyone could see that the houses occasionally collapsed, crushing the people inside. Even so, new residents would come and take over the ruins, salvaging the iron and wood, and building shacks,

4

shops, hash dens, and workshops for spray-painting, locksmithing, and metal-working in the clearing. Boss Galal, who ran the most famous hash den downtown—if not in the entire city including the suburbs—was the man whose lead they followed. And follow they did because Egyptians have a peculiar fondness for thuggish crooks, and many derive great pleasure from doing what they say and submitting to them. Maybe even going so far as to try to outdo one another in vying for their affection; maybe they do it to get on their good side, or maybe so they can count on their backing when something comes up. Boss Galal was the most famous safebreaker in Egypt. Paroled from a life sentence, he was ready to gut any police officer who tried to get in his way, or keep him from earning a living, or who simply irritated him. The police were all scared of him so they just let him have his hash den, figuring that was better than him gutting anyone or cracking any safes. His hash den was really nice: it was clean and orderly and it felt like a coffeehouse with its proliferation of chairs and colored tablecloth-covered tables lined up in rows in and around the large shack, which was as big as a soccer pitch. There was a counter made of marble and tile that was fitted out with all the nicest cups, kettles, copper trays, ashtrays, and water pipes used exclusively for smoking molasses-steeped tobacco, in addition to the coconut bongs used just for smoking hash. The boys who worked there were relatively clean and genial looking, but having a powerful and influential boss had made them rude and arrogant. They'd raise the price of each bowl from half a piaster to a piaster, which was double the price of other dens, and the price of a tea to two piasters, in order—so they claimed—to preserve a certain level of clientele and keep the lowlifes out. The Boss, owing to his tact and the experience of a commuted life sentence, had succeeded in attracting a select group of customers. Only the most respectable types, the most prone to looking stylish and showing off, showed up: journalists, artists, public-sector grandees, business men, and the sons of wealthy Revolutionary Officers, who'd taken the place of the pashas' sons, and who liked to tip excessively from a supply of unknown provenance. This got them the best service, and that set them apart from everybody else. The rest of us had to wait for the boys to serve the beys, who liked to take their time. If you had a problem with it, well—pardon the expression— but don't let the door hit you on the way out. A lot of serious hash smokers, including our circle of friends, avoided Galal's den even if they were friends of his. They were bound to get the best service if they went to smoke when Galal was there, but during the day when he was fast asleep, they were captive to the whims of the malicious little bastards whose attention could only be got with money. The way our group saw it was that getting high in a common coffeehouse—or somewhere like a common coffeehouse—took half the fun out of it. It took longer for you to get to the stage of being properly stoned because the crowd made the smoking a lot slower. The bowls would come ten at a time no matter how big the group, so each person would only get one bowl to smoke each round and by the time the next ten came and the water in the bong had been changed, and the coals broken up into smaller pieces because the last round's rips were so weak, your high would've already worn off. But then if someone dared to tell the boy to hurry up or order another bowl, he'd be told off: patience is a virtue, and God helps those who wait, and the world hasn't flown away yet and it isn't going to, and there's a silver lining in every delay, and on down the list of ever-ready, infuriating platitudes. The staff were all a bunch of no-good, disrespectful thugs. Plus, they always had the radio turned up as loud as possible and there was no hope of getting it turned down because everyone had the right to listen. At the same time, everyone had the right to talk, but with the radio at full blast, everyone had to shout. The racket alone guaranteed that you'd end up coughing away the deepest hits and get a headache no matter how good the hash was. It was all in Boss Galal's interest, of course: you could never get stoned so you'd just go on smoking and smoking. Serious hash smokers like us preferred to smoke in a no-frills hash den that was nothing like a coffeehouse, where even if they did serve tea and coffee, it was a service on the side—one that could be canceled at any moment for any reason. The closer the den came to being like a cave or a crypt or a burrow, the better the high, the more tickled the imagination. It doubled a hash smoker's enjoyment to be sitting there—wherever he was—doing nothing but smoking hash, hemmed in by a lot of stimulating limitations. No-frills hash dens, like bars, didn't try to do anything else. As soon as the customer sat down, he'd get one set of bowls after another with a steady frequency that didn't waste a minute. The workers all had specific tasks: there was one to clean out the bowls, one to pack them with tobacco, one to stoke the coals and break them up, one to change the water in the coconut bongs, and one—or more—to serve the customers.

These guys would kneel down on the floor in front of the customers, holding the bong in one hand and pushing coals down on top of the bowl with the other to make sure the hits were strong. Because they depended on tips, they were the lowest paid of all.

DOWN PAST ALI MANGO'S

Off Antikkhana Street, there was another way to Hakeem's den, but there was embarrassment to be had in that direction as well. Boss Ali Mango had a small store on the corner where he sold cigarettes, packaged sweets, and soft drinks, but it was all a front for his real business: dealing hashish and opium. Boss Ali Mango was a clever guy, but opium had made him thin, and a succession of jails had chewed him up. He was famous across every far-flung neighborhood in Cairo for being hyper-thorough when it came to his superb product. His specialty was a top-grade hash called Blue Powder. He always stuck to the same variety and only ever did business with the same grower in Lebanon. He was constantly inspecting each crumb he sold, too, even when the customer was in a hurry and didn't really care. The problem with Ali Mango was that he'd suck your blood and pretend he was doing you a favor. He was—of course—insistent, crusty, and transparent, but he was also as smooth and as poisonous as a desert snake. He was so frail and his wormwood-colored face so lacking in lifeblood that you almost couldn't see him. He had thick lips, rotting teeth, and a chronically dry throat from the fat, unfiltered Wings cigarettes that never left his lips. He had hawk eyes, too, and was always alert. Buried behind a glass counter adorned with jars of toffees, caramels, fondant bonbons, mints, gum, lollipops, firecrackers, and balloons, he'd spy one of us walking past on the sidewalk across the street and reel us in with a somber and peremptory wave of his veiny arm and a smile like a crushed tomato that still managed to brim with hospitality, decency, generosity, and glittering promise as though he were about to give you good news or an expensive present. His smile would win you over, like a hook snagging you by the neck so that if you ever did try to get away, it'd hurt and you'd give up. You'd have to say hello to him, Brother! (which was what he'd undoubtedly say to you) for no reason other than to be polite; that was the lie you'd tell yourself anyway. "So I guess we only know each other when there's business to do, huh?' he'd ask. "Aren't we supposed to be men, fella?" As soon as he saw you heading toward him, he'd get up, leaning on his crutch, and dart through the gap in the counter toward the red refrigerator that stood beside the cigarette display case outside the shop. Ignoring your protests that a treat was wholly unnecessary, he'd open it and move a slab of ice out of the way. Feeling to see which of the bottles were cold, he'd pull out the coldest one. In the blink of an eye, *chikk* . . . "Here you go, Bey. Drink up"—and as you took the bottle, he'd always add, "Drink up to cool down! Ha! It's as hot as fire today! May God protect us from the flames of hell." As you began to sip from the icy bottle, he'd rub his long fingers against the back of his ear and, in less than a moment, stretch his hand out toward you. On his thumb, there'd be a lick of opium smelling pungently of a freshness that was both alluring and harrowing, like the freshness of sin.

"Give me your mouth and take this kiss," he'd say.

The rumor among novice opium addicts was that soft drinks ruined the effect of opium, and Boss Ali Mango was always joking about how gullible they were: "God bless the Prophet! What are they on about? There's nothing that can spoil honest-to-goodness opium, not even lemons!" You'd continue standing there in spite of yourself and try to think of a way out. Veterans like us would advise you—heads up, indeed!—that the longer you stood there, the more screwed you were because next he was going to offer you a joint: "This hash is brand new. You can't even buy it yet. May God bless you and help you get your hands on some! I wouldn't put it past Him." Working on advice you'd been given, you'd ask him—grudgingly, no doubt—for a quarter qirsh, or maybe even an eighth. You'd apologize for the paltriness of the order, saying something about straitened circumstances right now, and you were bound to add that you didn't like buying on credit and didn't believe in borrowing, not a piaster. You had to be extra careful not to sound wishy-washy or tentative when you said it because he'd do his best to confuse you with encouragement: "Don't worry about the money. Since when is money the only goddamn thing that matters? We only know each other because of money? What's up, fella? How much do you want?" He was certain his loan would be repaid because you had no choice but to smoke the hash in one of the dens in Marouf, right under his nose, right in the Mayor of Marouf's backyard as it were. Boss Ali Mango had all the hash dens under his thumb and he could get at them any time he felt like it. There was nothing to stop him popping up when you least expected, like a heart attack. Being forced to pay up, or else being humiliated, was as insupportable as it was insulting. If you ever did get made a fool of in a hash den, even just once—and especially if it were over money—you'd never ever be able to get your honor back, no matter how much money you spent. The real problem was that Ali Mango would sell you a quarter qirsh for forty piasters—cheap as can be—but at the same time, his ex-wife Umm Yahya would sell it for only twenty-five. And it was the same hash, maybe even a lot better. Umm Yahya was very generous, too: her hash looked reassuringly plentiful and made you feel like what you were getting really was a quarter qirsh with a little extra thrown in to be nice; you could easily get ten bowls out of it. But he—God help us—had a toxic touch and was always taking a little off the top of the quarter qirsh till it ended up the size of a shriveled old fava bean, which he'd wrap in a quarter-sheet of cellophane in such a way that it was impossible to open up, unless you did it slowly after you'd left, but by then there'd be no point in complaining or throwing a fit. All you could do was get angry about what'd happened, so the best thing was to appreciate the wisdom of those who say, "Don't push your luck and leave it in God's hands." And so, walking past Boss Ali Mango's stand was risky, awkward, and totally frowned upon.

UMM YAHYA'S ALLEY

There was a third way to get to Hakeem's den, around the back of the mosque off Marouf Street, down a narrow, twisting alley, crowded with groups of children sleeping naked on the ground, encircled by their own shit now infiltrated by armies of hoary old flies, lizards, beetles, and flying cockroaches. Women squatted in front of laundry basins and primus stoves heating up big cans full of water they'd fetched from a charity tap on the edge of Bulaq Abu al-Ila. Old women with their spreads of sweets: sesame-seeded halva, molasses sticks, and cotton candy all being swarmed by flies. Mangy strays licked at the bottoms of both children and plates and when they got hit by surprise smacks, barked and recoiled in pain, carrying their screams of agony with them a short distance away. A man and his children sat around a bowl of fuul midammis, scarfing down bread and spring onions. Another man who'd made his bed in the street, slept deeply, looking to all the world like a mummy escaped from the Egyptian Museum just a few steps away.

It took some practice and a certain acrobatic ability to navigate the alley, but even then you couldn't help but look—to a distant observer—as if you were dancing on ice or through a field of thorns as you made your way to Umm Yahya's house. Her vicious dog—son of a wolf—was always chained, very securely, to the door to warn Umm Yahya of the arrival of any strangers so that she could be ready for them. He was unlike any other dog: he never grew fond of anyone, not even customers who came by dozens of times a day. That dog always gave the customers a hard time. He was so awful that even when he saw an old customer he recognized, he'd just tuck his head between his shoulders and roar, glaring at the customer, looking ferocious and intimidating, ready to pounce at any moment. He'd go on roaring and growling until Umm Yahya yelled to silence him from the second-floor balcony, which was really no more than the remains of a protruding floor that had once been surrounded by a wooden screen behind which the women of the house would look out from.

Umm Yahya greeted the customers she knew with a smile and those two dimples in her full and fleshy cheeks. Her round red face shone beneath the hand-embroidered edging of her headscarf and her soft locks, which were mixed in with some gray. She was pretty with that round face of hers, which had retained its allure and spoke of a bygone beauty that—you could be sure—had once been captivating. With a steely assurance, she'd yank the rope beside her, undoing the latch on the gate to the street.

You had to walk backward through the gate because of that damned dog. There was a staircase directly in front of you; of course, you knew it perfectly well, but it still got your attention as though you were seeing it for the first time. The steps looked more like boxes or crates stacked up edge to edge. One, two, three landings and then you were up above the roof, overlooking emptiness on three sides, half the walls having collapsed to expand the vista. Umm Yahya would be waiting for you on the last landing, holding a heavy cloth bag tied up tightly with the ribbon threaded through it. You were supposed to hold the money out as soon as you got up the stairs and with a quick glance at the amount in your hand, she'd see how much you wanted, open up the bag, and pick out your order. In a split second, the bag disappeared into a magical vault somewhere in the rubble piled up around her. She'd stay there by the top of the stairs, bellowing at the dog, until she'd made sure you'd reached the bottom and then she'd lock the gate behind you and completely forget she'd ever had the pleasure of your visit.

A few steps past Umm Yahya's, you came to the Muarraq hash den and you had no choice but to walk past it. It was nothing more than a tiny, gloomy storefront, leaking damp and putridity, hordes of ants and flies, and rivers of spit and phlegm coughed up out of the chests of disgusting hash addicts, who laid swollen, suppurating sores down onto the black surface of the floor, and no one, it seemed, ever thought to paper them over with a little dirt. Your eyes couldn't help but be drawn instinctively toward Hakeem's den, which lay directly in front of you, with its sweet, familiar scent.

Nevertheless, going down that alley was also frowned upon unless you only went to buy hashish from Umm Yahya and then immediately turned around and went back the few meters you'd gone because if you carried on down the alley, you'd walk past some sluggish young slackers, their eyelids sore-ridden from too many late nights and too much crap hash, their bodies hollowed out beneath their patched, colorless, shapeless, unrecognizable clothing. Yet all the same, they were good guys, if unfortunate and unscrupulous. All you had to do was walk past them and one of them would stick to you, regardless of whether you'd even looked in his direction. Inevitably, he'd impose both his companionship and his services on you any way he could, not giving a damn about your objections or grumbling, nor even your revulsion. God save you from that kid Sooka, for example. He wasn't a professional den bum, or an out-and-out thug or anything, he was—and this was what really piqued your interest—a decent guy. You couldn't help but like him and feel that he simply was an all-right guy who wanted to do you a favor: what he meant by that, of course, was that he wanted to be the one to hold the bong for you because he knew how to smoke you out so well that two bowls from him would be a better blessing than a hundred at the hands of those thieving, no-good den boys, who didn't have their hearts in it: the coals weren't hot enough, they didn't clean the bongs well enough so the smoke didn't flow properly, and on top of that they wanted tips! Come on, already! Those guys are crooks, kind sir; trust me. The kid puts his whole mouth over the bowl before he puts the coal on—he says he's blowing the leftover smoke out of the bong, and you, no offense, think he's actually unclogging the bowl by blowing on it, but—the truth is, believe you me—that the bastard (and I mean every last one of them) sticks out his tongue—which they really ought to cut off!—and licks the hash right off of the tobacco and no one's the wiser. Then all he has to do is stick the coal on top of the bowl and you're just smoking plain old molasses tobacco. You get the wind knocked out of you from all that inhaling, but in the end you've got no divine high from on high to show for it! I mean you pay for that hash from the sweat of your brow and then this son of a whore goes and steals it and tricks you into smoking plain tobacco? You see, by accusing others of doing what he does himself, he reveals the secret of his own scam.

By the time you made it to the entrance to Hakeem's den at the end of the alley, you'd inevitably be surprised to find yourself being escorted by either one, two, or three guys walking alongside you as if they were your pals. They'd come into the den with you and sit down close by, running up their tab so much it almost put your fears at ease; they might even argue with one another about who was going to serve you. Most of the time the arguments were hostile, albeit suppressed through use of their shared secret code: it'd usually end quickly with the weakest soon withdrawing. But when they were equally matched, they had to hurry up and make one another understand with a practiced look so that without any violence or disagreement one of them would step forward and the others would remain close by, maintaining a slight distance— not out of respect for you, of course: this negligible separation allowed them to claim they weren't part of the party if the police should suddenly raid the den, and raids could happen at any moment. The guy who held the bong for you would simply shake the bowl out when you were done, which meant that he'd suck up the remaining smoke in the bong after you'd smoked your fill. This was the smoky soup—when the coal got mixed in with the hash and the scent had burned off and the oil had started to sizzle—and you simply couldn't hold it all in your chest. Although his lungs were totally fresh, the kid wouldn't be able to inhale the whole soup either because it was so thick and went on for so long; instead he'd just toke quickly and hand the rest to his two friends. He'd occasionally also give his friends—with sir's permission—a bowl for the two of them to kill.

You were bound to get annoyed at having them around because of their constant, painful mooching after no more than five minutes of having them sit across from you. From his seat behind the barrels of bowls in the far corner, Hakeem the streetwise den owner was the only person who could sense your annoyance even before it showed. He'd twist his mouth, tightening it two inches, he was so irate. The boys who worked at the den—the legit ones—would glare discomfortingly at you and them, ridiculing you for having been so gullible, so easily taken advantage of, and yet to get back at you for bringing these guys in the first place, they'd cheat you, too, if you asked them to serve you.

And so entering from this alley led only to aggravation and was an all-around buzzkill. The best thing was to get your hash from Umm Yahya and then turn around and head back toward Marouf Street to look for a better entrance.

THE OPEN APPROACH

So it seemed that the only safe way to get to Hakeem's den was through the exposed opening off of Champollion Street, but that wasn't completely gossip-free either. On the corner, there was a shop that sold brooms, brushes, and general cleaning supplies, whose owner only ever liked to sit in the airy entrance to the alley, smoking a water pipe in the company of a friend or two. His little soirees exercised a gravity, attracting passersby to join in and take a seat. The ever-changing faces of the party were made up of either people from the neighborhood or customers, and they were so curious it was intimidating: they scrutinized everyone who went into the alley as if they were sheep up for sale.

Beside this shop, there was a smaller shop that was once just a tiny empty space between the protruding supports of two attached buildings. It was reclaimed by a retiree called Hawda al-Masarawi, who used to work for the city. He boxed up the empty space and turned it into a neat little kiosk where he sold cigarettes and soft drinks; neither the buildings' tenants nor the owners minded. Hawda al-Masarawi's son was a famous lawyer and a member of the Central Committee of the Arab Socialist Union—a professional leftist.

Naturally, Mr. Helmi al-Masarawi, the lawyer and member of the Central Committee of the Arab Socialist Union, was very fond of the proletariat and he also had a great fondness for restrained political debate. His apartment was on Champollion Street right across from his father's shop so he used to hold his nightly gatherings of nocturnal creatures— journalists, artists, poets, politicos, veteran lawyers and trainees, new literati fresh from their far-off villages who'd come to experience the Cairo night— on the sidewalk, which, incidentally, boosted his father's business. They discussed politics—especially foreign affairs—and literary and artistic matters. They listened to the poets' poems and the literati's tales in an open-air pseudo-salon where anyone who sat down and put one leg over the other could come and vomit up everything he'd ever learned from books that'd stuck in his head, to utter profound judgments in grand words and with even grander enthusiasm, and, what was more, it didn't cost a thing!

Each day, the gathering attracted new and easily forgotten, anonymous faces disguised as poets, writers, critics, and literature lovers. The rumor was that they were informants sent by the government to root out the secrets of the people at the gathering and, at the same time, to examine everyone who went down the alley—especially the intellectuals, and even more especially those with names people actually knew—so they could file reports about them. Whether or not the rumors were true, the ugly searching looks of suspicion and superiority from those pretentious, if tragically dressed, loudmouths gave everyone who turned down the alley an icy chill. None of us gave a damn about them or anyone else anymore, though, because the whole intellectual community—according to firm, reliable rumors—was a nest of spies, everyone volunteering themselves for nothing in return. The climate had infected them all with a disease that compelled them to snoop eagerly and doggedly and gather information about other people and their secrets, not with a view to writing reports there and then for one of the concerned organs. No, it was so they could store up the information in their diseased minds for the time that everyone was anxiously awaiting: when you got wind of news—whether true or false—that the other guy had stabbed you in the back with a report, or an impolitic word in a private meeting, or some dirty trick at work. The intellectual community—no matter what the level—had become a battlefield of one-sided oral reports offered up by everyone against everyone else like a cold war: everyone tried to terrorize the other before he could terrorize him first. Little by little, backbiting and defamation became the norm and nobody was safe; there wasn't a single person in the whole country who everyone could agree was squeaky clean.

Everyone was already vilified in the eyes of everyone else—even when they were genuinely innocent—so we could all just get on with doing what we wanted to do without the slightest worry, saying, "Who gives a damn!" and going off to find our high, taking the alley that led us where we wanted to go. It was also true that the passage off Champollion Street was both the easiest and quickest way to get to Hakeem's cherished, magical, sleepless hash den.

THE DEN

The hash den was essentially an Upper Egyptian-style country house built out of mud brick over the rubble of an old city house that had been knocked down years ago, back when the government said it wouldn't be responsible for the residents because—according to a decision made by the revolutionary government shortly after taking power—the whole neighborhood was at risk of collapse. There were two adjacent rooms, one to the right of the front door, one to the left, divided by a wide corridor that carried on into the house, where, in a pool of sunlight that poured through the vent in the ceiling, a mud staircase appeared, at the top of which, like in all Upper Egyptian country houses, you could see the edges of piles of straw and firewood heaped on the roof, which was made up of doors, shelves, and old car roofs thrown here and there over thick wooden rafters and a few iron supports. Beneath the rise of the staircase, there was a large earthenware amphora on an iron stand, which looked more like a straight-beam balance; the ground beneath it was wet from the dripping water. Next to it were several two-handled jugs, large basins, and rusted pails. Troops of chickens, ducks, geese, and rabbits ran, squawking and whooping in a cheerful, clamorous symphony every time Hakeem's wife looked out of the solitary inner room where Hakeem and his family all slept.

The two rooms of the den were plastered with mud and straw and there were benches made of the same mud built in along the walls. There were some old chairs on wrecked legs whose seats had been fastened with tiny nails, like a prank, which conspired against the trousers of customers who tried to sit down. There were also some boxes and upturned pails for the boys to sit on while they served the customers. Both rooms had windows that looked out onto the annexed courtyard outside the house, but the windows were shut except for a small strip at the top that looked like a circle of crepe through which flowed air, light, dust, the snorting of grouchy vendors, and the coquetry of brazen women slinging insults at one another. It was also through these two small strips that the customers could throw their hashish out onto the street if they were caught unawares by a perfidious police raid, which was as constant a worry as death.

Some of the die-hard hash-heads found the room to the right of the entrance cozier because they didn't give a damn about anything except being able to smoke a lot of hash as quickly as possible. Their solution to the quandary of how you could get high under the police's nose and get away with it was to leave the scene of the crime early. You could see them smoking intensely, completely focused—I swear if they'd worked a quarter as hard as that at their jobs, they'd have been superstars—and because they each wanted to slam down thirty or forty bowls in half an hour max they made the den maddeningly hectic and that always made the boys grumble and prone to snap at one another. This was the room where the packed bowls and coal brazier were kept and where the boys would sit when there were no customers. It was where, if a customer were in a hurry, he could reach out and grab himself a bowl ready-packed with moist, fresh, molasses-steeped tobacco and there was no shame in getting up yourself to break some coal up in the ladle and wave it around to get it good and hot. You could just carry on tending to your own needs until one of the boys took notice, or if not them, then one of the locals who were always hanging around, waiting for a generous customer to lean over and hand them a bowl, or to let them serve them in exchange for getting to finish the bowl off.

The courtyard was more enchanting than the den itself, especially right before sunset and at night. The small passage in front of the entrance to the den was once a narrow alley like all the other alleys in the Marouf Quarter, but the house directly opposite the den had collapsed years ago. All that remained was the base of the rubble walls, which were about two meters high, but the bricks, cement, and gravel that had once made up the ceiling had piled up inside the square made by the four-meter long walls. Feet and dirty water chucked onto the rubble from every direction had turned the ruins into a muddy mess so the outlines of the house had come to look more like a lofty, squared-off hill. It was then reclaimed for the best purpose of all: it'd been made into a refreshing spare den for summer evenings. It gave the whole place this artsy feel, this magical down-home atmosphere with its scorching stink giving off a depravity in which it took the utmost pleasure; it instantly disarmed its enemies and it was too powerful for even the most polished of preening gentlemen to resist its charm.

Wicker chairs were set up on the hill at twilight as the sky was dyed blood-red and the blushing sun began covering its face with the corners of its veil and withdrawing quietly into the chamber of the moon. This was the climax of the evening for the guys who worked as bodyguards for upper-crust businessmen and big shots and their friends. They sat in the chairs on the hill to pass a quick evening's amusement before they returned to their shops and offices. To them, the sky, the atmosphere, the whole visible world was spray-painted in bright and cheerful colors. The chairs on the hill were occupied all night long: one group handed off to another only to return after midnight, or a little bit before, to take back their spot.

Our circle was made up of writers, poets, artists, journalists, and a few university students, and we preferred to sit outside below the windows of the den. To our left, we could see the Muarraq den and its customers and to our right, a breezy alley that ended in an outcrop of ruins, where someone had set up a paint-spraying workshop, only to be cursed superlatively, all night and all day, by stoners who couldn't smell their hash over the permeating reek of paint that stuck in their noses even after they'd gone home. The people who sat on the hill looked to us like actors on a stage—especially in the evening—and we were the audience whether we liked it or not. They, in turn, couldn't help but feel a bit like actors before an audience so they constantly chatted with us, teased and quarreled. Often we'd all get into a boisterous, happy groove, insulting one another over Ahli and Zamalek soccer matches.

The energy of the gathering cooled somewhat at sunset, flickered between sunset and evening prayers at the Sheikh Marouf mosque, and was momentarily extinguished after the evening prayer, only to blaze once more around ten at night when communication between the hill and the alley was smooth, active, and focused. No one in either camp went over the line because everyone could see everyone else, and excessive flattery between hill and alley increased. Packed bowls were handed down from the hill to the people sitting in the alley below the windows of the den and the same, but packed even more generously with hash, were passed back up from the alley to the hill. Late at night, though—the very last phase of night to be specific—the hill took on a guise of magic, mystery, and secrets. Sitting in the alley, we might not even realize that a group of our closest friends, who preferred quiet, steady rotation, and being apart, were sitting in a far corner on top of the hill, where in the pitch-dark you could only see specters of the seated; and though the coals in the ladle and on top of the bowls were like stars falling at our feet, we still couldn't make anything out, and in the dark, the cloud of thick smoke was an undulating gloom, and while it flowed and some of its darkness dissipated, it returned, growing even thicker.

THE BOSS

Hakeem, the owner of the hash den, was an Upper Egyptian from the Asyut countryside. He didn't like to give the name of his village in conversation unless it was absolutely necessary, or unless he got talking with people who he could sense were from near his hometown. Otherwise, he figured that the name of the province, Asyut, was more relevant as it was bigger, just as a family name signals membership in a larger group. He owned some fields on reclaimed alluvial land in his village on Awlad Ilyas Island. He'd had it for a very long time: first he'd squatted on it and then he'd undertaken to improve the land, widening and filling it in, and planting pomegranate, orange, tangerine, guava, and mango trees. In a corner of the field directly above the riverbank, he built a nice, brick, four-bedroom house with wrap-around balconies like a village elder's house. His mother, two little brothers, and three sisters nearly of marrying age lived there and tended to the trees and grew radishes, rocket, and tomatoes. Every summer, Hakeem went to stay with them for a month at most. He'd sell off the best of the harvest and set his sights on another piece of land. He'd negotiate patiently, calmly, using his ever-present supply of cash and his readiness to pay up-front against the owner like a weapon since it wasn't at all common among his neighbors who'd stayed right there where they'd always been. In Asyut in Upper Egypt, the money he made from the hash den in a year—during which he always wore the same, surprisingly ever-immaculate, gallabiya be it summer or winter—became farmland and weapons to add to the arsenal he'd need when, one day, the exile would return to his hometown an eminent and respectable landowner.

Hakeem closed the hash den while he was away so we'd go and peek our heads into various dens that held no attraction for us. We took refuge in dens we didn't even find relaxing and our consternation ended up putting us in twice as bad a mood. For a whole month, we'd try—each in his own way—to discover unknown dens in Bulaq Abu al-Ila or Zaynhum or Gayyara or even in Gamaliya, Darrasa, or Nabawiya: those were the indiscreet and dangerous quarters. Occasionally we'd come across new dens here and there that we thought were real finds, but then when we got together in those places, it simply wasn't the same. We felt like strangers wherever we went. See, if a hash smoker can't get comfortable in a place, can't make the kinds of friendships that are necessary to maintain his dignity and sense of self in that strange, stoned world where one bong is shared between a philosopher and a man in the street, an intellectual and a thug, a ministry official and an office boy, a bey and a shoeshiner, his spirit will inevitably sink and be crushed.

When Hakeem returned, we'd always throw a big party that went on till sunrise. He'd provide the molasses-tobacco and take part in our drink and high. Some of us really loved having a beer when we were getting stoned on hash so long as the beer was ice-cold just like how Hakeem chilled it in his big washbasin full of ice. To prove just what a badass he was, Hakeem liked to hold up a brimming glass crowned with a head of white froth, take a big hit from the bong, hold it in, and then placing his mouth on the brim of his beer, exhale through his nose as he drank with the pleasure of the perpetually thirsty.

He was tall and thin, but solid. He had wide, lean shoulders that were slightly bowed as though he were carrying something very heavy; what was most likely was that the pail of concrete he'd had to lug around when he worked as a laborer had left its mark on his shoulders and he probably always felt as if he were still carrying a pail full of cement and gravel around with him on his back. His face was round and flat, dark like whole-wheat bread, his cheeks stuck out around his wide mouth with its old crone's smile. It had probably frozen that way and then spread, his cheeks swelling around it as if his lips were bracketed by big parentheses. His eyes were narrow, but he had excellent vision. Countless sleepless nights had wounded his eyelids and plucked out his eyelashes and brows, but his eyes were ever deep and bottomless. They bespoke a certain naughtiness: a shade of universally recognized mischief, much shiftiness, a certain torpor in the nerves, and an unwholesome glimmer that came and went, revealing—even when it was there—that he was a snake in the grass, that he had some buried, mysterious, perplexing secret, that he could murder someone and attend their funeral, and this was made all the more compelling because he was so taciturn we almost forgot what his voice sounded like.

We loved him. We loved being with him; maybe it was because he was such a good guy, or maybe because of his long, reassuring silences that always, and suddenly, alerted us to the dangers of idle talk. We could never control ourselves in that relaxed, casual atmosphere, but we'd restrain ourselves after a long spate if only for a brief moment during which we could hear ourselves or Umm Kulthum singing on the radio, which had apparently been on for some time. But because Hakeem was so quiet he became the repository of all the group's secrets and those of all the other groups. Everyone discussed their most private issues with him without the slightest reticence and he never held back on advice and suggestions, or even assistance if they should need it. And when assistance reached the point of lending money, he was extremely patient when it came to asking to be repaid; all he'd say was, "Faith is the patience of Job." He might not ever have asked you for it, whether directly or indirectly. He believed you couldn't put a price on knowing people: any one of us could fall victim to bad luck or a crisis—even the government occasionally found itself having to beg from other countries or having to borrow money at high rates from the World Bank—it happens to the best of families and we're all the children of Adam and Eve. Full will always fill empty, but what really mattered was that you didn't get embarrassed and go to some other den to get high because that was the only thing that could hurt him: to have lost your business with his own money. That meant death and bankruptcy.

The group he considered his best friends—our group—was made up of around thirty people with similar dispositions and the same taste in hash and drinks. We had a professor, writer, poet, artist, actor, journalist, antique-shop owner, composer, street magician, singer, songwriter, theater director, manager of a firm that sold Egyptian products, accountant at the National Bank, novice lawyer, clerk in the public prosecutor's office, secretary at a government grocery co-op, and a chronic university student who was addicted to student union elections. We'd all gone to Hakeem's den solo at first, a few of us having fled dangerous, depressing, despicable dens, others of us debts we couldn't repay. A few others simply loved searching out ancient places in tumble-down worlds and a third group were always looking for the cheapest price, for well-oiled rotation, for heavy highs, for friendly den employees who could be trusted to go buy hash for them, and so on.

Thanks to Hakeem, we became an affectionate, amicable crew. If you came to the den when all the boys were busy, he'd pick—based on a snap judgment of your personality, which he'd had absolutely no experience of, and yet his evaluations were usually always spot on—a respectable customer who he thought was your equal; and even though neither one of you had ever seen the other, Hakeem would smile and put you at ease, graciously saying, "Please sit down here, sir, so the boy can serve you both without any interruptions." You'd get up, not feeling the slightest bit awkward, and he'd follow after you, carrying your tray of bowls. He'd introduce the two of you and because—ninety-nine percent of the time—he knew the other guy already, he'd present him to you with all due dignity. You'd then quickly introduce yourself.

"Hello."

"Nice to meet you."

And take your seat on the bench beside him. The server would swivel the stem of the bong back and forth between you, using one of the other man's bowls, then one of yours, and Hakeem would return to his post on the other side of the cobbled-together counter where the bowls were refilled, but he'd never take his eyes off the two of you. He wouldn't relax until he was certain that you'd become the best of friends. The other guy would offer you one of his bowls so you could try his hash—after all, he did value your opinion—and actually, his opinion of your hash mattered to you as well. Both of you had to reassure the other that the dealer hadn't ripped you off. A few minutes and a couple of tokes later, no one cared anymore whose bowls were whose. Both of you would race to top the bowls off with hash and fight over who got to cover your combined tab. A new relationship meant a new branch of the group and we were always working to keep things fresh for as long as possible. Hakeem's sincere and ebulliently positive estimation wasn't intended to make you look good in front of the other guy or to make him look good in front of you; he simply gave you each a nearly synonymous description of you and the other guy's best qualities. But you couldn't help but be surprised—or rather amazed— by his uncanny ability to put his finger on the essence of your personality and uncover qualities you might not have even realized you had. Inevitably you'd fall for his description of the other guy, as well, and begin to play up to the qualities he'd said you had. Through Hakeem, you'd come to like the other guy and he'd come to like you, and it was as if, to him, we were all his children—though he was younger than some of us—and all he wanted, with the purest intentions imaginable, was to raise us as best he could. He epitomized that remarkable Upper Egyptian genius for putting together a network of support, nurturing it, and strengthening its bonds. As an Upper Egyptian exile living in this vast capital city—which, for all its minarets, was ungodly to its core—he couldn't be certain about anything in life, especially since he'd chosen this dubious and dangerous career for himself, unless he could manage to turn his customers into friends, into a claque who could provide moral support and assistance if ever he should need it.

Whenever you showed up at the den on your own, Hakeem would put on a grave voice and tell you so-and-so was in here asking for you, that he was dying to talk to you. The thing was that the whole time we were sitting there, he'd never stop telling us—in brief snippets between long bouts of silence—a long list of things that you—as a friend—surely wanted to know: so-and-so's coming tonight at such-and-such a time; so-and-so wants you to come to his birthday party tomorrow night; so-and-so scored some hash that's coming straight from Beirut in a diplomatic pouch and he wants you to try some before it's all finished; I told so-and-so that you'd been sick for a couple of days; so-and-so came back from the village yesterday and left you a large cream and honey mille-feuille, but the hoggish builders said you never had any trouble getting your hands on village delicacies and wolfed it down themselves; so-and-so got himself into a bit of trouble and we have to help him get out of it; so-and-so asked me to find him someone reliable to paint his apartment because he's getting married soon and I looked for this kid I know, but I couldn't find him and I'm going to try again with you here so you can vouch for me that I really did try to find him; by the way, so-and-so is angry at so-and-so so we're going to make them make up whether they want to or not—I mean we can't go around acting like children—and I really need you to be there; so-and-so's mother has come up from the village so he's got his hands tied; so-and-so's really put out because his manager's constantly harping on him—you don't happen to know anybody higher up at the company who can put some pressure on the manager to cool it a bit, do you?; so-and-so . . . so-and-so . . . so-and-so.

No, no, it was never gossip, never slanderous, never backbiting, it was all just friendly news that helped keep the family close together no matter how remote we were. If he got the sense that you were at all interested in discussing someone who'd done something you didn't care for—for one reason or another—he'd try to explain to you the circumstances behind that unquestionably unintentional act and why the guy was someone you'd really like. A solid guy, like that, he'd say, sticking his thumb straight up in the air to signal that someone was good and trustworthy through and through. The guy's heart—he'd say—is as pure as milk and, just so you know, he likes you and he always asks about you.

We became one big loving group of friends, just like a family. We visited one another's homes and workplaces, exchanged invitations to parties and weddings, some of us helped others when they got into trouble or had dilemmas, gave one another expensive gifts, loaned and were loaned money. We shared our hash, too: each of us would buy as much as he could for himself and the others without any expectation of repayment and, really, so what if everyone had bought some for everyone else and we ended up with a dangerous surplus? That was all right: not even genies could find Hakeem's secret hiding place. When someone turned up or another got up to leave, we'd make them take an arriving or parting toke or two. We all lived through one another's problems as if they were our own. A spirit of brotherhood, solidarity, sympathy, and cooperation emerged among the members of our crew, proving the fact that human beings love belonging to a group. It soon dawned on us that getting stoned was no longer the primary reason we all got together, it was simply a good excuse; a little rose-water poured on the friendship to moisten its roots and freshen its leaves.

THE GREAT LEADER

As if we needed one more reason to link us all to Hakeem's den, as if the den and Hakeem's leadership, his wisdom, his talent at creating that perfect Upper Egyptian atmosphere with its barely suppressed Sufi undercurrent wasn't attractive enough, as if smoking hash and hanging out together in our own little support group, as if all that weren't enough, we were shown one of the den's most significant revelations: Rowdy Salih. He'd been an essential component of the place ever since it opened, and moreover, a notable figure in the Marouf-Antikkhana Champollion district.

He certainly was a fixture in the den, but back when we were going there as mere individuals, sporadically, each of us going when he could, with no set time for friends, he was always hidden away. There was no doubt that we'd each seen him working inconspicuously in the den more than once; you couldn't help but notice him. But then after we'd become a friendly group who got together every night to get high, after everyone's passions, jobs, and traits mingled, our viewpoints converged, our eyes learned to communicate with mere looks, after we got to be like that, that was when Rowdy Salih really came on to the scene. It wasn't simply because we'd started fixating on him, because he'd become our amusement, our topic of conversation, the star of our jokes and stories; rather it was because—in addition to being all of that—he also possessed something of each of us, more than just one thing. He'd often act as if he were all of us and we'd often act as if we were him. The truth was that he'd become—though we didn't know for how long—the main attraction for all the den's customers because he brought a certain virile, mischievous, warm and brotherly, attractively lunatic ecstasy to the place. Everything he did and said made us laugh because we thought it was a slice of utter insanity, but we soon realized that it invigorated us; it was everything we wished we could do or say. We obsessively repeated the things he said no matter what they were and claimed them as treasures of a living heritage. We started citing things he'd said in conversations about every aspect of life; we even used them as authentic examples of the vernacular language to which we could apply our artistic and literary theories and we discovered a depth of eloquence and innate wisdom in them. We occasionally got the feeling that Rowdy Salih had actually studied art and literature, had, in fact, actively participated in every single movement, but that history had passed silently over his involvement just as it passes silently over so many things.

Rowdy Salih had this extraordinary ability to calm you down no matter how agitated you were. It was as if he himself were a powerful sedative, a pill that affected you as soon as you swallowed it. There was a warmth and intelligence in his emotions and he was wholesome and innocent as if he were actually just a one-hour-old newborn and not a hulk in his mid-forties.

He was from Aswan and had bronze skin. A black seed planted in a clay pot had produced a unique color: he was neither dark black nor pale white, he was more like the color of soaked earth. His hair, on the other hand, was white like the sky and stood straight up at all different lengths as if he'd just fallen from heaven with a rope of cloudy string attached to his head and as he approached the earth and gravity began to pull on him more the nearer he came, the threads had split at random and the roots were still stuck to his head. Yet his hair looked nice, distinguished; cropped from his forehead down to his temples as if it'd been cut by a celebrity hairstylist. He was always clean-shaven and clean-cut except for every once in a while when his hair would spread down over his temples and round his chin, weaving a net of matted white wool that made it look as if his face were encased in rough slate. He had a smooth, youthful, beaming face and there was a deep-seated, natural grace, and dignity—without the slightest hint of affectation—in his eyes. Yet there was a humility there so great that it all but curtailed his sharp vision; he never looked past the work that was directly in front of him. His face was long like an oil-lamp and he had the firm features of one grown sedate and content by true satisfaction. He had a long, bulging neck with veins that protruded where it met his chest and shoulders like the roots of a great big tree. He had a barrel chest, wide shoulders, and muscular arms; he was fit and if he'd entered a bodybuilding competition, he'd have been crowned the winner after the first move.

He wore short trousers—undoubtedly borrowed from a dwarf or bought off a rag-and-bone man—and a collared shirt that seemed at least ten years old and had lost all its color and shape. The shirt was torn at the shoulders, but through its long acquaintance with his body and its sweaty, grimy, intractable filth, it'd become a second skin; a coarser, more enduring one. And yet you never got the feeling that he looked grungy; in fact, it was exactly the opposite. Whenever you saw him, you had this overwhelming feeling that you were standing before a nobleman out of history to whom time had not been kind and who'd lost his ability to look haughty and disdainful. All it took was one look and you'd instantly lose the nerve to offer him charity or new clothes—not even as a gift between friends.

His job in the den was quite basic and limited, and everything else he did was the result of his good manners and willingness to help for the love of God. But his job came first and it was backbreaking work that required both patience and diligence: he was the one who packed the bowls. He'd take a big barrel filled to the brim with about three thousand burnt-out bowls—two days' and nights' worth—and he'd have to scrape them clean with a knife, unclog them, and wipe them down with a damp rag. Then he had to drop a sherd in each one that was the exact right size for the hole at the bottom. For the third phase of the operation, he had to pack each bowl gingerly with the molasses-steeped tobacco he'd very carefully got out of the packet so as not to waste even a single strand. He'd line the bowls up in rows on wooden trays; each row had ten nails on which the bowls were set to keep them from being shaken or falling over and he'd stack the wooden trays up beside him, erecting a down-home skyscraper that didn't lack for style. The boys who worked in the den never dared approach the stack until the one he'd packed two days before was completely finished. And he always announced the number of bowls as they went out and came back so that both owner and employee knew what was what.

He was so patient he could pack two stacks in one day if he worked through to the next morning and that was what he usually did. That way he could get his salary from Hakeem: eighty piasters all told—which was a huge amount, if only ye knew. Rowdy Salih would tuck the money into his underwear band and calmly walk off, looking like a swaggering giant coming down the aisle, even looking like he'd locked arms with an imaginary bride. He'd squeeze down the narrow entrance to an alley, which to an outsider looked more like the front door of a house, and after a few steps, climb over a mound of hardened, packed rubble only to descend a few seconds later down the other side so that the only thing left showing was his white hair, as if a swan had taken flight low to the ground and then dived down into a deep valley. If we followed him down—which we didn't do very often—we'd see him stop at the remains of a demolished house: only the walls remained, there was no roof and the doors and windows had been ripped out. The floor, though, was still level and tiled. He'd take the folded-in-four copy of *al-Gumhuriya* newspaper out from under his arm and unfold it, pulling apart the sheets and spreading them out on the ground. Then he'd grab two big bricks, set them side by side, and lay the remaining sheets of newspaper on top of them. He'd lie down, his right arm draped over his eyes, and fall instantly into a deep sleep, whose depth soon turned into a piercing, earthshaking racket when he began to snore as loudly as thunder on a stormy night, rather as if bombs were exploding everywhere. If you ran over to see where the roar was coming from, you wouldn't find a house collapsing or a water buffalo being slaughtered; all you'd find was Salih lying there comatose with noises coming from his nose, throat, and ass. Your mind would struggle and fail to understand how someone could sleep so deeply through all those explosions, but it was a sleep he simply wouldn't be stirred from; not for seven full hours, and the alarm clock in his brain kept time better than a watch.

In the last minute of the last hour, he moved his right arm and opened his eyes: they were free of any sleep, but they looked like little mussels floating in demitasses of vinegar. Thrusting his chest forward, he sat up and cleared his throat with a dry cough, hacking a glob of spit through the air like a chick taking off from a roof for a split second before crashing to the ground. He slipped his iron-nail fingers into his breast pocket and pulled out a folded oval Hollywood cigarette, which he straightened out and stuck between his lips. He lit it with a match and took long, deep drags that he positively gulped down. By the time he'd finished his cigarette and flicked the butt through the air, it'd done the work of washing his face, opening his eyes, and squaring his vision. Then he collected the sheets of newspaper and folded them up like a little envelope, which he tucked under his shirt. He stood up and stretched his long leg through the window, which overlooked an alley that led to the heart of Marouf Street, and as soon as he got outside, he crouched down and pulled the rock off his hidden treasure: an empty beer bottle wrapped in a brown paper bag. He sauntered off in the direction of the European grocer on the corner to buy a half-liter of denatured alcohol, a bottle of Pepsi, two piasters' worth of white cheese, two piasters' worth of eggplant and pickles, and two pitas. He stopped by the falafel stand to get two piasters' worth of fresh hot falafel and then went over to the offal cart parked beside Cinema Odeon and handed the man five whole piasters and the two pitas. The man took the pitas, opened them up, and stuffed them with tripe, lung, mumbar sausages, manyplies, tongue, eyes, and animelles. Salih took the pitas with a bowed head, with a sweet shyness and a smile of the politest thanks that only an aristocrat could pull off.

Rowdy Salih headed back to Hakeem's den with his purchases and holed himself up in a distant corner; he didn't have time for anyone at that moment. He mixed the denatured alcohol with the Pepsi, spread his food out on the ground, borrowed a cup from Hakeem, and then began to pour into the cup and into himself constantly as he ate. Everyone was cautiously getting ready to watch him out of the corners of their eyes, with a combination of apprehension and mirth, because now Rowdy Salih . . . well, he was about to get rowdy.

GETTING ROWDY

He'd start to get rowdy when the effect of the denatured-alcohol-and-Pepsi cocktail made its way through his veins up to his brain, which wasn't as quick to respond to the call to rowdiness as it had once been. There was one brief instant when Rowdy Salih would be afflicted by an unexpected bout of violent dizziness, which his body—despite its enormity—was unable to resist. Supporting himself on his elbows, he stretched his legs out on whatever rolled-up rags he could find and disappeared into the Kingdom of God, separating himself completely from the world around him, and no soul dared disturb him, touch him, or talk to him when he was in that state because that was when he was at his most rabidly violent and readier than ever to do something unthinkable: to hit someone with whatever he could get his hands on, demolish the den with people inside, or set it alight. The danger wasn't merely that there was no knowing what he might do, the bigger danger was that it would escalate into an uncontainable disaster because Rowdy Salih just didn't know how to stop himself when he was out of control. If it were to kick off with a fire, say—he always got off to a sudden and decisive start as if he were already in the middle of a previously disguised rage—soon enough he'd be picking up whatever he could find—human, animal, or mineral—and throwing it into the heart of the blaze. And if he ever did raise his hand to punch someone, punch he would; even before he'd raised his hand, the punch was predestined. He had a clumsy punch and if it didn't kill you, it would at least give you a permanent injury. When he erupted and began shouting insults and curses, his booming voice brought people from nearby streets, people who came to double their pleasure by watching as well as listening to an interlude of creative, clever insults, which painted a surreal portrait that won bursts of frantic laughter. The first reason they were so funny was that they could only be partially understood because of all the foreign phrases in English, Italian, Turkish, and Nubian they included, and which were shouted at the top of his lungs, his voice adding an air of gravity and dignity. It carried the seal and sign of greatness and the rhythms of gentlemen who, when they spoke, found people listened. He had that gentlemanly ability to mock with pitch and reproach with tone so he didn't even have to use words with clear social referents to get his point across. His transparent, lilting vocal rhythms made his point for him, especially as his voice had such great range and was filled with layer upon layer of both soft and coarse commanding tones. All he had to do was untie all the ropes of his voice at once and the tonal layers would wander over one other until politeness mixed with brusqueness, command with request, and censure with apology, so that nobody knew anymore if their ears were telling the truth or their eyes were lying. Their ears knew for sure that they were hearing an aristocrat, but their eyes tried to convince them that it was only a beggar suffering from an alcoholic's delusions of grandeur. If, at a moment like that, he happened to call to a friend to ask for a friendly favor, and even though he sincerely wanted to put as much good feeling into his voice as he could when calling to his buddy so-and-so, when he shouted, "How's it going, Ace," he couldn't help but making it sound like, "Hey, fuckface!"

These kinds of discordances came out one after the other, causing laughter to erupt all around him, but in hushed voices for fear of upsetting him. None of this meant that he was vicious, or dangerous—after all we spent lots of time with him and knew the score—it was just that when he drank what he drank to get rowdy, it was as if he strapped a heavy, pointless burden onto his shoulders, which only got heavier and more insupportable as the flame of denatured alcohol spread through his veins.

The heavy burden was his constant fear of being mocked, the fear that contemptible people—whom God had created no differently from him except that they wore posh clothes and had money to spend—would look down on him. Although he'd managed to hold all the snobs in check and commanded everyone's respect, he still had to keep an eye on them when he was drunk because Salih knew full well that all those fancy suits stuffed with human meat, with their perfume of cologne and cash, were cowards, every last one of them. In fact, we noticed that when he cut loose, he only interacted with certain types of customers and that made us curious—what did they have?—so we studied them and came to realize that they really were cowards to some degree or other, but that all cowardice, even the scantiest, rouses a taste for vengeance in like proportion, and Salih could smell fear in a person even when they hid behind imported clothes, high rank, or safes.

"Who do they think they're talking about? Those sons of bitches better realize I know what they're playing at. I don't get drunk! And when I do get drunk, everybody'd better show me some respect! Whether they feel like it or not. I don't care if I only get one carat of respect from them when I'm sober; when I'm drunk I expect them to give me twenty-four-carat respect. And that's that! No offense, but I mean if you act like an asshole, I'm going to burn you. I'll see to it that you don't get an inch out of life. What, just 'cause I drink denatured alcohol? It's all denatured alcohol, all of it, even whiskey and champagne. To hell with the names they make you pay high prices for. It's true they make for nice drinks—I'm not denying that—but all they're selling is fancy packaging and people are paying their life's blood to get it!"

He reached for another cigarette and straightened it out with a gentle flicker, then he lit it with the previous cigarette, exhaling with untold contentment.

"Listen, boss. The world's a rowdy place and it's filled with rowdy people. Everybody here's rowdy. They're all rowdy 'cause all they want to do is get rowdy and they either get to or they don't. And everybody here's run-down. But they're all run-down in their own way. And me, I'm the king of the run-down 'cause I'm run-down in every which way."

This rowdiness, which never lasted longer than two hours, allowed Rowdy Salih to lay a foundation and assert his power and dignity. We all went off to see to our affairs, promising to meet up again at night when Rowdy Salih would have entered phase two of his mirthful hellfire, when all that remained was his hilarious and constant laughter of the highest degree of purity, vigor, and brilliance. Everyone who he felt had turned their noses up at him somehow and whose snobbish, extravagant, and sissified look he didn't care for and who'd unintentionally mistreated him once would all be sitting up on the hill, smoking hash, and listening in. Now he had the upper hand and despite their elevated and distinguished position, which gave them the theatrical prerogative over those seated in front of the den, they became the audience. Rowdy Salih, with his excellent eyesight, was the only person who could make out their silhouettes in the pitch black; he knew them by name, profile, and shape. It was true that—just like any drunk—he liked to tell himself he wasn't drunk even when he was totally smashed, but this was the only time he liked to make it obvious that he was drunk so he could take advantage of the fact that drunks have no shame. As soon as he heard the voice of someone he'd had stored in his mind, he'd fire back a flaming, spot-on retort, and he'd be the first to bust up with a carnivalesque laugh, filled with unbridled, gleeful, maniacal sounds, so that nobody could tell whether they were laughing at the brilliant snap or laughing at him for being so completely absorbed by his own laughter, at that horrible racket.

THE CREW

When he wasn't getting rowdy, Rowdy Salih was very well mannered and shy. Our friend Qamar al-Mahruqi used to call him *al-gentleman*, intending every last dimension and shade of meaning the term implied. Qamar al-Mahruqi always loved to pick out the exact right word for a thing and ever since he'd started working for the American University, he'd become obsessed with the meaning and etymology of words in Egyptian Arabic. He was a research assistant to one of the academics working on the Egyptian Arabic–English dictionary project, which the American University was putting together to lay the groundwork for an imminent American takeover of Egypt.

Salih had actually been very deserving of the epithet when Qamar al-Mahruqi called him *al-gentleman* because the people who'd had to suffer his ripping the night before had just come into the den and he'd greeted them warmly, graciously dusting off the bench with the end of his shirt before they sat down: "Would you like some tea? Oh, you haven't got any hash with you? No problem! I've got an eighth on me. Take it. You can have that for breakfast until the dealer wakes up." He said it as if he hadn't just spent the day before ridiculing the posh customer and making the whole world laugh at him. The customer looked Rowdy Salih right in the eye, but he couldn't detect any trace of the night before, as if it'd been someone else who'd done what he'd done. This polite and affectionate Salih could never have been so rude.

It was this deep-rooted innocence—and this innocent assuredness—that allowed Rowdy Salih to dispel any residue of the past and made it impossible for anyone to bear him any ill will. But if someone—either to joke or tease—reminded him of something rude and cutting he'd said about the man the night before, Rowdy Salih's face would immediately flush with embarrassment and denial. He'd shake his head like someone quite refined and express an intense disgust at simply having heard such a shameful thing repeated. He seemed totally convinced of his own disapproval and revulsion, drooping his head and in that big, warm voice saying, "No, no, no that's not right! There's no need for that sort of talk. How could someone have said that to you, sir? I swear I'll cut his head off! You know it's better to be polite than clever. All a man's got is his word. Your word's like your horse, if you treat it well, it treats you well, but if you abuse it, it'll get you back. What would you like to drink, sir? It's on me. No, I insist. Come on, don't embarrass me here." This would make a few of us start philosophizing about split personalities and schizophrenia, and all those other terms that everyone seems to be using these days.

Talat al-Imbabi was a lecturer in history at Cairo University and was obsessed with a branch of a sub-discipline of psychology called Political and Social Psychology, meaning, for one thing, that he read more Erich Fromm than Toynbee. He was always cautioning us against diagnosing Rowdy Salih with a split personality, or paranoia, or even melancholia. In point of fact, Rowdy Salih had a completely balanced personality: he did everything he wanted to—whether he was drunk or sober—and with absolute freedom. It was just that he chose to do some things subconsciously, without really knowing it. But then why did he do those things at all? Obviously, he had rational motivations that grew out of his conscious awareness. Talat al-Imbabi, perceiving the crux of the puzzle like a scientist, went on to explain that Rowdy Salih was actually more balanced than any of us, that he was different because he didn't suffer from any of the psychological complexes the rest of us did because he always did what he wanted to do without any hesitation. He'd chosen to live this way: Rowdy Salih wasn't obliged to do anything, he wasn't coerced, he wasn't faced with exigent circumstances. No, he could've worked at any number of jobs. He knew more than one trade, which would've allowed him to feed himself, wear nice clothes, get married, and sleep on a soft bed in a clean, safe home; the only thing was—to put it simply—he didn't want to. Not because he couldn't—you could see he was a bull—and not because he was lazy—you could tell he was as active as a bee—and not because he was stupid or slow either—you knew he was brilliant, clear-thinking, quick-witted, and that he could do complicated arithmetic without pen, paper, or fingers. What it all boiled down to—as you could see for yourself—was that he'd wholeheartedly chosen this life. As for why and how? Well, that was what we had to investigate.

Talat al-Imbabi's analysis was utterly convincing; his conclusion seemed—to us, at least—both solid and reasoned. He was, of course, an avid reader; he had a huge library piled up in the big new apartment he'd recently rented in a brand-new neighborhood called Mohandiseen. He was married to a young Italian woman called Matilde, who was thick and plump, and whose white skin was mixed with the faintest red and gave off an unsettling, primal femininity and proclaimed her link to a clan of her color in the Italian countryside. Nevertheless she was an academic, an intellectual, and a Marxist, who sought to further the Internationale with her political work, and along those righteous lines, had no objection to living in whatever country she felt like and marrying any man so long as she thought he'd help her further her ambitions.

Although Talat was a Marxist at heart, he hadn't been involved in politics and he'd been hoping to get into it once he'd accomplished his academic goals: a PhD in the material history of developing nations. He hadn't gone to Italy just so he could come back with a white woman for a wife like all the other Egyptian students who'd been sent abroad to study did and had done ever since the beginning of the modern era. No, he was a brilliant kid and an all-around fireball; even in middle age his rapid-fire conversation constantly took off on tangents about the lunacies of change and innovation, about modernism and post-modernism, about the hippies, the Beatles, and the angry youth. He was a devotee of the younger generation's favorite philosopher, who'd recently become famous in the west: Marcuse, author of *One-Dimensional Man*. Many different influences

41

from philosophy, history, psychology, literature in all its short-story, novel, and poetic varieties, fine arts, cinema, theater, and classical music had stuck in his wonderful, clever mind and taken root, melding together in the crucible of his passion. He had profound and polarizing views on all those topics—as well as disappointing creative attempts in all of them—and so he excelled in his studies, overwhelmed his professors, and earned their trust and admiration.

He could expound masterfully and coherently about any subject we were interested in: about the difference between Sartre's existentialism, Albert Camus' absurdism, and Gabriel Marcel's faith; about the difference between Baudelaire and Rimbaud, Toynbee and Bertrand Russell, Sophia Loren and Claudia Cardinale, Colin Wilson and Marcuse, Louis Awad and Muhammad Mandour, Muhammad Anis and Abd al-Rahman al-Rafiʻi, Yahya Hakki and Yusuf Idris, Adel Kamel and Naguib Mahfouz, Muhammad Hasanayn Haykal and Ahmad Baha al-Din, Mustafa Amin and Muhammad al-Tabiʻi, Rose al-Youssef and Fatima Rushdi, Ihsan Abdel Quddus and Yusuf al-Sibaʻi, Gamal Abdel Nasser and Tito, all the way down the list to the difference between an Ahli–Tersana match and a Zamalek–Ismaili match. Of course, these revelations always led us back to a discussion of the differences—the essential ones this time—between Hakeem's den and Galal's, between Umm Yahya's hash and Ali Mango's.

So how then did it come to pass that Talat al-Imbabi, the son of a moderately well-off farmer from the village of Warraq al-Arab, should marry an Italian intellectual working for the international leftist cause and earning a living by teaching languages and literature at foreign-language schools, which you could find in every country; everywhere you looked there was an Italian school or institute looking for teachers.

These were the kinds of questions a naive person would ask about the members of our group, though embarrassment usually halted the questions at the glimmer-in-the-eye phase and they were rarely given voice. How, one wondered, did apple and orange come together? It was true, of course, that Talat didn't know a single word of Italian, but his English was very good and he was planning to improve it in Oxford or America soon, and although his wife's mother tongue was Italian, she was also fluent in English, French, and Russian and she spent a lot of her free time—what little she had—translating works of literature, journalistic pieces, and

42

reports and declarations from diplomatic organizations in the many countries in which she'd lived. This was in addition to the fact that she spoke Arabic—Egyptian Arabic to be precise—with an attractive accent and if she couldn't find the exact word for what she wanted to say in Egyptian Arabic, she'd finish her thought in English, the *lingua franca*. All of which was to say that the loving couple faced no obstacles and were as well matched as two bunches of jasmine.

Talat al-Imbabi's close friends scoffed at these kind of absurd questions with the sort of open ridicule that Talat himself could take in and laugh at with a decent amount of pride and hardly any embarrassment. They mocked the idea that the marriage was anything at all in comparison with Talat al-Imbabi's actual ambitions because, we all knew, that the only thing that could've stood between him and his goals was an obstacle so crazy that it was just asking to be bowled over. His ambition was as unstoppable as one of those Hungarian trains that only stopped at big cities, and it came wrapped in a dangerously charming, sweet, polite tenderness.

Talat had that quintessentially Egyptian stature; just like a pharaoh out of a relief, somewhere between tall and short, with thin, strong bones, a face as round as a saucer, a wine-colored complexion, and eyes so powerful you'd think they were his most prominent feature. He reminded you of one of those legendary highway robbers: wiry and iron-willed. His features were angular, but complimented by a suppleness that occasionally gave his skin a green patina like the leaves of a castor oil plant and that, together with his cusped mouth, gave him a look of implacable resolve. He had a measured, confident walk, but when he was wandering away from the hash den, he'd swagger off like a strutting man-about-town or some famous fop—in his tight jeans, springy imported rubber ankle boots, a thin, cream-colored linen shirt with nearly all the buttons undone, and a russet St Michael wool pullover, with the sleeves rolled up in anticipation of the appallingly changeable weather—and headed toward his blue Volkswagen Beetle, which still worked like a charm after all those years.

To tell the truth, he'd never made an effort to get married, not to Matilde or anyone else. He'd never planned to get married before carrying out the first stages of his plan, but then the opportunity presented itself on his doorstep, peeled and ready to eat. Matilde had been married to an

Egyptian, a friend of ours named Ahmad Asim, who was the son of the dean of Cairo University's venerable Law School—a very learned man, one of those extraordinary geniuses whose narrow academic specialization couldn't keep him from immersing himself in the study of the Arabic language and its literature, or from editing a few classical texts and earning additional graduate degrees in Arabic. His son Ahmad was obsessed with all things cinematic even though he'd graduated with a degree in the sciences. So fine, let him go do a degree in filmmaking, it was said, but Ahmad wanted to travel, to get away, maybe even to escape, and he thought the Egyptian Film Institute was backward and that it wasn't going to give him any knowledge or experience to add to his ambition; they had no equipment, no labs, no film sets except for some basic gear that simply wouldn't satisfy his hunger. That was how he explained the situation to his father, who worshiped at the prayer-niche of learning, so he had no objection to his son traveling abroad on the sole condition that he didn't spend beyond his means. Ahmad assured his father that he'd get a job to cover the costs of living and studying. Italy had always held the greatest attraction for him because he was crazy about Italian cinema.

Ahmad was an open-minded, worldly kid and he soon got addicted to student elections at university and became a pro at winning every year. He had firm ties to underground leftist groups, including those that had connections in every corner of the world. Nothing was easier than to get a letter from a comrade back home and deliver it to another comrade in some other country and then to find himself inundated with people offering to help set him up with a job and get ready for his studies. On his journey, he discovered Matilde, or perhaps she'd been thrown in his path. They met, grew fond of each other, and he found in her the foreign white woman that would make him proud when he returned to Cairo with her on his arm, like Taha Hussein, Hussein Fawzi, Yahya Hakki, Futuh Nishati, Abd al-Qadir al-Qitt, and others before him. For her part, she got a hot-blooded, tough, and thrilling Oriental, who combined an instinctual cleverness with the strong Islamic values he'd been raised with. Although she was four, maybe five, years older than him, he proposed to her and she accepted straightaway. She introduced him to her well-off family and put their fears to rest. They set up house in an apartment she owned in the Italian capital and she soon became pregnant. She chose to come to

Cairo to bring her baby into the world in the embrace of his pharaonic forefathers, but no sooner had she got her figure back after the pregnancy than they drifted apart for reasons entirely unknown even to them. Neither of them could give their friends, who were trying to get them back together, genuine and convincing explanations as to why they'd broken up. It seemed to have been an acute break, arising from quintessential and sensitive causes, which were difficult to identify and put into so many words. Therefore the split was both sudden and smooth, and there was a remarkable degree of give and goodwill on either side. Talat al-Imbabi and Ahmad Asim had been friends since they were kids; they went to the same exclusive nursery, primary school, high school, and university. Ahmad's sister, Mahasin Asim, was also a classmate of Talat's from the same faculty and department. How many long, perfect, exhausting nights had they spent studying together! He was there when Ahmad and Matilde began to drift apart. In all honesty, he went to great lengths to keep them together because he thought that the marriage was good for his friend whichever way you looked at it. He also thought that no one else deserved her, that she'd find someone who wasn't right for her and get caught in his snare. He completely lost it when he saw that they were going to go through with the divorce and was overcome by a strong and sudden urge to keep her under his control for some time longer in case one of them— she or Ahmad—came to their senses and things went back to normal. So he moved her to an apartment in the same neighborhood and got a nanny to look after her child while she was at work at the Italian Institute Dante Alighieri, just a stone's throw away from Hakeem's den. And when, after a few months, he could see that both parties were content with the separation and had completely forgotten about the other, he proposed to Matilde and told her he was more than happy to adopt her child.

A very small number of our circle knew some of the details; I was perhaps one of them, owing to my close relationship with our friend Qamar al-Mahruqi in whom I found a deeper, more sophisticated, and more open-minded literary taste than that of Talat al-Imbabi, who had a historian's disposition and was rather closed off from the human spirit. Qamar could've been a great writer of short stories and novels if only he weren't always so busy and hadn't scattered his interests in so many different and opposing directions. Qamar al-Mahruqi, who was married to Mahasin Asim and with whom he'd had a beautiful daughter named Nahla, explained his brother-in-law and ex-wife's relationship: leftist circles that inclined toward internationalism dismissed any difference between people of varying classes, races, and educational backgrounds except when it concerned personal behavior. We might have thought that as communists prone to dissolution and atheism and because so many of them embraced an anarchic lifestyle free of all moral and religious restraints, they could be rather indulgent—and maybe they really were when it came to their own relationships—but the one thing they could never tolerate was lying and cheating, and other manifestations of wretched behavior. Consequently Qamar al-Mahruqi couldn't rule out the possibility that his brother-in-law had misrepresented himself to his Italian ex-wife. He must have given her the impression that he was like her: from a wealthy, well-respected family, that he owned this and that, that he was just as well off as she was. Matilde—according to Qamar al-Mahruqi—had absolutely no problem with letting the man she loved and with whom she'd had a son spend as much of her money as he liked, but with the condition that she be allowed to make her decisions based on the truth and to have all the facts before they were officially bound together. If he'd simply been honest with her from the beginning about his background, there wouldn't have been any problems, especially as she didn't even believe in private property. But to tell her he was going to bring her from Italy to meet his family and see the matrimonial house that would be hers and his family's farms and estates just as she'd shown him her family's possessions and the farms of her father, who was an agricultural engineer, only to arrive at his father's modest apartment, which held none of the world's treasures except for her, and see his family's very modest state—the whole lot of them spent less in a month than she did in a day—and then to be told that he couldn't afford to resume his studies and that he was trying find work for them both in Cairo, well, that was something Matilde could never forgive. Plus what did she need him for? She was supporting him under his own parents' roof and it would only take her a few hours to get herself a decent job. Qamar al-Mahruqi explained that she was from a different culture, one that didn't allow emotion to dominate reason as ours did and didn't leave its hardships on God's doorstep and sit there calmly bewailing the good fortune of much misery and thanking God for bestowing it in such abundance. "No, my dear, I don't let *bye bye* get in the way." She wasn't going to lose: look, there's another suitor in the wings, ready to submit to all her conditions, including giving her the right to initiate divorce proceedings. Qamar said Talat was more of a man than Ahmad; there was no question about it. He was more active and smarter, too, tougher, wealthier: at least his family actually owned farms and could give him hundreds of pounds followed by hundreds more without any grumbling. He took on respectable work he dreamed up for himself for the leftist crowd and the embassies of communist countries, he translated articles for the Russian Sharq publishing house, which were published in the Arabic edition of *al-Sharq* magazine edited by Muhammad Mandour, he wrote historical pieces for Egyptian periodicals and magazines and reports on literary happenings for Arab newspapers, he traveled to universities in Libya, Kuwait, and Algeria to lecture, teach, and deliver papers at conferences. Therefore he always had money coming in and he'd built up the kind of image and reputation that allowed him to borrow money from the well-off without any embarrassment, to buy a car from a dealership with financing, and to save up enough for the key money to a big apartment in a nice building in a respectable neighborhood. He was more sophisticated and self-assured than the lot of us and he had a way with money: he knew how to make something big out of not very much, like he'd be out walking with Matilde past the antique shops on Huda Shaarawi Street and spot a valuable, antique sitting room set that he knew would make his apartment look like some important government minister lived there. It was obvious that Matilde was head over heels for Talat; she'd say his name with a sweet, musical tenderness: "Oh, Ta-laaat," she'd say, and we'd get high for free.

Another friend of ours, and a member of the group's inner core, Mustafa Lami, was a sculptor who'd recently graduated from the Department of Visual Arts at the Fine Arts College, and who was himself married to a Czech woman though we didn't know how, where, or when they'd ever met. He had a different take on Talat al-Imbabi, Ahmad Asim, and the leftist Italian intellectual. We liked hearing his opinions; he was one of the cultural-literary-artistic leaders in our big crew full of its varied personalities, goals, professions, and aptitudes. Mustafa Lami had a predilection for solitude that bordered on a complex. He even went so far as to isolate himself from the five or six of us who wrote, read, painted, and published. That wasn't to say that he sat by himself; it was just that he was a recluse even as he sat among us and shared the same bong and the same hash. He rarely took part in our discussions or expressed an opinion on a topic of general interest. It may have been because of the fear that had been instilled in the minds of young intellectuals—especially those from poorer backgrounds, who'd had to kill themselves to finish university—about the epidemic of reports and informants, which got so bad that they could get between father and son, husband and wife, even between a person and himself. And, don't forget, these reports were then used to arrest the innocent and get them thrown into internment camps in unknown locations.

Yet Mustafa Lami would often raise his head up unexpectedly, wave away the smoke pouring deliciously and deliriously from his nose and mouth, and grace us with a well-articulated, succinct comment on the subject we were discussing. What he said might turn the conversation on its head, or divert it toward another, more reasoned, more pragmatic—maybe even more dangerous—course, or it could kill the conversation dead. In that way of his, constantly holding words back, always seeming to think that allusion and hints were enough, leaving it to you and your intellect to finish the thought or discern the right context so that you were always responsible for the final picture, Mustafa Lami said, "What are you all getting so excited about? Have you lost your minds?"

"What do you mean?"

"Marriage . . . love . . . lies . . . betrayal . . . children . . . I mean all that stuff."

"What *exactly* are you getting at?"

"Listen, you idiots! Communism is international. All these countries that bought into the idea of what they call Internationalism are exactly like all of you: you know, delusional. Do they think that if the workers take control of the world that, you know . . . all this time-wasting and head-scratching . . . "

"What does that have to do with what we're talking about?"

"Do you want to know what I really think?"

"Please humor us!"

"In a few words . . . to put it briefly . . . the thing is . . . well, the people who work for political parties and secret organizations are . . . they've taken over positions in the country . . . especially women. They just use marriage as a pretense . . . an excuse to take up residence in the country!"

Occasionally at times like these, Talat would show up carrying a big tome written in English—most likely the plays of Shakespeare, or even likelier, one of his wife's purchases—a silver medallion key-ring full of strange keys of different sizes and shapes hanging from his other hand. He'd slip the ring around his pinkie so he could run his fingers through his thick mustache, which was rounded off at the mouth, making his chin look as small and pointed as a worn-down scrap of perfumed soap and giving an impression of strong will. Mere surprise became astonishment when we caught sight of Ahmad Asim, his oldest friend and his wife's ex-husband, and they sat with us or on the hill above us—it's fine, no big deal, just until a few people leave and free up some space. You could tell from Talat's eyes and his beige, impish face that he knew exactly what we'd just been talking about. His brilliance lay in the ability to discern your honest opinion about him even when you said exactly the opposite. He also couldn't be bothered to correct people's opinions of him even when they were unmerited. As far he was concerned, everyone was entitled to their opinions just as everyone else was entitled to do whatever they wanted. And plus he was a member of an emerging worldwide rebel youth movement that denounced everything it didn't believe in, or in its efficacy, even if it was something holy, which fought to allow people to live their lives the way they wanted where they wanted without interference from ancient laws, worn-out customs, dried-up mores, and diseased traditions, which had built up a historical prison that stifled human liberty and artistic freedom. As a member of this movement and as someone who sympathized with its many diverse communities, he didn't simply demand the things he demanded; rather he lived by the new philosophy because he believed it was an attempt to liberate human beings from stagnation and eclipse. Anyone could say whatever they wanted however they wanted about whomever they wanted; but in reality, it should've been the opposite: people who didn't do it openly and directly were betraying themselves as well as humanity. The only condition should've been that opinions had to be expressed in the open, boldly and objectively, because if they were uttered behind people's backs then they weren't opinions; that was gossip and it was unworthy of a response. It merited only condescension and disgust.

Ahmad Asim sat beside him like a dandy, like a little boy clinging to his older brother's side as he taught him how to behave in the company of men. There he was, his hands on his knees, lifting his pretty, dainty head with his perfectly symmetrical haircut—the work of a talented stylist, no doubt—his long, pointed nose, and his white, rosy face with its delicate, symmetrical features, which nonetheless evinced an obvious virility. Quick to smile, quick to grimace, as if with those two signals alone he could join in any conversation going on around him; he only used words when either smile or grimace required clarification. He held the stem of the bong with the tips of his fingers in a grip that put to rest the dandy comparisons and took deep drags like an expert stoner, looking—in the thick cloud of smoke—like a Neapolitan down-and-out or a bumboat captain in a far-flung port somewhere.

"Italians are hashheads too, man!" Mustafa Lami said, looking at him cheerfully.

From the distant, silent corner where he was busy converting some jars into bongs for a quick smoke, Hakeem piped up: "What do you mean, boss? That dude over there's a big-time stoner! I've known him for years. He used to come here all the time. And he used to always bring foreign ladies with him. He's a tour guide, isn't he?" Having asked his question, he turned toward us, eagerly awaiting an answer, and Qamar al-Mahruqi let out a throaty laugh; as did Talat al-Imbabi, with the same sounds and rhythms—they were a lot alike. Most of the time we couldn't figure out who'd influenced whom. They both had that same skinny body-type, too, although Qamar was slightly taller and slimmer. Mustafa laughed his familiar laugh, too, clenching his molars and baring his big, crooked teeth, and when it was a particularly hearty, uncontrollable laugh, bobbing his head in time with his emphatic, if silent, giggling.

"Actually, Hakeem," Talat al-Imbabi said, "he's a cinema guide . . . you know, kind of like an usher!"

Rowdy Salih had been busy with his bowls, working himself to exhaustion, but as soon as he heard the last bit he raised his head from the pile in front of him and studied Ahmad Asim's face covertly, glancing from under his forehead which was both concave and convex, and then in that thick, soft voice he said, "You know, I think I saw sir showing some people to their seats at the cinema. Are you an usher at Cinema Rivoli just here in front of the High Court? The guy who runs the concession stand at that cinema is a friend of mine; I mean I pretty much raised him."

There was an explosion of laughter that shattered and threw dust up into the air, breaking through the cloud of blue smoke and dispersing it. Talat al-Imbabi leaned over to Ahmad Asim, rubbing his mustache with his fingers, his key ring around his ring finger, and said, "That's Rowdy Salih. I'm sure you haven't forgotten him."

Ahmad Asim shook his head and blushed, beaming and speaking in a pleasant tone that was all welcome and repose: "Of course, I know Uncle Salih! I've known him for the longest time."

Laughing courteously, Rowdy Salih said, "Please sir, next time you all show a good action film, you've got to get me a ticket."

Qamar al-Mahruqi said, in an affectionate shout—he was the only one who had a special bond with Rowdy Salih that allowed him to talk to him however he pleased—"Hey, buddy, get it through your head: Mr. Asim's a film director. He's the one who makes the films, he doesn't show people to their seats!"

Rowdy Salih's face flushed; bronze turning to the color of a child's face when he's made a terrible mistake. He pointed toward Talat al-Imbabi and stuttered, "No offense, sir. It's just he said you were a cinema guy."

"I meant he guides the ideas, like an artist. Now do you get it?"

Rowdy Salih nodded and his apologetic expression made it clear that he'd indeed understood.

"Between me and you, there isn't a big difference. The guy who makes the film is the one who puts people in the seats, not anybody else," Mustafa Lami said under his breath.

"You've got that right, Moos," said Ahmad Asim.

Talat al-Imbabi clapped his hands gleefully, mixing sophistication with an appealing childishness: "Salooha, I've got a feeling today's going to be a good day, God willing! Do you have any plans?"

Hakeem looked at him with slight apprehension, and Rowdy Salih joined him with a meaningful glance, which all but cursed such a stupid question and its clueless questioner, as if to say "You're looking at my plans!" Talat seemed to pick up on the meaning behind the glance and to

51

have been hurt by its bite. "I meant after you're done with work."

The permanent smile on Hakeem's pursed lips spread and as if answering a question that required absolutely no deliberation at all, he said, "He's going to get rowdy of course."

"Tonight?"

"Is he going to finish tonight?"

"Well, when's he going to finish?"

"Why? Do you need him for something?"

"Yes, as a matter of fact."

"You have something you need done at home or something? An errand?"

"No, nothing like that. I want to invite him over."

"Invite him? Over to your house?"

"What's so weird about that, Hakeem?"

"There's nothing as queer as folk!" replied Qamar al-Mahruqi in a suggestive, sarcastic, secretive tone. Talat turned to him to enlist his help.

"You know, Qamar, you could probably convince him, and convince Hakeem."

"To do what?" he said, leaning back against the wall and crossing his legs, looking noticeably taller. The cuffs of his black trousers pulled away from his soft white woolen socks that stretched up out of the wide opening of his sturdy English-style black shoes. The collar of his burnt umber checkered jacket—with elbow patches—spread apart and the bones of his chest showed under his beige wool turtleneck like sturdy strips of plywood. He reached his long fingers into his inner jacket pocket and pulled out a metal cigarette case; it looked like it was made of gold, which wouldn't have been a surprise with Qamar, and it also contained a magically concealed lighter. He elegantly plucked a cigarette out and placed it between his lips, then he pressed the side of the case and a knuckle-sized cover sprung open to reveal a flame. All this while waiting for Talat to light the bowl and answer his question; he took a deep drag from his cigarette. The boy Sabir handed him the stem of the bong and Qamar held it between his index and middle fingers where the cigarette was. He started smoking, his face turned toward Talat, keen to hear exactly what it was that Talat wanted his help with. But Talat said, "Why aren't you talking? You didn't say whether you would or not."

Qamar pulled the stem, which was still held snugly between his two fingers, to the side and said, "I still don't know what you want me to do, smart guy!"

Talat stroked his mustache thoughtfully and said, "I'm thinking about inviting Rowdy Salih over to my place for a few days, or a week or two, whatever he wants."

"What's the occasion?" Qamar asked, with some difficulty because he said it through his nose while trying to hold the smoke back so it came out like a sharp buzzing, like the creak of a jammed country door.

"Nothing in particular," replied Talat dismissively.

Qamar al-Mahruqi's face turned red, giving him the appearance of a carrot. He smiled, his gaunt, sunken cheeks receding and disappearing completely behind the long wrinkles that cut across his face. His wide mouth and his prominent white, symmetrical, beautifully formed teeth seemed his most remarkable feature. His mouth was so wide it made his eyes narrow and they only got narrower as he spoke, disappearing completely when he smiled, the only things still showing his eyelashes blinking and shooting out sparks. It was with these that he turned his whole body toward Rowdy Salih and centered his sight on him: "Are you going to come, Salih?" he asked with an intense neutrality.

With an even more intense shyness, Salih smiled and without taking his eyes off the bowls he was cleaning out said, "I'd be honored, sir, but— . . . ," finishing his thought with a glance in Hakeem's direction. Hakeem looked suspiciously at him out of the corner of his eye and then turned to Qamar.

"Okay, but what about his daily bread?"

"It's no big deal. I'll pay him his wages as if he was working," yelled Talat across to him.

Hakeem was confused. "You mean as if he's not working? Or is he going to be working?"

"Of course, he's not going to work. He's going to sit on his ass like a pasha. He'll eat with us and drink with us and sleep in a clean bed, and he'll get paid for it, too! And his hash, cigarettes, and booze'll all be on me."

"Is that all?!"

"No more, no less."

"Salih's mom must have been praying for him, the lucky bastard."

"Out with it already!" said Mustafa Lami, winking at Salih as if to signal to the spectators that he was trying to get under Salih's skin and turn him against Hakeem. Salih looked up and responded with all seriousness, "Out with what? He's going to make me work till I drop."

Equally serious, Talat tried to clear up the potential misunderstanding: "Absolutely not, Uncle Salih. I'm telling you you're going to be my guest. How could I put a guest to work? You're going to come to my house as an honored guest and you'll be well looked after. You'll be waited on hand and foot."

"Aha! So you are going to put me to work. What you just said is work to me. Hard work, too!"

"When did I say anything about work?"

"Hear me out here, sir. Right now, I'm Rowdy Salih the guy who works at a hash den, right?"

"Nothing's going to change."

"No, but I'm going to be a guest. My whole job will just be to eat, drink, get high, get drunk, go to sleep, wake up, eat, drink, get high, get rowdy, go to bed. Honestly, now, what job could be harder than that? I'm not even sure I could last a whole day."

The waves of a sea of laughter swirled and eddied. Hakeem stared at Salih and mumbled, "What an ingrate! You even think lounging around is work?"

Ahmad Asim nodded. "I know what Uncle Salih's getting at. He's trying to say that he's the kind of guy who's used to a hard day's work so his body doesn't even know how to relax. Lots of people are like that."

Rowdy Salih waved his dirty, crooked arm and shouted, "Sir, you're just not getting it. You make movies, right? Well, then, you've got to understand what I'm saying. Anyway let me break it down for you: You're saying that I'm going to go to his house and play the part of an honored guest with no responsibilities except for eating, drinking, smoking hash, getting rowdy, and sleeping in a clean bed. Am I right?"

"Right."

"Well if I want to do a good job of it, I'll be exhausted. For starters, I don't even know how to act. And secondly, a role like that needs practice. Practice I should've started on thirty or forty years ago so that when I get myself into a jam like this it'll be obvious that I really am the kind of respectable guest who deserves an invitation like this."

"Son of a bitch! You're something else," said Talat al-Imbabi in a whisper only we could hear. Then out loud he said, "Who said you'd be acting? It's the complete opposite: we want you to be yourself. Our house is your house and you're like our big brother. That means all you have to do is take it easy and not lift a finger."

"You mean you just want me to be Rowdy Salih like I always am?"

"No more, no less."

"Well then, as God would have it, I won't be respectable, honorable, or dignified."

"Says who?"

"Says my brain! You all—and no offense—have no choice but to treat me like Rowdy Salih in your house, and not like anyone else. Rowdy Salih from the hash den who's never been respectable his entire life—to people like you that is. You know, respectable people."

"But we do think you're respectable, that's why we're inviting you to come stay with us for a few days—or months, whatever you want."

"That's nice and all, but—"

Qamar al-Mahruqi interrupted him to put an end to the headache: "We've been down this road once already, Salih. Why don't you just try it? What have you got to lose?"

"Ha! Of course, I've got something to lose," Salih said, hiding an embarrassed smile on his tell-all face. He continued, laughing throughout, "On account of . . . if I lose, I lose . . . . Don't you see?"

Qamar al-Mahruqi peered at him, certain that there was likely to be something deep in those words and that it was important for us to know what it was. Qamar al-Mahruqi was always telling us that he was like a novice when it came to Rowdy Salih, the teacher, who possessed a lifetime of experience, parables, and wisdom. "What are you going to lose, precious? Give us a hint," Qamar said to rile him up.

"To tell you the truth, Qamar, I don't think I can. I know you don't have any problems understanding, it's just me. I don't know how to say what I want to say even though it's on the tip of my tongue. It needs getting rowdy, but at the moment I belong to Hakeem. I'm not my own master to go get rowdy right this instant. Especially since we're getting rowdy enough right now as it is. Let's keep at it. This rowdiness beats mine, I think we can all agree."

"You're one of a kind, Salooha," said Mustafa Lami, exhaling smoke. A deep silence ran through the party for a brief moment, but it was interrupted by Rowdy Salih, who gave Talat al-Imbabi a look of extreme gratitude, backed up by a sweet smile.

"In any case, Talat, sir," Rowdy Salih said warmly, "I put myself in your hands. When I'm done with this chore here, I'll go with you wherever you want and we can give it a try like Qamar says. And now we've told Hakeem so he can plan to make do without me for a day or two."

Talat and Ahmad both seemed pleased, exchanging ecstatic looks with the others, delightedly proud and wicked. But none of us had the slightest idea why.

THE WINDOW MAN

Ibrahim al-Qammah was a prominent member of our esteemed group, but if you saw him sitting with us, you wouldn't be able to pick him out. He certainly wasn't an intellectual—he didn't even know how to read and write—but he was usually the most elegantly dressed of us all, both in terms of taste and cost; he wore only the finest shirts, trousers, leather jackets, pullovers, shoes, socks, sandals, and slippers straight from the shop windows downtown. He smoked imported Rothmans, the strong, stinging kind. As far as language was concerned, he was more articulate than many who had certificates attesting to their brilliance and diligent study, even more than many who'd worked in politics at the national level. He used all the same tending-toward-High-Arabic words the rest of us did, the same terminology we used peppered his speech, and all the same eloquent clichés, both classical and contemporary. He listened assiduously to poetry and really understood it, appreciating the images and meanings as well as any poetry buff. His passion for world cinema qualified him to tell you to go see a new film called *The Visit* starring Anthony Quinn and Ingrid Bergman: "It'll blow your mind"; or *Beckett*, *The Great Gatsby*, *A Man and a Woman*. If you asked him about a new film playing in one of the cinemas downtown, he'd screw up his lips in disgust or wave his hand dismissively, and that was all the reason you needed not to go see it.

He was also a connoisseur of female beauty. It wasn't just any woman who turned his head, no matter how loudly her body or accoutrements screamed. And yet sometimes he just stood there, dazzled, muttering to himself: "Good Prophet of God!" though the woman or girl that had just walked past you hadn't caught your eye at all. To him, she was the beauty of an age, and when you turned to examine her silhouette as it faded in the distance, you could see that the man had a finely attuned taste, stemming from a pure and enlightened soul.

We'd taken notice of him even before he'd become one of us. It wasn't on account of his elegant bearing or his exquisite dress sense; no, it was more on account of his eloquence, his carefully worded, brilliant diction, his grace, his intense economy with all but the most necessary words: there was no small talk, no solecisms, no pretension, no hyperbole. We were certain that he hailed from a wealthy family, that he'd done graduate studies in London or Paris, particularly as his face said as much. His face was red like a caramelized pastry; round with plump cheeks and bulging temples, which pulsed with all the blood that flowed through them, and met in a nice beard, in the center of which was a dimple like that of a tender newborn. He had a thick neck, barrel chest, and a wide brow that looked like a bundle of crescents beneath a vault of short ginger hair parted far to the left. His hair and brow were like a hat that shaded two big eyes—as seductive as those of the female genies of legend—with long, straight eyelashes. He was short and sturdy, with a firm, slender waist, his body growing wider toward his chest and shoulders, where a forest of curly hair poked out of his shirt's buttonholes and covered his wrists and arms. On his left arm, he wore an engraved silver bracelet that looked like what was called a stone bracelet and, unlike most people, he preferred to fasten the leather strap of his watch around his right wrist. He was meticulous in his comportment, his expenditure, his smoking: he'd smoke ten well-packed bowls and then he'd leave and come back a few hours later for ten more, then another ten at sunset, and then around midnight he and a couple of friends would come and smoke any multiple of tens.

For fun, we tried to figure out what he did for a living; whether he had a trade, or a job, or a career. Qamar al-Mahruqi said he looked just like an architect, or so, and Mustafa Lami nodded his head in agreement, adding that, to be more specific, he thought he was an interior designer and perhaps he'd been a colleague of Qamar's from the College of Applied Arts. Talat al-Imbabi rubbed his mustache and stared subtly at the guy, suddenly proclaiming he'd cut off his own arm if the guy didn't turn out to be a photographer with a back-alley studio, citing as evidence his habit of shutting one eye when he focused on something, the inevitable result of working with cameras for a long time. Zaki Hamid, the hardworking, up-and-coming actor, said, "You can all relax, this guy's one of those extras who dream they'll be discovered by a director one day and that's why they're always so concerned with how they look." Al-Uqla, the caricaturist who'd begun publishing his work in a few newspapers, said he was certain that the guy was a member of the famous top one-half of one percent, the class of jobless heirs, who had enough money to last them forever and save them from the indignities of work. Just look how good his hash is, and how much he smokes, and his fancy clothes and his posh way of talking, his self-esteem. But Faruq al-Gamal, the vernacular poet, laughed with that Alexandrian lunacy of his and eyes that shone blue like the sea despite his dark complexion: "Whatever he turns out to be, he looks perfectly pleasant and nice enough to me."

Scoping out the customers and trying to figure them out and guess their backgrounds was one of our favorite den pastimes; we found it much more enjoyable than gossiping like other people. Thus we had no choice but to ask Hakeem for the lowdown on the clean-cut young man. Our motivation was confined strictly to confirming the accuracy of our individual certainties and our respective talents at unlocking people's secrets from a distance. Hakeem hesitated for a moment and it seemed that—for the first time in history—he himself was out of the loop.

"Now, I don't want to tell a lie, but what I heard from his friends was that he works in retail and apparently he does very well. More important than anything, though, he's a stand-up guy. He always leaves a big tip and he doesn't like to make a fuss about things. You can tell he's an all-right guy from how nicely he treats the creeps," he said, jerking his head in the direction of Wagih Farhan, who sat in a distant corner of the second room, hunched over a notepad balanced on his knees, lost in thought, occasionally scribbling down a word: he wrote poetry in Egyptian Arabic.

He had a very expressive face and never appeared to feel awkward in any way; nothing in the world embarrassed him. He was always borrowing money and going around from place to place trying to hock his poetry, song lyrics, vignettes for radio, or slogans for political campaigns. Yet all the same, he did—regrettably—possess some talent, it was just that his personality wasn't in the least bit genial. In no time at all, he'd set off your anxious suspicions; there was just something about him that made you reluctant to become his friend. Of course, there were rumors about his ties to the intelligence services, the secret police, and the censors, but those were the kinds of accusations that were thrown at a wide range of people indiscriminately so we never believed the rumors unless we saw reliable, material evidence. This, then, wasn't a good reason not to include Wagih Farhan in the group even though he wrote good vernacular poetry and had the right kind of rebellious, indignant, cynical soul. He tried to flatter us as much as he could and we immediately returned his compliments twice as good as we got, but we never invited him to sit with us. If he came over on his own initiative—which he often did—or came in when we were already there and joined us, we simply ignored him, not telling Sabir to include him as he passed the bong stem around; if Sabir did it on his own, we mostly didn't say anything. If Talat al-Imbabi were there, though, he'd hand the stem to the person whose turn it was, deliberately and rudely skipping Wagih, but at the same time he'd draw attention to his actions with a loaded apology: "Pardon me, Wagih," as if to say, "Get lost!"

Wagih never got upset, though, not even if you said it to his face. No, he'd just break out his teeth-baring, neutral grin and say, "No big deal. Sabir, bring a set of bowls just for me." If he wanted to antagonize us, he'd stay there beside us with his bowls, or if he wanted to signal that he was passing us over in turn, he'd get up and sit somewhere else.

I often felt bad for him on account of the cruelty of it and I myself struggled to understand the reasons behind it. I always tried to wipe out the residue of those painful moments by being very nice to him in conversation, saying hello or warmly returning his greeting, offering him a cup of tea, or a bowl of smoke, or a cigarette; I never hesitated to pick up a costly tab. One night at around two in the morning, I was surprised by a noisy ruckus at the entrance to the Hotel Imperiale, a pension on Ramses Street where I had a room on the second floor. I heard the commotion through the light-well where the service stairs ran past my bedroom window. I could hear my name being repeated in the clamor and I worried that it was a delegation from my hometown come in the middle of the night to tell me about some disaster. Then there was a scrum and a lot of footsteps running up the main staircase accompanied by jabbering, shouting, threatening voices. Then the door to the wing where my room stood smack in the middle, overlooking a narrow corridor, was yanked opened and there was a knock at my door. I dragged myself out of bed and opened the door to find the narrow corridor brimming with people, including the custodian on my wing, the security guard, the concierge, Wagih Farhan, and a young lady: a floozy who couldn't help but look like she'd been around and suffered much.

"What's going on? Wagih, what is this?"

The angry concierge stepped forward, gesturing: "This fella's been pestering us saying he wants to bring this girl up to your room! 'Just tell him I'm on my way up,' he says to me."

Wagih started shouting at him, almost coming to blows, "Watch it! I already told you *this girl's* my wife. What don't you understand? Here's the marriage license, buddy. Now do you believe me?"

He flipped through the folder he always carried around with him under his arm until he found the marriage certificate and started waving it in our faces: "See! See, anybody want to say something 'cause I'll stuff it in their face. How come none of you believe me? Is it because we look hard-up? That's not our fault. That's your fault for judging us, and you know exactly what I'm talking about. We had nowhere else . . . I don't want to go into it."

The concierge made a gesture of desperation as if to say, "I guess I have to deal with this lunatic tonight and I have a feeling it isn't going to end well." He looked at me once again imploringly so I turned to Wagih Farhan, sparks of anger shooting from my eyes: "What does of any of this have to do with us? Why are you coming to see me at this time of night anyway? We're not even friends. This is taking inconsiderate to a whole new level."

"Take it easy, pal. Tonight's my wedding night—I wish you all the same good luck very soon—and I couldn't find anyone to celebrate it with, but then when I was passing by here, I remembered that I have a dear, sweet friend—in the true sense of the word—who lives in this pension. I

61

thought I'd take the opportunity to come tell you the good news and that we could hang out and celebrate with you till the morning. If you want to go sleep, that's fine, we'll just sit here—it's no problem at all . . . and all will be right with the world!"

My patience was running thin so I extracted myself: "Don't you worry, all *is* right with the world. Now, take your wife and get lost. You ought to know that sort of thing isn't allowed here."

I shut the door and went back to bed, relishing the sound of the security guard braying at him in his Upper Egyptian accent: "I don't want any trouble out of you."

I could hear heavy footsteps retreating until finally they disappeared. The strange thing was that when I saw him the very next day at the hash den, he returned my greeting with a smile as if nothing had happened, and that same day Hakeem told me that there was some tart sitting on a chair in the alley waiting for "your friend." Things progressed from there and next thing we knew she was sitting beside him in the den. Then, because Hakeem was embarrassed by the look of her, he invited her to sit in the inner room with his children. The invitation tickled Ibrahim al-Qammah's wit and playful, sardonic spirit and he quipped, with a wink of his pretty eyes, "Now you're guaranteed to get your money."

We all broke out in laughter because we were well acquainted with the familiar daily ritual: in a few minutes, Hakeem and Wagih Farhan would start arguing about the bill, each accusing the other of trying to cheat him and in the end, after a lot of badgering and headache, it'd become clear that all Wagih had left in the world wasn't enough to cover the whole bill. Eventually, and always, Ibrahim al-Qammah would calmly place his wide hand over his broad bulging chest and nod at Hakeem, which meant the poet's tab was on him.

Ibrahim al-Qammah was the only member of our circle we hadn't met through Hakeem. We met him by chance on a gently breezy autumn afternoon when he came up and found us sitting in the alley under the den windows with an empty seat just beside us. He peeked into the den and saw it was full of a lot of rough types, so he said hello and gave us a shy, mild-mannered smile, his eyes slanting toward the empty chair as if to ask about its status. We all gestured to him at once, saying, "Please . . . " He sat down, leaving only a few centimeters between us and him. We'd smoked our fill, but still we hung around, hoping that the kid Tooha would show up with a new type of hash called Blue Powder that claimed to "make every night a full moon." When the bowls were brought to Ibrahim, he began to cut up—with his fingernails and not his teeth—a clump that looked like the size of a lemon in his hand. You could see how supple it was and you could almost make out the hairs at its green heart. He sliced off generous servings, which, when flattened out, nearly covered the entire bowl. Sabir came over with the bong and the coals, and when he handed the stem to Ibrahim, he pushed it toward us and looked at Sabir with a reproachful glance as if to say, "Where are your manners?"

Sabir brought the overturned pail he sat on over to us and said, "Mr. Ibrahim says 'Good evening' . . . "

"Thanks so much, Ibrahim. Thanks a lot."

We all took hits without any hesitation and when it was his turn, he inched his chair over a little so that he was sitting with us and from that moment on, he became a notable member of our group; if it hadn't been for his modesty, he'd have been our recognized leader.

Not two days later, as we sat in the same spot in the alley under the windows, looking with interest suffused with delight at a poem by Faruq al-Gamal in *Sabah al-khayr* magazine that spread over two whole pages accompanied by a brilliant illustration by a famous artist—it was so beautiful it almost distracted us from reading the poem—Ibrahim al-Qammah turned up and made to go into the den out of habit, but then immediately changed direction and came over to us. "Hello. Hiya." He shook our hands one by one, and he must have sensed the warmth of our welcome because he pulled up a chair and sat down. We noticed that he was being quiet and it seemed that he didn't want to be nosy, to distract us from what we were taking such great interest in, so Qamar al-Mahruqi showed the magazine spread to Ibrahim and pointed at Faruq al-Gamal: "That's our friend Faruq al-Gamal and this is his poem!"

Ibrahim blushed and gave Faruq a look of admiration and joy, and then he bowed his head with a cheery smile: "Hello! It's an honor to meet you. I've loved poetry and poets my entire life although it really eats me up inside. I wanted so badly to become a poet like Ahmad Rami who writes songs for Umm Kulthum. My heart's full of things to say. I just don't know how to say them in meter."

We exchanged a knowing glance, which Talat al-Imbabi translated into words uttered in a neutral tone, "And Jackpot."

Then in a split second devilish temptation danced over his face like neon-light adverts flickering green, red, yellow, and white, and he took the magazine from Qamar al-Mahruqi and handed it to Ibrahim, with profoundly mischievous respect, as though he were handing his supervisor his master's thesis, "Here you go. Read it so you can tell us what you think about it. Your opinion means a lot to us."

Ibrahim's face grew only redder and he looked like he was about to burst into flames. He was struck by a childish, exceedingly innocent silence and a genuine sadness, and then with a regret that broke your heart, he said, "I wish I could. It's a great shame but I don't know how to read or write. I barely know how to sign my own name. I know how to write numbers and add, subtract, and multiply, but still at the end of the day, my mind's all the capital I've got."

We were like marionettes whose invisible strings had been cut, falling down into our seats, creating a muffled echo. We didn't know how much time we passed in that state, until Mustafa Lami, who was sitting right beside him, brought us back to our senses. He took the bong stem from him and asked affectionately, "What is it you do for a living, Ibrahim?"

We all sat up in our seats and looked at him, pleadingly and pitifully, but he just smiled and with the simple ease of someone very proud of his work said, "I design shop windows."

"You design what?' Faruq al-Gamal asked.

"Shop windows," the lot of us chimed.

"What exactly does that mean?"

Talat al-Imbabi pursed his lips and shrugged as if to admit his own ignorance. Ibrahim al-Qammah chuckled politely and then said as if by way of apology, "Truth be told, it's not a very well known profession, although it's been around forever. There are so many jobs in life you never hear about even though people go and get doctorates in them."

Qamar al-Mahruqi waved his long arm, fairly exasperated: "What don't you all understand? The job's in the name."

Ibrahim al-Qammah turned to him and said, "Well, yes, but it's not very clear."

"Okay, then please explain it to us." Ibrahim nodded to Faruq al-Gamal to acknowledge the invitation, and turned to us: "You should all know that window design is both an art and a science. It's more than simply being clever. Not just anyone can design a shop window, even if they're an interior decorator."

Zaki Hamid the actor asked, concealing his sarcasm, "What kind of shop windows are these exactly?"

"All sorts: fabric shops, shoe shops, smallware, clothing, stationery, bathroom fixtures, anything that's for sale. Windows are a shop's face. They're a bit like its calling card. They have to be arranged in a studied, artistic way so that people who walk past stop to look whether they want to or not. That matters to me more than it does to the shop owners. Now getting the customer to stop, is that it? What's he going to look at? The merchandise the shop sells: like the new models. How can we arrange them in such a way that it tempts the customers and gets them to come inside and buy one? How can we dress a mannequin in a shirt or a pullover or a dress or a suit and then pose it in a particular way to best show off the suit? How can we get a pair of shoes to look as pretty as a doll in the window? Two things are of the utmost importance: beautiful presentation that attracts people and pleases the eye! And number two: the window has to be big, large enough to accommodate a lot of items. Sometimes the merchandise is rubbish, but an elegant presentation can make it look like the absolute top of the line."

Talat, Qamar, Mustafa, Zaki, and Faruq all looked convinced, like they'd discovered a new source of wonder and admiration. Qamar, his eyes sunk, said, "You don't say! It seems there's a lot going on in the world that we're clueless about, even though it's right in front of us."

"You know, they study this subject in Europe. It's called the Art of Display," said Mustafa Lami.

"Okay, but is this the sort of job that pays well, Ibrahim?" asked Talat al-Imbabi.

Ibrahim nodded, gesturing as if to say it had no shortage of benefits: "I'm the one who planned and designed all the shop windows downtown. You've got to remember there are only a few of us. There's probably only five or six of us in each city. Plus, it's not like every shop owner knows how to arrange a display."

"So how long does it take to design a window?" asked Zaki Hamid.

"Could be a day. Sometimes it's two days if we're in the middle of the season and we want to really pack the models in. But setting up a shop window from scratch, I mean, for the first time ever or at the beginning of a new season, that can take ten or twelve days."

Mustafa Lami was looking at Zaki Hamid with a look of good-natured mischief that was borne out by the question he asked next, "But tell me something, Ibrahim, are you sure you've never been a film extra or something?" As if he were accusing Zaki Hamid of being stupid and narrow-minded for having insisted that Ibrahim here was nothing more than human scenery.

We laughed begrudgingly, but Ibrahim said, "I've tried everything and I wanted to be a lot of different things, but never an actor. I've never thought about it; it just never occurred to me. God's good to those who know their limits. Take sports; I won several club championships."

"Championships in what exactly?" asked Talat.

"Boxing for the Ahly Club!"

"Why'd you give it up if you were winning, champ?"

Ibrahim pointed to his nose and laughed. "I got my nose broke three times and my jaw dislocated once. It was brutal. I also took a couple of shots to the eye that could've blinded me. The guys I used to fight always wanted to pummel me however they could; the only thing they cared about was hurting me because I had good form and knew how to throw a sly punch. I was going to win the decision even if my nose was broken. After a while, I found myself boiling over from all the injuries and every match I went to I was ready for a brawl, take-no-prisoners like! Then I heard some divine voice saying, 'Why don't you give up this violent and tedious game, Ibrahim?' And it made me understand that it was actually against my nature. It wasn't for me. As luck would have it, I took a jab to the gut that had me laid up in bed for two months and I never went back into the ring. That was about three or four years ago."

Qamar al-Mahruqi, who always liked to keep things as informal as possible, teased him, "Well, it's obvious you're quite old, Ibrahim, even though you still look young."

Ibrahim chortled. "None of you guys are older than twenty-eight, right? Me, I'm already three whole months into thirty-three."

"Yeah, but we can tell you've been a stoner since forever," Mustafa

Lami teased affectionately.

"You know when I started coming to this den? Twenty years ago! I was only twelve years old when I started getting high in hash dens. The first den I ever went to was Hakeem's; back when Marouf Street was just behind the den. I wandered near and far and ended up right back where I started."

"'Reckless youth makes rueful age,'" quipped Talat.

Qamar al-Mahruqi sat up, blinkingly searching for his eyes behind wrinkled eyelids. "How'd you know how to come here alone when you were only twelve? Only pros come to this place. Were you born cocky or what?"

"No, not at all. You know who it was who brought me here? Rowdy Salih! I swear to God. I bumped into him on the street and he said, 'Where you headed, Ibrahim?' So I leveled with him. I said, 'I'm dying to smoke a couple of bowls, Uncle Salih,' so he brought me here and he bought me some hash out of his own pocket, too. I've been addicted to Hakeem's den ever since—mainly out of love for Rowdy Salih."

"You mean you knew Rowdy Salih from before?" asked Talat.

"I've known him since I was five," said Ibrahim, pointing backward.

"How come?" we all asked at once.

"Rowdy Salih was my boxing coach from day one. He's the one who taught me the ABCs of the game, got me to fall in love with it. Trained me at the highest level."

"Our Rowdy Salih?"

"Yeah, the same Rowdy Salih. What's so weird about that?"

We froze for a second, but soon burst out in heavy, hysterical laughter. Talat al-Imbabi wiped the tears from his eyes with the silk handkerchief he kept in the back pocket of his jeans and asked, "What the hell does Rowdy Salih know about boxing, man?"

"What do you mean what does he know?" Shouted Ibrahim al-Qammah. "That was his job back in the day. Boxing coach."

Qamar al-Mahruqi slapped his forehead audibly and exclaimed, "No way! That's nuts! Nuts!"

Ibrahim al-Qammah continued, "It's obvious you guys don't know Uncle Salih very well. It's because you only know him from here, of course."

"Then please tell us a little about him," pleaded Talat al-Imbabi in a flat voice, devoid of any attempted provocation.

"Rowdy Salih used to be a boxing champ. He was Egyptian national champion in '47. In '48, he had his military service and when he finished, they made him a policeman. The Policeman's Club was supporting him so he could carry on practicing every day. Oh, it's such a long story I don't have time to tell it right now."

Qamar al-Mahruqi half-stood up and implored Ibrahim al-Qammah to tell us about Rowdy Salih, to tell us every major and miniscule thing he knew about him. Ibrahim said he was sorry, but the story was longer than the Epic of Bani Hilal, and maybe even more important. It needed time and clear heads, not simply because so much happens in it, but also because the person telling it has to enjoy the telling, has to be able to hear himself telling it so he can learn the things he'd failed to learn from Rowdy Salih the first time around.

Talat made him swear on his father's grave; Qamar beseeched him, almost kissing his hands; Mustafa Lami warned him not to jerk us around about this topic in particular; Faruq al-Gamal told him he was expecting an epic poem starring Rowdy Salih; but all the actor Zaki Hamid did was smile—maybe for the first time ever—and look at him sweetly. Ibrahim al-Qammah put our fears to rest by explaining that he personally derived great pleasure from recounting Rowdy Salih's life story and that he was even keener than we were to hear it, especially since it was what linked him to this place; it was just that he had work appointments that he couldn't break. If we met back up again at night, he said, we could all watch the film of Rowdy Salih together without having to worry about any bastard censors cutting even a single scene.

BORN UNDER A FATED MOON

O f all the kids who worked at Hakeem's den, Sabir al-Assal was the most active. One could've easily used the famous verse *If I hadn't addressed you, you'd never have seen me* to describe him except that Sabir didn't usually address you. He knew what a hash den employee's limits were and he was always careful to keep to them. He never involved himself in things that didn't concern him, and not even in those things that did concern him, if the people discussing them were the people he was responsible for serving. The customers themselves may have been down-and-outs with no real pedigree to speak of, maybe even actual lowlifes, but because they'd sat down and ordered, as soon as he knelt down in front of them to hold the bong and the coals, they immediately became his betters. He had no business joking with them, or smoking a bowl without their permission; that was how he was raised and he'd learned from experience that it was better to spare himself the headache.

Sometimes we didn't even see him, or we'd ask after him while he was kneeling right in front of us, serving us. He was a phantom; a mass of smoky cloud that poured out of the two fountains on his face. Smoke never stopped pouring out of his nostrils as he dispelled the thick smoke of the long rips he took to finish the bowl off after the stoners had smoked, or to make sure that the bowl had actually run out. We often tried to take as deep a hit as we could, all the while exasperatedly scrutinizing Sabir—minding his own business—so that there wouldn't be any dregs left in the bowl for him to finish off. But as soon as he put his burnt lips on the stem, the thick cloud of smoke told us that the bowl wasn't out yet and that Sabir—God grant him health—had only now got it going and burning at just the right high heat.

Sabir al-Assal was unlike any other hash-head phantom we'd seen. I often had to wear my reading glasses in order to make out his face during those quiet mornings that lasted till the midday heat mainly because Sabir specialized in a specific sort of customer: groups of fifty bowls or more. Groups like that needed a dynamic, experienced, good-natured kid, who knew how to transmit his own personal blaze through the bong he was holding to the customers so they'd mindlessly order more and more. Holding the bong was itself a skill: the kid had to kneel down so the smoker could take his hits comfortably and be able to expand his chest, all while nestled in his seat, and didn't have to bend over and struggle to smoke, not to mention not to have to deal with the bong, constantly unclogging and cleaning it. All these concerns formed the basics of the trade that Sabir knew perfectly well and proved the wisdom of the catch-phrase he constantly repeated: "Two bowls are better than ten," which meant that one bowl served well could get you high all on its own, and kick-start your toking appetite, and do the job of a hundred un-served bowls.

All the same, when I was by myself I preferred to be served by one of the other boys, and not Sabir because he'd take me for a ride. He'd make me smoke fifty or sixty bowls in no more than half an hour whether I could handle it or not . . . . No, thanks, man, no way! I'd rather he sat next to me as a friend and smoked with me at my preferred unhurried, stoner pace, which was easier on my lungs. When he did join me, Sabir would huddle up on the bench, even at the height of summer; it was obvious that he'd simply got used to all that crouching in the cold every winter of his life, so that he no longer had any choice but to sit like a hedgehog, nearly burying his entire head and thin shoulders between bent knees. I liked studying his features, or rather, I mean, the remnants of his features, which were completely worn away like an ancient copper coin and lost between his sunken cheeks and gaunt temples and made his mouth look like an arch stretching between two dried-up lakes and his thin nose like an imaginary bridge spanning two embankments. It was as if his face were a yellowed old map with torn-off corners and rubbed-down folds, which despite it all was still a documentary record of the destruction that had spread through the Marouf Quarter since the middle of the century. The quarter whose sons refused to leave and even though the government brought its bulldozers in to knock them all down every few months, they were still shocked to find that they'd sprouted up again and grown tall.

I looked into Sabir's eyes and I could see they were sleepy as usual. Even when they were open, they were ringed by twin bridges of sticky sleep, between which two black ships sailed over two tiny ponds of still blue water, but despite the movement of these miniature ships, the burden of nights so long they turned into days had given his eyes a permanently lifeless glaze.

People only called him 'boy' while he was at work because he was at least fifty years old; a few years older than Rowdy Salih. And yet all the hash den regulars and the folks from the neighborhood would address Sabir as 'Hey, Boy' while at the same time addressing Rowdy Salih as 'Uncle Salih.' It wasn't simply because one had totally white hair and the other hid his beneath a woolen skullcap that hugged his ears and brow, or because Salih was a giant and Sabir was a scrawny little rascal whose age was hard to pin down or even approximate. The difference between them was in the person itself. Rowdy Salih—despite his ratty clothes and generally repugnant appearance—had this inborn gravitas that compelled your respect, maybe because, to you, he was the living embodiment of the phrase, 'fallen on hard times,' whereas Sabir was the consummate sarcastic smart-ass always sneakily laying malicious traps to catch out any silly idiot dumb enough to fall into one. Plus he adored the name 'boy,' thinking it a good omen, since by God's logic we'd all been boys once, not to mention the fact that the nickname 'boy' suited his latent man-child's desire to be as naughty and mischievous as an orphan, especially as he'd suffered two tragedies as a child: he wasn't only an orphan, but a foundling, too.

We sensed a certain affection between Rowdy and Sabir al-Assal. Perhaps what linked them to each other and to Hakeem the den owner ran deeper than affection, and they had no problem talking about it openly in front of Hakeem as if he himself knew. When Qamar al-Mahruqi asked

Hakeem about the secret he allowed the smile trapped between the corners of his mouth to defy its shackles, to plan its escape, and he released it just slightly, almost let it get to the gate of his pursed lips, and then seized it and threw it back in its cell, calling out as if saying hello again to one of the most important principles he'd been taught as a child in Upper Egypt and always respected whoever abided by it: "It's because they're both from the same village. Children of the same spot of earth and born in the same house. They used to play with each other when they were kids." His mischievous smile grew agitated behind the iron bars of his cheeks and looked out through the windows of his eyes, wanting to expose something; that much, at least, he'd failed to hide and it piqued our curiosity. Hakeem went on, finishing his thought and pretending to ignore the smile that had escaped his grasp and run off in all directions over his face, "Lord knows what they used to do to each other when they were little. God protects and forgives!" Then he successfully tracked down his smile and reined it back in. At that point, a resounding laugh roared out of Rowdy Salih's chest. Calmly and regally, he looked at Hakeem, radiating an instinctive dominance, and in a rueful tone between peals of laughter, he said, "I swear to God the only person who ever did anything to me was you. You're the one who took my virginity, dammit. You tricked me and then you raped me. Got me to work for you for free. But as soon as I get my head together a little bit, I'm going to get you back for all of it and more! The problem is, gentlemen, that every time I get my head together, I go and get rowdy. But don't you worry, there's still plenty of time left for me and you. I'll make you sell all that land you've got in Upper Egypt!"

On Sabir's face, the bridge spanning the two sunken lakes of his cheeks collapsed, exposing the rusted iron struts that straddled the foundation of his two rows of blackened teeth, and we instantly understood that he was trying to laugh, but the long rips he'd taken from the bong weren't helping him; all he could do was jabber confusedly. He swung his scrawny arm up beside his ear, showing us he was swearing by the Almighty, He Who inhabits the Highest Heaven: "Yeah, Hakeem's never going to get into heaven. He made me and Salih sign in less time than it takes to blink. He bought me and Salih out dirt-cheap."

"Don't say 'bought,' Sabir! You got to pay money when you buy something? Are you saying what he gave us was *money* now?" shouted Salih, who was busy packing tobacco into bowls. Then he added, underlining his point with two big fingers, "We each got three measly pounds!"

"I didn't even get my hands on that. He paid me in opium. You know, he used to be a small-time opium dealer back when he first got here from Upper Egypt fresh off the felucca." He was going to say something else, but Mustafa Lami cut him off, jerking his hand backward: "Hold on a sec. Are you trying to tell us this den we're sitting in right now used to belong to you and Salih?"

"Of course," said Sabir proudly, perhaps even craning his neck. "Ask anybody in Marouf and they'll tell you."

"Not just us," Salih explained, "But he only bought me and Sabir's shares. This whole space from the door to the rowdiness inside used to be a three-bedroom apartment. Sabir inherited one room and the woman who sells radishes on the corner made up a space for herself in the living room. But, get this: she was the only one who put her foot down and got her fair share from him, and how! Poor me and Sabir here ended up giving him the whole kit and caboodle!" The smile had finally disappeared from Hakeem's face, leaving only a pale flutter over his bronze skin. He stuck out his arm and nodded dejectedly: "Why don't you just say I stole your inheritance?! These two were born here in this house. Both of their dads had rented rooms from a previous tenant and then the landlord died without any heirs. The house was falling apart so the government ordered it to be torn down. People who had their old rent contracts could get the equivalent in public housing, but the government told the sub-letters 'We don't owe you anything,' just like the World Bank told Nasser. The house used to be divided into two huge apartments, four stories high, but the only thing left was our friends here living dangerously in the apartment on the ground floor. Every time a car passed by, the walls danced and the roof clapped to keep time. You know, if the place collapsed and killed them, it would've been their own damn fault because the government had already kicked them out once. So I come along and take pity on them, and build this place with my own money. Do I deserve to be blamed for that?"

We laughed. With obvious sarcasm, Talat al-Imbabi replied, "Good God, who would blame you? Of course not, you should be thanked."

"But how'd you know the landlord's dead? Couldn't he just turn up here someday?" asked Qamar al-Mahruqi.

Hakeem's smile fell down dead before he could save it so he mixed it into the mound of molasses-steeped tobacco on the large tray where he cut the leaves and softened them up so Salih could fill the bowls with greater ease and more economy. "You know who the landlord was? He was from our village and I used to come here to visit him when I was a kid. I heard all the news about this place as soon as it happened so I came and I brought cash. If he's a real man, he can climb out of his grave and come find me!"

"Surely, he can't, though," said Mustafa Lami. "He's scared of you."

"Wait, you used to be young, Hakeem? You know, like, you were a baby once?" Faruq al-Gamal asked.

"Hakeem's always been a devil just like he is now," Talat al-Imbabi interjected.

Wala al-Din the short-story writer—a marginal member of the group, rather like his starkly emotionless modernist stories—laughed and pointed at me: "Me and this bastard have known Hakeem for ten years and he hasn't changed one bit. Remember? We used to come here and each buy a grain of opium off of him for five piasters. Hakeem was the one who got us into that nasty stuff."

"Thank God we gave it up!" I said with a disapproval I hoped would disguise my shamefaced lie.

Qamar al-Mahruqi was smiling absent-mindedly and contemplating Rowdy Salih. Then he began muttering to himself, "So Rowdy Salih was actually born in this house?"

Sabir pointed: "In that corner over there, right under the stairs. That's where his father's bed used to be and that's where his mother had him." Then suddenly he sprang to life and sat up straight, a feverish enthusiasm rushing through him. It was the first time I'd seen any signs of life in his eyes; the first time I'd ever seen a sign of anything in his eyes. Around his eyes and nose I saw marks, like fingerprints, showing his age. We'd all turned to look at him when he suddenly sat up in his seat. He began to shake his head, his hands gripping his knees: "Would you also believe that Rowdy Salih was born on the Night of Destiny? I swear on the Quran! Salih who's sitting right here in front of you! His mom, my aunt, Montaha, God rest her soul, waited right until the Night of Destiny to have him. She sat up on the roof waiting and when she saw a shooting star in the sky, she said, 'Lord, all I want is a boy after all these daughters!' And the All-Hearing decided that she'd give birth to Salih here on the Night of Destiny. Now you all know just how truly blessed he is!"

We were all completely enraptured as if we'd just discovered some ancient treasure, but the pure manic laughter flooding out of Salih brought us back to reality. "My dad got real rowdy that night. You probably think I'm lying when I say I could hear him in my swaddling clothes. I got rowdy, too: Waa waa waa! My dad said to my mom, 'I hope you enjoy your son, lady. You could've asked for some money or a nice house.' And then she told him, 'This is how it always is: *you ask for money, you get advice,* so I said I'll just ask for some advice and maybe He'll give me some money just to spite me.' The world was totally rowdy back in those days. Everybody was at each other's throats. King Fouad had a chronic case of one-foot-in-the-grave and then when he died, they said I brought him bad luck. My dad was mad 'cause I'd just turned up and my mother told him, 'Look at that! Five boys in a row, and before that, six girls.' My dad left home and ran away to Sudan, but my brothers were even bigger jerks than he was. They waited right up until I went to do my military service and then chol'ra wiped them all out. Well how come that son-of-a-whore chol'ra didn't take Hakeem out? I'll tell you why: because he's just like chol'ra himself, only he's more choleric!"

A storm of laughter shook the corners of Hakeem's smile, but he took his annoyance out on the molasses-tobacco he was de-clumping. "Oh, you're an ungrateful one! Mr. Talat wanted to take you to stay at his house but you couldn't cope with the luxury. Poverty's just the cure for people like you. But then again I don't think I've ever seen anyone quite like you."

Salih exploded in a roar of purely manic, cheerful laughter, but there was something else there. We got the feeling he was using it to say something that shouldn't be said. But all the same it was clear that the laughter was meant to mock Talat, for his house and the supposed luxury, and Hakeem, too, for his trivial idiot's imagination. The amazing thing was that Salih's laughter had an undeniable effect on Talat. His eyes were downcast and his fingers twiddled with his mustache in obvious discomfort; he wiped his brow with his palm as if trying to wipe the embarrassment from his face. Finally, he gestured and gave a look meant only for us, as if to say, "There's no call for repaying a gesture or pointless bragging." Then in a tone that only confirmed his wholly unintentional failure to avoid bragging, he added, "Forget about that now, Hakeem. It was an honor to have Uncle Salih. My house was happy to have him and he's welcome anytime."

The words slid off Rowdy Salih's tongue, "Thank you, Talat Bey. I told you before I went I wasn't going to make a respectable guest. Not because I'm not respectable, but because the invitation itself made it perfectly clear that I'm not respectable. I got the chance to be respectable for two or three days and I tried like I promised you I would, but I realized someone who's not respectable one place isn't going to be respectable in another place. It was a draw, you know."

"What do you mean?" Talat asked, shaking his head as if trying to think straight.

"Explain it however you like and I'll go along with it."

Hakeem stared at him in disgust: "Hey, you know what? You're an ungrateful waste of space."

Mustafa Lami exhaled smoke in a disgusted sigh and pushed the stem away roughly. Sabir al-Assal noticed so he stood up, shaking the laziness from his crooked back, and tapped the boy who was serving us on the shoulder. "Sorry, Sooka. I let you serve these gents so you wouldn't say I keep all the best customers to myself. Don't take it the wrong way but these folks here, nobody knows how to take care of them quite like I do. It's just I've known them forever, pal, and anyway don't worry, you'll get your share of the tips." He took the large, deadly bong and started cleaning it out, washing it, getting the rhythm of the water just right so it sang like music in our ears. He broke up some new coals in the ladle, pulled his own personal pail over and sat down. He threw his arms wide and waved to pull us in closer, as if to say, "Now we're going to start getting stoned for real; all that stuff before was just to clear our throats and empty our lungs."

THE WHIP AND THE LAW

In 1930—according to Sabir al-Assal—Rowdy Salih was almost seven years old and the calmest, meekest, most likeable little boy in all of the Marouf Quarter. In the first apartment on the ground floor of the house that was now Hakeem's den, Sergeant Abd al-Birr Salih of the Camel Corps lived with his family. The apartment was made up of two rooms, a hallway and a toilet, and there were—God bless the Prophet!— thirteen of them; six girls, five boys, and the man and his wife. The man was rarely there, though, since he was always away on missions with the Camel Corps and didn't seem to mind being away from home very much. They might spend a whole month in a village until it became safe and stable again after some long intra-familial conflict peppered by murders, arson, and destruction. Then they might get orders to leave suddenly for some town, to crush a protest or impose martial law with tyrannical, unconscionable force; those missions could easily spread from one town to the next with no end in sight.

A Camel Corps soldier has no friends except for his camel and his long Sudanese whip, made from animal tails soaked for ages in oil, long enough so that when it comes down, it burns and splits human skin right open no matter how much you covered up with clothes and cushions. The soldier was entrusted with his camel and had to be ready to hand it over at any moment. He was entrusted with his whip, too, but he could leave it with his camel after work and it wasn't the end of the world if he lost it so long as he bought a replacement. Moreover, everyone knew the government whip was licit and its flaming sting caused people to flee before they could be seriously injured; that was one of its features, you see. The hardened veterans in the Camel Corps derided the government whip. To them it was a child's toy; barely even suitable for a female entertainer to whip her donkey with as she traveled through villages trying to make a living. It could never do the job of imposing the strength of the Camel Corps and enforcing the law against people who were apparently—as the government had told to them—law-breaking riffraff including some with criminal inclinations and who were in dire need of stamping out. So the members of the Camel Corps all bought genuine Sudanese horsewhips—even better when they were made from crocodile tails! Some soldiers knew how to make them so they'd make them for themselves and others: these were real top-of-the-line whips; the kind that left their mark on a citizen's body for the rest of his life after a single encounter and ensured he'd never think about making trouble again.

No one would deny that the Camel Corps were good guys when they weren't using their whips to carry out government orders, and Uncle Abd al-Birr Salih was proof of that. You only had to ask any of the sons of the Marouf Quarter, whether those who lived in the high-class apartments near Suliman Pasha Street or those who lived in the traditional apartments near Sheikh Marouf's tomb in those old-style buildings with their ancient windows and verandas and washing hanging down from clotheslines, and which on the inside were little more than shacks and huts and talismans. The people from the proper buildings and the people from the shacks all thought that Uncle Abd al-Birr Salih, the Camel Corps sergeant, had a good heart even though he never went anywhere without that Sudanese whip under his arm. Only the children were scared of him because the constant scowl on his face looked like a round loaf of bread when the dough gets knotted up before it goes in the oven and it comes out scarred by long grooves; he looked to all the world like an ape, hissing and baring its teeth.

Nonetheless, having a good heart was one thing and being good at one's job was another. In the evenings, when he'd lay a burlap sack down in front of the house beside a water jug, a tea set, and a bong made out of a tin can, he attracted a big group of neighbors around his age. They all chipped in for the tea and the molasses-tobacco to enjoy the company of Uncle Abd al-Birr Salih and his wonderful stories about everything he'd seen in the lands of God's creation where the government had sent him. He'd get sidetracked and start talking about the whip, pulling it out from under his thigh and resting it on his knees as he waved his hand in the air above it as if to cast a spell:

A whip has to be able to set fire to the body because it's the government's reputation, its honor, and we in the Camel Corps are nothing but veins and the blood of the government's orders flows through us, and—just so you know—if we do what the government wants and put down a protest or break up a conflict, we're going to have to cut people up and throw them to the dogs until the mission succeeds. So, you know, it's in our interest—O Camel Corps Soldier—that our whips be forceful and decisive so we don't have to resort to killing or dragging people to death. For that reason, Brothers, a whip can be the most useful method of suppression because just one lash will do a great deal more damage to a person's emotions than to their body. After just one lash, a person won't be able to muster the slightest bit of humanity with which to defend himself or even protest; all he can do is scream or groan and run away frantically like a frightened animal looking for somewhere to hide.

These were the things that Uncle Abd al-Birr Salih of the Camel Corps used to say and which Sabir al-Assal still remembered, could never forget, not even a thousand years after he'd heard them on one distant childhood night of mischief, after he'd escaped from the shelter and come to stay with his ailing widowed mother and several half-siblings she'd had with a man who wasn't his deceased father. His mother would lock him out of the house to force him to go back to the shelter because she had enough on her plate, and her new husband had had enough, too. So Sabir, who had nowhere else to go, would sit there with Uncle Abd al-Birr Salih on the burlap sack in the alley beside his house and volunteer to serve him and run some errands for him as a gesture. But those moments with Uncle Abd al-Birr in the neighborhood were few and far between, usually lasting a day or two—four at most—before he'd get an order to appear at the Security Directorate ready to depart for some village somewhere. That was why Uncle Abd al-Birr didn't have his own bed where he could sleep during his brief furloughs. About two years after his son Salih was born, the bed was sold, then the wardrobe, then the copper basin and the laundry pot, and then all the cooking pots because, honestly, Uncle Abd al-Birr's household didn't need to cook anymore now that they'd got so numerous that they'd need the payroll of the entire Camel Corps to support them. All they needed was a few plastic plates because all they ever ate anymore was fuul midammis bought from a cart, or potatoes they fried in an old pan borrowed from a neighbor, or—on paydays—a dish of lentils cooked in a clay pot over their mud-brick hearth. Their bodies melted into one another's, each of them sleeping in whatever spot they could find. The girls slept all in a row from one wall across to the other while their mother slept crossways in front of the doorway so she'd be the first to wake up if—God forbid—someone tried to intrude upon her girls in the night. Salih and his brothers, on the other hand, were left to sleep in any spot—whether in the living room or in the alley—where there was enough room for their bodies, even if they had to sleep curled up. A scratchy woolen blanket made from strips of burlap sacks covered the girls, but it was nothing more than a gesture at preserving modesty. For their part, the boys waged war against the cold in the alley all day and night so there was no place left for it to sting them that wasn't shielded by a blanket of filth and mud thicker than a suit and overcoat, plus hood, since soap had never once touched their bodies and water never ventured past their faces.

Ever since he was a little boy, Rowdy Salih—God's truth—adored his mother and her circumstances upset him greatly. He did everything he could to try to bring home a piaster, sometimes even two. That good little poor boy hung around the Marouf market, helping to load up vegetable and fruit carts, staying up all night with the fruit vendor, taking one guava, apricot, or date at a time and arranging them on the cart artistically, but solidly so that it would hold together for days until the fruit was all sold out. Behind those arrangements, they hid the halfway-spoiled fruit, which the vendor sold for the same price as that written and stuck to the front of the display, so the customers would think he was giving them the same-quality fruit. At the end of the night, Salih would take whatever fruit the vendor had been ready to throw away back home to his mother. He often had to smack his brothers when they talked back to their mother or asked her for something she simply couldn't provide. He spent his entire childhood asking when the Night of Destiny would come so he could climb up to the roof and wait for the sky to smile on the lucky ones. Salih had only one wish: that God would bless his mother with a lot of money so that she could buy them new clothes and kebab, kofta, halva, and tahini sweets.

Aunt Montaha, Salih's mother, could see that her condition was only getting worse and that Uncle Abd al-Birr's salary—minus his expenses on those permanent sojourns—wouldn't even cover the cost of bread, to say nothing of the food they wanted to eat with it, or the rent, or kerosene for the lamp and the primus stove, and it would never stretch to pay for a single aspirin or Epsom salts, or a spool of thread to mend clothes, or a glass cover for the lamp, or anything along those lines. Those worries all made up one mountain and keeping a close eye on her daughters made up a whole other. Aunt Montaha was dark-skinned, you know, that dark Aswan complexion, but she had pretty features and a feminine body like that of the queens of Old Nubia, like Anas al-Wujud herself whom Uncle Abd al-Birr used to love to tell stories about. But her daughters—goodness gracious!—were the spitting image of Uncle Abd al-Birr, real apes. All they'd got from their mother was a supple softness, her slender neck, her round, proud breasts, her slim waist, and her slender hips on remarkably long, thin legs so that even the youngest one, who wasn't quite nine years old yet, looked like a camel and its teetering load when she walked down the street. Their marriage dilemma was that all the young men in Marouf had known them since they were children and had taken great care in memorizing their faces so that they could avoid them when trying to choose a bride from a respectable family. Yet when a stranger to the Marouf Quarter saw one of the girls from behind, his spine would stiffen with a frantic lust and he'd wish that he'd been born a dog, or a donkey, or a bull so that he could take advantage of the permissibility of mounting whatever looked good to him wherever and whenever he pleased right out in the open. This sudden and overwhelming lust would run away with him and he'd start thinking about renting this poor, unfortunate woman an apartment and taking care of her so that he could have her as his permanent, if unofficial, consort, but then he'd speed up—this was what usually happened—to try to catch a glimpse of her other side to round out

81

his ecstasy only to be confronted with the sight of a monkey or a gorilla; no more, no less. He'd inevitably freak out, perhaps scream in horror, or gasp, his face and entire body recoiling from the unpleasant surprise. All the same, they were very decent young ladies and their reputations were as good as gold. A few men came around asking for their hand in accordance with the custom of God and His prophet, but those guys were all bottom-scrapers who couldn't even afford a single meal. Aunt Montaha knew that her daughters were in a tough spot because of their looks, but she was convinced that there were some people out there among God's faithful, who still valued inner beauty, a good upbringing, and chastity, and that they would come in time. The only problem was that she had to see to their needs and protect their reputations by providing at least the bare necessities to save them from ridicule.

Aunt Montaha had a close relation who was married to the doorman of a big building in Garden City and who knew lots of people and could count on all the building's residents and their guests for favors. She was broken up about Montaha's hopeless situation so she tried to help her as much as she could, but what good was a drop of water in a drought? She met a big-shot lawyer from Shibin al-Qanatir to the east of Cairo on his frequent visits to the building in Garden City to see his sister who'd just got married to one of the tenants. She found out from the sister that he was single, in his sixties, widowed, and all his children had married and moved away. He could deal with the loneliness, he'd got used to it and discovered it possessed a certain sweetness, but he wasn't used to doing housework. He didn't need a live-in maid because between the refrigerator, canned food, and restaurants, his food needs were taken care of, no problem; all he needed was a trustworthy, clean, well mannered, and decent woman to sweep the villa, dust, mop, change the linens, do the laundry, and cook him a week's meals so that his butler only had to warm them up and tidy the rooms. He would send his driver to pick her up at the door of the building every week on Thursday morning and bring her back Friday evening or early Saturday morning if necessary, and he'd pay her ten pounds a month. Aunt Montaha danced with joy and prayed to God to look after her relation and make sure she'd never be forced to depend on others. The two women agreed they'd keep the job a secret strictly between them so that Uncle Abd al-Birr Salih wouldn't find out, and Montaha insisted the older kids pretend not to know what was going on and to carry on as if nothing at all were happening. Every Thursday morning she'd put on her black cloak and her plastic slippers and head to the building in Garden City with her son Salih in tow. They barely had time to finish their cups of tea—with milk—before the driver came to pick up her and Salih, who never left her side. On Friday evenings, they'd return to the neighborhood looking quite clearly revived.

Those were the happiest days of Salih's childhood and of all his siblings, as well; their new blessings showed. The girls' faces became pretty after they encountered fragrant soap, combs, hairpins, kerchiefs, and new colorful dresses, for the first time, to say nothing of the glow they got from three square meals a day. The mother found her way to the shops that sold china and aluminum pots, and headscarves and kerchiefs, which she bought in anticipation of her daughters' future nuptials. Salih—for the first time in his life—had a shirt and trousers to wear after a lifetime spent in the same dingy gallabiya that had dissolved into rags. His body was introduced to sweaters and pullovers, even to a spiffy overcoat like respectable folks' kids wore, and his sullied, swollen, torn-up feet finally submitted to shoes after having gone barefoot for so long. That was all made possible because the lawyer came to love Salih like a son. He bought him clothes and gave him pocket money to spend as he liked—his mother had no part in it. He played with him, affectionately as if he were his own grandson, and he insisted that his mother feed him—and herself—from the food she prepared for him. The man was fond of her, too: he respected her for her modesty, trustworthiness, and cleanliness both on the inside and out, and also because her cooking could stir his appetite from miles away. Thus he decided to keep her on and he never nitpicked with her about anything until she eventually became the master of his domestic life. He even started calling her 'Nanny' and he never bothered to inspect what she'd bought. He grew accustomed to her and he was generous; she was simply overwhelmed by it all.

Salih loved that man so much he worshiped him. He would tell Sabir al-Assal and the other kids in the neighborhood that he knew being born on the Night of Destiny had made all the difference, if only because God had given him a new father—a real-life pasha!—who loved him and taught him about the blessings of the world and the bliss of being someone's son.

His mother often let him stay at the lawyer's for a week or two during which time he'd go along with the lawyer to his office and run his personal errands for him. To him, the office was as big as a city: hundreds of clients coming in and out and hanging around. The office clerk met with all the clients to hear about their complaints, which they spelled out for him in boring detail, while he ran through every trick he knew to see if there were some loophole in the law that would kill their chances. Salih listened intently for hours and absorbed an astounding range of information that he later trotted out when he went back to the neighborhood to show off to the other kids. To put it plainly, the lawyer was the greatest, most important man in Salih's life; his only teacher. He imparted a conscience, and knowledge, morals, and virtues that Rowdy Salih would otherwise have never learned, not even if he'd gone to university. The seeds of everything good in Rowdy Salih, in his behavior and beliefs, were sown by the lawyer, who'd taught him that he, too, was a human being and that he deserved as much respect and dignity as anyone else. Salih wanted to teach the lesson that he'd been taught to all the other kids in the neighborhood and if he'd only been able to stay at the man's side until he reached adulthood, his life would've taken a radically different path.

The lawyer was deeply involved in politics, an important member of the Wafd Party, and he was well known across the country because there were branches of his firm in every provincial capital. He was always writing for the newspapers and he'd been a member of parliament for several consecutive terms, having been up for ministerial positions more than once. This was in the early forties during the Second World War when the whole world was topsy-turvy and Egypt had its own headaches as a result of the decision to join the war in Britain's interest when really we should have been fighting against the British! In any case, there then began an alarming number of strikes, from railway workers to the workers in Kafr al-Dawwar and al-Mahalla, till they reached every worker in every factory in every town. Everything came to a halt, and protests grew in number and became violent, and then the judges and lawyers in Shibin al-Qanatir—or rather, in the district around there—went on strike. All the townspeople went out into the streets to protest against the occupation and its puppets—meaning King Farouk and his men—and the notable leaders all made speeches. The police tried to disperse the crowd, gently at first, and then when that didn't work, they started beating them, but the people fought back courageously as if they were fighting against the occupying forces. Many prominent families had their pride injured that day, their superiority and standing assailed by the beating and mistreatment of their elders at the hands of the most extremely ignorant and stupid. Everyone lost control and the police grew more violent, but still they failed to rout the families and had to wire for the Camel Corps. Nevertheless, all the male citizens occupied the town square and demanded that the public prosecutor and the prime minister come and set down exactly what the people of the entire area were owed for the wealth and lives lost because of the idiocy of the police and their unjustified violence. The tumultuous sit-in was run by a group of notables from the district led by Abd al-Megid Bey al-Aryan, the big lawyer-politico, the man with the brave and stinging pen, who was a member of parliament to boot. They figured—owing to their high opinion of themselves—that even if the government didn't comply with their demands—although they represented an entire district—then they'd at least send a proper delegation to negotiate a settlement in a calm and civilized manner. They could never have imagined just how different the picture that arrived in Cairo was from what they might've expected. The news that arrived at Government HQ, the Royal Palace, and al-Dobara Palace was of a vicious revolt that had embraced the path of bloody struggle on a campaign to reach the heart of the regime itself and instantly everyone went mad, abandoning whatever common sense they had left. They considered sending an army tank battalion to level the town, but a sensible group put a stop to that lunatic plan before it got off the ground, and they had to satisfy themselves with sending a huge division of the Camel Corps to teach the scum some manners and keep them in their houses until all the masterminds could be quietly rounded up. But to leave them there sprawled out in the town square—even if it were a silent protest—well, I mean, that would have impugned the honor of His Majesty himself.

The Camel Corps detachment descended on the town square with a vicious attack, protected at the rear by cavalry on fierce, intimidating horses. The whips began to fall: on faces, napes, asses, and thighs without discernment; more like an unbounded frenzy. At that moment, Salih was standing behind the man, all but hanging off the fabric of his coat; he'd been stuck to him like a shadow since the beginning of the crisis though he could barely grasp the nature of the conflict and its causes, or appreciate its dreadful scope. But he was amazed by this giant of a man who didn't give a damn about the government or the king himself or the British and their awesome power, and who was facing them down, almost at blows. Yet this proud amazement was matched by a fear for the man's safety that grew and had now crystallized before his eyes as an imminent and life-threatening danger. Salih wished he could steal a revolver and empty it into the heart of anyone who tried to hurt his teacher-father, who possessed all those virtues that made him, in Salih's eyes, almost a prophet. But there he was lost underfoot, unable to tell camel hooves from Camel Corps soldier boots. All he could do was cling to the man's clothes and try to shift him with his entire body, to get between him and the fiery sting of the whip, but then suddenly the godless whip wrapped a belt of raging hellfire around the man's back; an audible whizz and then a crack, the sound of flesh ripping beneath the whip. Salih couldn't even bring himself to groan as he cradled the man against his little chest and the streaming blood made his clothing cling to his body. He vowed that if he survived, he'd memorize the face of the man who'd wielded the whip and kill him with whatever weapon he could find—yes, he had to kill him. The only thing that could satisfy his thirst for revenge was to kill the beast that had lit a blaze of agony in his veins. He turned his head, his eyes wet with hot tears, to see the face of the man with the whip, to plan how he could pull him down off his mount by his feet, to make him kneel before him, and then to tear out his windpipe. But he'd only just moved his head slightly away from the man and laid eyes on the feral soldier when the whip again began to strike his face, his nape, his entire body. The lawyer cried out in pain, tearfully begging God to protect him from the accursed devil. Salih screamed and threw himself on top of the man, not simply to protect him with his own frail body but to flee the horror that had struck him when he laid eyes on the attacking monster. It was his father, Abd al-Birr Salih. Are you such a cowardly beast, you fake of a father? Have you no mercy or compassion? Have you no heart? No emotions? He turned to show his father his face to put an end to the violence, but his father wasn't himself at that moment; he couldn't see, or feel, or hear. He was wholly absorbed in his violence like a participant in a Sufi ritual totally consumed by God's sublimity. The

broken-hearted boy shouted so his father would hear him and as plainly as he could he said, "Father, it's me, Salih! Stop hitting us." Uncle Abd al-Birr stared at his son and then reached his long arm down and snatched him up off the ground, throwing him behind him on the camel's back. Then he set off, hurrying the camel into a gallop toward open country and he didn't let the camel slow down one whit until they got to the entrance of the neighborhood, where he grabbed Salih and threw him to the ground. Then he told him that now wasn't the time for his reckoning, and went back the way he'd come.

That strange day many years ago split Rowdy Salih's life and personality in two. The person he'd been before was completely unrelated to the person who was born that day. Ruin took hold of him and failure followed him no matter where he went. He started to crack, but the strong foundation the lawyer had laid down in him was what saved him from complete madness. The first thing that changed was that Salih now hated his father with such a blind rage that he seriously contemplated killing him. About a week after the incident, Uncle Abd al-Birr returned. He'd inquired, searched, investigated, and eventually linked his children's new and improved appearance to his son's presence in the embrace of that man whose identity and station he'd found out about after the incident. He came home to put his ill-fated wife on trial and to serve as prosecutor, judge, and flogger. Salih stood there waiting for him, a knife concealed in his pocket. He'd grown taller during those days of plenty and more intelligent: he understood things better than his father now; he knew things that he didn't. Sabir al-Assal could still remember those few moments before Salih followed his father into the house: The marks the lashes had left on his back, chest, face, and thighs looked more like speed bumps, like bridges blue and puffy with blood and perforated like a sieve. He was in such a state he was on the brink of madness, telling Sabir, "But Sabir, the thing that really gets me is what was the point of hitting those people with whips? It would've been cruel enough if they were animals. How can that man be a father and a godless monster at the same time? How does he hide his inner beast? Why'd my mom agree to live with a man who'd have no problem cutting her up with a knife if the government told him to? What gets me even more though, Sabir, is they think people'll take a couple of lashes like I did and not say anything! How? Now that I've tasted the whip, I think I'd rather they just executed me. I mean, it'd be more merciful. It's more dignified to get hanged than whipped. God, Sabir, if only you'd seen Mr. Abd al-Megid when he was whipping him like a pig. I'm going to make him pay. No, Sabir. Don't say, 'He's your father.' I'll wipe him off my birth certificate!"

When he followed his father inside, he saw his poor mother trembling and cornered, his sisters wailing but daring not to make a sound, and his father, poised to strike, screaming at his mother like a madman, "Say something, you bitch! What do you and your son have to do with that lawyer? You working as a maid behind my back?" Then when he saw Salih approach, he shouted at him in disgust, "Here's the little prince now! So tell me: was this bitch working as that lawyer's maid or—"

Salih's heart broke out in flames and he began to tremble. He stretched to twice his normal size, his features morphed, his skin turned blue, and he shouted, rattling the windows and shaking the ground, "Hold it right there! She's not a bitch. This woman's better than you and your whole goddamn country. She wants to bring her children up with clean money earned from the sweat of her brow because the monster who married her and stuck her with all these mouths to feed is a disgrace. All he does is get her pregnant. What's the problem with her going to work for a respectable man if I'm always with her? She's not a bitch; the real dog is the guy who tears at people's flesh when they've never even done him any wrong!"

He was overcome with emotion and began to weep as if lamenting the memory of his miserable childhood and the loss of a light that'd brightened his life for a brief moment before this man-monster had smothered it. Salih refused ever to call himself his father's son again. "What did this guy whose good graces fed and clothed your kids ever do to you? Why'd you have to beat him so viciously? Why'd you have to humiliate him like that? The government told you to drive the people away, not to tear up their flesh. Is the government the only thing you obey? What's the point of obeying them when you're flat broke? You're not even human! If that decent man dies in the hospital or if he's permanently injured and unable to work, you'll have ended up harming the government you were supposed to protect."

Waves rose as Uncle Abd al-Birr Salih waded through an ocean of astonishment until he could no longer keep it together. He stood there dumbfounded, frozen, the end of his whip hanging loosely in his hand, his eyes like two blood-filled saucers, his gorilla features relaxed in a desperate attempt to disguise his anxiety about the surprise shot he knew was going to have to come. He began looking the boy up and down with his fiery glance, and then a sudden burst of energy flowed through him and he grasped the whip tightly. There was a glimmer of deceit in his eyes but when he saw his son getting poised, fully expecting him to try some dirty trick and getting ready to give it right back to him, he saw he was no longer the son he'd known. With his slave's malevolence, he drew out the ruse so that he could take him by surprise with a decisive blow; if it killed him, so be it. He clung to a lingering residue of fatherhood in the hope that it might have some impact on this mule, who he'd never once noticed had grown so much. He muttered as he stood there, faking composure: "You talking back to me, you dog? Standing up to me? Well, of course, you're her son and you two plot together. Like mother, like son." What Uncle Abd al-Birr Salih hadn't counted on was that his son was even more malicious, even wilier and trickier than he was, for in the blink of an eye and without the slightest forewarning, Uncle Abd al-Birr Salih found that his whip was no longer in his hand, and that it was now in the possession of his son Salih. Salih held the handle tightly and wrapped the whip around his solid hand, holding it like a pro who knew exactly how to place the tongue of the whip on whatever part of the body he aimed for. Uncle Abd al-Birr Salih stood there powerless, completely helpless as Salih began to wave the whip at him menacingly.

"I'd love, just love to give you three or four good ones like the ones we took, me and that good, decent man. I'd love to make you taste the fire as it eats through your flesh. I'd love to make you understand just how degraded this whip of yours can make an innocent person feel. I'd love to show you how one lash from this can damage a person's dignity for the rest of his life. I'd love to, I'd give anything to, but my heart won't obey me. It's not because you're my father or because I give a damn about you. No! It's because I can't stand to see someone's flesh—I can't even stand to see an animal—get torn up by a whip. I'm not like you. I'm not a monster. I'm so lucky I didn't turn out like you. I didn't inherit anything from you. I took after my uncle on my mother's side, on the side of this woman, who saved your children from hunger and ruin and who—despite all that—you were coming to whip. You'll never get your hands on this whip again. I swear I'm a woman if I don't make you pay."

Uncle Abd al-Birr exploded with rage and pounced on his son like an old leopard. He wrapped his long hands around his son's neck and thrust his nails into the flesh. He began shaking him violently, baring his teeth and shouting, "Oh, so it's come to this, has it, you son of a bitch? You son of a whore! I swear to God I'll choke you dead right here."

If a plane buzzing overhead could shake the Muqattam hills, Salih would've trembled in his father's clutches, but he was planted as firmly as a mountain. He didn't want to have to lay a hand on his father, but when the nails pierced ever more deeply into his neck, he pushed his father away with a modicum of gentle restraint, and a great deal of suppressed anger, but still Uncle Abd al-Birr was launched backward through the air like a storm-blown feather. He only stopped when he slammed into the wall and fell to the ground in a heap. The old man was still strong, though, solid and nimble. He got himself together again and stood up, sparks shooting out his eyes, and pulled a switchblade out of his vest pocket. He flicked it open lightning-fast and ran forward, pointing the blade straight at his son's heart and he'd have landed it home, too, if only Aunt Montaha hadn't screamed and alerted her son. At the crucial moment, he jumped out of the way, straight through the door, and then whipped out his own knife, but Sabir, who'd been crouching in the alley beneath the window and had seen all the action through the iron grate, valiantly leapt up and snatched the knife from Salih's hand: "What do you think you're going to do? Get away from here as fast as you can!" Then: "Uncle Abd al-Birr, take it easy now."

Salih could see that his father was a moment away from throttling him so he grabbed him by the arms and shoved him backward; Uncle Abd al-Birr went reeling, flailing in the air. Then Salih bolted and Uncle Abd al-Birr ran off behind him, waving his switchblade, Aunt Montaha behind them shouting, and all her wailing daughters hopping behind her like frightened ducks, while the younger boys ran off after their mother until they all disappeared into Marouf Street and their voices drifted off as if plunging down a well.

Salih ran ahead slowly so as not to demoralize his father and to draw him into running after him and he led the whole circus of runners, switchblades, and shouts to the Qasr al-Nil police station where he ran right inside. The oaf was so fixated on chasing his son down no matter where he went that he ran after him straight into the police station, brandishing his switchblade. But then when he suddenly found himself in the chief inspector's office and saw his son handing the man his whip, he felt a sudden horror. He didn't know what to do so he just stood there, switchblade in hand, looking around him, appalled at his wife who stood beside him, shouting, wailing, and slapping her face. The chief inspector stood up and walked over to him calmly, then he took the switchblade out of his hand and placed it on the desk beside the whip. They eyed each other warily as Sabir al-Assal peeked out from behind the wooden screen, wanting both to advertise his presence and hide at the same time. In truth, he was firmly on the side of Salih and his mother after having heard and seen the man's despicable brutality.

Salih filed a formal complaint against his father, detailing everything that'd happened. He didn't exaggerate, but he was firm; his incensed tone must have given the complaint an air of credibility because the chief inspector listened to him closely, with compassion and interest, even going so far as to silence the father every time he interrupted his son. The chief inspector was amazed by how clever Salih was and by his way with words; he even repeated some of Salih's phrases with a dreamy air. He took up half the police report dictating Salih's testimony word-for-word. "Write: 'improper use of a government weapon in the abuse of his children. Evidence: a network of swollen blue bridges all over Salih's body; attempted murder of his own son with a switchblade including insistent pursuit in the course of which the suspect even broke into a police station; brutal assault on the person of the lawyer and prominent politician, Abd al-Megid Bey al-Aryan, who lies presently in the hospital between life and death on account of lashes received to his ears, eyes, and breast, and note also that the son of the accused was an eyewitness to this.'" Salih was sent for a medical examination and the prosecutor ordered Uncle Abd al-Birr to be detained on the basis of the investigation's initial findings. Salih went directly from the public prosecutor's office to the hospital to see how Abd al-Megid Bey al-Aryan was doing. It was obvious that Abd al-Megid Bey was suffering from a number of problems, the most obvious of which was the previously undiagnosed diabetes that was making it harder for his wounds to heal. A team of doctors had worked through the night and he was saved by some divine miracle, but he was permanently injured and could never fully recover. He no longer needed a maid; he needed a whole team of nurses, and he stopped going into the office except for the odd brief visit.

Salih, who'd been profoundly saddened by what had happened to the man, cut himself off from the world; he was no longer interested in anything, not in eating or getting dressed, nothing at all. He stopped shaving, refused to change his clothes; he refused even to wear clothes unless they were ragged and filthy like he was. He cried a lot when he was alone, looking to the sky and reaching out. He walked the streets, wanting nothing more than to kill the gloomy sadness that now plagued him. The clerk at Abd al-Megid Bey's firm offered him a job as an office assistant.

"You mean you want me to come here every day at a certain time and leave at a certain time?"

"Of course. It is a job, isn't it?"

"And wear a suit like the other assistants?"

"It doesn't have to be a suit. You just have to look presentable."

"And you're going to give me orders: do this, don't do that?"

"Which you'll follow to the letter."

"No, thanks."

"We'll give you six pounds a month."

"Trust me, I'm not worth half a piaster."

"Why would you say that? You're a good kid. You deserve it."

"The problem's me. I can't stand to have anyone control me anymore, not even to make a living. Even if you offered me a salary to do no work at all, I still wouldn't take it. I'd rather be dead than be a freeloader."

"Well, it's up to you."

"But I do want to ask you for a favor."

"Fine, but make it quick."

"My case against my father is coming to trial soon and I'd like one of the lawyers here to represent me."

"Of course. We'll take care of everything."

The lawyer who represented Rowdy Salih at the hearing laid into his father, using the worst possible language to describe him and showing the judges the lingering traces of the whip on Salih's body and making reference to the medical report. In his fiery summation, he went on to say that this was the monster who'd assaulted Abd al-Megid Bey and that the time had come to put an end to this blight on humanity and finally do away with these brutes who terrorize the innocent.

The court sentenced Uncle Abd al-Birr to six years' hard labor on both counts and permanently barred him from military service. Salih was livid. The truth was that—despite his deep loathing for his father—he'd never wanted him to suffer such a cruel punishment. He immediately pleaded with the lawyers to appeal the ruling, but the appeal ended up getting his father an extra year. And so Uncle Abd al-Birr was taken to prison and his whip seized just as Salih had vowed it would be. The family unit broke down completely. His mother did what she could to earn a living: from selling vegetables that were past their prime to selling ladies' goods door-to-door and working as a washer-woman in other people's houses until—by dint of backbreaking work alone—she was finally able to marry her four girls off to laborers from Upper Egypt, just like Hakeem had been before he'd settled in the den.

All this time Salih was adrift, floating through the streets of the Marouf Quarter and its hash dens, training himself for what he believed was the most important game of all, one which every decent man had to learn: to renounce, to compel one's body with an implacable force not to desire anything at all, to train one's soul—which, God tells us, leads us to evil—not to order you to do anything, but rather to obey you and your wishes and to carry them out.

He would tell Sabir some of the things the voices in his head had told him, but it was all a load of impenetrable nonsense no one had ever heard out of him before. Yet every time Sabir al-Assal decided that Salih was crazy for sure, no doubt about it, something he said would strike him; it'd confuse him at first for being strange and shocking, but soon enough while he was getting stoned, it'd dance over the flame of the bong and stick in his mind because really it was an entirely rational thought and a most perfect distillation of wisdom. But who—Sabir asked himself—was strong enough to put those grand words into action? Salih, though, was the type who practiced what he preached.

Once, after prayers at the mosque of Sheikh Marouf, Salih stopped the imam in front of all the worshipers and said, "No offense, sir, but when you start practicing what you've been preaching to us about for the past hour and a half, and giving us all headaches, then you can come and warn us about evil. Why've you been trying to scare us with stories about what happens to thieves after they die? Didn't I see you last night taking change for a pound from Azuz the grocer when you never gave him the pound in the first place! I saw it folded up in your palm with my own eyes, but you just kept arguing with the guy and saying, 'I gave you the pound,' and lying through your teeth. Just drop it, man. Give us a break!"

Everyone just froze, stunned, as though they were deaf, dumb, and blind. The preacher was taken completely by surprise. He had no idea how to respond so he simply turned and stepped over the threshold of the mosque to get his shoes. Salih, though, just giggled innocently and patted him on the back, whispering in his ear, "Hey, don't let it get you down. Just don't do it next time and always remember: God sees us with our own eyes, which means he's got to put someone like me there to see you, and if someone sees you, you know he's going to let you know he knows, even though he really ought to just stop you." The preacher couldn't bring himself to look Salih in the eye and as soon as he got his shoes on he ran off, disappearing down the nearest alley.

On the day Salih was called up for military service, Sabir had already dodged the first medical test because he knew he'd pass with flying colors. He also knew that they could never catch up with him because he used so many pseudonyms, all of which were recorded in logbooks at the many police stations he'd been hauled to for a variety of different offenses. Nowadays, though, he regretted it; if only things had gone according to plan, he'd have been a policeman by now. Salih, on the other hand, completed his military service, serving for many years in the Medical Corps Support Brigade. They lost touch with each other during that period, but Sabir and all the other sons of the neighborhood always reminisced about Salih and his funny stories and the things he'd said, and then they'd laugh and cry out, "God bless you, Salih, wherever you are!"

CUT OFF

One day I went to the hash den by myself very early, which was unusual for me, at around eight in the morning. The Marouf Quarter was half lifeless, many houses had only just shrouded themselves in sleep at this hour after a night's backbreaking exertion in hash dens and in the market, in coffeehouses and on kushari and kebab carts. White-collar employees of every grade, on the other hand, were rushing off to work, sleepy and squinting. Coffeehouses received new staff for new shifts and fuul midammis carts spread along Antikkhana, Champollion, and Marouf streets. The air filled with the smell of morning, and radios blasted the Quran in Sheikh al-Hussari's voice on his show, *Scripture Recited*. Sitting on a bench in Hakeem's den at an exquisite moment like that you could reach the most perfect highest of highs.

That wasn't why I'd come, though, on a solo visit so early in the morning. What I really wanted was to get Rowdy Salih all to myself at that time of the morning, when there weren't any customers, or noise, or even Hakeem himself; not a soul, no one but Salih, who liked to get his work out of the way early so he could have his evenings free to sit there as a customer like the rest of God's creation. I, too, had become a devotee of Rowdy Salih, and my enthusiasm had begun to overtake that of the other members of our circle. I'd noticed that each of us had his own link to Salih and that each was unique. I mean we each had our own special relationship to Rowdy Salih. We could all sense it in ourselves and our connection to him was determined by how deeply we thought the feelings ran. For my part, I embraced this link, which to me epitomized my love for pure observation, for feeding off everything I saw and discovered, because I felt that perhaps there was some value hidden in this example of primitive humanity that deserved to be respected and appreciated, to be discovered and drawn out. I also felt that I needed to embrace all the other links, as well, in order to understand the true secret behind each of our relationships with Rowdy Salih. I knew these were all highly personal psychological and spiritual relationships and that they were motivated by undeniably dissimilar reasons, which, however, had to be formidable because they'd transformed our initial enthusiasms into abject devotion. How else could you explain the fact that almost every member of the group was sure that his relationship with Rowdy Salih was the most solid, and loyal, and affectionate, and intimate? Thus I found myself, in some way and to a certain degree, implicated in all of these relationships; I'd become a participant in the experiment as well as its observer. But even if I failed to find out the truth about the other parties involved, then at least I was certain to succeed—with their help, of course—in uncovering some of my own secrets.

As luck would have it, I found Rowdy Salih sitting on a burlap sack in the corner. He was dressed in a tank top and plain white trousers, both of which were dingy, but against the darkness of his thighs, legs, arms, shoulders, and chest, they looked as white and pristine as could be. The cup of tea beside him steamed in the morning air and through his sleepy eyes, he began to scrape out the bowls with an ancient table knife. Hoping to share in the emotions of daily life, I'd brought along a load of fuul, falafel, and eggplant sandwiches, a paper cone of pickled vegetables, and a bundle of green onions, making allowances for Salih, who I was going to insist have breakfast with me. I was a bit disappointed when I saw the cup of tea in front of him, but I put on a brotherly tone and called out to him, "Have you had breakfast yet, Salih?"

He smiled politely. "I don't usually eat breakfast, to be honest."

"What about lunch?"

"Ha! I don't really get rowdy about making appointments for when I eat."

"Well, why don't you come do all this food a favor? I need some help here."

"Even if the sky was about to fall, I still wouldn't ever do anything I didn't feel like doing."

"So when are you going to be hungry then?"

"If it weren't for getting rowdy, I'd never get hungry."

"You mean getting rowdy's the only thing that gives you an appetite?"

"No, not at all. It's just I eat to give the alcohol something to land on."

"Well, you know what they say: 'Hungry is healthy.'"

"Hungry'll make you good, but being full will lead to sin."

"What do you mean?"

"It's like this, see: somebody who's always used to being full will do wrong if he has to miss even a single meal! All these guys who're stealing from us are the ones who're used to being full all the time and they're paranoid it'll stop. Lord protect us from the evils of the stomach! Real men ought to do like I did."

"What was it you did?"

"I taught my stomach some manners! I taught it not to ask for anything and that I'm the one who's going to give it what I feel like when I feel like it. It'll go to bed whether it's eaten or not and it knows I think it's worth less than an old shoe. If my stomach thinks it can use its animal urges to get me to disgrace myself and mistreat others, well, fuck that!"

I confess I put aside the food I'd brought with me, even though my mouth had been watering when I bought it. The only thing I craved at that moment was a cup of tea. Salih had got two sets of bowls ready for me and set them down beside me, waiting for me to top them off with hash, but when I didn't, he asked sweetly, "You haven't got any hash?"

"No, Salih, I don't."

"I'll go buy you some."

I'd also seemed to have lost my appetite for hash and I was thinking about what Salih had said a few moments ago about conquering his stomach, mind, and body so that nothing could ever enslave him and damage his dignity. Even getting rowdy wasn't something he was addicted to: he did it because he wanted to, and often when he didn't feel like getting rowdy, he didn't. I was confronted with an urgent and unsettling question: if Salih could overcome any need for food or a bed, what fraction of his boundless strength would I need just to give up hashish? But when he stood there beside me and held out his hand, I gave him the money for the hash and for the first time in my life, I tasted the bitterness of repugnant submission.

I sat there in the den by myself, blind to the world around me as Rowdy Salih's words floated back and forth in my mind trying to get even more of my attention. For a moment, I'd relent, only to ignore them for much longer, figuring they were no more than noisy flashes like firecrackers and children's snaps, which were damned annoying when they exploded, yes, but everyone knew they weren't dangerous. Nevertheless I still feared them and fought to keep them out of the sensitive sectors of my mind so they wouldn't stick there like they'd stuck in the minds of my friends, who found in them a sort of virgin wisdom, a manifestation of the first encounter. I told myself that this was one of those times when you really needed to know what *reason* actually meant: when it meant taking control of disruptive ideas and re-aligning one's behavior with the norm so that you could tap into the reasoning collective. That was when the mind got adopted into the collective, which would punish it, restrain it, and impose its backwardness and status quo on it until it could be completely reined in. A lot of us sympathized with those who— in our stead—broke bonds of every sort to escape authority. Yeah, all right, sure, but what was all this daydreaming before I'd even smoked a single bowl? Rowdy Salih broke through the mental fog, his poignant words ringing in my ears:

God made the world a rowdy place and then he filled it with rowdy people. Everybody here's rowdy. They're all rowdy 'cause all they want to do is get rowdy and they either get to or they don't. And everybody here's run-down. But they're all run-down in their own way. And me, I'm the king of the run-down 'cause I'm run-down in every which way.

My attention was drawn to a looming shadow on the ground and I looked up to see my good friend Qamar al-Mahruqi standing before me, laughing that clarion laugh almost exactly like Rowdy Salih, with its succession of interrupted *ah*s and ending with a drawn-out, blissful cry, which rested on individual letters to sound them out and give a joyful melody: *G . . . e . . . . t I . . . . n!* Nobody actually knew what 'Get In!' meant. Rowdy Salih was the one who'd come up with it. Did it mean 'Get in on the rowdiness?' Or was it just a stand-in for 'Heads Up!'? Whatever it was, the thrill of imitating his laugh and shout took our minds off the search for its intended meaning.

I raised my head, attempting to survey Qamar's tall stature, his narrow hoopoe-ish head, his delicate features, his sunken cheeks, and his pleasant, cheery face that turned to pure joy when he laughed. He was wearing a black coat over an open-necked—no tie—cream shirt and gray flannel slacks. He was carrying a folder with 'American University in Cairo' printed on it, which held a notebook and a copy of an English book I'd heard he was planning to translate into Arabic. I struggled to read the title just so I wouldn't have to ask him about it. The book was called *To Hell with Culture* and because it was popular at the time I could easily make out the author's name: Herbert Read. A mechanical pencil—you know the kind where'd you squeeze down on it to get the right amount of thin lead to come out—was clipped on one of the pages. In addition to his passion for all kinds of polemical books, Qamar al-Mahruqi loved elegant and expensive objects. You always saw him with the most luxurious pens from global brands like Parker, Sheaffer, and Trupoint, and with Ronson lighters, and he wore Persol glasses and silver rings with gems, and he had amazing leather briefcases in all different sizes and a gazelle-skin wallet. He'd been like that his entire life: beautiful and beauty-loving, but he was quick to overdo it, all of it, and quick as well to drop something for something else no matter how rare or expensive it was. Possessions made him instantly happy and he grew tired of them just as quickly.

He tucked his folder under his arm and began to clap his two long hands excitedly: "Bravo! It looks like today's going to be a good day." Then he sat down beside me on the bench and leaned over and we kissed on the cheek as if toasting this unexpected, lovely morning. He spotted the row of bowls filled with molasses tobacco on the overturned pail at my feet and instantly understood that I'd sent someone to go buy hash, so he stretched his long, delicate finger, like an octopus's arm, to the bottom of his coat's magical inner pocket and pulled out a piece of rolled hash about the size of a knuckle. It was a dark olive color and it looked delightful and delicious. Qamar, owing to his great generosity and squeamishness, never sliced hash with his teeth; he objected to this vile practice because it made the hash smell like saliva and ruined the flavor. Rather he'd cut it with his ever-clean fingernails and that was why his pieces were always big and thick and completely covered the tobacco. As he was topping off all the bowls, he said, "There's no one here, I guess."

"No one but Salih."

"He's the only person brave enough to wake Umm Yahya up at this time of the morning."

"He's the only person who's friends with her dog."

"You know, I think Rowdy Salih's one of the world's greatest logicians."

"Logicians?"

"You know, it's possible his logic doesn't sync up with most people's and they hear him talking and they think he's crazy, but if you really think about what he says and parse it bit by bit to understand it, you'll see that really our logic's the one that's fuzzy; his is crystal clear."

He stood up and walked over to the bongs, picking out the best one. He pointed the stem at the ground and water began to pour out in a thick stream. He began writing on the ground in a large thuluth script and as I followed it I saw it spelled: "Oh Happy Day." Gracefully, he filled a tin cup with water from the amphora and filled the bong up, sucking on it and blowing out excess water until he got the bubbling rhythm just right. He set it on the floor by the bench and walked back to the brazier of coals that were about to go out. He picked up the big tongs and picked out a coal about the size of a pomegranate and dropped it into a pan then he took the iron hammer and broke it up into smaller pieces, which he emptied out into the strainer. He swung the strainer about like a pro until all the ash had blown off and the coals were blazing and then he sat down, holding the bong, and pointed the stem at me, bringing it closer to my mouth and giving me a smile that was all sweetness and goodwill: "Oh Happy Day!"

With great gratitude—and rather than getting up and embracing Qamar—I took the stem in my mouth and began to smoke, feeling refreshed and full of hope. Just then and for just that moment, an idea struck me as if it were the hash sizzling and glowing beneath the blazing coal and spreading its perfume and rejuvenating enlightenment through my mind. I was so tickled by the idea, I asked myself how I'd failed to realize it before: I'd determined, without recourse to any deep investigation or comparison, that my dear friend Qamar al-Mahruqi, whom I'd been close to for more than ten years, was—in fact—a clean-cut version of Rowdy Salih. This version had received a higher education and been exposed to a huge swathe of intellectuals, and it didn't matter—at least, not for the moment—whether this educated version represented progress or the opposite, whether it was more correct or corrupted. My mind ran after its discovery with unbridled enthusiasm and I gave myself the benefit of the doubt that Qamar al-Mahruqi had clued me into this breakthrough himself by performing the role of the hashish waiter with consummate skill and without the slightest shame—it was that last bit that really brought out the similarity between him and Rowdy Salih. No, that couldn't be the reason: I myself did exactly the same in those rare moments of brotherly intimacy and served Qamar. But still I wondered: Was this a case of influence leading to conformity? Or was Qamar al-Mahruqi really cut from the same cloth as Rowdy Salih?

Qamar al-Mahruqi smoked me out one bowl after the other in the best morning session of my entire life. He was drifting in and out of my mind's eye: he'd come apart and come back together, to come apart and come back together once more. He was there copied and multiplied in various shapes and colors from ever since the first time I'd laid eyes on him in the Barabira coffeehouse in Zamalek one bright morning just like this one. It was a book that brought us together that moment when he came in and saw me absorbed in a huge tome. The coffeehouse was full of empty chairs, but when he came in, a leather file with a little triangle of yellow celluloid sticking out the top under his arm, he walked past all the empty chairs and headed straight toward me as if I'd been waiting for him.

"Hello there."

"Hello."

"Do you mind?"

"Please."

He pulled out the chair across from me and sat down and then he ordered a tea with milk and began flipping through *Sabah al-khayr* magazine, but I could tell he was watching me with interest, and my suspicions were borne out when we locked eyes and he broke the ice with a smile so soothing it was like a balm. He pointed to the book laid out in front of me.

"*War and Peace?*"

I was amazed he could tell what it was without even looking at the cover. "How'd you know?"

"I've read that edition more than once, but you know it's a shame that Dar al-Fikr only published two volumes because Edwar al-Kharrat stopped translating it. I heard that Dr. Sami al-Droubi—do you know him? He's a Syrian writer—apparently he's translated the whole thing. People who've read it say it's better than Edwar's translation because al-Droubi was able to capture Tolstoy's style, too, whereas Edwar translated the book in his own style, which means what you're reading right now is the Edwar of *High Walls* and not Tolstoy."

I learned he was a student at the College of Applied Arts and that he'd been trying to write a novel, but he wasn't happy with what he'd come up with and decided to tear them all up and give himself a break, except that lately he'd begun writing a novel based on the life of the actress Nagla Fathi, which he'd got to see up close and in various contexts, and in which he'd found the sort of uplifting values that were so tempting to a storyteller, and so he was optimistic that this time he could make a serious go of it. In return, he learned that I'd recently been attached to the Court of her Majesty the Press but that I hadn't been hired anywhere yet, even though I'd been given many reliable promises of that happening very, very soon at *Gumhuriya* newspaper where I was an apprentice, and also that I—like he—had tried my hand at writing short stories, but that I'd had a few published in the literary supplement to *Sawt al-uruba* newspaper. "What's this *Sawt al-uruba* thing?" he asked and I explained that it was just a throwaway paper run by a friend of mine so he could fill it with editorial advertisements, and in exchange for publishing my stories, he had me do the layout for him.

That day, we had a second round of tea and then a third and we smoked half of a big pack of cigarettes. He insisted on paying the bill, but we made a plan to meet the next morning, each of us planning the exact same surprise for the other. I went first, partly to thank him for his kindness the day before: "I've got a feeling you're a hardcore stoner like me and I want to treat you to a couple of bowls."

He laughed and said he'd been planning to suggest exactly that to me. "In that case," I said, "let's hurry up and go treat ourselves." One short shortcut brought us straight to the heart of the complex of alleys in Bulaq Abu al-Ila. The whole neighborhood was made up of hash dens of various types and classes: from shack-dens to coffeehouse-dens to house-dens, which were apartments where the owners gave you the absolute top-of-the-line service, but they were the most expensive since they were residences and the police couldn't raid them unless they had a warrant from the prosecutor, which, by the time it was issued, the owners of the apartment would've already heard about and have had time to take precautions. There was no shortage of hash dealers and they could be found in every den. What was even better was when the den owner himself dealt hash because then you were guaranteed to get some real dank stuff and the guy who sold it to you was always right there ready to be held accountable if it disappointed. That day we each got a faithful portrait of the other; each of us plumbed the other's soul, mind, and life story. I told him about my family in the countryside around Fouadiya and about my political, poet father, who was burdened with his many children, old age, and poor eyesight. He told me about his family in the countryside around Mansoura, about his mother, who was upset that he'd gone against her wishes by not studying medicine, and about his mother's brother, the famous doctor and poet. From that moment on, we hung out together every day, without exception, for years and even when we were angry at each other for some reason, we still had to meet up so that one of us could express his anger in a practical way and the best thing about it was the delightfully childlike nature of it all.

He'd been peculiar his whole life—at least in the eyes of people who didn't know him well and didn't really get him. One day he went with his college to visit one of the high-ups at the Youth Organization to have a discussion about the condition of university students. Even though Qamar was—if only on paper—a member of the Organization, as were most young people, he asked for permission to speak and was granted it. Then he improvised a grandiloquent speech in which he passionately attacked the Organization, the tamest of his accusations being that the Organization was in fact nothing but a fifth column whose mission was to defend the revolution against the masses despite the fact that the masses were the true guardians of the revolution. Neither the official—nor anyone else for that matter—had been expecting a surprise attack quite like that in such a setting. The official was horrified, his skin pallid, his lower lip turning blue, but he was calm in the way that only powerful people who knew exactly how to lure a speaker into getting himself into deeper trouble than he already was could be, so he growled menacingly and said, "Huh? So what? It's just talk. Idle talk. Why don't you tell us what evidence you have for these dangerous accusations?" Maybe the man knew perfectly well that Qamar al-Mahruqi was the sort of person who was quick to react when provoked and that a threat—no matter who it came from—would quickly demolish any reticence he might have clung to because he soon let rip with an enviable audacity. He claimed that he himself was the best evidence for what he'd said because he'd been a member of the Organization and he'd dropped it and tried to get as far away from it as he could ever since the leadership, Messrs. So-and-So, So-and-So, and So-and-So, had tried to get him to snoop on countless decent patriots and to file detailed reports about their private lives. They hadn't stopped there, but had intimated to him—motivated, it seemed, by nothing other than pure evil—that those he'd been asked to spy on were among the most dogged enemies of the revolution and that they were currently conspiring against it. But when he told them that he knew all those people—his neighbors and teachers—better than well, they accused him of being naive and politically unaware. They—in short—painted people with the brush of their choosing and mesmerized the young with the trappings of power so that they'd write secret, entrapping, volatile reports about all the people they didn't like. The tragedy was double-sided, too: those who wrote the reports were transformed into professional spies and acquired the adversarial, distrustful souls that went with the job and pushed them to slander the innocent with their fabrications, which, in turn, gave rise to a climate of anxiety and fed the people's latent hostility to the revolution. And those about whom the reports were written had their lives ruined, were thrown into prison, lost their jobs, and so on.

Qamar wasn't arrested that day, but he was subjected to relentless harassment after that: lots of investigations and chilling threats. He had to suffer dawn raids and had his apartment searched countless times; he was thrown in jail either for weeks or months, emerging each time more of an anguished wreck until finally they succeeded in breaking him. Even his friends abandoned him because they feared his extremism. He'd been driven to the brink of madness, but he fought against it with sarcasm and hashish, even though his wounds never healed over. He always felt as if people were avoiding him so he was often the one who cut himself off from others to protect his pride. At other times, he wanted to avoid even his closest friends, but this only came about when he was feeling like no one understood him. The tiniest thing set him off: he merely had to get the sense from what you were saying that you didn't really understand him or that you had a shred of doubt about something he'd said, but his 'pity parties' didn't normally last more than two days, after which he'd be back to being his cheery, expressive, welcoming self.

The incident at the Organization had disrupted his life completely, cut him off from the world, but he himself had been stubborn and tough and spoiling for a challenge, and it was in that challenge that he discovered himself. It got to the point that he simply disdained everything and reduced everything to everything else so that, to him, death became life, prison became freedom, setbacks became progress, success became failure; that was all anything ever came to in our country. He lost confidence in all intellectuals and political types. He was condescending about them and categorically rejected everything they represented and called for. He became an uncompromising nihilist. Often when you were talking to him, he'd get lost in his own thoughts for several minutes during which you'd think he'd flown off somewhere far away and when he finally snapped out of it, you could detect a hint of contemptuous indifference in his eyes. He was excitable, often paranoid, quick-tempered, and always primed to stand up to the anonymous enemy he was constantly expecting would spring up on him from out of nowhere. After he graduated and found himself blacklisted from all government employment, things only got worse.

He eventually found a job with a construction-engineering firm. He would draw up the diagrams, plans, and models, which the senior engineers had outlined. Soon his job colored every aspect of his life. He started carrying a fancy leather travel bag around with him that had several pockets to store all his things because he was always on the move and never home for very long. There were certain pockets that were never opened, or only very rarely, because their varied contents were mildly embarrassing: takeaway food, shirts, socks, underwear, but the rest of the pockets were filled with sketching paper, blotting paper, tracing paper, rulers, triangle scale, and every type of pen in every color he could find. As soon as you started talking to him about anything—anything at all—his long fingers would start to reach into the bag and take out his elegant notebook with its special paper and a pen and draw you a diagram to explain the 'issue' in all its dimensions and to focus the conversation on the question at hand no matter if you were talking about where a shop was located, Rowdy Salih's face, or what have you. When he was doing a calculation, he'd draw a diagram of the money and all the different directions it moved in, and if you complimented his hash, he'd draw you a diagram of how it was produced in the fields and then brought over from Lebanon as a brick. His conversation, too, was littered with scales, lines, foci, equilaterals, and such.

Many months of that went by and we started introducing Qamar al-Mahruqi to our new friends as the construction engineer. When the friend happened himself to be a construction engineer and discussed any aspect of the profession with Qamar, he'd always come away astonished by the range and depth of Qamar's knowledge. The most likely thing would be that Qamar would lead the friend off on compelling tangents, which would distract him momentarily from any too serious job-talk until the hash kicked in and put the topic of conversation to rest once and for all. But then one day he surprised us all by turning up looking newly made over. He'd traded his coat and European dress shirts for American jeans and a short-sleeve knit shirt, collar undone, either side splayed against his chest, and over that a thick-pile wool sweater, which he occasionally changed out for a gray suede jacket. He almost looked like he was overdoing it. His travel bag had shrunk to a quarter of its previous size, but it was the same bag so we inspected it to figure out the secret and we discovered that it was just the spawn of the bigger bag.

In our carelessness, which we were loath to admit, we hadn't noticed that the big travel bag was really made up of four smaller bags of varying sizes held together by hidden fasteners *in order to handle all your carrying needs*! Even more attention-grabbing was his vocabulary, which had been infiltrated by a whole new set of terms that soon predominated, and yet, we still didn't realize that he'd left the construction firm and taken a job at a land development firm headquartered in Heliopolis. The company was actually German, a new chapter in the history of the old Imperial Capitulations. Our daily conversations adopted new, trendy words like potter's clay, greening, drought, desertification, deluges and drizzles, genetic engineering, hybrid fruits, and greenhouses. The really delightful thing was that suddenly all the corners of Hakeem's hash den were taken over by flowerpots full of moist soil and plants and green shoots and strange varieties of flowers and roses, all of which had started out as seeds brought by Qamar, who tended them as if they were his own children. A fast-growing hyacinth bean-vine stretched up to the ceiling, wrapped around the top of the door, and hung over the benches and windows, its drowsy leaves breathing in the smoke alongside us and tickling the backs of our necks until we pushed them gently away, shyly as if humoring a naughty child in front of its father. Interestingly it was Rowdy Salih who was responsible for caring for the plants in Qamar's absence and he watered them with care and love, mothering them, running his fingers over each and every shoot to check how it was doing. If he saw that one of the shoots wasn't doing very well or that a branch—God forbid!—wasn't getting enough water, he'd begin to despair. One time he shouted at Hakeem and threw a bong bowl at him because he'd smashed one of the flowerpots to make pebbles to go in the bottom of the bowls even though the flowerpot was already cracked. Before Hakeem could even open his mouth to start protesting, Salih shouted him down, "Shut it, you run-down old bum! You think you're the big man around here? Think you're the boss with that elbow-looking mouth of yours? What did that flowerpot ever do to you that you had to go and break it? We've got a hundred broken bowls here that would do just fine for pebbles. No, the thing is you just don't have a heart. Don't you know pots can feel pain, too? Me, when I see a bowl break, I get upset. I'd rub it with a balm to soothe it if it weren't for people teasing me. It's not like I just go and break it 'cause I think it's worthless. It has to break on its own before I think it's right to go and make pebbles out of it."

Hakeem could do nothing but stare at him with a fake smile plastered on his monkey-esque mouth. Yet eventually the den's plant-fever died out and was replaced with an enthusiasm for ceramics of every kind: flowerpots, casseroles, pots, plates, even bong and water-pipe bowls. Our conversations were dominated by talk of the fine art of ceramics, porcelain, and earthenware. They even branched out to a discussion of the origins of man and how our great ancestor Adam had himself been formed of clay. Our conversations were always open to everyone; Rowdy Salih, Hakeem, and Sabir got involved, as well as the bums and layabouts who always hung around looking dejected a few steps away from us, as if penned in by an imaginary cage, waiting for Qamar to send over a bowl, which he'd remind them was for them all to share. Out of the blue, Salih said that the scientists these days who claim that man originated as a primate were one hundred percent correct and if you wanted proof, you just had to look at Hakeem's face. Hakeem just looked at him and gave him a shit-eating wink, then he pointed backward and said, "God have mercy!" We all understood he was making a joke at the expense of Salih's father and sisters, who all looked like gorillas with the gift of speech.

Rowdy Salih, though, simply ignored the winking provocation and laughed: "The thing is, when the world was first created it was all rowdy and all the creatures looked the same."

Hakeem frowned, his face trembling, its color draining: "Give it a rest already!" The group resumed its buzzing conversation, but it soon died down and then was completely silenced by the arrival of a new and unexpected delegation. Usually the newly arrived brought a new topic of conversation with them because those of us sitting there depended on them for fresh news. One of the newly arrived that time brought news that was news to us: he shed light on the mystery of why we'd been having so many conversations about ceramics lately. The newcomer was a colleague of our friend Qamar al-Mahruqi at *the company*. Which company, you ask? Lotus Ceramics, which had a factory in Fayoum, head office in Giza, and a downtown showroom full of pricey dinnerware, demitasses, cups, and vases. In the days that followed, we could tell that Qamar al-Mahruqi's inventive genius was in overdrive; he'd sit there for hours at a time, bent over a stack of papers under a plastic plane called a 'planchette,' sketching diagrams with his fine-pointed mechanical pencil and jotting down numbers and notes in the margin with a ballpoint pen. Then when he was finished, he'd tear the page out and stick it in his folder and draw the diagram all over again, but this time more complexly and with more circles, triangles, and quadrilaterals until it took on the appearance of a city all built-up with houses stuck together and streets one on top of the other.

We tried and failed to uncover the secret of what Qamar al-Mahruqi was so assiduously and stealthily working on, but we did notice that he occasionally brought some new young guy with him to the den, whom he'd introduce only by name, but in a tone of some solemnity as though he were presenting a celebrity who required no introduction. And yet the guys he introduced us to—there were three of them in total—were clearly somewhat well-off, and their appearance, the way they spent money, and the large sums that danced lightly on their tongues made it inescapably obvious. We Egyptians don't usually need someone else to make introductions—we're very quick to introduce ourselves just as direct and practical as can be—so it didn't take very long before we learned everything about the guys that Qamar had started bringing with him to the hash den, usually one by one but sometimes all together.

One of them, a guy called Walid Rashid, was short and husky and had a plump, mildly ruddy, mildly handsome face. He was about seven years younger than we were and was in his final year at the Faculty of Physical Education, even though his true passions were singing and acting and he insisted that his voice—taut and strong as it was—would win him great fame in the world of music in the next few years. His father had passed away, leaving him a small tract of agricultural land, but it was obvious from the way he spent, and his new Fiat, and his fancy clothes that he could rely on a source of income that wasn't running out anytime soon. The riddle was easily solved once we learned he was from the village of Mit Rahina and owned a papyrus factory. Talat al-Imbabi stroked his mustache and said that since the guy was from Mit Rahina, it was obvious that the family house had been built over an ancient cemetery, and we all agreed with him because there was no way that a small agricultural estate and a papyrus factory alone could give one member of an entire family such ostentatious affluence.

The stocky, olive-skinned guy, who couldn't shake off his country-boy air even though he wore a wool coat with a heavy-knit collar, a thin white scarf, and a thick shirt over wool trousers made by a British brand called Hield, was called Mursi Khallaf. There was a slight and appealing severity to his voice, which gave a warm, confidence-inspiring tone to everything he said. He was generous, and generous with compliments, too, sweet-tongued you could almost say. Qamar introduced him to us as if he were famous, only mentioning that his brother was Nosshi Khallaf, who'd been off in Germany for years studying filmmaking and was about to come back a major director. It was easy enough for us to figure out that Mursi Khallaf, whom they all called 'Sir Sapper,' had studied automotive engineering but that, despite his privileged position, he'd never got more than a high-school diploma. He apparently had a job working for the Traffic Authority in one of their licensing offices. He was quick to insinuate himself with others and no international con artist could match the way he gained your complete trust in just a few minutes. Like when we met for the first time and he smoothly found his way to the seat beside me so he could pitch me an idea for a book, which—to put it briefly—was going to be a how-to manual entitled *How to Repair Your Car Yourself*, in which he'd give detailed explanations of how a car's engine works and how all the different parts relate to one another and also discuss all the things that could go wrong and how to identify and repair the fundamental problem yourself instead of having to take it to a mechanic. What he needed from me was a brotherly favor: to put the book into crisp, clear language that anyone could understand, but he was clever and good-hearted enough to realize immediately that he wasn't going to get what he wanted out of me so he backed off coolly, without taking the slightest offense.

That left the tall, reedy young man, the one whose thick hair flopped childishly over the left side of his forehead. All his features were childlike to a certain extent. He was hyper-finicky about his clothes and only wore the most shamelessly effeminate, floral-print shirts in the loudest possible colors with bright plaid trousers. His name was Wagdi al-Wakil so at first you thought he was related to Mustafa al-Nahhas's wife, Zeinab al-Wakil, you know, from a grand and illustrious, wealthy family known to everyone. But you only had to sit with him for a few minutes to know that not even in your wildest imagination could he be part of that family, or any family at all for that matter. It was merely coincidence: same name, no relation, although you could tell that he tried subtly and subliminally to exploit it with his over-the-top chic and his coiffure, to make it look like he was the son of respectable folks. He was a good guy—there was no doubt about it—and much put-upon, but he had that enviable lucky streak you find in so many people who do well for themselves without any mentionable exertion or exceptional skill. His talents all boiled down to the fact that he was a good salesman and his specialty was ladies' shoes.

The shops downtown and in Heliopolis all fought over him because he was said to have the golden touch, but the truth was that it wasn't just his touch; his comportment, the things he said, the tone of his voice, they were all imbued with an instinctive gentility that mesmerize women of all ages in a flash. There wasn't a woman on earth who could go into his shop and leave without having made a purchase. What's more, he'd invite them in graciously as they were passing by, "Come in, Ma'am," and even if they had absolutely no interest in buying shoes, ninety-percent of the time, they'd take him up on it and stride into the shop, sometimes shyly, other times beaming with pride. And then Wagdi would go to work, taking the woman in hand and carrying out what essentially amounted to a sexual repertoire that reduced teen girls to putty and rekindled the sensual fires of women long past their halcyon days. He'd escort her to her seat with abundant courtesy and a fair bit of hot-making, accidental grazes and then he'd go into the storeroom to pick out styles that he knew—through a combination of talent, intuition, and experience—would be perfect for her; no, rather to be more exact, would be what she'd dreamed of for herself. Then he'd kneel down elegantly at the woman's feet so that all her well-guarded charms would be laid directly before his eyes, which gave off chaste, charming glances that could revive a weary heart with the fresh, thrilling murmur of adventure. Then came the process of taking the smooth, soft foot in hand and slipping it into the shoe with tremendous care, all the while keeping one hand on the woman's calf, and then he buckled the shoe and turned to the next foot, always rubbing his hands on the woman's feet as if to convey a worshipful affection for those outstanding legs and the honor they paid the shoes. Most of the time, the woman wouldn't take the new shoes off, she'd just tell him to wrap the old ones up, and she wouldn't dream of haggling with him; rather she'd happily pay the extravagant price and throw in a generous tip just for him. After all, even though he'd got her to pay an exorbitant amount, he'd at least given her a truly reliable pair of shoes, which would retain its value for years to come. This was why he didn't take a salary, but preferred to work on commission, and he'd managed to squirrel away a healthy sum in the bank that he could've easily used to open his own shop downtown, but he preferred not to since he was already making several times what the shop owner took home after deducting the considerable overhead.

It didn't take us very long, then, to figure out what had brought apples and oranges together. What Qamar al-Mahruqi had actually been doing when he was up to his ears in engineering diagrams was inventing a brick-making machine. All you'd have to do was feed in the alluvial mud, or just plain mud, that was already mixed with clay, and the machine would form it into bricks that would then be dried out and fired electrically, or baked, and emerge as dried bricks as solid as stone. The machine could produce a thousand bricks every three hours, but if you wanted a higher rate of production, you just had to scale the design up into a bigger machine. Qamar al-Mahruqi had been looking for investors to put his project into action and he'd ended up with these three guys: Walid Rashid, Mursi Khallaf, and Wagdi al-Wakil. To tell the truth, we envied Qamar his brilliant technical mind and his knack for invention, but we weren't thrilled—although we may have been amazed—about how he'd hid everything and managed to keep his idea and its implementation a complete secret from everyone in the old loyal group. Of course, when the three youngsters got good and high, they couldn't help but drop ambiguous hints about the project, what would be good for it, what would ruin it, but we didn't care much about any of that; if the project had turned out to be a complete bust and wiped out the combined savings of all three of those guys, we wouldn't have ever heard about it. Nevertheless, we got routine reports about how things were progressing from their bad moods, disappointment, and occasional rudeness. They'd been so sure that the invention was foolproof, they'd had it built precisely down to every last detail in one of those big machine shops, they'd bought all the necessary equipment, they'd built a base for the machine in a location they'd chosen specifically for it in a village in Fayoum, but then when the machine was assembled and plugged in, it just wouldn't work. They'd taken Rowdy Salih along with them that day to help and to fetch things for them and when he saw them all standing there—including the inventor himself—puzzled, unable to unlock the mystery of why it wouldn't work, he went up to the machine and began examining it, trying to account for all the different pieces. Eventually, he put himself in God's hands and announced, "This machine's missing something, Mr. Qamar."

They exchanged a sarcastic, bitter, shamed glance as if to say, "Right, all we need now, Rowdy, is for you to come give us your opinion on these technical schematics, too!" Rowdy Salih didn't have to see their expressions—he could sense it instinctively and in any case, he'd been expecting it—but he'd long since got used to not caring about what people said, be it negative or positive. He only ever dealt with hearts anymore, a subject he was an expert in; his predictions were never wrong. He simply ignored the sarcastic look on Qamar and his partners' faces and gave a shy and tender smile: "Pardon me, Qamar Bey, I don't mean any offense to you all, but just humor me for a second. This machine here—as far as I can tell—is missing something that's downright worthless, but important nonetheless. I mean without it, the invention's not an invention. When Qamar Bey was designing the machine—and you know, I'm sorry, but the pen makes mistakes, too—he forgot to include something to connect the gears all together so that one gear can drive the others."

"What gears, you jackass? You think this machine runs on gears?"

"Maybe he thinks it's a flour mill!"

These were the reactions of Mursi Khallaf and Wagdi al-Wakil, with Walid Rashid joining in in spirit, but Qamar al-Mahruqi's eyes sunk deeper than usual and he just stood there looking dumbfounded. Rowdy Salih laughed.

"It's just . . . . Now . . . it's plugged in and the machine's on, twenty-four-carat-like, but . . . then when you try to feed the clay in, it doesn't take it and it just sprays all over us until it's used up. So that means there's something inside the machine that the electricity isn't getting to. The only thing that's working is the motor, not the machine. How come? Well, that's what I don't get."

Qamar's petrified body finally came back to life and he started pointing his index finger. His face was pale and his throat dry as he muttered, "Indeed. Exactly. Rowdy Salih's right. Well done, Rowdy. I know what's missing."

He opened his travel bag and took out the diagrams and then he squatted down, hunched over, and began to examine them all. Finally, he leapt to his feet with a throaty cry of victory, "The problem's in the manufacture, not the design. I've got everything accounted for here from A all the way to Z. I bet you! Look, here's how everything supposed to move, here, I've got it all worked out step by step."

An exasperated Mursi Khallaf put his hands on his hips and asked, "Well, what are we going to do now?"

"We've got to take it apart and then put it back together piece by piece."

They spent several long months taking it apart and putting it back together, and taking it apart again and putting it back together again, but in the end all they could do was pile it up in the courtyard of Walid Rashid's family home in Mit Rahina and wait to sell it to a junk man for scrap. Walid shouldered the brunt of the loss because for one thing he'd been the most enthusiastic about the project, and for another, he was the wealthiest. The strangest thing, though, was that they didn't love Qamar any less, and in fact, they adored him even more for having brought out the adventurous little boy inside them all.

Before the incident, Qamar al-Mahruqi had accepted the invitation of his friend and ours, Talat al-Imbabi, to attend some cultural events being put on by the Soviet Cultural Center: talks, screenings of Russian films, and concerts, and it was there that he found an opportunity to express himself freely and say what he couldn't say anywhere else. He took to them and became a regular and eventually met Mahasin Asim, the sister of our friend Ahmad Asim, who worked at the center. She'd been admitted to the School of Humanities to study history, but she was obsessed with French and everything to do with France so she also enrolled in a French institute to take language classes and ended up spending a lot of time, money, and energy on that. On top of everything, she was a real scatterbrain. She spent several years doing the final year of her history degree, and when she felt like she was never going to pass, she put her studies on hold and took a decent-paying job at the center.

Mahasin Asim was a very nice girl—as her close friends could confirm—so nice that she sometimes came across as ditzy. Her whole problem was that her thought process was interminably slow even though she was quick to understand. She spoke very slowly and softly, but at the same time she'd struggled to pronounce foreign letters ever since she was a child so she ended up coming across as a thoroughly Egyptianized foreigner. She wasn't pretty like her brother Ahmad either. Her face was quite plain and her pale skin and ruddy cheeks didn't make for a nice combination. Her figure was quite boyish, not at all sexy; it didn't even turn the heads of men who liked their women a bit gamin-esque. Perhaps this explained why she didn't have any relationships with young men except for those with whom she worked, although in those situations she was as nice and affable as could be. As soon as he met her, Qamar al-Mahruqi devoted himself to her alone and she to him automatically. After only a handful of meetings in quasi-romantic locales, they each decided rashly and resolutely that the other was their soul mate. They became the closest of companions and any trepidations they had were put to rest; their views on life, art, and other people all in accord.

Finally Mr. Mustafa Asim could relax now that his daughter Mahasin—after endless despair—had finally broached the subject of a potential fiancé who was planning to propose to her. All he asked his daughter was, "Do you love him and do you think he's a good person?"

"Of course, of course," she answered with confident exuberance.

"Well then, I wish you both the best of luck. You can tell him to come see us," he said, but just to be certain he asked his son Ahmad to find out some things about this Qamar al-Mahruqi. This investigation was carried out during one of our meetings in the alley at the foot of the hill accompanied by much giddy, light-hearted laughter. Ahmad reported back to Mr. Asim that the 'kid' passed all the tests of manliness, salary, and reliability, and Qamar called his mother's brother—a senior doctor-writer whose name carried the most weight with Mr. Asim's family and that was the sort of thing that made things go even more smoothly—and asked him to divide his share of the family inheritance from his mother's. To solve the problem, his uncle bought out Qamar's share of the agricultural land for a few thousand (i.e., countable on two hands). But that was enough for Qamar to be able to buy a respectable apartment near Ahmad Urabi Street in Mohandiseen and Mr. Asim helped his daughter out with the cost of furnishing the apartment to a suitable standard. In no time at all, Qamar al-Mahruqi was transformed into Mahasin Asim's loyal, docile husband, and then again in no time at all, he became father to a baby girl called Dalia. His father-in-law, though, didn't much like how Qamar was always bouncing from one job to the other so he called in some favors to old students of his, who were now professors at the American University, and they got him a job in a position that had been invented just for him: 'expert consultant.' This new stretchy job title came with a decent salary, but his actual job was to assist a team of researchers at the American University by collecting material—specialist and colloquial vocabulary—they could incorporate into the new Egyptian Arabic–English Dictionary they were preparing.

However, Qamar soon tired of married life. He began to detect profound and essential differences between him and his wife in all aspects of their personalities until little by little every bond that had once connected them was severed. He couldn't find a way out. He started spending the entire day and most of the evening away from home and he retreated into his former loneliness. Even when he was at home, he slept alone on a mattress on the floor because—he explained—he'd always hated beds. Nevertheless, thanks to Mahasin's remarkable patience, which was helped by the fact that Qamar never stopped giving her the respect that was her due as his wife, their life together continued. Nor did either of them forget that she herself was even more prone to seclusion and long, but never boring, bouts of solitude than he was.

"Ggggeeeeeettttt iiiiiiiiiiinnnnnn!" Rowdy Salih shouted when he came in and saw Qamar on that early morning. His ecstatic voice had this intimate, friendly ring to it, and Salih and Qamar gave the words 'Get In!' a tone of warmth, affection, and utter jubilation.

"Ggggeeeeeettttt iiiiiiiiiiinnnnnn," responded Qamar, intentionally echoing the intimacy.

Salih handed me a quarter qirsh of hashish enshrouded in crimson paper and said, "Do you owe Umm Yahya any money?"

The staples in the paper pricked my hand as it rested against Qamar's folder. "Ten piasters all together," I said frowning and cracking my knuckles. "Why? Did she ask you?"

"Well, she asked me who the hash was for, so I said it was for Mr. So-and-So and then she told me to tell you 'Umm Yahya says hello.'"

"Is that all?"

"Umm Yahya never says hello to anybody just to be nice, you see."

"Why'd you have to tell her the hash was for me?"

"You know I can't tell a lie, sir."

Then he noticed that Qamar was holding the bong and coal for me and that I was insisting that he come sit down and take a turn smoking a bowl himself. Salih smiled at us, singling Qamar out with a special look of appreciation for his skill at running the bong, and headed for the door, "I'll go wake up Sabir."

Qamar, suddenly crestfallen that our party might be joined by a fourth, turned and called to him, pleadingly, "Do us a favor, we don't need anybody else. This here works just fine. We're only going to smoke a couple of bowls and then we're going to sit here and read." Salih relented and you could tell he understood. He took the burnt-out bowls with him over to his corner and sat down on his old straw cushion where he once again resumed the work of cleaning and refilling bong bowls.

CONTRABAND

Marouf Elementary School—which by the grace of God exists to this day—has produced students that have gone on to do great things, including a serious journalist, movie star, army general, police chief, doctor, and engineer. This school also produced Rowdy Salih, who never went on to become anything at all, and yet had still managed to achieve a resounding fame among all the hashish smokers of Cairo, which equaled about eighty percent of the male population. But what was he famous for? For what qualities or distinction? For what? It was a question you couldn't answer and yet he was famous and that was all there was to it. He didn't go out looking for it and it didn't make him particularly happy.

He could still remember each of his classmates from Marouf Elementary School by name and nickname, but they'd certainly all long since forgotten about him. By Rowdy Salih's own account, told over countless sessions, celebrations, and moonlit nights perfumed by the scent of hashish as it sizzled on a gentle flame, our living moments feeding the fire, he'd received a diploma from the elementary school whose walls— only a few meters away from Hakeem's den—could hear our conversation. You can't even imagine what a diploma meant back in those days, at the end of the thirties! They read English novels: *A Tale of Two Cities* by Charles Dickens—maybe some of you eggheads have heard of it—and Shakespeare's play *King Lear*—you've heard of that one surely; they're always talking about it in the newspapers. And they read means they *read*: a student would stand up in front of the class and read out pages from the book in correct English and then explain what he'd understood. Rowdy Salih himself had a part in *King Lear* when the students acted out the play. "You know, the school theater club, like for the graduation ceremony." He could still remember a few snippets of dialogue, but he didn't like to show off: "So what if people find out I know English? Screw them."

But when some of the new-fangled college boys would take him for an ignoramus and speak English in front of him, thinking he was just some lunkhead who couldn't possibly understand what they were saying, he'd get so excited. He couldn't think of any way to quench his desire, except to laugh hysterically, which only seemed to confirm their mistaken assumptions about him: that he was nothing more than an ignorant doofus, a howdy-rowdy type. What he wanted more than anything was to correct them when they parroted certain English words without knowing how to pronounce them or use them in the right context. But he frequently had to stop himself at the last moment because he didn't want to give the game away since it would only lead to him being mocked or insulted, which in turn would lead to him getting good and rowdy with them, which could only end with him smashing the brains of the one and ripping open the belly of the other. It was more important to keep them in the dark so that he could find out more about their true natures.

"You see, sir, the best thing's for everybody around you to think you're not that smart. They'll be nice to you; sweet as can be. They know they don't have to worry so they'll forget about you and let you be, and that means you've won already. They'll talk in front of you openly. They'll start going into the closets where all their skeletons are buried—maybe even corpses of people they've killed—or maybe all the bad things they've done or had done to them, maybe, maybe, maybe, there's no end to it. But you got to play it cool. You can only listen in, that's all. Don't even think about saying a single word. Let yourself become one with the—no offense— doofus. Listen, so you can learn how to do this and not do that and if you end up doing it, then how to do it properly, and why, and for what. Do all the long divisions you have to in your head to find out the true nature of the person sitting right in front of you, and whether you ought to become his bosom buddy or simply throw him out in the garbage and be done with him before he can start making trouble for you, which is the last thing you need. You should know, by the way, that playing the fool—no offense— is an art. You've got to work at it. Me, for example, when I find out someone's true nature, you know, like if he deserves respect, I'll respect him a hundred percent, but if he doesn't, I never let him know that he doesn't. I mean if he found out that I think he doesn't, that'd make me a real dumbass of a fool. A clever fool never shows his hand because even if it's just by accident, you'd be letting the enemy win. Of course 'cause it's only natural that no matter what, the other guy's going to get upset and think you're looking down on him or that you don't respect him. Sure as hell, I don't respect him, but only on the inside, and if I've got to serve him, I'll give it my twenty-four carat best, but then if he treats me like a two-bit nothing and tries to show off like he's better than me, well then I'll know exactly how to put him in his place. Listen, sir, what's the point of finding out the truth about somebody? Well there's at least one reason: to know how to protect yourself. Let me tell you what I mean. See, the whole time I'm sitting there listening silently, I'm going through all their closets and having a look around. I mean I'm finding out where all their hot-button buttons are. I don't touch 'em just yet. I trace all the darkened paths that lead to them, but I keep my distance. You see, sir, you've got to know: evil's right there, walking next to you in the street, working alongside you, sitting beside you in the coffeehouse, maybe even sharing your bed. The thing is, though, you can never know when it's going to turn against you. When it's going to attack and reveal its red eyes. But if it can tell that you know about it, that you understand what's up, that you can see it, well, then you've become its number one worst enemy. But if you're clever, you'll realize that you've only got two choices—just the two—when it comes to evil: either you're strong enough and you face up to it and resist, in which case everything you picked up when you were sitting there quietly will come in handy, or you're too weak and you have to give into it in that typically Egyptian way; well, even then everything you picked up, you know—knowing where all the hot-button buttons are—can also help. You know why? So you know how to avoid them!"

Salih sat there silently for a little while and then he started up again. "Once upon a time, there was a man called Status Quo. Yeah, yeah, that's what his parents named him, Status Quo. Anyway, this guy Status Quo got married and he had two sons, Getting Better and Getting Worse. Getting Better got married and had one son whom he named What's Right. Getting Worse also got married, but he had two sons. He called the first one Decline and the second one Screw It. What's Right was a good guy, decent and pure-hearted, but his only problem was that he figured that as long as he was an upright do-gooder then he'd be taken care of and no one could do him any harm. He put all his faith in his father Getting Better and that was what he relied on most for support. His cousins, Decline and Screw It, thought he was a real boob. They said, "That guy What's Right is such an idiot Whoever heard of such a thing as What's Right?" So they took all his money and invested it and ended up wiping him out. That left just the two of them. Decline started plotting against Screw It, but apparently Decline was even dumber than his cousin, What's Right. He did his best to make up with his brother and become friends with Screw It. I mean, Screw It was the world's biggest conman, a genuine descendant of wind, fire, and ice. Decline figured he'd keep an eye on him, but at the same time, he'd rely on him for help. Our friend totally wiped him out, though, and ever since then this has been the state of the world: most people are friends with Screw It and turn a blind eye to all the misery around them, you know, life goes on. Begging your pardon, but I think 'life goes on' is the dirtiest curse word I've ever heard in my entire life."

Rowdy Salih began to despise his diploma almost as soon as he'd received it from his alma mater, Marouf Elementary School, because it reminded him of all the other students who'd also received it. They'd all stereotyped him as being unruly and kept him at arm's length, operating according to a delusional prejudice that said that all dirt-poor, black-faced little boys, who dressed in rags and had calloused hands, had to be evil and boorish and badly brought up.

At first, he tried to use his diploma to get a job and he sent applications to several governmental agencies and national organizations, begging and pleading with them for the sake of his family who counted on him for support, but it was so much wasted breath. Finally he got tired of buying stamps for all those applications and refused to have anything else to do with any agencies, or the nation itself, and stubbornly insisted that he'd turn down a job even if it landed on his doorstep. He bounced around from trade to trade; the longest time he ever spent in one job was the five years he worked as a carpenter and that was why it was the only trade he'd mastered and why he could custom-build cabinets, beds, and chairs. But then he was called up for military service and he went off happily and willingly even though he loathed order and severity. And at the end of every service period, he'd sign up again as a volunteer because in the army he could pocket his whole government salary since food, drink, shelter, and clothing were all taken care of, not to mention the little tips that occasionally found their way to him.

Because he loved the Nile so much and believed that it—unlike all the other rivers of the world—had something divine about it, he couldn't stand to be away from it, not even for a single day, so the two of them had a firm daily date that he could never miss. Plus, was there anything better than putting on a clean white gallabiya and a big white turban and carrying his net and bait with him as he walked on his pilgrimage to the banks of the Nile outside the city, where he'd always sit on the same rock in the same distant spot, which he preferred, though he didn't know why, to all the other spots along the long, drowsy riverside? Was it because the rock was as tall as a young tree and kept him high enough off the ground that he was safe from a crocodile suddenly leaping out of the water and dragging him to the bottom? Or was it because the rock was smooth and beautiful and wide at the top even though there were mysterious grooves running down the length of it as if it were a column leftover from an ancient palace that had once stood there? Or was it because he considered the rock's bare perch a kingdom of unsurpassed pleasure with room for him to spread out his napkin and his provisions: bait, stove, kettle, cup, tea, sugar, and loose tobacco, and where he could assemble his fishing pole, which was made out of reeds that were attached with metal screws according to how short or long you wanted, and cast off and watch the cork dance on the distant waves like an acrobat, bobbing and sinking, hinting with celebratory winks? No, that wasn't the only thing that drew him with such irresistible yearning to that place and caused him to pine every day when evening signaled the end of his fishing fun. The greatest attraction was hidden inside the mud-brick hut that was only a few meters away from his rock.

From his seat on the rock, he could look down on the back fence of the hut, wrapped around a wide, uncovered courtyard with young trees among furrows planted with rocket and parsley. A clothesline stretched across one corner of the garden, and in another, there was a run full of ducks, geese, and hens. From where he sat, Salih could see straight into the hut through the door that looked out onto the backyard all the way down to the corridor that ran the length of the house with two rooms on either side and ended at the bathroom. He came to feel as if he were part of the family. He could tell that the tall, full-bodied man was the owner of the hut and that he'd squatted on that patch of riverbank and that the thin woman, who breastfed one child and had another child on her shoulders and a third clinging to her skirts and was constantly shouting at them to keep away from the river so the crocodiles wouldn't snatch them, was certainly his wife. But the heavenly angel, the statuesque young lady, who stood up straight like an army officer and had a perfectly expressive, almost ideally perfect, face and body, had to be the man's sister for the resemblance was clear. They even walked with the same rhythm as if one of them were impersonating the other. He could hear them calling to one another so he learned that her name was Wahiba and the wife was Umm Hasan and the husband was called Mekki. Whenever Wahiba spoke, her voice turned his attention from the flashes of the winking cork and his heart flashed, too, every time Wahiba's voice rang through the hut.

Salih saw that the owner of the hut had been keeping an eye on him for a while and that he'd decided that Salih was trustworthy and wasn't after anything besides a little fishing. The man would often come by for no other reason but to say hello. "Ten times a friend," he'd say, and Salih would reply warmly, "A hundred times yours." From time to time, Salih would invite him for a quick cup of tea and they'd have a little chat. Mekki was quite obviously pleased and relieved to hear that Salih was Egyptian. He told him that he, too, was almost totally Egyptian as he'd been born in Shalateen in Egypt and had an older sister who was married and lived in Cairo and an older brother, as well, who worked as a doorman in Zamalek. How'd he end up there then? Oh, well, that was a long story and yet he told it anyway, leaning his elbow on the rock, cup of tea in hand. Mekki had an uncle, who lived in Shalateen and worked as a landscaper and gardener for the big estates there. That uncle had a daughter, who'd been born soon after the Urabi uprising and was nearly twenty years old by then, and he had his heart set on her marrying a government employee with a steady wage. Then one day that government employee—a guy who'd signed up for the army and then gone onto join the security forces—turned up. He was actually from Halayeb, but he'd seen the girl at the market in Shalateen when he went to visit some of his relatives who were traders there. They got married, but after a few months the government sent him to some town far away; no one really knew their new address and none of the letters he sent ever reached them. Then it all got even more complicated when Mekki's uncle left Shalateen for a job in Khartoum working for a wealthy family, who had great big gardens and needed a caretaker to live on the grounds. The uncle had done his sums: in Shalateen he had to pay rent and his wages were measly—and intermittent at that—plus, he didn't have any family in Shalateen except for his older brother, Mekki's father. But in Khartoum, he'd get his own house and his food, drink, and clothing would all be taken care of. Mekki's uncle spent months kicking the idea around in his mind until one morning broke with the sound of his brother screaming and his sister-in-law wailing. The brother had been bitten by a horned viper while prostrated in prayer on top of a pile of dried corn stalks out in front of his house. The viper itself had been searching for a way out from underneath the stalks, which had been thrown down on top of it, when the uncle's brother, bleary-eyed in the dawn twilight, pressed his forehead right down on top of it. Before he even knew what was happening, a fiery iron spike pierced his forehead and his head imploded—what an awful morning it was!—and by evening, the brother was dead. There was no cure for a viper's sting, especially not when it got you right in the head. The uncle saw evil omens everywhere and was overcome by loneliness, depression, and despair so he took his wife and decided he'd try his luck in Khartoum. God smiled down on him, sure, but it caused a lot of confusion and letters got lost in the mail, addresses being forwarded to other addresses that eventually returned to sender. In the end, communication between Mekki's uncle and his daughter was completely cut off and neither of them had any news of the other. This caused the uncle great sadness for the rest of his life until he was afflicted by an illness—God protect us!—that made him bleed like a woman. After several years, Mekki was surprised to receive a letter from his uncle asking him to come live with him in Khartoum because the work was getting to be too much for him and he needed an assistant. Mekki was twenty-five years old at the time, he'd already been excused from military service since he was his parents' only son, and he was a farm worker, who'd work for one day only to spend the next ten idle, and he, too, had rent to pay. What's keeping me here, he asked himself, when I can go work for my uncle? So he took his mother and went to Khartoum to the house his uncle had got from his employers; it was large and could fit an entire family—no, more like a whole clan. Mekki was pleasantly surprised to see that his cousin, who'd been just a child back in Shalateen, had blossomed into a lovely and marriageable young filly. His uncle had still been hoping for a son, but his wife ended up giving birth to their third daughter, Wahiba, the gorgeous girl who lived with them. Mekki wasn't silly enough to let his cousin, that eligible bride from his own blood, get away so he had a word or two and before you knew it, the official came and they were married. The next day he consummated his marriage to the bride, who lived with him to this day and had filled his life with the blessing of many children. Their life together was as happy as could be until they were taken unawares by a plague they'd never even heard of before: cholera. The uncle and his wife died on two successive Fridays along with dozens of other poor people. Mekki inherited the man's job and responsibility for Wahiba, his cousin and his wife's sister. His sly and cunning uncle had taught him to stay a couple of steps ahead of fate and helped him—with the assistance of his employers, members of the Khartoum elite—to get his hands on that piece of riverbank. The first thing he did was put up a fence, then he kept himself busy, building the hut little by little until he had a few rooms, and finally turned his attention to the garden, digging trenches, laying down fertilizer, and watering it until it bloomed with God's blessings. Now, Mekki could finally rest assured that he was going to be able to leave his children something so that they'd never have to suffer the indignities of begging.

That story, like a pact of honor, sealed Salih and Mekki's friendship.

"Good evening, Egyptian."

"Good evening, Mekki."

Salih, perched on his rock, would occasionally turn his head and lock eyes with one of Mekki's family members behind the fence, and they'd smile and exchange greetings and wave. Then there were the pleasant, rather astonishing, surprises, like when one of Mekki's sons would surprise Salih with a tray bearing a brimming teapot or a plate of special, homemade halva or a bunch of fresh dates. Back in those days, Salih caught about four pounds of fish a day. He usually picked out the best ones and took them to his old English boxing coach, who'd been assigned to train the guys on the army team. Salih would grill the fish himself and prepare his coach's meal. But then he started dividing the fish between his coach and Mekki's family each day.

The English coach liked Salih for lots of reasons, which he and his assistant were always listing, among them the fact that Salih understood the coach directly without a translator and the coach was comfortable talking to Salih, especially about the speech and customs of the people of Egypt and Sudan, and whenever he tested the guys he was training to see who was the toughest and showed the most potential for living up to the physical and mental demands of pugnastics, Salih always came out on top. "Have you boxed before?" he asked him.

"Yeah, in elementary school when I was a kid."

The coach was obviously surprised: "But you move like a trained boxer and you know the game through and through." Salih laughed bashfully and explained that he'd known a big-shot lawyer-politician when he was a boy and that he used to go with him to the Ahly Club when he went to exercise so he could watch the boxers train. He'd fallen in love with the game and started training by himself according to the directions he'd heard the coach giving the boxers, and then after the people at the club realized he had a close connection with the lawyer—who was on the board of the Ahly Club—he started getting treated like a VIP and was allowed to come to the club by himself whenever he wanted and attend any training session he liked. The English coach told Salih, "You love the game and that's the first step on the stairway to success," and then he said he'd take him under his wing and he promised him that he'd be damned if he didn't make an international champion out of him in no time at all. He designed a training plan and diet that Salih stuck to religiously and he earned every piaster of the incentive pay he got for going through that serious, disciplined training. Salih also decided that he wasn't going to think about women at all, or getting married, because he didn't want to get involved in anything that could get in the way of his sporting career.

But then when he laid eyes on Wahiba and met her cousin-cum-brother-in-law Mekki, he began to feel—for the first time in his life—that he wasn't suited to the austere discipline he'd imposed on himself. He was torn up by the fear that he'd have to lie to Mr. Heath, his English coach, who'd been especially keen on the rule about keeping away from women. But what could he do now that Wahiba's eyes had hooked his heart, which remained there in the water, pained by every passing wave? His attraction for her was fierce, tempestuous, and it quashed all resistance. He wasn't attracted to her alone, but to the whole hut and all it contained, and that was why he'd appointed himself the ever-watchful lifeguard of the children so that they wouldn't roll down to the river because he could see past the surface of the water with his acute, practiced eyes and make out the silhouettes of spiteful, blasted crocodiles creeping toward the banks, hiding beneath the swamp grass, getting ready to leap out and pounce on a child in the blink of an eye. More than once, Salih had got up and dived to save a child, ecstatic at its ability to run, barreling down toward the river in pursuit of a squawking duck, and right when Salih grabbed the child's arm, the duck would vanish, only its squawks echoing in the jaws of the predator beneath the water as it was pulled down to the depths. Then Salih would carry the child back to the hut to deliver him—by hand—to his mother, or sometimes his aunt. Salih could hear his heart pounding like a drum when Aunt Wahiba opened her arms to take the child, and Salih's hand would unintentionally graze her chest and he'd nearly faint from the intense heat of the hidden treasure he'd felt with the back of his hand, his heart a heady din of ululating dancers, clinking finger-cymbals to a rhythm as euphoric as he. He felt that Wahiba was like that child, that there were crocodiles along every shore stalking her because she was so good-hearted and innocent, like a vulnerable prey easily got, and as soon as the thought occurred to him, every muscle in his body shuddered and he lowered his gaze in shame. "Don't mention it. But keep an eye on those kids," he said as he turned and walked away.

He returned to his perch, feeling as if all the blood in his veins had been renewed, heated up, come to life, and he asked himself as the fishing rod bobbed and quivered beneath his thigh: Could it be, my boy, that it's your destiny to live with this beautiful, enthralling knockout with her sweet, truly innocent face? Why not? You're a big strong man, Egyptian, enlisted in the army, you get a government salary at the end of each month you could spend on a wife like that. You've been anti-marriage your entire life, but maybe because on some level you've been waiting for Wahiba. Who knows? Maybe when the two of you share a bed in your nuptial home you'll become—with her and for her—the world champion Mr. Heath, your English coach, wants you to be. Yes, Wahiba was put here to make you stronger, to help you put your life together and be the best you can be.

Later one tender afternoon, Mekki and Salih were having a friendly chat. "I bet you're sick of your rations already!" Mekki said to Salih. "Don't you ever feel like some home cooking?"

Salih reacted immediately as if the gates of heaven were opening for him, "Oh, Mekki, you have no idea. I'd give anything to smell some frying onions."

"How about coming to my place for dinner tomorrow?"

Salih bought several parcels of fruit and found Mekki waiting for him at the door. A warmth that proclaimed the beauty and splendor of the whole wide world had settled over the courtyard and a reed mat was spread out between the young trees and palms bearing young dates. A low table was laid out and the delicious, rich aromas of roast duck and a huge pot of fatta shrouded by a veil of tomato sauce and fried onions sent out waves of delirium and rapture. That generous supper put an end to Salih's hesitation and a few days later he cut to the chase: he asked for Wahiba's hand according to the custom of God and His prophet and his request was welcomed heartily. The only costs of the marriage were the necessary furniture and all was made even happier and more auspicious by the fact that wily Mekki, who was smarter than to have given up his departed uncle's old rented house, gave Salih and his wife two of the rooms.

The honeymoon outlasted one moon; it lasted a whole year, which passed like a brief moment as if no more than a dream on a moonlit spring night. Salih could never forget Wahiba's embrace, no, nor her perfumed breath that spread like fire all over his body. Wahiba was the greatest wife a man could ever hope for: she didn't tax her husband, she never ceased to treat him like a slave treats a master, she raised birds, was frugal, bought her clothes from door-to-door saleswomen on reasonable installment terms, and when the two families got together, which was most days, they were like one big, happy household. Mekki discovered in Salih a brother to keep him company, to revive the past and bring it roaring into the present. They both enjoyed talking about the old days in Egypt and they were both sorry to hear their wives—the two sisters—talking every evening about their third lost sister, who they only knew lived somewhere on Egyptian soil. Is she dead, they wondered, or still alive and well? What's she like? Does she have a lot of kids? Where are they? What do they do? etc., etc., down the long list of questions, which led to new questions and grief, distress, and the memory of separation. Mekki and Salih decided to search for the older sister and to find her even if they had to plumb the depths of the earth because they knew that rediscovering the sister would double everyone's happiness, especially if they found out that she had *grown children*.

They each began to search for leads. Salih went to see his Egyptian friends of Sudanese descent and asked them—feigning genuine interest— about their hometowns. Mekki, on the other hand, found his way to an ancient man from Shalateen, who'd known his uncle well and was once a member of the Camel Corps. It turned out that he knew the husband of Mekki's uncle's eldest daughter Marzuqa Wahdan, who was also called Montaha. What was more, he even knew Marzuqa herself through one of his sisters who was a doorwoman in Cairo and he gave Mekki her address. Mekki chose not to tell the whole family about it because he didn't want them to get upset if it turned out that the old man was talking about someone else. Meanwhile, Salih had lost hope in the whole venture and thought it was no better than looking for a needle in a dust pile, but he didn't know that Mekki had written a letter and sent it off to Cairo registered express. When Mekki got a letter back and knew for certain that his uncle's daughter was alive, he was wise to keep it a secret for a little while. He learned from the letter that his cousin's husband was fed up with life in Cairo because he was out of work and had no money to come to Sudan so Mekki rushed to send him some money by postal order and told him to come to Sudan as soon as he received it. He promised he'd be able to find work, a place to live, and a good life there and then he explained how to get there by way of a particular Nile ferry captained by so-and-so. Mekki began to keep an eye out for the ferry each day as it came to town at the quay and on the day they finally arrived, he was standing on the quay and calling out as loudly as he could: so-and-so! And there he was, so-and-so, weaving through all the disembarkers, rushing toward him, and embracing him. He was a middle-aged, broken-down man and the woman who followed after him was thin and shabby looking, dressed in a black shroud and old worn-out shoes. Pushing the woman out in front of him as if she were something he'd been entrusted with and was now returning to its rightful owners, the old man said, "Here, boss! This is your cousin. Families always come back together!" Mekki leapt into her arms, weeping as she patted his shoulder with great emotion and then he took them both back to the house.

An exhausted Salih had just returned from training and was stretched out half-naked on the rope bed as his wife massaged his arms and shoulders with warm oil and he fought the desire to make love to her right there and then because the house was full of children and someone could knock on their bedroom door at any moment. And so it was because not a moment later they heard a ferocious banging at the door born of great exuberance.

"Who's making all that noise?" asked Wahiba, almost in protest.

"Wahiba, your sister Marzuqa and her husband are here!"

Wahiba abandoned Salih's body and ran off, screaming in excitement. Salih sprung to his feet and searched clumsily for his shirt and gallabiya. He was blown away, he could hardly believe that an idle wish had become reality just like that. Then he remembered something Mekki had said to him one evening, "I can tell you're a lot like me and my family, and your name doesn't sound strange to me at all. You being here is what's brought the past back to life."

When he stepped into Mekki's living room, he tripped over his own surprise. He saw his wife in her sister's arms, both of them shouting and jabbering. He couldn't see the old woman's face, but he froze where he stood, shell-shocked, and after a deep sigh that was almost his last, his face turned pale and his throat went dry. He was staring at the strange, muttering man who'd accompanied her. *Impossible! No way!* But there was no denying it: all evidence pointed to the fact that the man standing before him was his father. Therefore this woman was his mother and somehow he'd gone and married his aunt!

The shock was echoed on the faces of his father and his mother, who, for her part, shouted in a mixture of joy and terror and grabbed her chest: "Salih? The army sends you to Sudan and you don't tell us? Shame on you and your cruel heart!"

The father barked, "What's this boy doing here?"

"He's my husband. We're married," answered Wahiba, proud and confused all at once.

His mother beat her chest and screamed, "Good Lord in heaven! Your husband? How can you marry him? You're his aunt! His mother's sister!"

"His aunt? Salih's your son, cuz?" shouted Mekki.

His mother wept and slapped her cheeks, his father slapped his hands together: "That boy's been bad luck his entire life. But, I got to say, this is the worst it's ever been!"

Wahiba drooped like a wet rag, falling to the floor, one arm draped across her face. Saliva pooled in Salih's mouth until he was finally able to unsheathe his voice: "What's all this nonsense going on here? Is my mom's name Montaha or Marzuqa? I've never heard this Marzuqa before. Was my grandfather's name al-Khisht or Mahran?"

His mother wailed, "Dear Lord! After this long life of mine, my oldest son doesn't even know my name is Marzuqa Wahdan al-Khisht! I mean I'd forgotten about it myself. Nobody ever calls me that. It's all my mother-in-law's fault! She's the one who started calling me Montaha and it just stuck for the rest of my life."

"What are we going to do about this mess?"

Salih was frightened to see that Wahiba had fainted and gone stiff. He beat his head against the wall, he bellowed and cried and tore at his clothes. His head started to bleed, he grew weak, collapsed, and fell into a long coma he wished he'd never come out of. The truth was that he'd never woken up from that coma, not even to this day, because he was never really clear about the details of what happened after that exactly. He did remember that the official came and legally separated the incestuous pair and he also remembered that Wahiba never recovered, that she became scrawny and pale, the features of her face disappeared, the curves of her body erased. It was because of the strain—they said—because of the sudden shock and the subsequent fever, which she survived only miraculously. Still she pretty much lost her mind and then she got hooked on zar ceremonies. He could remember going to see every sheikh of every sort to find a cure for Wahiba in their books and to seek out a penitence he could perform to be granted God's forgiveness for his inadvertent sin. He himself went slightly mad: he gave up training, he didn't want anyone to see him he was so ashamed, he asked to be discharged from the army, and he returned to Cairo. He spent a long time jobless and homeless until he realized he could always get a job with the police and so he applied and was hired as a ministry guard.

His job was to stand at the door of the minister of labor's office and after he settled into his new job, he returned to his love of boxing. He went down to the Policemen's Club and signed up and threw himself into training with the team that was preparing for the Olympics in Spain. He did end up traveling with the team and he came home with a gold medal! He was surprised one day to discover that his Excellency the Minister of Labor—whose door he stood guard at—had seemed to take a liking to him: one time, he asked him to go buy some things and deliver them to his house in Garden City and he tipped him a whole five pounds, which was more than what Salih got paid in an entire month; another time, he gave him a suit, a pair of black and white wingtips like he'd never worn before, and a European dress shirt and tie; a third time—this was at the Feast of the Sacrifice—he gave him about half a sheep and three pounds and he started calling him 'Uncle Salih' even though he'd only ever called Salih 'Private' before. These niceties eventually started to worry Salih—it was simply his nature to be suspicious of people's intentions because he knew that gentlemen's hearts weren't naturally filled with compassion for their servants—so a wary Salih began to search out the secret behind these dubious new developments. It didn't take him very long either. One day for some reason unknown to Salih, the minister threw a fit and a memo was issued saying that the canteen staff weren't allowed into his office anymore and that only Salih could handle the office's tea and coffee orders. In no less than a week, Salih became, for all intents and purposes, a waiter in a policeman's uniform. One time as Salih was collecting demitasses on his tray to take them back to the canteen, the minister stopped him with a congenial smile: "Salih, are you, uh, married?"

Salih was surprised by the question, but simply laughed politely, "No, I'm not, Your Excellency."

"Why not?"

"Why should I be?"

"Don't you like women?"

"Not one bit—no offense."

The minister didn't know how to react and just stared at him. Salih could feel the man's eyes boring through his face and neck and then his entire body. The minister finally spoke: "Can you tell me why, Salih? Maybe—"

"Its just . . . It's just . . . "

"You know if you get married, you'll get a bigger salary. And things'll get better. You'll find you like women."

Salih nearly told him the story of how he'd married his aunt and how that cursed marriage had sealed his heart and mind off from all worldly joy, but he stopped himself before he could even start. He had a sudden sense of foreboding, which looked to him like a column of black smoke. It worried him, put a stop to the laughter in his throat, made him go pale. The minister took Salih's sudden discomfort for prudish embarrassment regarding the subject of marriage—that was all there was to it—so he nodded soothingly: "Think about it and when you convince yourself, I've got a bride for you. I raised her myself and I don't want to lose her to somebody I don't know. I want her to have a solid future with a stand-up guy like you. Think about it, Salih, and keep me posted."

Salih nodded gratefully as he couldn't think of anything to say and pressed the tray against his chest to keep the cups from chattering as he struggled to hide the tremors that had come over him. Later, after he'd regained his composure, he did as the minister had advised and considered what it might be like to marry a woman his Excellency the Minister had set him up with. Even if she were only his maid—as Salih suspected—she'd still be quite a catch and there was no doubting that the minister would give him a raise and help him find a place to live. Salih found himself walking around the minister's neighborhood more and more. The doorman at the building where the minister lived knew Salih well because Salih always liked to make friends with doormen; he thought of them all as family. Salih took the doorman to a coffeehouse on Qasr al-Aini Street and treated him to a cup of tea and a couple of rounds of water pipe. A word here, an anecdote there, and a joke to top it all off were all Salih needed to get every last detail of the story out of the doorman. It was exactly like it happens in the movies, and a disbelieving Salih had to ask himself: Do films borrow from real life or does real life borrow from films? Then he wiggled his finger, laughing, and said that they both borrow from the other, but what real life gets from films is more dangerous than what films get from real life. Then he slapped his hands together, shocked by man's capacity for cruelty and injustice, and carried on with his story: the maid—that is, the bride—had indeed been brought up in his Excellency the Minister's household and as a result she'd had a despicable upbringing. As had the minister's good-for-nothing reprobate of a son who'd been left unsupervised in front of this feminine feast. His precocious virility had grown up on her chest and belly and had then come into its own in the little room where she slept beside the kitchen on the servant's staircase. The girl had to have more than one abortion.

His Excellency the Minister, though, was content just to cover the whole thing up, and he didn't want to get rid of the girl because he didn't think he could find a substitute as clean, trustworthy, and obedient as she. But then when his villager relatives found him a girl that was her equal in every way, His Excellency the Minister decided to get rid of her in a way that suited his position and which would convince the new girl that anyone who served him obediently would leave his house for a suitable home as a happy bride, not wanting for anything. Thus the minister had set his eyes on Salih and planned to fix them up on false pretenses. "Don't do it, Salih. Don't you dare. God loves you, that's why he made you ask me," warned the doorman, pointing, his eyes gleaming like crystal balls, like peeled onions.

After he found out the truth, Salih was simply unable to go on acting like he'd always done. His attitude toward His Excellency the Minister changed completely: his hand, which had grown used to saluting the minister as he approached, refused—on its own, without any mental intervention on his part—to move, and his face, which had grown used to smiling whenever he saw the minster, had chosen to turn itself into stone rather than smile at the man; even his ears grew deaf to the sound of the minister's bell.

The minister's chief of staff shouted at him, "What! Are you sleeping? His Excellency rang for you!" He went into the minister's office wearing a frozen, stern, and gloomy expression and stood a few steps back. The minister looked him up and down and was quiet for a long moment, perhaps searching to find that old Salih he knew. Finally, he shouted at him, maintaining a shade of tenderness, "Where were you?"

"Nowhere."

"Didn't you hear the bell?"

"I heard it."

"Why didn't you come then if you heard it?"

"No offense, but why should I?"

"Aren't you supposed to bring me my coffee?"

"I'm a guard not a waiter."

"You . . . . What is it? What's the matter?"

"Nothing."

"Fine, go! Get out, you animal!"

"I'm a human being just like you, maybe better."

"Get out! I don't want to see your face in here again."

Salih bolted out like an arrow, curtains flapping, doors screeching, keys jingling, drawers slamming, cups shattering, papers flying. Everyone who worked in the minister's office wanted to find out why His Excellency the Minister was angry with Salih since they knew he'd taken him under his wing. More than one of the senior office staff tried to get Salih to tell him something, anything, about the sudden upheaval, but Salih kept his counsel. The minister, though, seemed determined to find out what was behind this volte-face and so he called Salih into his office two days later and tried buttering him up:

"When a minister orders you to do something, you do it."

"Your Excellency can only order me to do things that are part of my job."

"You're an ingrate!"

"And you're a slave driver!"

"Rude, too? I swear to God I'll teach you some manners."

"You won't and you can't. I already know my manners, for one, and you couldn't even teach your own son any manners. Why don't you just let sleeping dogs lie, Your Excellency!"

The minister leapt to his feet, came out from behind his desk, and walked straight up to Salih—preceded by the sparks shooting out of his eyes. He reared back to plant his fist on Salih's temple, but—to his surprise—Salih caught his fist in his hand andbegan to crush it, then he let him go and the entire room filled with his frightening roar, "Nobody lays a finger on Salih Abd al-Birr. He's the one who hits and he never gets hit. And you ought to know: if you try any tricks on me or try to start something, you're going be the one who pays a heavy price."

Salih turned and walked away calmly, shutting the door behind him, and headed for his usual spot and stood there, feeling for his regulation sidearm. Not ten days later, Salih was summoned to the headquarters of the Greater Cairo Security Directorate and there he was informed that a decision had been taken to transfer him to the Darb al-Ahmar precinct where as a punishment he'd be demoted to the post of nightwatchman. Here came long nights spent between Bab Zuwayla and al-Ghuri Palace, where being a watchman meant taking nighttime walks in the park, armed with a sidearm and petty bribes from the vendors who'd wrapped their wares up in tarpaulins and left them in the street overnight. The only problem as far as Salih was concerned—rather, the dilemma—was boxing practice. How could he work his beat the whole night through and still make it to the Policemen's Club mornings and evenings to train? If only he could've trained by himself, but the annoying hang-up was that the club managers had asked him to train a bunch of young recruits who were hoping to box in the local leagues. It wasn't like he was going to get paid for it, but what could he do? God knows, he adored the pugilist arts, but there was something that mattered even more to him than boxing, something that mattered more than life itself: freedom. To wake up whenever his body had slept its twenty-four carat fill exactly. To do what he wanted to do, not what others wanted him to do. To say what he was thinking, not what other people wanted to hear. To act when he felt like it, to fulfill his own desires, not to be the slave he was, to be told what to do, to have his freedom curtailed. No! No, no, no! To hell with boxing, to hell with work, to hell with the whole damn world! "Tomorrow I'll show them exactly what I think of them!" He sat back on the sidewalk in front of the Palace of al-Ghuri, rubbed his coarse beard, and lit a cigarette as the muezzins' voices from atop the mosques of Hussein, al-Azhar, Abu Dahab, al-Ghuri, al-Salih Talayi, and Bab Zuwayla flowed together harmoniously in a wave over everything in a carnival of jubilant song as if to proclaim the resurrection of fuul carts, milk shops, falafel stands, coffeehouses, and the shaking, clanging wheels of animal carts. Salih was filled with a desire to get rowdy! As soon as the sun rose up over the shoulder of the clouds, he ran to a shop and bought a bottle each of denatured alcohol and Coca-Cola, then he stopped by a fuul cart, and finally he sat down on a bench and began to drink and eat rapaciously. He headed back to his home on the roof of a crumbling house in an Upper Egyptian enclave right beside the Security Directorate and changed his clothes. He wrapped up his government-issued uniform and sidearm in a bundle, which he stuck under his arm and then he went out. He stopped at a coffeehouse for a coffee, black, shot the bull with the other customers, laughed, joked, and had a generally noisy good time until he had to go to training. He proceeded to the Security Directorate and handed in his kit, telling the office he no longer needed it. "Why not?"

"I got an important order I can't ignore."

"What order? Who from?"

"My conscience. It said, 'To hell with this job, Salih,' and I replied, 'To fucking hell with this job, Conscience!' So I'm here to hand in my kit and to tell you all I'm resigning and you can give my beat to someone else."

"Are you nuts? You think this is a bakery you can just quit whenever you feel like it?"

"Whatever. Maybe I am nuts, but I'm sure as hell not going to work for you all anymore."

Long story short he succeeded in getting a receipt that certified that he'd returned his kit in full and then he took a streetcar to the Policemen's Club and strode right into the cafeteria, ignoring the looks he got from some of the employees and patrons when they saw him sit down in the first seat he came to and cross his legs as if he were the General himself. When he called for an extra-strong coffee, the surprise in their eyes became shock and if eyes could speak, they'd have said, "First, you come late and now you're acting like you own the place?" But they moved on, though bitter and grumbling, and a second later the manager came over pompously, the ground shaking beneath his heavy footsteps. He glared at Salih: "Well, well, would you look at that! What exactly are you doing here, Your Imperial Highness? Aren't you supposed to be at training? And don't you think you're overdoing it just a little? Or is there no such thing as respect anymore?"

"Of course there is. How could there not be?"

"Stand up, boy, when you speak to me."

Salih wiggled his finger and said, "Impudence, I simply won't tolerate."

The manager was at a loss for words. He looked as if he were comparing his own strength (waning) to Salih's (waxing) and he seemed wholly convinced that hitting Salih would only lead to his own dignity being dragged through the dirt. He turned around without saying a word and walked off. Salih had almost finished the last sip of his second demitasse of coffee when he saw a whole host of club officials and athletes dressed for training coming toward him like a band of scouts, trying to scope out all possible risks before a full-scale attack. They were led by the club director, who evinced a practiced, diplomatic calm. Salih felt as if he were tottering in the director's incredulous vision, but nevertheless he held his position. Trying to muster as much contempt as he possibly could, the director addressed Salih, "Would Your Honor mind standing up to speak to me?"

A cloud of alcohol fumes parted before Salih's eyes and he suddenly realized he was dealing with the general, the venerable club director himself, who'd never done him wrong, who'd actually often been very kind to him and embraced him after every fight he'd won. He felt that he owed this man in particular his respect so he stood up, but he tried to keep his distance so that the unmistakable smell of denatured alcohol emanating from him wouldn't cause him to lose all face. Confidently and respectfully, he said, "I'm sorry, General, sir, I haven't slept in more than two months. From duty to training, from training to duty."

The general smiled wanly as if to signal he was amenable to coming to some understanding and said, "How can a champion athlete like you talk back to the manager? How can you sit there all full of yourself when we're standing right in front of you? You're obviously not normal."

"Quite right, General, sir, I've got things wrong with my brain."

"Have you been drinking, son?"

"You have no idea, General, sir! But why are you calling me *son*, too, General? You're killing me."

"I can tell you're a thug. What you need is someone to control you."

"It's the opposite, General, sir. My problem is there's no counting the number of people who want to control me. Everywhere I go, I bump into somebody who wants to control me. At every step, there's two or three people who've got to give me orders and I've got to get their signatures. And I've got to salute them and ask them if I can go to the little boys' room, if I can eat, drink, sleep! I'm sick of it, people! I can't take it anymore! I've decided this isn't going to work. I've got to be the one who controls me for me. What's wrong with that? I don't want to have to subject myself to anyone else! Is that my right or isn't it? You say 'Job'? I don't want to work. I don't have to! You say, 'Boxing'? I don't want to fight. Who's with me?"

The general looked around him, his head whizzing like a motor. "Is this the attitude of someone who's contending for a major world championship? Are these the values of someone people have their hopes on?"

The manager looked at Salih with a mixture of pity and contempt: "All the guys he's going to fight in the tournament are midgets compared to him, but I guess he's chosen to commit suicide."

The general waved the man off exasperatedly and said, "He can go to hell for all I care. Let's cut to the chase: Are you going to apologize to the manager and go to practice or not?"

"Not! Not!" Salih said and stormed off, cutting a path straight through to the front door without once looking back. If he had, he'd have seen that they'd all turned toward him, frozen in shock, following the back of him with pale, idiot grins, soaked in the sweat of frustrated vengeance.

Salih never went back to the Policeman's Club after that. He received notice of his dismissal from both jobs and he took it the way a prisoner takes news of his release. He went to claim his remaining wages and he saw the ironing man waiting for him at the pay window. Salih owed the man more than three pounds: his share of the rowdiness they got up to together every few days, which the ironing man would pay for and then calculate Salih's share and note it down in his ledger of customer tabs. That left Salih with about a half pound so he threw his arm around the ironing man and they went to al-Ghuri Palace together, where they got seriously, elaborately rowdy. Salih had to sleep it off for a few days, which were also the last of his rent-paid stay in the rooftop shack he called home in the Upper Egyptian enclave. Little by little he began to wake up from the nightmare of employment, to free himself from the noose of strict work timetables, from all shackles. He started giving boxing lessons to enthusiasts in poor neighborhoods and public squares in exchange for cigarettes and the money he needed to get rowdy. At first, he was a loyal, generous trainer, but he soon got sick of training because it, too, tied him down with appointments and routines he simply couldn't put up with anymore. He surprised even himself when he decided he wasn't going to go to the square anymore and then eventually he stopped going to any appointments at all.

EARLY MORNING HEP CATS

The changes that had come over Mustafa Lami were striking. He'd abandoned his classic style, which was at once modest and elegant—you know, the way a man wouldn't look respectable unless he were dressed in a blazer and tie free from any shiny, embarrassing sweat spots. He, too, had started wearing coarse, ratty, jeans, with loads of pockets and bright yellow copper rivets, but he still retained a certain stylish distinction. Over the jeans, he wore a knit shirt and a wide-necked wool sweater capped off by his shirt collar. On his feet, he wore black shoes so shiny they looked like they were covered in plastic. Thus Mustafa Lami started looking like Talat al-Imbabi, except that Talat was tall and reedy and Mustafa was shorter and relatively stocky. Likewise, he turned against people who stuck to their conventional styles and he made fun of their fossilized minds, or rather their bourgeois minds. They were as worried about maintaining conventions as they were about preserving their reputations and dignity, which in the past had meant success and a place at the vanguard of society.

Clothes—of any kind—were not the sort of phenomenon that could hold our attention for very long, especially not since we'd discovered Rowdy Salih, who'd demolished the myth of 'the clothes make the man' for us once and for all. We no longer took any notice of his appearance, which was drowned out by his character, and it never occurred to us that he was shabbily dressed even though his clothes never left his body except in one tear after the other until he was left naked, or nearly so, and he had to hurry over to Wikalat al-Balah to buy a secondhand shirt and pair of trousers. He presented us with damning evidence that a human being was his character, not his clothing, and that people who thought differently were—in his opinion—idiots, duped by the scams of a frivolous society.

"No offense, but this society's nasty. How do you expect me to respect it? You should just respect God for your own sake and leave it at that. Got the hang of it? Well then the hell with all the rest! Boss, our society dresses itself in fairy dust. Everybody acts like they're respectable. Everybody wants to scare everybody else with their fancy-schmancy clothes."

Interestingly, this sentiment got us to look at how the tourists dressed and we got the impression they were of the same school as Rowdy Salih: they wore raggedy, torn-up clothes, but they carried expensive books around with them so that they could seize any opportunity to read. They also seemed to be imbued with the same character as Rowdy Salih, especially as they knew their way to dens in the twisting depths of old, run-down alleys; they even knew their way to the hash dealers in al-Batiniya, Zaynhum, and al-Gamaliya. Hakeem's den got the largest share of the hip tourists because it was in the heart of downtown. We'd usually see one of the foreigners, his chest, back, shoulders, and arms bare, dressed only in an undershirt and ripped-up trousers, missing at least half of one of the legs, wearing flip-flops or ratty sandals on his feet, with an overgrown, nasty beard, generally filthy or crusty from so much walking around; maybe they'd come all the way from Paris or London or Berlin on foot! They all took their small piece of hash in hand and cut off a slice and then they'd grab the bong stem excitedly and take the same strong, satisfied, stoner hits as we did. They even managed the same holding-the-smoke-in technique that we Egyptians were certain we'd invented: we'd hold the smoke in our throats as we were inhaling and we'd force it out through our noses, causing a sharp screech like the sound of a car doing what the kids called an 'American peel-out.' The foreigner would sit there, cross-legged, not minding that half his thigh was exposed, or that he was barefoot and looked a right mess. He'd just sit there getting high and absorbed in his book. We envied him and pitied ourselves for not enjoying time, life, and travel like he did.

It always surprised us when Salih went up to one of those foreigners, who'd then pull himself together and stand up, smiling and shaking Salih's hand warmly. The foreigner would pull a chair over so Salih could join him. He'd tell the waiter to give Salih a go at the bong and Salih wouldn't make the same excuses he made to us: that it wasn't his poison, but would happily take some hits and soon fall into a friendly conversation with the foreigner that seemed quite intimate and private. We'd be dying to know what they were saying because it looked as if they'd been friends since childhood, as if they were reminiscing, laughing gaily, giving each other five after every joke. That sort of thing happened with more than one foreigner and it got Talat al-Imbabi to modify his position on the activities of international espionage. To American central intelligence, or the CIA, he added the Israeli Intelligence Agency, Mossad, especially as the prevailing not-at-peace, not-at-war situation had the whole country on a sharp edge, which wasn't getting any blunter, and everyone had this suppressed rage inside of them; no amount of hash could make the burden any lighter. There were no solutions in sight. The only thing that had been the least bit successful during the war of attrition between us and the Israeli enemy were some of the self-sacrifice operations carried out by our sons. There wasn't a single family that didn't have one son or more serving on the front lines ever since the absolute and overwhelming defeat in the June war and Anwar Sadat didn't look like he was planning to make use of the mists that had begun to encircle the horizon. Nevertheless, life was tolerable and none of us was out of work. Mustafa Lami was working as an artist for a children's magazine, Qamar al-Mahruqi for the American University, Talat al-Imbabi was teaching history at Cairo University, Zaki Hamid had a bunch of supporting roles in radio and television programs, Faruq al-Gamal had been taken on by a famous weekly as a political and social caricaturist, Ibrahim al-Qammah was in demand as a display designer, and Ahmad Asim was trying his hand at documentary filmmaking. Those were the core members of the crew and the affiliates—meaning the guys we saw only once a week or so—were all making a living one way or another. We were all better off than government employees, laborers, farmers, and artisans, who were facing serious hardship. Their wives and mothers had to stand in line at the government co-ops to buy a kilo of meat or rice, or laundry detergent, and they still might not have even got their hands on any one of those things when it was finally their turn because the co-op employees would secretly sell three-quarters of the stock to black-market dealers and door-to-door saleswomen. And yet no one could explain where Egyptians got the money for the hashish they burnt day and night. Sure, it was the only thing in the market that never ran out, but it still cost the stoners a lot in terms of den expenses.

"We're dying to know what you and the foreigners talk about when you hang out," Qamar al-Mahruqi said to Rowdy Salih. Our ears all pricked up.

"Which foreigners?" Salih asked.

"That last foreigner, for example," said Qamar.

"That foreigner's sly. A real troublemaker."

"What did he say to you?" Talat al-Imbabi cried out impatiently, desperate for evidence to back up his theory.

Salih smiled: "This last friend of ours, here, asked me, 'Why were Egyptians so sad when Nasser died?'"

This sudden turn in the conversation got us all sitting up in our seats. Fiery sparks shone in Talat's eyes as he scanned our faces as if to say, "I told you so!" Zaki Hamid the actor rested his cheek in his hand and fixed his strong, piercing gaze on Salih: "And what exactly did you tell him, if I may ask?"

Salih laughed, his nerves like cold steel: "I told him the truth, of course. You know . . . my opinion about stuff."

"We'd like to know your valued opinion!" cried Mustafa Lami sarcastically.

Salih laughed. "I told him that the Egyptians are a great people. 'Great at what?' he says to me. So I tell him, 'At everything.' Great in age, great in rank, in intellect, understanding. 'What does that have to do with being sad about Nasser's death?' he asked. So I said to him, 'Think about it, Whitey! If we're great at everything, we're going to be great at grief as well! The thing is, we loved Nasser because Nasser, my western friend, was as great as the Egyptian people. He was on our scale. He was great in every way just like us. Egypt, we put our trust in him so he became Egypt and Egypt became him. The foreigner didn't know what to say to that . . . ha ha ha! Get out!'"

We all shared in his raucous laughter, adding the words 'get out!' at the end, which was how he liked to cap things off; like a full stop at the end of a sentence.

A LOSING BET

Despite the fact he could neither read nor write, Ibrahim al-Qammah had this profound perspicacity and intelligence and it was he who'd first noticed that something was amiss in Talat al-Imbabi and Rowdy Salih's friendship. Only a few weeks before, during a brilliant session with both bowls and bong smoothly making their rounds—and quickly, too, because there were only a few of us there that evening—Zaki Hamid the actor winked at me and said, "I guess Talat doesn't say hello to Rowdy Salih anymore."

The wink almost passed safely home unnoticed, but it was Talat himself who ended up getting our attention. His face went pale at first, but then the blood surged to his cheeks, leaving a suppressed, worrying trace. He seemed uncomfortable and he began denying the suggestion earnestly in a faint and rusty voice, "Not at all. Where'd you get that idea? Salih's a very good friend."

If only he hadn't done that. For one thing, there was a tone in his voice that confirmed the resentment he was trying—an failing—to hide, and for another, his self-deception caused him some confusion and he asked Sabir to take a bowl over to Salih as a small token, apparently having forgotten that Rowdy Salih didn't smoke hash. He must've realized his mistake, though, and a yellow smile stretched over his plump lips as if he were dying to cry out: "Yeah, things have changed between me and him. Anybody got anything they want to say to me about that?!" But he said nothing of the sort, he simply retreated into a moment's silence and then it was his turn at the bong, which rescued him from the embarrassment of a longer silence. He took the stem of the bong calmly, and slowly began to crack his knuckles in preparation for the long rip after which there'd be no more hits. That was his preferred style of smoking and it always reminded you of a soccer player taking a few steps back before running up to shoot a penalty kick.

I'd gone to the den earlier that morning to smoke a quick ten bowls before heading to the Broadcasters' Club between Elwi and al-Sherifein streets to attend the first read-through of a five-part radio play I'd written. I found Qamar al-Mahruqi and Mustafa Lami there. They were both deeply engrossed in a stoner's tête-à-tête with Rowdy Salih, which is to say a discussion about politics. At the time, Qamar al-Mahruqi was constantly telling us that the nuts of his brain were coming loose because of Sadat, who would erase a page or two from the history of the July Revolution every day and at the same time blather on about how he was following the course set by the Departed Leader. The building of the Revolutionary Command Council was demolished and the old enemies of the revolution were released and given high posts, including those who'd been guilty of blatant treason. People who'd been affected by the nationalization measures were allowed to sue the government and some of them won, allowing them to re-amass their estates, and the government returned the assets of others. Stars of the old regime were allowed to publish poisonous books impugning the honor of noble Nasser, who went to the grave a poor man, and they were allowed to go even further in the prostitute press, benefiting from their monopolies and beginning to criticize the gains made by workers and farmers both in terms of their standard of living and their political representation. They attacked free education. They greedily denigrated the Land Reform Law, which had broken up the old agricultural oligarchy and led to troubled harvests and chaos in the agricultural economy. They slapped themselves and tore at their pockets because they thought the High Dam was a disaster, the biggest trick ever played on the Nile, and that it would transform it into a eunuch with no desire to fertilize the land anymore and that it would soon overrun its banks and flood cities and sweep buildings away. Every day in his column, Anis Mansour would try to tempt people into emigrating, telling young people how great it would be to get out of the country and go find opportunities for a happy future in the United States and Europe. All that and a lot more, Qamar al-Mahruqi explained, were the reasons why the nuts and bolts of his mind were coming loose.

As I neared Hakeem's den, I could make out Rowdy Salih's voice the best; it was clear, booming, deep, manic, friendly, vivid with genuine emotion. It emitted a certain ominous majesty that put you in mind of Tiresias, he of the shocking prophecies in ancient Greek plays.

"If Sadat loses his mind and starts taking the public sector apart, you should all march up to him and tell him, 'Hold it right there!' Anything but the public sector. What will people have left if he takes that from them? I swear to God Almighty we won't be able to buy a fuul sandwich, or a shirt, or a shoe even! How are people supposed to buy their kids new clothes at the holidays? How are we going to afford butter, oil, eggs, frozen fish, frozen chicken? Laundry detergent? Can any of you all afford to buy a kilo of meat from the butcher's? Maybe you all can, but the people can't. The people can barely afford to ride the bus where they get crushed and insulted and have the dignity of their women trampled on. What are they supposed to do? If the public sector's broke, why don't you all fix it? Take out those thieves you put in and it'll get better."

I met cheering applause as I entered the den to join the party. During his tirade, Salih had got up and walked past his station toward the far window of the den to grab the pick he used to unclog the bowls, but in the heat of the moment he stayed standing there, mindlessly cradling the pick under his arm like a field marshal. When the applause shook him out of his reverie, he just laughed a long while and then walked back to his station in the corner and sat down and started cleaning out the bowls as if nothing had happened. I suspected that Qamar and Mustafa hadn't noticed me come in, so I announced my arrival: "What? A seminar on an empty stomach?"

Qamar laughed and sucked his cheeks down into the void of his wide mouth and growled as he held the smoke in his nose: "Rowdy Salih's upset because Talat isn't speaking him to anymore."

Mustafa elaborated, "You know, the cold shoulder. He won't even make small talk with him anymore."

"It's like he doesn't know him all of a sudden," Qamar confirmed.

"That's how Salih feels anyway. It's his impression," Mustafa added circumspectly.

"Fine, but what does that have to do with Salih's rant?"

Qamar growled, or maybe it was a laugh: "One subject led to another! That's Rowdy Salih for you."

Mustafa's constantly hidden, considered smile grew: "But it's on topic. It's always on topic."

"Rowdy Salih's one-size-fits-all; he stretches to fit all sizes. To him, everything's interconnected: a piece of bread's connected to parliament, and oil, soap, and fuul are connected to Gamal Abdel Nasser. To him, Muammar Gaddafi, Sadat, Yasser Arafat, Saddam Hussein, and the USA are all one big happy family! King Hussein calls the British 'Granddad,' He thinks Mustafa Khalil, Abd al-Aziz Hegazi, and Mustafa Amin are the sons of the Burji Mamluks. I swear you missed out: you should've heard the speech from the beginning. His anger at Talat was what got him started."

I was in a hurry so I didn't have time to delve into the story, but I'd noticed that Talat al-Imbabi often went through periods of wanting to be alone, but because he was so fond of noise and company, he usually resisted them, merely choosing to sit there lost in thought for hours, focused only on getting seriously stoned and not saying a single word. His features would get even more delicate until they almost faded away and the only thing left of his face was a pale shadow, extremely thin, on his reed-like body. During those spells, he could easily forget a whole host of social dos and don'ts, like returning greetings, offering you a tea when he ordered one for himself, making you look for his keys for two hours because he'd left them some place. He was always the most devoted, most affected, the closest of us all to Rowdy Salih, so it never occurred to me that he could ever turn his back on Salih until I bumped into Ibrahim al-Qammah the next evening when I was at the den by myself. He fired a surprise question at me: "What happened between Talat al-Imbabi and Rowdy Salih?"

His question worried me mostly because he was so sincere. "I don't think anything could ever happen between those two," I said. "I mean, you know, sometimes Talat's got his head in the clouds."

Ibrahim wagged his finger in confident refutation. "No, there's definitely something going on here that's not normal. Thing is, he was just here. I was here when he came in and I was sitting here when he left and he didn't once say hello or goodbye to Salih. Even when Salih said good evening to him, he ignored him. I tried to draw him into talking about it, but he didn't give me a chance. He completely stonewalled me!"

"That's weird. Maybe he's got something on his mind."

"Maybe . . . . But I know Talat. He's got big ambitions, and people who've got big ambitions are fast talkers. I bet you he's planning to become a minister some day."

"No, no. Talat al-Imbabi would never settle for anything less than the presidency of a large country like the Soviet Union or something."

We giggled hysterically. Ibrahim said that perhaps that was the source of the disagreement: Talat was worried that Rowdy Salih would try to take the presidency away from him. Two days later, I bumped into Qamar al-Mahruqi at around ten in the morning. I was coming out of the metro station in Bab al-Luq and he was coming from Tahrir Square on his way to the American University building where his office was. We embraced as if we hadn't seen each other for years and immediately after our warm hug, we instinctively turned back toward Tahrir Square and from there to Antikkhana Street on our way to Hakeem's den. Suddenly, he stopped: "Damn! I don't have any hash on me."

"Me neither," I said. We were in the middle of Bassiouni Street. Qamar pointed and so I followed him down an exceptionally elegant alleyway, which wound between buildings as if it were actually a fissure and led to Qasr al-Nil Street. I was taken aback; I hadn't known about this kiosk that took up almost the whole alley and sold antiques. It was actually just a look-out kiosk set there by the hash-dealing owner of the coffeehouse in the alley. We got our hash from Fouad the coffeehouse owner and carried on. During that short—both in distance and duration—trip, Qamar told me the story of what had happened when Talat al-Imbabi invited Rowdy Salih over to his house for a few days. Qamar was also concerned about the sudden chill in the relationship between the once close friends so he'd done some investigating and had finally arrived at an unbiased, verified story he felt comfortable sharing with me.

All of Talat al-Imbabi's wife Matilde's friends were also friends with Mahasin Asim, Qamar's wife. One of them was an amiable woman called Hayat al-Barri who worked as an administrator at the American University. She was a remarkably active translator of English-language political articles and, occasionally, literary criticism, which she published in Arabic periodicals. She was divorced, thirty-five-ish, dark olive skin, attractive, as thin as a slice of pizza, and yet she still gave off this alluring femininity, if only when you were up close to her and the finely drawn features of her body—those sexily symbolic curves—became clear. She was—so people said—as the rather down-market expression has it, in heat; that is, she was in a state of sexual excitement that simply wouldn't be tempered or worn down. She'd love to— according to the same people— do nothing more than lie on her back in bed, only ever getting up to wash in preparation for the arrival of a newcomer. That was why, perhaps, she'd had three failed marriages; we'd had front-row seats to the last one. We all knew she was generally considered to have been slumming it by agreeing to marry the last guy, who was a novice journalist in the foreign affairs department at the Middle East News Agency. Her first husband had been a very famous movie star, one of the most important, and senior, innovative filmmakers in Egyptian cinema. People said she knew that he was a confirmed homosexual; they even said it made her happy because— according to the rumor—homosexuals went to the greatest lengths to satisfy a woman sexually. She ended up leaving him, though, because on one of their trips abroad he tried to take her to an orgy at a nudist club. She left him right there and then and came home on her own. They were formally separated a few days later. Her second husband, on the other hand, was a deputy at the Ministry of Education whom she'd met because he was the guardian of his sister's daughter, a student at the American University. She eventually separated from him after a whole lot of pain and suffering caused by his backward, traditional, and rigid thinking. Her third husband, the up-and-coming journalist, would drop by the hash den from time to time and we'd press him, quite doggedly, for details of the break-up. He only ever said very nice things about her almost as if he were reciting a poem in praise of her sweet disposition, character, and scent, and her bedroom kindnesses, but apparently her voracious, bordering on bestial, appetite—although very sexy—soon came to seem more like a scandalous liability to the man who bore the burden of that sponge that never would stop sucking.

Nevertheless, Hayat al-Barri was simple and pure; she didn't suffer from any psychological complexes at all because she wasn't repressed, she was liberated in the true sense of the word. She did whatever she wanted confidently and without hesitation. Her talk was smooth, her thoughts organized, though they weren't devoid of emotion, rather—and who'd have thought!—some people described her as angelic. Anyone who saw her would immediately forget everything he'd heard about her; he wouldn't believe it, he simply couldn't imagine that this modest, sweet, wholly innocent woman could—despite her great height—be folded up by a man like a cash-note and stuck in his small pocket to be saved and not spent. She didn't use any makeup or cosmetics except for that dizzying scent that always clung to her body. She was honest, direct to the point of dangerously blunt; if a man tried to flirt with her, she'd pierce him with the two sharp arrows of her wide eyes and their brandished lashes. Then she'd knock him over onto the battlefield of his own despicable behavior and no amount of reserve, dignity, or stammering could save him. She never needed more than a few quick words to reject you and would slam the door of pursuit right in your face. One time some jerk asked her why she divorced the novice journalist so she shut him up with a cutting reply, "Because he was just like you: not all man and not all woman."

Hayat al-Barri was from Upper Egypt; she'd been born in Minya and her father, who was the head of the post office there, had her enrolled in a foreign-language school when she was a child. Then she went on to study English at the School of Humanities. Her father died during her first year of university entirely unexpectedly and left her with nothing besides his meager pension, but she was stubborn and tough. She started working for an import–export firm, drafting and translating foreign correspondence, and she was able to finish her degree and graduate with honors. Her still young, thoroughly chaste mother seemed to be rekindling an interest in men, but Hayat didn't mind because she knew there was no use in a vivacious woman remaining a perpetual widow. She told her mother she had no problem with her getting remarried and after graduation, Hayat settled in Cairo and began working as a secretary for the owner of a famous film production company, who adored her for her fluent English and wide

151

knowledge of art and literature. She worked for him, earning a considerable salary, up until she married the famous filmmaker who helped her get an administrative position at the American University.

She knew all sorts of people. She had no end of friends and acquaintances of all nationalities who respected her and they all shared a remarkable intimacy. As soon as one of them—man or woman—saw her, they'd let out a shout of delight as if they'd come across a precious find. She knew Matilde even before she'd married Ahmad Asim; this was because Matilde was a noted member of the Italian Communist Party and very active in international women's organizations, and Hayat had translated some of her articles from an English magazine and published them in an Iraqi communist magazine. She got in touch with Matilde, who'd asked for her address, and they began to correspond in English until one day she was surprised to hear from her Italian friend that she'd married an Egyptian and accompanied him to Cairo.

Ever since then Hayat al-Barri had felt at home in Talat al-Imbabi's house, not simply because Matilde was her best friend but also because Talat was encouragingly hospitable, although the real reason behind that was because Talat was a ladies' man unparalleled by any in his generation. That shifty little beanpole had no qualms about committing the riskiest of capers even if he wasn't totally sure they were going to get him the woman he desired. From the first time he laid eyes on her that day when she came to see her Italian friend and meet her Egyptian husband, he knew he wanted Hayat al-Barri. To him, she was sex personified, all that he'd longed and hoped for especially since Matilde—and he'd married her despite the fact—wasn't sexual at all. She was just white, somewhat pink, flabby, the parts of her body wildly out of proportion: she had a huge ass and a body like a horse-drawn carriage! Not to mention the fact that he thought intellectual women weren't cut out for sex, let alone this one, who was involved in the highest levels of international politics. His desire for Hayat only grew the longer he was married to Matilde; he began to crave her with all the strength and energy of his sexual imagination.

One time as he was trying to seduce her, she told him as plainly as she could, "I'm a sensual woman and you're not a sensual man."

"What makes you think that?"

"Call it a woman's acute intuition." She explained, "A real man doesn't even have to seduce a woman. He gets rewarded for keeping the woman at arm's length, for demonstrating his virility." Then she chose to go further and crush the remaining remnants of his stubborn, pleading lust for her once and for all: "You're barely enough for modest Matilde, who doesn't give a damn about sex. I doubt you can even satisfy her."

"Don't knock it till you've tried it."

"Even if your conscience . . . your twisted conscience would permit you to betray your wife with her friend, I'd never betray a friend with her husband." The cocky playboy was reduced to a frightened rabbit. She knew that he'd been lying when he'd said that Matilde was expecting her for lunch, so she put the phone down and went over there immediately to find that Matilde had extra afternoon lectures that day and that she'd be stuck at the institute until eight in the evening. All the same, she pretended to believe him when he said that Matilde had just called and apologized for not being able to make it. Suddenly he had an idea.

"What do you say we go get stoned?"

"Where? At Hakeem's?"

"Is there anywhere better? Have you ever laid eyes on Rowdy Salih?"

"I went there with Qamar and my ex a few times, but I never saw him."

"I bet you he's just finished up his chores about now and he's starting to get rowdy. Come on, I'll show him to you."

At Hakeem's, he led her to a far corner but as soon as she saw Rowdy Salih at his post, diligently lining the bowls up in rows, she was overcome with curiosity and forgot about Talat completely. She crawled over and crouched down in front of Salih, watching him intensely, which only made him giggle and the prominent Adam's apple beneath his beard shuttle up and down like a sieve being shaken about, and the fine flour of his laughter, which had started out coarse in his chest, was sifted out dustily onto Hayat al-Barri's face. She got tired of crouching so she moved to the bench across from him where we always sat, and Talat had to pick up the rack of bowls and walk over to her. What choice did he have? He sat down in the trap he'd been trying to avoid in case a nosy member of the group should come in and ruin his plans. Hayat got stoned hard that day; she kept up with Talat, taking hits and holding them up in her nose like veteran stoners.

She was out of her skull, her whole body on fire, and she was revived by Rowdy Salih's charming conversation; it had set her imagination alight. She fell in love with him, she felt that she'd been transported to a primitive world of fantasy and sex. All of a sudden, Adam, father to us all, was right there in front of her, face to face, banished from heaven to this hole-in-the-wall. She secretly felt that she herself was Eve, her personality had been wiped out, her ID card a blank, and what's more her clothes melted away and this nudity, she felt, made her happy. More importantly, she took Rowdy Salih for a wellspring of elegance and sophistication, the likes of which she'd never seen in anyone else her entire life; and that was to say nothing of his affably genuine modesty. She told Talat that she'd give her life to live with that man for as long as she could: she'd wouldn't live by any restraints, or traditions, or habits; rather she'd wash herself clean of all the learning she'd acquired, for all new knowledge is but one more restraint on a man's freedom. When Talat insisted that they had to leave, she went to say goodbye to Rowdy Salih. She put out her slender, soft hand, but he was embarrassed by the state of his, dyed dirty by molasses tobacco, pebbles, and bowl scum, so he wrapped a tissue around his hand—the very picture of humility—and took hers in his warm and friendly grasp. She could only stand there, intoxicated, until Talat pulled her away and they went off. She put her arm in his, not minding if his elbow rubbed against her breasts, and leaned over to whisper to him as high as a lunatic, "You'd never believe it, Talat: that's the man I've been dreaming of. If only I could get him to agree to come live with me, but on the condition that he remain exactly the way he is."

Despite the shock that shook Talat to his very core, he found the irony tasted sweet like a pleasant pain, although—it was true—the blow hadn't quite bashed his head in just yet. As if trying to extract the sharp blade from his heart, he said, "Why wouldn't he agree? He should be so lucky!"

"I don't think so. People like him, they look simple, but it's a trick. Deep down, he's very complex. Most of the time, it turns out they're hardwired for a highly specific lifestyle. A specific routine that they find impossible to abandon, or else they die like a fish out of water. If this Rowdy Salih of ours ever left this place to go live in Montazah Palace, he'd die. To him, a palace is like a prison. Even if I offered myself to him, he might say no; either because he's afraid of sin or because he's insecure."

"No way. Anything but that. He was about to eat you up. I swear, if you two were locked in a room together, he'd pounce on you and gnaw you to the bone! Guys like him are animals and it's only being poor that makes them lose their claws. Considering the sexual repression and lack of release that Salih has to live with, there's no question that he's absolutely ready to seize any piece he can get his hands on. It's only logical."

"You're wrong; it isn't logical. It's simply what you think. You go around judging the history you study without a real awareness, and your mind ends up more busted than it was to begin with. Look at you, you treat people like they're all sheep and you think all the people in a given group are exactly alike. The approach you've adopted focuses on the masses and a material explanation of history, but unfortunately it's incapable of understanding the masses. Me on the other hand, I'm a student of literature so I'm interested in individuals. Trust me, I know that people are as different as their fingerprints, even if they're twins."

"Are you trying to tell me that if you offered yourself to Rowdy Salih, he wouldn't drop what he was doing and jump on you and eat you up bones and all? Who'd believe that? I'm a married man with plenty of experiences and I couldn't . . . "

She pulled her arm away gently to point, "You yeah, but not him. He might have a thousand reasons not to say yes. Even if he wanted to and could, his desire might instinctively suppress itself because, in the end, he can't bring himself to put it into words."

"That's if it were mere instinct. We're talking about animal instincts. The more educated you are the more your mind can keep those animal instincts under control. You just said yourself that all new knowledge is a newfound restraint on personal freedom."

"What about you? You've got this highly developed intellect, but I mean, come on, your instincts are running around like a whole zoo up there! It's not that, it's something else. It has to do with the values a person grows up with, Taloooot."

"Fine, you want to bet?"

"I'll bet you."

"For what?"

"If Rowdy Salih takes me up on my proposition and agrees to sleep with me—he only has to agree, the rest doesn't matter—I'll give myself to you for one night. But if Salih backs out like I predict he will and restrains himself—for whatever reason—then you have to stop thinking about me forever or else I'll tell Matilde everything, and you know I will."

He scratched his mustache, nervous and pale: "Okay, but how can I agree, or how can you agree to sleep with someone like that?"

"Who said that was going to happen? I'm just going to test him. I'll see how far I can get him to go and that's it."

"Are you sure you want to go through with this?"

"Definitely. And if you don't want to do it with me, I'll do it by myself. Or with somebody else, like Qamar al-Mahruqi, for example."

"Fine, but this is going to take some planning: a script, direction, acting."

"So what? Invite him to come stay at your house for a few days. Once he gets settled in, we can take him to my place and put the plan into action."

"Alright then. You're crazy, and I'm even crazier."

Salih did indeed go to Talat al-Imbabi's apartment as the guest of honor. The apartment was always full of young people, mostly women, both foreigners and Egyptians. They were all members of various Marxist organizations, which one of the French cells was trying to unify so they could better support them during crises. With the arrival of Rowdy Salih, the atmosphere in the apartment grew even more frenetic, with a joyful clamor that nearly reached the point of pandemonium because of the arrival of this strange guest. To them, he was like a rare animal-human descending directly from our primate forefathers, as if he'd been isolated for all these centuries in a jungle somewhere before turning up there in the apartment. Everyone congratulated Talat, who'd proven himself profoundly streetwise for having discovered this specimen of earliest humanity. Some of them immediately started studying him and examining his social and cultural background to try to link him to primitive societies that had managed to mirror certain achievements of modern science.

Others enjoyed listening to his pleasant conversation and catching glimpses of his strange thoughts and opinions that were replete with lived experience and never-ending wisdom. Others still—loudmouths with theoretical minds—made fun of everyone else for their painstaking attention and unusual interest in this throwback of a man who had nothing to do with anything. Matilde—Talat's wife, lady of the house, and the payer of the rent—was herself happy to have Salih there and welcomed him with an entirely unanticipated serenity. Mischievous and cunning as she was, she even went to Wikalat al-Balah to buy him trousers, a shirt, and a pullover, all secondhand, because he—as she'd expected from her seasoned knack for dealing with the third-world poor—wouldn't feel comfortable with new clothes. She was also the one who taught him how to operate the shower and bathtub and how to bathe with the loofah and soap she'd bought especially for him. Her happiness wasn't diminished at all when she saw him come out of the bathroom dressed in clean clothes because she trusted her instincts and knew that a bath and a change of clothes wouldn't affect Salih's authenticity; rather, it made it stand out even more.

At first, Rowdy Salih was happy with the unusual attention. He slept soundly at the crack of noon after having eaten a nice breakfast of fried eggs, fuul, and a variety of white, yellow, and red cheeses, in addition to a whole helping of jam, honey, butter, white coffee, and tea. He'd wake up at the call for the afternoon prayer and sit down to a delicious lunch of beef and poultry cooked in inventive ways, which he remembered from his childhood when he'd worked as a helper at the Greek restaurant beneath Cinema Odeon. In the evenings, he'd drink whiskey, or rum, or wine brought by the crowds who wanted to have a look at Rowdy Salih and talk to him. It wasn't very long, though, before his patience ran out. He began to feel very confined by these sessions that were centered around him day and night because people found him a strange and peculiar wonder of the world. He began to tire of all the questions and the trying effort of replying as honestly as he could. An irritated Salih couldn't help but start to grumble. He began talking about how much he missed the Marouf Quarter, how he much he missed getting rowdy. He didn't hide the fact that he wanted to get rowdy because, as he explained, the whiskey, rum, raisin wine, and date wine had absolutely no effect on him. This was exactly the opportunity Hayat al-Barri had been waiting for. She explained to everyone that Rowdy Salih needed a change of scene and said she'd take him to get some fresh air and clear his head and bring him back better than she'd found him.

Talat had gone ahead to Hayat's apartment and hidden in the office. He locked the door and threw himself down on the sofa, happy to find a copy of the book he'd been reading at home: Spinoza's *Theologico-Political Treatise*. He picked up where he'd left off, careful not to mark the pages with his pen as he did with his own copy, but he was very agitated, he was panting, and his thoughts drifted. As soon as he sensed them entering the apartment, he put the book down. He almost coughed, but he stopped himself. He had a momentary fright, but then he smiled and stretched out, telling himself that there was still a lot of time before the experiment got to the implementation phase.

Hayat al-Barri, although she was an intellectual, always dressed in the newest and most elegant fashions and used the most expensive perfumes, the kinds that evoked both bliss and sexual suggestion. She could read and speak two foreign languages—English and French—in addition to Arabic, she loved world literature, and had translated many stories, poems, and plays, and had opinions on a wide range of political, cultural, and social issues, which she could express precisely and concisely. But deep down she had a wild, earthy, intensely animal nature. Her love of foods like salted fish, sardines, and aged mish cheese hearkened back to our distant animal origins, back when we used to eat carrion. Her sympathy for everything primitive and unrefined wasn't unique—most people shared that predilection—but Hayat al-Barri was brave in that she was completely open about it and she lived by her philosophy without the slightest reservation. The way she saw it there was no such thing as real sex in marriage, which was a mere biological relationship between two parties, a sort of partnership based on a mutually agreed contract, which put both parties' anxieties to rest and enabled them to produce children. True fun was anti-marriage, anti the kind of stability that breeds familiarity and appetite-killing routine like boring—sometimes even revolting—leftovers. She often cited examples from animal sexuality, especially dogs because, according to her, sex among canines resulted from a genuine attraction between two partners: the bitch spreads the scent of her desire in the air and eager groups of dogs come running and fight over her (doggedly!) while she—the desiring bitch—lies there like an empress. She waits to see which one will come out on top, and if she's so inclined, she gives herself to him, or else she just runs away and abandons the whole lot of them and they withdraw calmly and civil-like. No matter how crazy any of them gets with desire, it never results in rape like it does with humans. There's no power on earth that could make a bitch submit to rape no matter how weak she were or how strong her rapist. She has her own criteria for choosing and she submits only to her desire. This—Hayat explained without any embarrassment or reservation—was sex as God created it: two parties, similar desires, they come together, and the pleasure's outstanding. To her, the failure of the institution of marriage had been proven long ago, even in terms of its most basic goal, which was keeping lineages straight.

Talat al-Imbabi had heard all of this already and he knew for certain that she was very liberated, but he also knew that she was crafty and that it wasn't very easy to know what she was really thinking. She'd suffered a great deal at the hands of hired thugs employed by vengeful leaders and big shots in the communist movement, especially from the anarchists who'd joined the movement without really understanding its essential qualities; they just used it as a pretext to throw off restraints. They'd all taken turns attacking her and left her to tend her own wounds, and after that pattern was repeated countless times she lost all confidence in the leadership and its boosters. Nevertheless she remained locked into the same social sphere with that crowd because people who enter the communist movement have a hard time getting out, and they can get stuck in vise-like situations and relationships. Likewise, they get addicted to being part of that crowd, where they only know one another, and only find pleasure in one another's company. Talat knew that she'd long since abandoned her beliefs, but that at the same time, she couldn't fit in with new, different types of people. She didn't feel herself unless she was among those types, even if they cheated her and lied to her in the name of principles and the future of the working classes. She no longer resented them, she was no longer appalled by them, maybe because she'd started behaving the same way toward them. If one of them promised to meet her the next day at such and such a place at such and such a time to take care of such and such a thing, she'd listen earnestly and promise to keep her end of the bargain, but it was only talk and she forgot all about it as soon as she turned around. She wouldn't go to the appointment because she knew for sure that the other guy wasn't going to turn up. She'd also grown used to the war of rumors and backbiting; she'd been inoculated against it and it could no longer do her any damage. Whenever and wherever she bumped into a fellow comrade, the conversation would be limited to tearing up another person behind their back, but she knew not to trust what anybody said and they knew not to trust that she trusted them. If that weren't enough, she didn't even trust her own gossip because she just said it out of habit to keep the conversation going. As far as she was concerned, it didn't matter what directions the conversation took so long as she only did what she wanted to do in the end. She only went to meetings when it was absolutely necessary.

After presenting an analysis of Talat's character and his understanding of Hayat's character, Qamar said that when Hayat made a bet with Talat over Rowdy Salih, she was actually hoping deep in her heart for Talat to win the bet: that Rowdy Salih would pounce on her and ravish her because she really did crave him and that special, delirious drunkenness she'd detected in his rancid scent. The idea of the bet appealed to her and she decided that she wanted to have him—the charm and novelty of it!—on her own turf even if it meant stooping so low as to rape him. She didn't care whether Talat won the bet or not; the important thing was for her to win the day and be transported to the furthest reaches of this mad intoxication. That was how a distressed Hayat put it anyway when she confessed the adventure to Qamar over a couple of spliffs in the garden of the American University.

Her apartment in Roxy in Heliopolis was made up of two big rooms: one beside the front door was the library-study, and the other—the bedroom—was in the interior beside the bathroom and kitchen. The front room was more like a belly, curved and wide, comprising the living room, dining table and six chairs, and a glass china case; velvet curtains hung over the door and there were two windows, one overlooking the light-well and another between the foyer and the corridor that led to the kitchen, bathroom, and bedroom.

Hayat and Rowdy Salih sat in the foyer. She got a bottle of Coke and a bottle of denatured alcohol out of the refrigerator and laid them out in front of him with a carafe, a glass, and some mezzes.

"Now you can relax, Salih dear."

She disappeared behind the hallway curtain, which was heavy like a wall, and Salih got busy mixing. He drank with relish, the burn scraping against his throat, scalding it; he loved that. Then the numbing of his mind commenced and his eyes dreamed up a cloud of fog. A dazzling perfume wafted over him and filled the air with a feminine scent as grand as the universe. He began to tremble. Old sensations, which he'd thought had vanished, were roused in him. His emotions were carrying out hidden maneuvers and he felt as if tanks and armored vehicles and battalions of heavy artillery were pushing through his veins. He suddenly discovered that he was a young man of twenty-five, not forty-five like his birth certificate said. He looked up to face the phantom, the intoxicating scent, and he saw Hayat al-Barri looking completely different. He saw something even the most proudly pious would be powerless to resist: a body lithe and balanced with divine precision; a miracle whose manifold details could be seen beneath the black, see-through nightgown—as if it were no more than a gossamer cloud of cigarette smoke. Her svelte abdomen was taut and in the middle there was her navel like a nibbled coin; below that her lovely vulva, like a puffed-up pita, was obscured slightly near the bottom as its bulge receded between her thighs looking like a guava wrapped in a pink silk handkerchief, which was woven through with straps that wrapped around her slender waist and attached in the back around her round, cleaved bottom, which was set on thighs like marble columns and oh, if only you'd seen those lovely bare calves!

That vision etched itself onto Salih's eyes and nailed him to his seat, ashen, dry-mouthed, panting. She approached him, flirtatiously, sensuously, and in a voice softer than her silken bedspread, said, "Feeling better, Salooha?"

She sat in his lap and wrapped her arms around his shoulders, leaning down slightly so that her coal-black braids spread over his face. Her breasts, loose beneath the thin fabric of her backless, sleeveless nightgown, spilled out. They were splayed out like loaves of dough before they've gone in the oven, sticking to each other—except for at the bottom—and against the wooden baker's peel. They were full of life though and her nipples were hard, they poked through the flimsy material and burned like two coals against Salih's shoulder.

He was confused and started to laugh nervously, which brought out in her a profound anxiety that gave her the look of an idiot. He was dressed in a white poplin gallabiya with a collar and cuffs. Hayat al-Barri surprised him by jumping to her feet and standing there, shocked, her eyes bulging with a lunatic glint. He could see she was staring at his lap. Salih felt

161

intensely embarrassed and tried to hide it and forget about it. Hayat straddled him. Salih began roaring with buffoonish laughter, doubled over, trying to push her off like a child being tickled. Salih tried with all his strength to push her off, "Please, lady, I'm begging you. Let's get things straight first at least."

She was panting so hard she couldn't find her voice, so she just hissed and wrapped her arms around his neck. She began rocking back and forth on top of him, nimbly vigorous and skillful. He could find no escape but to stand up, carrying her in his arms. He staggered forward a few steps as she shouted and pleaded, "My bedroom's down the hall."

But he'd settled on the long sofa. He leaned over and set her down on top of it, freeing his neck from her grasp, and then he retreated wheezing and sat down in the chair beside her, his chest heaving, a grin chiseled into his face, speechless. He lit a cigarette and gobbled down the smoke. Hayat felt like she'd fallen from the peaks of Olympus to the Qattara Depression. She felt like a straw blown in the wind. But she'd always been good at picking herself back up at embarrassing moments. She put out some of her fire and buried the rest of the coals under the ash of her steel nerves, which had been fortified by detentions and police raids. She turned to look at Salih, seriously this time, with new eyes, humane eyes trained to soul-search—and criticize—and give in to defeat with a sporting spirit, like a champion who's lost a match and rather than curse his luck will seek to learn from it. She lit a cigarette and stared with her sardonic, black eyes, which were overflowing with the civil, sophisticated affection of Upper Egypt. It dawned on her that she really was in the presence of a human exemplar who deserved study, not merely a morphed animal and a subject of ridicule. A smile played on her lips, feminine glass shattered against the cold marble of her voice. Her gaze gripped him: "Are you scared?"

"Yeah, and twice shy."

"Let's stick to fear first. Why're you scared? There's no one here but us."

"And God?"

"What about getting drunk? God doesn't get angry about that?"

"No, but . . . I want to tell you something, lady. The Lord God in Heaven has better things to do than—no offense—sit there hovering over every member of the flock and tallying up his sins one by one. Our Lord's the Lord of our hearts. He sees and knows. My drinking only hurts me.

162

Even if getting rowdy's a sin, that doesn't mean I need to go and add new infractions to my file so I get even more punishment come Resurrection Day."

"Well said, Salih," she replied—as if only to herself—convinced, then she dusted off the cherry of her cigarette elegantly in the ashtray and took a long drag. She kept her cigarette held up beside her face as her thoughts drifted, then she continued as though she'd remembered something important: "But what's this will of yours? How were you able to control yourself? I could feel your body shaking and I was sure it was too late, that you were already in too deep and it was impossible for you to get out. I don't think I'll ever be able to forget that moment for the rest of my life."

"I wasn't in too deep, lady! I was taken in! You know, which means I can kick out whoever entered me as if I was no better than a building without a doorman. Miss, you have no idea how much that hurt me, what you just did. No offense but it's like you hit me with an old shoe. Ain't I a human being, too, lady? A man? It's my right to want sometimes and not want some other times. Or is this how it happens now without so much as a 'beg your pardon?'"

She groaned as she watched him with eyes clearly saying, "No, you're dead wrong. You're unlike any other man in the world as you've just proven." But she remembered something and pointed backward, "Let's talk about the 'twice shy' thing. What do you mean 'twice shy?'"

"No offense, but self-respect."

"Meaning?"

"Our folk used to say, 'When you eat out of a bowl, don't get it dirty' and 'Wipe your feet before you go into someone's house.' I brought my personality to your house, but I should've polished it up from the very beginning. This house has beennothing but nice to me, so how can I go and stab it in the back? Plus Mr. Talat's my friend and we get on well together, and you, ma'am, are one of his friends, which means I got to treat you like a treasured possession and not take any cheeky licks."

She'd been drawn in by the absurdity of it all and laughed thoughtlessly. She shouted loud enough for Talat to hear her, "You don't have to worry about that! Talat knows and he's fine with it and everybody's free to do whatever they want."

Salih's face broke out into flames, spittle spread over his lips, sparks flew from his eyes. "Mr. Talat knew that you were planning to do this and he's okay with it?"

She nodded, mumbling, "Uh huh."

"Well, then—no offense—but he's a twisted little son of a whore and I don't want to have anything to do with him ever again! What a fucking, piece of shit day! I was completely fooled: I thought he was an open-minded, respectable guy."

His anger was frightening as he slapped one palm against the other. Hayat immediately stopped laughing. She stood up, and seriously and with an unmistakable sincerity applauded him, then she bowed theatrically. She went up to him timorously. "You really are a real man, Salih. You deserve to know it. I'm glad you defeated me. At least you saved me from losing my bet; it would've killed me to have had to pay up. To be honest, you didn't defeat me. No. You gave me a victory. You proved my suspicions. Would you believe me, Salih, if I told you, I swear to God, I'd kill to marry a guy like you? But since that's not possible at the moment, let's be friends. And in order to prove my friendship, I'll drink some of your drink; from the same glass. See." She took the glass of denatured alcohol and drank from it, every muscle in her face scrunched up, and then she handed the glass to Salih, "To your health!" He also took a gulp as if signing his name to the covenant they had just sealed. She got up and darted behind the curtain, disappearing down the corridor, while he got back to drinking and smoking with an allegro tempo that nearly finished off the carafe and two bottles. Hayat came back in wearing a loose house gallabiya and looking like a completely different woman. She pulled the heavy curtain back and the corridor came into view. She called to him respectfully as if she were calling her husband or brother, "Follow me, Salih."

He stood up, drunk, nearly tottering, but smiling anxiously. He went over to her and she led him to the bathroom by the hand. She pointed to the bathtub: "Take a warm bath to clear your head so you can enjoy the meal. I'm cooking you a duck."

She didn't wait for his reply; instead she pushed him inside and slammed the door on him. Then she pretended to hear a knock at the door and called out, "Who could that be? One second!" She walked to the front door and opened it up exaggeratedly so it was audible, then she exploded in warm welcome, "Hello! Hello there! Brilliant timing! Come right in." Then she shut the door audibly again, perhaps even slamming it. She walked to the office and rapped at the door ever so quietly. The door opened to Talat's deathly pale face and his fingers rubbing his mustache in great anxiety. She whispered to him as she shut the door behind him, "You're the one who's just arrived, okay?" He nodded wearily and went into the living room where he sat and continued to smoke, sullen and silent. Hayat went into the kitchen to prepare the meal. Later when they were sitting around the table, Salih was the only one who ate with any appetite, but not greedily. As soon as he'd finished, he said, "A thousand praises and thanks, dear Lord." And a second later added, "The only thing missing now is a little fresh air."

"Like where?" Hayat asked. "The zoo?"

"No, Ma'am," Salih replied instinctively. "Somewhere fresh, like I said."

"Well, like where?"

"You know, Marouf Street!" Hayat and Talat could only exchange a dumbfounded glance.

From that day on, Qamar al-Mahruqi explained, Talat al-Imbabi hadn't stopped scowling at Rowdy Salih, or as Salih himself said, "He's giving me the cold shoulder."

"Couldn't it be that he's lost face, Salih? You know there are a lot more thieves about these days and they can steal the eye shadow right off your eyes. You ought to be patient with him until he finds it, not get mad at him," added Mustafa Lami guilefully.

Zaki Hamid the actor said, "Oh, but I'm dying to steal Rowdy Salih's face to act in a few parts. If masks were any good, I'd have brought someone here to make a cast."

Salih laughed and said, "You want me to wrap it up so you can take it to go?"

We all giggled. Faruq al-Gamal was about to say something, but Ibrahim al-Qammah—with the impudence only likable good-old-boys could pull off—said, "Uncle Salih has to tell us what happened between him and Talat. There must be a reason and you've got to know what it is, or at least have a guess."

Faruq al-Gamal furrowed his brow and piped up as if he were about to expound one of his highfaluting, acutely enigmatic vernacular poems,

"Surely we have a right to know, seeing as we're friends with both parties. Isn't that right, Salih?"

Qamar al-Mahruqi was struggling to hold back the secret he'd told me a few days earlier and which I, in turn, had told Mustafa, who'd told Ibrahim, who'd told Faruq, each of us making the other swear he wouldn't speak a word of the secret to anyone because there was no point in embarrassing Talat, who was our friend, and at any rate we'd all have been humiliated in a situation like that. It was obvious enough that the secret was eating away at Qamar, beating against his ribcage demanding to be set free, and when he gestured and opened his mouth, I was certain that he was going to spill the whole story so I ahem-ed at him and winked, silently pleading with him not to divulge it, to keep the matter between us alone, especially since Salih—even if we killed him—wouldn't have given up a single word about what had happened. Qamar took a step back: "It's a long story, guys. There's no telling it."

Right then Salih sat up straight and put his hands on his knees, hunching down as if about to stand, and then he said in a sincere voice, "It's not a long story at all, Qamar, sir. It's pretty basic."

"Fine, tell us then if you're such a man."

Ibrahim al-Qammah was hankering, "We need to know, please, to put our minds at rest."

"It's very simple, guys, I swear."

Mustafa Lami barked at him like a trial judge, "What's the story in brief?"

"Not in brief. We want all the boring details!" cried Qamar

Salih said, "All it is and all it was is that Mr. Talat got rowdy. You know, he was getting rowdy."

"What do you mean he was 'getting rowdy?'" Qamar protested. "Why would he get rowdy?"

"Because he wanted to get rowdy. You know—no offense—to get his hands on some good dough, to get himself an important job."

Qamar's expression changed and he began to listen intently and askance, "Get dough and a position from where?"

"From Iraq. In Iraq."

"I don't know what the hell you're talking about."

"Man, you got to know Saddam Hussein's getting rowdy in Iraq. He wants to get in on the rowdiness like everyone else. I know, I mean I saw a lot of him back when he was a student here in Egypt. I was working water pipes at a coffeehouse in Giza where he used to hang out with poetasters and political types. I figured him out straightaway and I knew he had the devil in his head. He thought to himself 'Gamal Abdel Nasser's dead so I'll take his place and rule the Arabs.' He had his eye on Egypt. He saw all the journalists and cronies around Gamal Abdel Nasser and he thought they were the ones who made Nasser the leader he was. He sent people here to come negotiate to bring them to Iraq to work for him and promote him as a great leader. A journalist's a journalist, a writer's a writer, and a schemer's a scammer, so what's the problem? Of course, they're going to be making loads of money."

"What are you on about? What does any of this have to do with Talat al-Imbabi? You think we're stoned or something?"

"I'm getting there. Talat's finished getting rowdy here about now and he wants to go get in on the rowdiness in Iraq. Wasn't Mr. Talat—no offense—a member of that group called the 'Vanguard'? Saddam's guys picked some of those guys to go work for Saddam. Journalists, broadcasters, professors, and people no one cares what it is they do so long as they sing the praises of Saddam and get down with his rowdiness."

"Talat al-Imbabi? He's going to go to Iraq?"

"He's been getting his passport ready for two months now and he already told the university he's taking leave. They took care of his flight, too."

"Where'd you hear about this?" A dubious Mustafa asked.

"He just let it slip, a few words here and there, and I picked up on it. 'You're going where?' I asked him, but he just gave me a silent shrug. His wife, though, she's a straight-talker and doesn't like to hem and haw. She told me the whole story, and I kept my mouth shut, but then he asked me what I thought so I told him as honestly as I could, 'You're dying to get rowdy. You've wanted to get in on the rowdiness for a long time. So fine, trust in God, and go wild.' He got angry and sullen. But his wife laid the whole case out for me in brief: 'Uncle Salih, we've got to be able to buy our own place and we've got to think about our future children and their future and live a life that suits us.' 'You're totally right, lady,' I said, but ever since then, he's been angry at me. What was I going to do, lie and tell him 'Congratulations'? 'Tell 'em straight and to their face' as the saying goes." Then he got up and went into the house to look for something.

Qamar stood up and started pacing back and forth, hands in his pockets, his color now a waxy, bloodless white. He started muttering, "How could he not tell us? You're one sneaky punk, Talat! Give us a hint, at least."

We shared a deep silence and something like sadness enveloped us; it was if we'd just heard news of a friend's death. I guess we were all sobered up by it, too, because the whole party began smoking again in unison frantically and intensely as if we were coming rapidly to the end of our stash.

SPECTERS OF THE ROWDY

Right after he graduated—at the top of his class—from the College of Fine Arts in the early sixties, Mustafa Lami was selected for a scholarship to study in one of the socialist countries on account of his prodigious talent as a painter. He waited a few years for his turn to travel and although he was pretty much certain that, in order to get the chance to go abroad before his classmates, he'd have to compromise his pride and some of his values: to fawn, kiss ass, beg, and volunteer to write confidential reports on the political activities of his colleagues and professors, he lived on in the hope that there remained some fair people in Egypt who'd give him what he had coming, even if it took a lucky stroke. But because deep down he knew that the age of justice on earth had come to a close and was never coming back, he began to drown his anxieties and confusion in hashish, with such focus and interest that he soon became a hardcore hash-head. The only way happiness and contemplation could reach him was through good hash, even though the reason he'd started smoking hash in the first place was because he wanted to see the different hangouts where people went to get high. He wanted to take in all the types, conditions, and people, and to plumb the entire constellation of those places, which were so rich and inspiring to a painter who wanted his paintings to reek with life.

At one point, he despaired of life in Egypt completely because there was simply no way for him to make it; he hadn't even been made an instructor at the College even though he certainly deserved it. He loved adventure and he had the constitution for it so what was stopping him? Thus he decided he'd travel at his own expense, partly to study and partly to discover other worlds, and he'd take whatever job he could find to help finance his studies. He didn't have the money for a ticket, but he did have two sisters who were married to successful husbands, and as he was the only boy in the family, and even though his sisters wished he'd stay in Egypt—in Cairo, to be specific—to help them get through life, they knew his future was more important than sentimentality so they agreed to lend him the money, which he promised to pay back as soon as he could. He went to Czechoslovakia, but as to why he chose to go to that country out of all the others, not even he knew. It all boiled down to the fact that he had some Egyptian and Arab friends living there and they could set him up with a job and a place to live—according to the correspondence they exchanged, anyway. And they did: they got him a job at an advertising studio that specialized in film posters and ads for films and plays in theater programs that were handed out to audiences for free. He also enrolled at the Arts Academy and picked as his research topic a subject that he'd been interested in all his life because of his long obsession with pharaonic reliefs and paintings: details of the human face as a representation of the environment in which one is born and lives and its imprint on one's genes and its effect on phenotypes, which allow us to know—simply by looking—a Chinese person from an Indian from an African from a European, and so forth.

He really liked it there; prices were reasonable and there was no shortage of goods in the shops. Life was very easy, no restrictions or complications about anything and as long as you stayed away from politics you were fine. The flipside of easy living were the easy relationships. So it was easily that young Barbara answered the call of his eyes, which had fallen for her at first sight. Barbara Smailovic was of mixed Serbian and Albanian descent. She looked familiarly eastern: fit and pretty, she had a slender waist, pert rear, swelling breasts, and long neck, and she was a fun and relaxed twenty-something. She'd taken a middle-of-the-road diploma, which led to a job at the same studio where Mustafa worked; she was responsible for distributing materials to the artists: paper, paints, brushes, and other things like that were all part of her inventory. After about five lovey-dovey months of taking each other out on dates around the capital and its suburbs, they got married among a large group of their co-workers and friends. He had her all to himself in a relatively modest apartment in one of the Prague suburbs, which they furnished together simply. The rent was reasonable and they had enough money except that he had to work so much to earn enough to cover all their expenses that it left him no time at all for study; there was barely even time for the body's required rest. On one rare occasion when he had a chance to go for a stroll outside the city he was overcome with stress and worry. He sensed an immediate, pressing danger that threatened his future, or rather that stood to destroy it completely: drawing adverts had begun to impose certain marketing techniques—like emotional duplicity and a disregard for the kind of aesthetics that gives meaning—on his brush and that if he kept it up for another year, he was inevitably going to turn into a hack—that's all, just a hack—like any illiterate painter who makes a living and not works of art behind which lies a vision, a philosophy, a spirit. Then he started thinking about how his current situation compared to his life in Egypt and he discovered with a horrified heart that the difference couldn't be reduced to mere homesickness, being far from family, friends, and his magical, captivating homeland, but that there, at least, he was somebody, even if only a very minor somebody. But in this foreign society, he was nothing: simply a worker in a studio; his only reason for staying there was to further his studies and get a doctorate and gain experience as an artist, but he wasn't sure that was even in the cards. The best thing, he decided, was to go back home a golden boy; at least there he could get a job with a magazine on a decent wage and carve out an artistic career for himself that was more in line with his ambitions. He didn't waste a moment: he sent a telegram to his elder sister to arrange an apartment for him and his wife, and good fortune had it that his sister was about to move to the Gulf with her civil-engineer husband on a long-term posting and she felt that it was better, both for its preservation and her peace of mind, that her only brother live in her apartment while they were away. So Mustafa Lami returned, but he was now three people: he, his wife Barbara Smailovic, and his three-month old daughter Sara. That same good fortune also had it that a large news organization had decided to set up a children's magazine called *Green Sparrow*, which seemed to have all his old university classmates on staff, and he joined the magazine two weeks after he arrived back in Egypt. He also became one of the most important founding members of the group who met every day at Hakeem's to get high. He was crazy about his daughter, who'd started to grow up quickly as though Egypt's glorious weather had imbued her with the spirit of its clement sun. Her features matured, taking on the look of his dear departed mother and some echoes of his departed father. His father had been the office manager at a famous downtown law firm and owned an old, tumble-down house in the Gamaliya neighborhood, which they now rented out for copper-working and gold-smithing workshops, but the whole rent wasn't even worth the trouble of going to pick it up. Almost as soon as life had started smiling on Mustafa, it began to frown: suddenly the news organization grew tired of the magazine's constant, and seemingly open-ended, losses and the new chairman of the board came to the realization that his news organization had been founded to play a political role and it couldn't stand to be distracted by a children's magazine. "What do we have to do with kids? Is this a news organization or a kindergarten?" Thus, with a single stroke of the pen, the magazine was shut down and because all the employees were on temporary contracts—six months with an option to renew—they were all let go, the loss of their talents not regretted.

A depressed Mustafa soured on the world during one long month when he was completely unable to cover his expenses. But then the next month he received a telegram from Libya inviting him to contribute his artwork to the *Arab Culture Magazine*, which the Libyan government had founded as a way of putting Libya on the map of Arab cultural activity alongside the likes of Egypt, Lebanon, Syria, Iraq, and Algeria. Their newspapers and weeklies also established illustrated children's supplements. All Mustafa had to do was get in touch with the Egyptian correspondent responsible for collecting the material from Cairo, get the stories and write-ups from him, illustrate them, and then hand them in to him. They paid very well and money once again began to run through Mustafa's hands. He started getting high, hard-hearted, and steely-eyed, but just as suddenly, life frowned again, and dark, menacing clouds loomed in the sky and blocked out the sun on the morning when he woke to find

172

his only, beloved daughter had caught measles. She was treated as if it were an acute cold, but no sooner had the depressing day passed steadily along with her rising temperature than the little girl calmly breathed her last the next morning. Her soul slipped stealthily out of her body during a nap that lasted no more than a few minutes and departed, never to return.

It was hard on everyone. The sudden shock of her death distracted us from Talat al-Imbabi's imminent departure for Iraq to go work for *Revolution* newspaper and write about Arab nationalism under the shadow of an administration whose leaders wanted to reclaim its mantle now that Nasser was gone. Our get-togethers were taken up with consoling Mustafa and trying to lessen his acute pain, but his grief was overpowering and it nearly killed him. He was transformed completely: he became a scrawny, permanently sullen man, his features swollen from all the hot tears. Pleasure meant nothing to him anymore, he no longer laughed at jokes, he sat there silently the whole time like a stone, broken-hearted, lost. Life in Egypt frustrated him: he'd had to abandon his dream of being sent to study abroad and he knew that it was all just a nightmare he could only escape by leaving immediately for somewhere far away. He must've revived some old negotiations with friends in various Arab countries about finding work because one day we were surprised to see the Egyptian correspondent handing him a contract he'd been sent from Libya.

None of us knew anything about the contract and Mustafa simply took the two copies of the contract, folded in quarters, and slipped them into the thick leather folio he always carried around with him, looping its leather ring over his wrist; it was where he kept his sketchbook, some charcoal pencils, passport, money, cigarettes, and house keys. He ignored the contract for more than two months without even bothering to read it, let alone sign it. On one moist and stifling August afternoon as we sat at the foot of the tall hill, the Egyptian correspondent turned up out of the blue with the Nubian singer—more famous for his political struggles than his music—Mahmud Zaghalil, a friend of Mustafa's and a colleague from the Department of Design. From the back-and-forth recriminations, we got the sense that the correspondent was fed up with having to chase after Mustafa and that the Libyans were anxious for them both—Mustafa and the contract—to arrive already. After failing to find Mustafa at home, the correspondent had turned to their mutual friend, Mahmud Zaghalil, whom he'd brought along with him, hoping to put an end to the whole business of the contract for Mustafa's sake.

Mustafa opened his folio and took out the contract that was folded up like a handkerchief. He handed it to the beaming correspondent, who unfolded it to separate the two copies—one for him and one for Mustafa—cheerily repeating, "Congratulations! I wish you all the best!" He flipped the two copies over, searching for Mustafa's signature, but he didn't find it. He frowned, a bit ashen, and laid the contract in his lap, peering at Mustafa as if he were one of the Seven Wonders of the World.

"Why didn't you sign it then?"

"I'm sorry, Salah. I'm not going to be able to sign."

Salah the correspondent took the news like a stone to the skull. He threw the contract down on the chair beside him and fell into a somber silence, clearly racking his brain for a fitting reply. We began to exchange dumbfounded glances, tongue-tied by surprise: on the one hand because Mustafa hadn't discussed the issue with us at all, and on the other because he'd refused to sign, coolly without causing offense, with a tone that echoed in our ears like someone clinging to the last column of support for his own lofty pride.

"May I, Salah?" Qamar al-Mahruqi asked, reaching out to pick up the contract. Salah didn't give him permission, but he didn't stop him either, and Qamar began scanning the contract. His face broke out in a frantic flush of joy and amazement and then he folded it and said, "But you simply don't have the right, Mustafa! How can you turn down an offer like this?"

Salah perked up a bit and nodded conciliatorily as if reinforcing Qamar's surprise. This was all the permission we needed to pass the contract around, studying it closely, searching for the one reason, whether obvious or obscure, to justify Mustafa's rejection. The only thing we found was a once-in-a-lifetime opportunity. The contract outlined how Mustafa Lami would be hired as a distinguished, top-grade illustrator at *Revolution* newspaper—there's a newspaper called *Revolution* in every single country, isn't there?—at a thousand Libyan dinars a month in exchange for helping with design layout and illustrations, stories, and sketches, and he'd also receive extra compensation for any additional projects he took on for any of the organization's other publications. The contract also stipulated that he was going to get six months' salary upfront to help him cover the costs of moving and arranging accommodation, and that this sum would be taken out of his wages in very manageable installments.

We were all looking at Mustafa, silently imploring him to explain the—undoubtedly precarious—reasoning that had made him refuse to sign such a contract, which even Ahmad Baha' al-Din might not have got. But our efforts came to nothing and silence overcame us for forty or fifty bowls, the effects of which we didn't even feel. Suppressed anger bound the faces of Mahmud Zaghalil the singer and Salah al-Sisi the correspondent in shackles of solid iron wrinkles. They'd given Mustafa sufficient opportunity in the hope that he'd back down or at least explain why he was refusing. Finally, after coughing and clearing his throat as if he were about to start singing, Mahmud Zaghalil said, "You don't like the contract, Mustafa?"

"No, actually, quite the opposite. It's more than I deserve."

"Do you have specific conditions? We can fax them."

"Not at all. I have no conditions."

"So what's stopping you from signing?"

"Personal reasons. Very private."

"Let's go, Salah," barked Mahmud Zaghalil, as if what he really wanted to say was, "Fine, to hell with you then!" But instead he stood up and said, "Ciao, everybody. Sorry to bother you all," then he took Salah by the arm and they walked off, disappearing down the short passage in the corner, and we knew without a shadow of a doubt that Mahmud was going to stop by Ali Mango's shop in the passage on the corner to get some hash because really how silly would it be to come all the way down to the Marouf Quarter and leave empty-handed!

"How could you refuse an offer like that?" Qamar asked. "Are you nuts?"

"What a waste," said Faruq al-Gamal, sighing.

Zaki Hamid stared at him with his fierce, ominous gaze: "Don't let this opportunity pass you by. You're being a fool. You'll be set for life. Listen to me: go catch up with them before they call Libya."

"You want me to run after them?" asked Ibrahim al-Qammah.

"No, no, no." Mustafa shouted decisively, holding him back.

Ibrahim twirled his fleshy hand beside his head and winked meaningfully: "So what's the story exactly? What's up?"

"I don't understand you, Mustafa," Qamar added. "A little while ago you were dying for a deal worth a quarter as much. And now when you get the deal of a lifetime, you're going to turn your nose up at it?"

Mustafa took a deep drag from the coconut bong and held it in; his face was sullen and looking fairly fetal. As smoke poured out between his lips, he spoke, "To be honest, I want to get away from all the rowdiness. I have no interest in getting rowdy. Not with *Revolution* newspaper. Does anyone even know what the hell Revolution means anymore? I don't know how to get rowdy and I don't really want to learn."

We didn't know what to think; we figured he was kidding around, and could only stare at him dumbly. When it dawned on us he was being deadly serious, Qamar pointed at him splenetically: "What the hell are you talking about: 'getting rowdy,' man? You're going to follow after Rowdy Salih? Rowdy Salih's going to be making decisions about your future now? Get a grip already!"

Mustafa raised his hand to silence him. "Hold it right there. I'm sorry if you guys all think what Salih says is just a big joke, but personally I really believe in what he has to say. I'm sick of all that stuff, especially now when everything's so damn awful. All these Arab intellectuals give me the hives. The whole lot of them! The ones who are rowdy because they're trying to get rowdy. They're all a bunch of lackey propagandists. Why would I want to go help them create the myth of a new leader? Don't we have enough of that already? The Arabs couldn't deal with one leader, how are they going to put up with three or four? Anyway you guys know that Saddam, Gaddafi, and Yasser Arafat are dividing the Arab intellectuals up between themselves because they've each got great rowdy plans in their minds and they need people to go out and make them even rowdier. Each of them's desperate for his rowdy plan to beat out the rowdy plans of the other two even if it ends up costing the treasure of Croesus. They want newspapers parroting their words in every country, radio broadcasts, television broadcasts, books, panels, films, plays. The intellectuals have all forgotten about their countries' real problems and spend all their time trying to make their leaders look good. And everything they do is in the name of the revolution. In the name of Arabism. Didn't you see how much money you can make off of Revolution? No, thanks, man. God'll take care of me."

Qamar was absolutely livid. "What's the matter with you? Did anybody ask you to kiss anybody's ass or praise the leader in print? What do you care? Why don't you just let leaders be leaders and yes-men be yes-men and get on with your job? Your job's self-contained: illustrating; no more, no less."

"You're wrong if you think that my work as an illustrator at *Revolution* wouldn't mean constantly having to suck up and propagandize and lie to myself. Plus you could never enjoy even a little freedom when you're locked up in the leader's cage. You couldn't have any ideas, or God forbid, a dubious thought you kept to yourself, or else not even you'll know where you are the next day. Qamar, take a look at the contract, look at the salary and the perks. I mean they're just trying to break you down ahead of time. Stuffing you quiet. Either you're grateful so you kiss ass, or you're an unfeeling idiot."

Although you could tell from his expression that Qamar agreed, he still threw his arms up reflexively and said, "So you've made up your mind, have you?"

"Personally, Mustafa's convinced me," Zaki Hamid chimed in.

Al-Gamal snapped his fingers excitedly. "I've got a new poem:
Rowdy Salih went charging into history
On a horse without reins or saddle He prods the joyful people in the castle."

Ibrahim al-Qammah added, "*And their cash drawers he swindles.*" We laughed.

"Their 'saddlebags' would be better," said Qamar.

"No, 'cash drawers' is more on the mark," said Zaki Hamid. "More poetic. It's a symbol of ill-gotten gains."

With faked glee, in a cracking voice, Mustafa Lami added,
"*And their cash drawers he swindles,*
handing out what's in them to the disabled."

We giggled uproariously and then Ibrahim al-Qammah snapped his plump fingers together like down-home boys do when they hear something they like: "Well done, Moos. You're a good kid, I swear, and you deserve all the best. I mean, come on, guys, we're Egyptians. Sons of the pharaohs. If the leader of the Arab nation isn't Egyptian, it just isn't going to work. Trust me. Do they think being leader is a game? It takes a man whose grandfather was Ramses the Second, and whose uncle was Khufu, for example, and whose mother was Hatshepsut, and whose cousin was Ahmose. You can call Ahmose Ahmad for all I care so long as it helps the Arabs." We enjoyed many pleasant evenings just like that one.

We'd expected that the Libyans' Cairo contacts would stop dealing with Mustafa once and for all as a punishment for ingratitude, but during those sweet evenings, we heard from Mustafa that they not only continued giving him work, but that they were still hoping that he'd come around and accept their job offer. The issue had split us into two camps: Zaki Hamid, al-Qammah, al-Gamal, and I all supported Mustafa's position in broad strokes and fine details; we were actually quite proud of him. But Qamar and Hakeem were hoping that Mustafa would see the light and seize this great opportunity. For his part, Rowdy Salih was the only one who sat the discussion out, saying—in his own words—that he was recusing himself. "Mr. Mustafa's going to do what he thinks is right. No offense, but he's plenty clever and there's no point in me telling him do this, don't do that. I think that'd be rude of me—no offense."

Qamar gave him a reproachful look. "Right. Well then, how come you gave Talat your opinion?"

"Because Talat Bey's different from Mustafa Bey. No offense, but Talat Bey's easy. I told him what I thought because I knew for sure he was going to go no matter what. Even if the sky were falling, he'd still go. Talat Bey wants to go to bed and wake up the premier of the Soviet Union so he can add Egypt and the Arabs to it. He'll take Khrushchev and make him Rector of al-Azhar and he'll put Podgorny in charge of Mecca and the Haram al-Sharif. Then he'll take the Rector of al-Azhar and put him in charge of the Kremlin!"

As usual, he wasn't thrown off by our hysterical, screaming laughter—accompanied by stamping feet—no, not even his own laughter could stop him: "Mustafa Bey's something else though. I can't tell him go or don't go because I know, I mean, I'm positive that he isn't going to go. He really has no business getting rowdy. He's not getting all rowdy in his head, you know, he's not all stuck up; he doesn't go around calling himself cock of the walk. And if he's not getting rowdy in the head then that means there's no rowdiness for him to go and get in on. All Mustafa Bey wants from the world is a brush and some paint."

Not a week later, we were surprised to see the singer Mahmud Zaghalil turning up with the sculptor Fakhr al-Din Shaddad, an old classmate of theirs. It took forty bowls—generously topped off by Mustafa—to properly welcome them and we were almost at a hundred by the time the immaculate deal, which we all celebrated, was sealed. The emirate of Abu Dhabi was setting up a children's magazine called *Malik*, and Fakhr al-Din Shaddad had been charged with contracting a team to move to Abu Dhabi where they'd have access to the most cutting-edge presses, not to mention all the great resources for planning, performance, and innovation that had been pledged to the publication. As the Gulf Arabs were free of any taint of leadership and rowdiness and the only aim of the project was artistic, Mustafa happily signed the contract even though the salary wasn't even close to half the previous offer. It was a lovely day when we all accompanied Mustafa Lami and Barbara Smailovic to the airport to bid them farewell and remind them not to forget to write.

CRACKED

Mustafa Lami left behind a great void when he left, which was exactly the opposite of what happened when Talat al-Imbabi went away. Mustafa had this affectionate side that people who spent a lot of time with him had a hard time giving up. A few months after his departure, one of Qamar al-Mahruqi's tag-alongs foisted himself upon the group: that was Mursi Khallaf the inspector at the Cairo Traffic Authority. Suddenly, he'd become a regular, always sticking to the group schedule, spending freely; of course that wasn't at all strange as he earned upward of five hundred pounds a day for turning a blind eye and approving cars that didn't merit their registrations.

Zaki Hamid, Faruq al-Gamal, and I weren't very happy about having to share our familial, familiar, supportive gatherings with Mursi Khallaf. We found it positively revolting how he'd always insist on treating us in that pathetic, hamfisted way of his the whole damn time: "Bring the beys such-and-such on me! Get the beys going first until they're all set! I'll give them some bud they've probably never tried in their entire lives! Nobody puts his hands in his pockets so long as I'm here! It's all on me! Let's use my stash!" etc, etc. We put up with it grudgingly since we knew the new-moneyed ranks were growing at a worrying rate back in those days. But meetings got truly ruined, rendered entirely tasteless and joyless, if we were joined by Walid Rashid and Wagdi al-Wakil in addition to Mursi Khallaf. It got to the point that we seriously considered looking for another den, but our loyalty to the place, that cradle of our treasured memories, prevented us from leaving it for some new den far away. Rather, that was what gave us the strength to go back there every day; it was as if we were in danger of losing it.

Apparently, the new-money threesome picked up on the fact that Hakeem was the only one who wanted them there because it wasn't long before they suddenly stopped coming. We'd barely had a chance to relax after they'd stopped coming before we noticed that Qamar al-Mahruqi himself began to disappear for long stretches, and it wasn't long before we lost track of him completely. The search for Qamar became a pressing concern: everybody asked everybody else if they'd heard anything about why Qamar had up and disappeared, and the link between his disappearance and that of Mursi, Walid, and Wagdi only added to our growing apprehension.

I went to his new apartment in his new neighborhood and climbed up the stairs to the third floor in the midday heat and knocked on the door of the apartment, which was just to the right of the landing. I heard a rude and arrogant voice, shouting from inside the apartment: "Who's there?" and then the door opened, revealing a huge, glowering man hurriedly doing up the drawstring of his trousers. He shouted boorishly, gesticulating, "What is it?"

In the most polite tone I could muster, I said, "I've come to see Mr. Qamar al-Mahruqi please."

Furrowing his brow, he put his paw behind his ear and shouted, "Come again?" I raised my voice over the din of my boiling nerves, "I said 'Mr. Qamar al-Mahruqi,' isn't this his apartment?"

"No idea. This is my apartment."

"Since when?"

"What's that? Are you questioning me?" he said before slamming the door in my face, causing the ground beneath my feet to shake. I hammered at the door with the heel of my shoe and shouted curses on his father and the father of the beast that'd given birth to him and on the vile circumstances that had brought him here. I went downstairs slowly, having made up my mind to hit him if he got any ideas about following me.

I took the same bus back to Tahrir Square and some time later stopped by the American University. The office Qamar shared with the other research assistants was completely empty and one of the custodians told me he hadn't seen Mr. Qamar for several months. He figured he was either on a very long vacation or his contract with the university was up. As I walked down the hallway on my way out, unease spreading through my thoughts and multiplying, I suddenly remembered our friend Hayat al-Barri so I headed straight for the other building where her office was tucked away in a wing of the library.

She gave me an exceedingly warm welcome and after we'd drunk our coffee, I told her I wanted to take her to Izavich for lunch, but she countered by inviting me to the Greek restaurant beneath Cinema Odeon because it was her favorite restaurant, and she had a monthly tab there, and—here was the reason of reasons—she was dying to see Rowdy Salih, who could be found only a few steps from the restaurant. She was very clever; she instinctively knew that I wanted to ask her about Qamar so she cut to the chase and thrilled me with her astonishing tale:

During those months when Qamar al-Mahruqi wasn't quite himself and had stopped paying any attention to his clothes, food, or sleep, and had started avoiding everyone, overcome by peculiar feelings toward his work and friends and wife, his erratic behavior raised eyebrows and was considered generally frustrating, although Hayat al-Barri thought he was simply helpless and put upon. He would invite his weirdo friends over to the house, the sort of people who could never fit in with Mahasin Asim's crowd. One of them, Mursi Khallaf, only ever talked about how much he'd spent that day on getting high, and God, how he'd pester anyone he knew had a car by offering his services for repair, licensing, and sales. The second guy was called Walid Rashid, and he was nice enough, sure, but was he was one hell of a shady character: he drove a Camaro, which the president of the American University himself didn't drive, and the amount he spent on hash, Marlboros, whiskey, and imported shirts and shoes simply wasn't normal for a kid who was still in college studying who-knows-what, not even if he'd inherited three acres of agricultural land between him and his four married sisters. Also his circle of foreign acquaintances—Hayat herself noted—was very wide, and despite his rather poor English, he was clever and could make himself understood with looks and gestures, which made it clear that he was selling expensive things at high prices. The third guy, Wagdi al-Wakil, was—according to Hayat al-Barri's spot-on description—a slimy, phony cheat who occasionally claimed to be the nephew of Zaynab al-Wakil, Mustafa al-Nahhas's wife, but then he'd forget and claim he was from the wealthier branch of the family, or he'd forget again and say there was no relation. Occasionally, he'd claim to own a shoe store on al-Shawarbi Street, but then he'd forget and say he was just a partner in the store, and then forgetting once more, he'd say he was just an employee, but that actually he was more important than the owner. They were a weird bunch and they got on Mahasin's nerves. She refused to entertain people she couldn't stand so she avoided them as much as she could, but she couldn't help but hate the idea of them being there. And when she confessed her disgust to Qamar, he defended them stridently and accused Mahasin and her friends of being a bunch of detached Marxists, isolated from real people as if they were living in a Jewish ghetto, and of having no clue about what Egyptians were really like, and maybe they were just Soviet collaborators after all. He said a lot of things out of the hash-den dictionary, which all boiled down to: the Marxists in the Arab world were getting rowdy because every last one of them was rowdy to get in on the rowdiness and after all their trouble they might not even get to get in on it because the rowdy Soviet Union itself had gone from trading in the pains and dreams of the world's poor and oppressed to trading in human destiny in an insane nuclear arms race that didn't give a damn about the future of the working class or the future of any of the world's classes. It was nothing more than an army now, breathing down the necks of all the world's people. Everyone who'd gone to Russia had seen with their own eyes that the wealth that the people of the USSR had broken their backs to amass was being spent by their leaders on a space war, while the people were abandoned to deplorable conditions, including famine and iron-fisted repression. Of course, if Qamar had asked Mahasin or Hayat al-Barri, for that matter, in a calm moment their honest opinion about the state of Soviet Marxism–Leninism—which was actually just the old Marxism holding a mask up to its face—then she'd have surely gone further than he had in condemning it, and she might have even cited official reports, testimonies, and studies that proved beyond a doubt that

Marxism–Leninism was headed for earthquakes that would inevitably destroy it. But for Qamar to roll out that boilerplate and use it to attack and insult his friends—including his wife—knowing full well that they weren't really Marxists any longer and weren't involved in any official organizations, only meant that he was cracked, lashing out, and deranged.

Whatever his problem was, she—Hayat—knew how to placate him. Like me, she truly liked him and thought he was one of the sweetest people she knew and that he was an honorable guy through-and-through—a *humane* being, you know—so generous. The thing was though—as Hayat had discovered—he had a problem with women. Although he was such a good guy, he had this awful image of women in his heart—Hayat explained—and deep down he just didn't respect them. All his charm and affability with the ladies was a show. He'd probably been bit by some woman in the past, and that experience had embittered him against all women. It didn't take much for them to annoy him and despite his model patience and reputation as a friendly, social guy, he had very little time for women's conversation. He always tried to cut his conversations with them short no matter how important the topic. He wanted to be the great decider and to have the last word no matter how wrong he was. He could've easily been Lord of the Manor, which was both his wish and his salve, with Mahasin's blessing, if only he'd been a little kinder to her, been a little more subtle about it. He could've convinced her to play nice with his friends if only for his sake and at the same time insisted that his friends be better behaved in other people's houses, but as soon as Mahasin started calling his friends boorish plebs, he blew up and started insulting her and the people she associated with. It was God who took Mahasin's side, though, one night, shaming Qamar and showing him that he was being bullheaded.

It was the night of her daughter Dalia's birthday and Mahasin was throwing a party to celebrate. Truth be told, Qamar hadn't spared a piaster on the party and had bought too much of everything, which was a giveaway that someone else was actually bankrolling the whole costly affair. He'd invited some of his friends over that evening just as Mahasin had invited some of hers. The party went on all night and Qamar's friends got quite unmistakably drunk. They started acting out of hand, swearing, saying lurid things to some of the women, and one of them even had the gall to goose the young maid, whom Mahasin had taken great pains to bring from a village in Fayoum. Unfortunately for Wagdi al-Wakil, the startled girl screamed and ran into the kitchen, making a scene, and Mahasin—naturally concerned and frazzled—ran after her and demanded that the young maid tell her what had happened. As the girl explained, her tongue trembling, her words shy and panicky, Mursi Khallaf avenged her honor right then and there, rearing back with all his might and punching Wagdi al-Wakil right on the jaw—bang like a gunshot! Wagdi fell to the ground like a stiff corpse from the horrible surprise alone, but that wasn't enough for Mursi, who then spat on his face, causing everyone there paroxysms of disgust. That could've been the end, but Mahasin burst out of the kitchen like a fire ball with octopod tongues, cursing, damning, spitting, getting it all out. She was an entirely different person: she was violent and they were all too afraid to face her. They submitted meekly to her rage and were getting ready to leave, but she'd let the rebel out already and there was no controlling it. It—and she—set off on a certifiably lunatic rampage, flipping the table over, bottles, glasses, plates of hors d'oeuvre splashing onto faces and elegant outfits. Hayat al-Barri stopped her as she was picking up the phone to call the police and took her in her arms and dragged her to the bedroom. She locked the door from the inside and tried to calm her friend down, begging her not make the evening into a bigger scandal than it already was. At that moment, Qamar came out of his shock-coma and found he could stand once again; he showed his friends out, escorting them downstairs.

Mahasin spent the whole night trembling and gripped by worry, for her terrified daughter Dalia wouldn't stop screaming and weeping and had completely forgotten that only moments ago she'd been celebrating blowing out her candles for the fourth time in her life. What a cursed, painful birthday it'd been for the little girl. When Hayat looked at her watch and saw that it was nearly midnight, she had a divine inspiration about what she could do to get the poor little girl's mind off her terror. She took Mahasin, Dalia, and the young maid, excused herself to the lingering guests, and bundled them all into her Volkswagen Beetle, which she'd bought from Talat before he'd gone abroad and had repainted in 'Diplomatic Black.' She drove them over to al-Sheikh Rihan Street where she knew that *The School for Troublemakers* would only be halfway through its first act by then. She was friends with Samir Khafaga and most of the members of Artists United from back when she'd worked as the famous movie producer's secretary. The employee at the door flashed her a smile and led them into the theater. Pushing Mahasin, Dalia, and the maid in front of her, she asked him where Samir was and he said that he was filling in for him that night and that coffee was on its way. Then he gestured to the usher and said, "Take Ms. Hayat to Mr. Samir's box."

Mahasin, Dalia, Hayat, and the maid all had a good laugh and during the intermission, they drank coffee and Cokes and Dalia had a chocolate bar on Samir Khafaga's tab. They strolled around backstage, saying hello to Adel Imam, Saeed Saleh, Younis Shalaby, Ahmad Zaki, Suhair al-Babili, Hassan Mustafa, and Hadi al-Gayyar. The most important thing about that fun, uproarious evening for Hayat—besides, of course, showing Dalia and her mother a good time—was that she discovered something very peculiar, something she'd never noticed before: Saeed Salih and Adel Imam—in particular—had a certain air about them, which, granted, was only fleeting, but was clearly modeled on Rowdy Salih, whom she was pleased to have got to know very well. So it wasn't only Qamar al-Mahruqi who'd been influenced by Rowdy Salih's personality. As a matter of fact, she simply couldn't tell whether it was Rowdy Salih himself who was this new, widespread, highly influential trend that had an entire generation in its throes or whether it was the people whom he'd influenced who'd gone out and created this trend, especially as every single comedian in the country played the part of the idiot, or the fool, or the guy who acts an idiotic fool so that he can get out of following any rules. They talked like Rowdy Salih, repeated some of his funny expressions, they thought like him when they were up on stage. There was no doubting that they'd all gone and smoked hash at Rowdy Salih's, but all they'd taken from him was an attitude and some cutting remarks, which they dropped into serious contexts to cause hilarious dissonances, but to Hayat, Rowdy Salih the man was himself a great deal more valuable than that when looked at from a certain angle.

Hayat worried that if Mahasin went back home she'd get depressed all over again, or that Qamar would come and let loose on her and the situation would only get more critical and complicated so when they got back in the car rather than turning around toward Qasr al-Aini Street, Hayat drove them to her apartment in Heliopolis where the three of them all slept in her bed.

The next morning, Hayat left Mahasin and Dalia at her place and went to the American University to pick Qamar up and take him back to her apartment so he could make up with his wife over a delicious lunch and so she could hand Mahasin and Dalia back over to him without any hard feelings as if nothing at all had happened. She didn't find him— naturally—so she went to see Dr. al-Nabawi Sharif al-Nabawi, the head of the dictionary project.

"Good morning, Professor."

"Hello, Hayat. Please, come in. How are you?"

"I'm fine, thanks. But I can't seem to find Qamar al-Mahruqi. Does he have the day off?"

The man smirked. "Mr. Qamar al-Mahruqi tendered his resignation."

"What? Did you say he 'resigned?'"

"Mr. al-Mahruqi told us we could take the job and shove it, then he tore up his contract and stormed out."

"When was that?" she asked, knitting her brow, suddenly pale.

"A while ago. Five or six months."

Her throat was as dry as wood: "Did something happen, Professor?"

"To be honest, his job was very difficult. He was pretty much the most important member of the dictionary team and I was trying to acknowledge that fact with bonuses and by covering all his expenses."

"What was his job exactly, if you don't mind me asking?"

"Collecting old expressions still in circulation in the popular quarters: in alleys, markets, taverns, coffeehouses, hash dens, and so on, and explaining what all these expressions mean or allude to. He filed expense reports for the costs he incurred infiltrating and taking part in these different environments and communities and I gave him incentive pay on top of it."

"I'm sure you were very supportive."

"One day, I stuck my head into his office and found him shouting at the office boys and the receptionist. He had this really shady looking guy in his office: ratty clothes, unkempt, filthy, greasy hair, you know, he looked like a bum. I mean the guy looked awful, real disgusting. You couldn't tell whether he was a thief or, a beggar, or a lunatic. Long story short: he simply couldn't be allowed in the building until he'd had a thorough going-over."

Hayat chuckled, beaming despite the unhappy situation, "That must've been Rowdy Salih. I'm sure of it."

"You know him?"

"You should know he's a good guy. Very respectable, maybe even more respectable than some of the clean-cut effendis who stroll right through here without so much as a batted eye. But anyway . . . "

"So I called Qamar in and I said, 'Who's that, Qamar?'

"'He's one of my sources,' he says. 'I'm recording him. Everything he says is full of terms and expressions that will form the core of the dictionary!'

"'Okay, Fine, but why didn't you give the receptionist his details?'

"'The guy wanted to throw him out because he doesn't have an ID card!' he said.

"'All right, but how come you're shouting and making a scene?'

"'Because they insulted my friend right in front of me!'

"'I'll be honest with you, I didn't care for the way Qamar was speaking to me in front of the office boys and the staff so I shouted at him and told him I wasn't going to put up with any theatrics in the office, but then he took it so badly I really started to worry. He yanked his contract out of his pocket—he'd only just renewed it—and rip, rip, tear! He threw it in the ashtray and—get this—he started ranting: 'Who do you all think you are? You should be thanking your lucky stars I even agreed to work on this project. This whole dictionary's a conspiracy! The rowdy Americans are the ones behind all this rowdiness 'cause they're planning to invade and occupy Egypt! They want to know the meaning of every single word Egyptians say on the streets so they can know how to control us! I refuse to continue helping you all with this crime! I'd rather make do with ten pounds from an honest job than all your rowdiness!' And then he just up and left and I haven't seen him since. I'd call his father-in-law, but the whole thing's too embarrassing."

Hayat exhaled cigarette smoke and all her sighs and in the resulting cloud, she could clearly make out the situation Qamar had found himself in: he'd become dependent on those friends of his to bail him out of the trouble he'd got himself into. Now, it was down to her. What would she tell Mahasin? She worried that if she told her the truth, she'd only upset her more. Sure, Mahasin had a job so she could afford to look after her daughter and cover the bills for things she'd bought on credit, but she couldn't survive like that for an entire month. Hayat decided that Qamar's chances of getting his old job back were good if only she could come to an understanding with Dr. al-Nabawi Sharif al-Nabawi. Like her, he was from Upper Egypt and they shared a warm friendship based on mutual admiration; they often exchanged books, reference works, significant foreign periodicals. But she still had to figure out how to get Mahasin to stay at her place for a few days until she could sort out this blasted crisis and also to figure out how she could track Qamar down as quickly as possible. She went over to his apartment and knocked and rang the bell until she grew despondent and she repeated that procedure morning, noon, and night, but nothing came of it. She suspected Qamar was actually inside but that he was refusing to open the door and face his visitor. She then went to Hakeem's den to ask after him and she made note of the fact that Rowdy Salih wasn't there either. She asked Hakeem about the both of them and he told her that Qamar had turned up for the first time after several months about ten days ago—that is, eight days before the fiasco—and smoked himself twenty bowls and then he took Salih with him and left. Hakeem hadn't been there at the time, but Salih had left a message for him with Sabir that Mr. Qamar and his partners had rented out an old house in Mariout near Alexandria and turned it into a workshop for pottery and ceramics, and that Qamar had hired Rowdy Salih to be the nightwatchman. Though Sabir suspected that Qamar had really taken Salih along to be their hashish waiter, Hayat had had all she could take so she went back to Mahasin and convinced her that Qamar was in a severely troubled state and that it might become a dangerous, full-blown nervous breakdown if they were to meet face-to-face just then. It would be better for them both if Mahasin stayed with her for a few more days or till the end of the week so that Hayat could have time to calm Qamar down. It'd be even better if Mahasin could take a few days off work. Hayat took it upon herself to call her office and tell them that Mahasin was very unwell and that she needed to rest at home until the end of the week. Then she got in her car and drove over to Qamar's apartment. She was planning to sit at the sidewalk café across the street so she could catch Qamar coming in or out, but she went up to the apartment first to double check. She put her ear against the crack in the doorframe, holding her breath, and she thought she could hear shouting and swearing in the course of a conversation that sounded more like a knock-down, drag-out fight so she knocked at the door. The voices went deathly quiet. She rang the bell; she rang and rang, but there was no use. She went downstairs, certain that Qamar and his friends were in the apartment, and it was then that she saw me going up to Qamar's apartment the day I went to check on him. She almost called out to me to tell me that Qamar wasn't there, but she thought it better to let me go ahead and see what would happen. When she saw me running out of the building, looking for a taxi, she thought about calling me over again, but she figured it'd be better if she were by herself. The people in the apartment—she assumed—were fed up with two rounds of insistent ringing, thinking that it was the same person both times, and the Gulf Arab wearing the dishdasha had come out to shut me up. Almost as soon as she'd finished her coffee at the café across the street, she saw Qamar al-Mahruqi coming out of the building with two other guys: one was the Arab in the dishdasha and the other was an Egyptian dressed in a shirt and trousers, who she thought looked familiar. She jumped up, threw a coin on the table, and ran after them shouting, "Qamar! Qamar!"

"Hey, Hayat!"

He left the two guys and walked over to meet her. She noticed that he was still wearing the same shirt from the night of his daughter's birthday party and that his hands looked rough and dirty. He didn't bother with pleasantries: "Where's Mahasin?"

"She's at my place with Dalia and the maid. She got very ill the night of the party and I had to get the doctor in to see her. I didn't let her go to her parents' house because I didn't want to worry them so I took her to my place."

"Thank God I didn't call them," he said wryly. "You'll have to excuse me now. I've got guests."

"But I need to talk to you. You've got to come see Mahasin. Dalia's had such a shock. You've got to come make up with her."

"I'm not going to see anybody. I'm not making up with anybody."

"Fine, that's not a problem. You stay here. I'll go get her and she'll make up with you."

"Let her stay at your place for a while . . . or with her folks. I'm going on a trip right now and she's better off staying with someone—like you, or the maid even—than staying by herself."

190

"Where are you going? For how long?"

"Alexandria."

"Oh, really? Not to the workshop in Mariout?"

"Ha ha! You've been checking up on me, haven't you?"

"Not on purpose. Okay, well, just tell me when you're coming back?"

"In a week. Now if you'll excuse me."

"Qamar!"

But he just waved at her and caught up with the other guys. The guy in the shirt and trousers said goodbye to them and hurried off, while the guy in the dishdasha walked over to a nearby Mercedes, opened the door, and got in. Then he opened the door for Qamar and they drove off toward some unknown destination. Hayat didn't know what to do; she went back to the café and threw herself down on a chair. She felt like she'd got herself involved in a problem that she simply wasn't up to seeing through. She ordered another coffee in the hope that it might calm her nerves before she got back in the car, and that maybe it'd help lead the way to some escape from this conundrum. She drank, smoked, thought, and tried in vain to steady her mind. Just then a taxi pulled up in front of the building and out came Dalia holding the maid's hand and Mahasin following behind them. She sprinted over to her.

"What are you doing here?"

"I missed my apartment. I'm so torn up and I don't know why."

"Qamar just left. He was with two Gulfies and he said he had to go to Alexandria for work."

"Who cares? He can come back whenever he feels like it!"

They went upstairs together and Mahasin took the key from her handbag, opened the door, and they all went in. Mahasin and Hayat sank exhaustedly into the sofa and sat there silently for a long while. Mahasin eventually got up and changed her clothes and told Hayat to do the same. She did and then they went into the kitchen and threw a meal together and then they all settled down to a long nap. At around four in the afternoon, they woke to the sound of a key turning in the lock and heard the door opening and slamming shut as if some uncouth beast had kicked it. They went out into the hallway in their nightgowns and what should they see but the man in the dishdasha following behind a Haram Street

191

prostitute wearing a ton of makeup, swaying her hips with every step she took. Mahasin screamed, "What's going on here? Who are you? How dare you break in!"

The astonished man froze in his steps. "Who am I? Who are you?"

"I own this apartment."

"I bought this apartment yesterday and I paid the rest of the money this afternoon. 36,000 pounds!"

"Get out! Get out of here before I call the police."

The prostitute wailed coquettishly, "Whaa! Police? The police are coming?"

"I'm going to call the police on *you*. How dare you come into my apartment when I'm not here?"

Hayat al-Barri went up to the man calm-cool-and-collectedly: "Sir, won't you please sit down?"

"Fine, I'll sit."

"And you, Ma'am, do you mind doing us the honor of getting the hell out of here?"

"You got a problem with me or something?"

"You go now, Badia. I'll call you later," said the man to the woman and she left in a huff, slamming the door behind her, her clunky sandals clapping against the marble staircase until they disappeared in the enveloping depths and only an echo remained. Hayat shot Mahasin a meaningful glance and winked.

"Come on, Mahasin, shake a leg! Take the phone inside and get a move on. Call a restaurant—doesn't matter what—and order something so we can offer this nice guest of ours something to eat."

"That's not necessary. Really, it's not. The important thing is that I bought this apartment here, furnished and with everything that's in it. What are we going to do about this situation?"

"We'll take care of it. We'll take care of everything, don't you worry. We're Egyptians: we've got everything under control, you'll see. Have something to drink first and cool down so we can all talk this through."

With her smooth talk, Hayat poured out the smooth wine of her smooth femininity that hid a smooth sting: a bottle of Coke, a cup of coffee, two spliffs, and the dolt drank and smoked without batting an eye. A couple of playful smiles from Hayat had him sinking lazily into his seat until there was a sudden banging at the door, and Mahasin—still in her nightgown—ran to open it. A police detective and his assistant came in and asked who'd called for the police. Mahasin stepped forward and introduced her friend, her daughter, and the maid, and then she pointed to the intruder. The policeman could see that everyone in the apartment—the woman of the house, her daughter, her maid, and her friend—were all dressed in nightgowns except for this big oaf so he knew that the break-in story was true. There wasn't anything else you could call it under the law and on that basis he submitted wholly to the woman who'd called in the crime with all due compassion. With inspiration and help from Hayat, he wrote a painstaking, extremely detailed, and damning report in which he recorded everything in the apartment that belonged to Mahasin, from her daughter's bed to her maid's clothes. For his part, the man presented a contract of sale signed by Qamar al-Mahruqi and witnessed by the real-estate broker, as well as Mursi Khallaf and Walid Rashid. The Dokki neighborhood police precinct didn't know how to respond to the man's exasperating threats of blowing the issue all the way up to a diplomatic incident. That night, they had a slapdash hearing in front of the public prosecutor, who forbade any tampering with the contents of the apartment and granted Mahasin permission to stay there. The public prosecutor told the man that even if the apartment hadn't been registered in the names of both spouses, in the event of a dispute between spouses when the wife has given the man children—even if only the one—it's the husband who has to leave the apartment. The prosecutor also seized the original contract in Qamar and Mahasin's names and the new individual contract signed only by Qamar and ordered that he be brought before him to discuss the validity of signature. He assured the man that he would see to it that his money was returned no matter what it took.

Hayat al-Barri finished her painful story and said that now it was up to us to find Qamar wherever he was so we could get his wife and daughter out of this embarrassing predicament. She also said that despite everything that had happened she wasn't angry at Qamar; no, to the contrary, she pitied him. Unlike what a hasty mind might think, his vengeful act wasn't intended to hurt Mahasin; rather, he was getting back at himself. Because he was so profoundly intellectual and open-minded, his emotions were totally pure, but unfortunately this was a defective emotionality and even when it came to his most fateful decisions, he didn't resort to reason. Then later, when his decision was transformed into action and even he could see that he'd made a grave error, he'd do a hundred-and-eighty-degree turnaround toward what he thought was the solution to the dilemma. Take his marriage to Mahasin, for example: he hadn't thought it through; it was an emotional, torrential impulse that he simply gave in to, eyes shut and senses numbed. And then after they'd lived together and it became clear to him that she had a strong, stubborn personality like his controlling mother whom he'd always complained about, he saw that there was nothing he could do; he wasn't the type to cut and run. But then he'd punish himself for these loony impulses, which had landed him between two domineering women, who wanted to control his freedom and state of mind. The danger behind these impulses of his was that their violence often swept away several absolutely blameless innocents in their wake. You know this as well as anybody since you guys have been friends for so long—and—as she'd come to learn—he wasn't the least bit malicious, he was just unlucky. Unlucky, I tell you; a mischievous, stubborn, unreasonable little boy who'd cut off his nose to spite his face and consequently put his family through the cruelest punishment. I told her that maybe we should go by Hakeem's to see what we could find out. Hakeem or Sabir must have got an address for Rowdy Salih by now, or else we could just go on hearsay and head to Mariout and ask people there if they know anything.

At Hakeem's den we were surprised to find Rowdy Salih sitting in his usual spot, filling bowls. As soon as he saw Hayat walk in behind me he stood up, smiling, and let himself hug her like a shy child in his aunt's embrace. Rowdy Salih said that the workshop hadn't got off the ground yet. The only thing that was there were the machines for mixing the material, cleaning it, and forming it into various shapes like the prototypes. He said he'd got sick of living in quiet, dead Mariout on the shores of the wild lake there. He missed the bustle of the Marouf Quarter alleys, despicable Hakeem, filthy Sabir, and the god-awful bowl-filling, but the bigger reason—now we're coming to the truth—was that he couldn't stand Qamar's partners bossing him around and being obnoxious. All he did was buy some denatured alcohol and Coca-Cola and get a little rowdy, but the whole village flipped out and the scene there in Mariout terrified Qamar so he grabbed Salih, marched him down to the Desert Road, stopped a car heading toward Cairo, paid double the fare, and told the driver to drop this guy off in front of the Hilton hotel. Salih fell into a deep sleep in the car and didn't wake up until they got to the hotel and then all he had to do was cut down a few streets to find himself in the Marouf Quarter once more. He recalled all these details over twenty bowls smoked by us and served by Sabir, and when Hayat explained to him that she desperately needed to see Qamar because his daughter was very ill, Salih said that he'd sworn to himself he'd never return to that place, but he was prepared to go back on his word—for Hayat's sake. He said he'd take her over there right then if she had her car with her. Hayat cheered and high-fived Salih elegantly—a joyful slap—and then she pulled him to his feet as he dusted off his clothes and got ready to set off.

THE DOVE

I hadn't seen Hayat al-Barri since she'd gone to Mariout, but only about three days later I was at the studio for my friend Mamoun al-Naggar's show *Airmail* on Sudan Division Radio to record some short stories I'd written. I was excited because, for the first time ever, the recording was going to take place at the studios in the new building in Maspero, near Hakeem's hash den, which meant that I could go get stoned right next to work—as if that morning weren't lovely enough already. I spotted Rowdy Salih sitting there in his usual spot, filling bowls, and as soon as he saw me, he grinned and gestured as if to say, "Oh, if only you'd been there, you'd have seen so much!" as though our conversation had only suffered a momentary interruption.

Whether it was due to his talent at transmission or mine at reception, I understood from his gestures that he meant what had happened in Mariout when he and Hayat al-Barri had gone there. I could see that he was happy to share in an innocent conspiracy against his friend Qamar al-Mahruqi in the service of what was right. His tone changed slightly, as if he were opening parentheses, or introducing a conditional clause, and said that when he found out from Ms. Hayat on the way over there what Mr. Qamar had done, he got very angry with Qamar and decided he never wanted to have anything to do with him again, but not to worry as his friend had put his mind at ease and got back on the right track as easy as anything. Salih's voice changed again as if he were closing the parentheses, or settling the unreal conditional, and started to recount all that had happened from beginning to end.

First, Hayat al-Barri had taken him to a hotel downtown called the Cosmopolitan behind the stock exchange—I think you know it, you go there occasionally to the bar to drink, don't you? She picked up the man in the dishdasha and he got in the car with us. I got out to let him sit in the front seat, but Ms. Hayat told him to get in the back. Salih looked awfully happy when he told me that last bit. The man in the dishdasha studied Salih's face and said, "I've seen you before."

"With Mr. Qamar," Salih replied, laughing.

He nodded and offered Salih a Marlboro, but Salih declined politely, explaining that it didn't do it for him like his acrid Cleopatra King Size and that all things from Cairo, the Mother of the World, tasted smooth and delicious just like it. Hayat smiled and the man said nothing as the Volkswagen took off like a jumping frog, shooting right and left until it reached the motorway and sped toward Mariout as quickly as it could.

They caught Qamar completely by surprise. He was sitting on the bench in the courtyard of the house with his three friends, Mursi, Walid, and Wagdi, who came to see Qamar every couple of days, partly for the pleasure of the open road and partly to keep up with their important project, which was still in its infancy. They were in the process of getting seriously stoned and drafting a production schedule, which they intended to implement very soon. Qamar froze in his seat, but his friends stood up boisterously, in raucous welcome, and the man in the dishdasha strode up and set about playing his part in the plan he and Hayat had agreed on during the car trip. He pounced on Qamar, grabbing him by the collar and shouting as he looked all around him, "Here he is! Here, sir, come arrest him! Here he is, Officer, go for it! You police can't hear me or what?"

The man shoved a trembling Qamar back down on the bench, his head slamming against the wall, and then headed for the front door, shouting for the police; he was laying it on a bit thick. Hayat cut him off at the door—a wonderful dramatic touch—and screamed at him, "Please! This isn't what we agreed to." She didn't have to fake her anger.

"What do you mean, lady? You expect me to find the guy who ripped me off and then just let him go? What was the point of bringing the police then?"

"The police are here just as a last resort. We agreed that they'd keep their distance and not get involved."

"Why shouldn't they get involved?"

"You know I promised the prosecutor that I'd solve the problem amicably, sir. The way to fix this is for you to get your money back, and if I fail to work out a solution, then be my guest, go get the police and they can arrest Qamar. But first give me a chance to talk it through with him."

"Okay, Fine! Let's see what you can do."

With that genius and genial boss touch of his, Walid Rashid sidled up to the man slowly: "Please, sir, come make yourself at home first. We'll take care of everything, money's no object. You think we're kids or what? No, we're men, real men, real stand-up guys. We know how to take care of business."

"Everything will be resolved, God willing," added Mursi Khallaf.

"First things first. What do you all feel like having for lunch? I mean, for dinner? We've got a blessed fridge-full here, or how about I roast you all a sheep? That'll be tastier and quicker," Wagdi al-Wakil said.

The man in the dishdasha looked at him nervously, unsure whether the word sheep was meant as a joke at his expense. Salih was the only one who picked up on the reason behind his anxious expression and he called out gaily, "Don't take it the wrong way, my Gulfy friend! No offense, but these guys mean what they say. There's no need to give them a wary look like that. I mean maybe you saw their cars parked outside—God in heaven!—it's all Mercedes and Peugeot and Volvo!"

"Why don't you go get us a fire started there, Salih?" Mursi barked at him.

"You mean you want a big fire?"

"I mean the kind of fire we can roast a sheep on."

Wagdi stood up and went with Salih: "Come on, I'll get you the sheep out of the big fridge." They walked off. Mursi Khallaf crouched on the ground and started rustling up the coals in the brazier around the teakettle, in which he'd begun to brew tea, and then he packed a bowl and handed the stem of the bong to the stranger: "Gooooooood evening, Najaf!"

The man pushed the bong away roughly, grumbling priggishly, "I don't use that shit!"

Mursi looked at him, maintaining a polite neutrality and then he gestured with an enviable calm and gave a wink to prove that he really was the most cunning of all God's creation. "No, of course, not. But we do use that *shit*! I mean it's not for all the great and good." Swallowing the smoke with extreme delight, he added, "People like yourself, I mean."

Wagdi al-Wakil came in carrying a whole sheep that had recently been slaughtered; the butcher in the house next door had cut it up so it would fit in the refrigerator. He brought it over to the man in the dishdasha: "What do you think?" he said, blowing a kiss off his fingertips. Then he turned, and with an air of mock lordship that managed to retain a great deal of charm, he commanded, "Come on, Salooha, light us a rager in the house, quick." He handed him the sheep and followed him inside. Mursi swung the bong over to Hayat: "Okay, Hayat, what's the deal?"

Hayat took a deep rip and blew out thick smoke as the man in the dishdasha stared at her with a mixture of amazement, suspicion, surprise, and confused desire. Weighing every word, she said, "Long story short: Mahasin and her daughter were sitting in their apartment and then the door opens and this guy here walks in with a prostitute."

Mursi's head drooped. Qamar's face went white and he looked completely crushed; he sighed deeply and muttered, "I told you to change the locks first thing, or at least put a new lock on."

"Why should I? I wasn't stealing anything!"

Hayat carried on, "So then he called the prosecutor and told them he caught thieves inside his apartment and the police came and took us all away."

"Why you?" asked Walid, who was following along earnestly.

"Because I was there with Mahasin at the time. Anyway, so they took us away and brought us in front of the public prosecutor."

"The prosecutor?" shouted Qamar—just like that—sitting up in his seat.

"Of course," she said, "It's a crime, isn't it? This gentleman showed them a contract of sale signed by Qamar, and Mahasin showed them the deed in her name and Qamar's, which means that the man's contract isn't valid."

Qamar seemed to be returning to his senses: "Get to the point already!"

"I'm sorry to say it, but the prosecutor ordered that you be brought in."

Walid was outraged: "How could you not tell us the apartment was in you and your wife's name, Qamar?"

Mursi elbowed him angrily: "Don't pick on Qamar. He's been through enough." Then he turned to Hayat, "You said you came here to figure something out."

"That's our only option."

"You mean if this guy gets his money back, the problem goes away?"

"Of course. And we'll write up an agreement and we'll all witness it and then me and this nice man here can go hand it in to the prosecutor. No harm, no foul."

With the look of a gang leader who knows no one's going to dare oppose him no matter what he says, but all the same in a warm, brotherly tone, Mursi looked at Qamar and asked, "How much do you have left over, Qamar?"

"Less than half. Maybe a third, I don't remember," replied Qamar with a dry throat, staring at the ground, barely able to hold his head up.

A charged silence fell over everyone; it was interrupted by Wagdi al-Wakil shouting cheerfully as he came over ostensibly to warn them, "By the way, there's a suspicious car outside that keeps driving back and forth. I guess they don't like the look of Rowdy Salih. They must think he's a tramp up to no good."

"Sit down, Wagdi. We need to talk to you," said Mursi.

Wagdi crouched down and looked at them, gesturing theatrically: "And here I am, ready and all ears."

Mursi looked back and forth between them: "Can either of you afford to buy out Qamar's share in the workshop? Qamar will stay on with us, of course, but as a manager on a salary."

They all took a moment to think. "Why don't we just divide it up between the three of us? We'll give Qamar his money and we'll all own the company equally," said Walid.

"All right, then! Everybody chip in." He took a fat wad of money out of his bag and dropped it on the ground in front of him. Wagdi looked at Walid: "You pay for the both of us and I'll settle up with you later."

"No prob."

Walid picked up his combination-locked Samsonite briefcase and opened it. He was uncomfortable for a moment and Hayat instantly understood why: she spied some very rare-looking pieces of jewelry—gold inlaid with genuine rubies. Walid knew how to take precautions, though, and he simply hid the contents of his briefcase under his arms and pulled out a wad of twenties and tossed it on top of Mursi's money.

Although he was trying to maintain a veneer of brotherliness, Mursi was stern when he said, "Qamar, give us the money you've got."

Qamar hesitated briefly, but then opened his travel bag and pulled out a leather wallet. He took out a sealed stack of bills: "That's ten, sealed." From another pocket in the travel bag he took out another stack; this one was unsealed. "That's twenty-five hundred." He put his hand in his jacket pocket and took out a handful of folded bills: "And this is five hundred, which makes thirteen altogether."

Mursi looked up and gave the man a defiant look: "How much you got coming, sir?"

"Thirty-six thousand."

He began counting and the man began counting after him, wad after wad, until the money was enough and more. Hayat immediately took out her leather pocketbook and began writing out a receipt for the money and a letter saying that the man had retracted his complaint and that he and Qamar had agreed to annul the contract of sale they'd signed. Hayat was getting ready to leave and tried to hurry the rest of them so they could get a move on, but Wagdi al-Wakil insisted they eat the roast sheep. With the first threads of dawn, four cars set off down the Desert Road, caravanning together and harassing one another, as the dew on the car windshields hinted that the sweating sun was about to rise in a foggy, disheveled procession like bubbles of fresh milk.

IMPERMANENT CHEER

None of the members of our circle had any problem acknowledging that there was something of Rowdy Salih about them anymore. At first, we teased one another when somebody did something that we realized—whether right then or only later—was a distorted imitation of Rowdy Salih. It got us laughing no matter how distorted an imitation it was. Then we began cheering on the people who were the most proficiently Rowdy Salih-ish like Qamar al-Mahruqi and Talat al-Imbabi, who were the real pioneers. Even Hayat al-Barri had become one of the strongest devotees in the cult of Rowdy Salih with a passion equal to that of her naive youthful exuberance for Marxist thought.

Hayat al-Barri became a regular at Hakeem's hash den. She would come by herself in the afternoons and sit with us, at the foot of the hill or on top of it, dressed in those jeans of hers, which clung tightly to her thighs and hips, looking sexier than she'd be if she were completely naked. She, too, had become Rowdy Salih-ish, inside and out, repeating his phrases passionately and affectionately. She copied his free-flying, stuttering laughter and she called him by his name without any formality at all. She'd say goodbye to him like he was her sweetheart, "Ciao, Salooha," and we'd fairly melt from a rush of delight and also, perhaps, from jealousy. She addressed us by name, too, not letting titles get in the way of intimacy, but there was a certain something missing—a certain emotional beat—when she said our names.

We all had a good relationship with her, and even the alley kids adored her. They fought over who got to run errands for her although she usually just made these things up so that she'd have an excuse to shower them with affection and small change, which never seemed to run out. She became the princess of the neighborhood: so-and-so washed her car, so-and-so changed the spare tire, so-and-so took it to get patched up and inflated, so-and-so ran to get us fuul and piping-hot falafel from al-Tabei in Bab al-Luq, etc., etc. The truth was that she'd taken the place of some of the missing members of the group especially since Qamar al-Mahruqi only rarely came anymore—and his absence no longer attracted any attention. When he did come, he'd come at peculiar times: early in the morning, waking Hakeem up from a sound sleep, or right before dawn after they'd already packed it in, or in the heat of the day when everybody was on their last nerve, and he was always in a hurry, anxious, he'd slam down twenty or thirty bowls in a row in a steady back-and-forth between him and the guy serving him. He hadn't lost any of his elegance even if he looked a little worse for wear, a bit scruffy. He didn't talk as freely as he used to, didn't joke around. He seemed more and more like an army soldier—a conscript—who's experiencing fatigue, exhaustion, graveyard shifts after a long life of luxury. He used to leave things in the den, little calling-cards we knew were from him: ceramics produced by the workshop, a buffed and shiny ceramic bong-bowl that looked like it belonged in a display case, big mugs with pharaonic engravings, dishes decorated with designs and Quranic verses that were for mounting. Hakeem pointed to them, his grin pasted on, asking everyone he saw, "You don't know anyone who wants to be a sales rep for a workshop? Mr. Qamar is looking for someone. He needs a clean-cut, educated guy to take some samples around to shops and earn a good commission. You guys don't know anyone?"

With credible earnestness, Hayat al-Barri said, "I swear if I had the time, I'd do it myself." All the den customers and the people from the alley were happy to have Hayat al-Barri in Hakeem's den, but it was more than just the pleasant novelty of having a woman there getting stoned with them side by side. It was because the day she showed up in Hakeem's den was also the day we had news, which Egyptians had been waiting for—with anticipation burning hotter than coals—for ages. Finally people could show some spirit, puff out their chests, raise their heads up again after such a long stretch of humiliated dejection. That first day she came to the den as a customer, looking to get high like all the other guys, she'd brought a palm-sized radio with her, which she clipped to her belt and flipped on every few minutes, changing the stations persistently as if she were searching for a specific bit of news. Eventually she jumped up and shouted for everyone to listen. She jacked the sound of the radio right up so everyone could hear the greatest news of their lives, of the whole modern era: our armies had crossed the Suez Canal, destroyed the impenetrable Bar Lev Line, and crushed the troops of the Zionist enemy, rounding up the retreaters as they scattered, and shook the earth beneath Israel's feet on Yom Kippur. Everyone was ready to hug and kiss Hayat for having brought us this victory in her wake. Euphoria came over the entire nation and the whole world shined its lights on us. Even people who sympathized with the enemy found themselves looking at us with a newfound respect and that only fed the fuel of our ecstasy and deepened it.

Even after the tide turned and the Third Army was encircled, even after the ceasefire and Sadat's speech in parliament, the masses were still in thrall to the glee they'd been deprived of for so many years. After they'd wept for the sons they'd lost in the Sinai deserts during the dreadful defeat of the sixties and the sons who'd served in the military all throughout the war of attrition, they began to boast about the medals they wore. It was true that the heat of victory soon cooled—froze even—and the elation was roiled when the enemy broke through and by the attempts to end the conflict, but still a new feeling had come over us. We were confident once more that the Arabs could be a powerful force again if only they united. Hayat al-Barri had her own opinion about whether the Arabs could become a powerful force again now that they'd regained the energy sources, water, fertile land, rare tourist sites, and mines hidden deep underground until that unknowable day, known only to the perpetual enemy who always held our destiny in his grasp. Hayat felt the so-called Arab reemergence could never happen so long as the Arabs still suffered from the ills of authoritarianism and the love of being the boss and bossing around. That they would forever remain at the mercy of foreign powers who allowed the pirates among us to rule us—and was there anything in the world more abundant than pirates, who would do anything to gain power—even if it only meant being mere puppets and tools for suppressing their own people?

We soon forgot about the October War, which—in the end—led to more grief and consternation than the June Defeat. We actually began to long for the Days of Defeat when prices skyrocketed and products disappeared from the market to the point of scarcity. Hashish was the most purely democratic high in the country. It was how people buried their anxieties so they could put up with life's bitter moments and earn their daily bread, minding their own business. The price of hash suddenly went up along with the price of gasoline as if it were a sort of fuel that society needed in order to run. It was brought about by the rise of the U.S. dollar and the steady decline of the Egyptian pound, which soon became the laughing stock of world currencies, because people said the drug dealers needed huge sums of dollars to import hash and opium. Yet, the people continued to smoke hash all day and all night; they just cut back on the costs of fire: that is the den-costs. The flow of customers became a trickle and it didn't help things that the dens themselves raised the price of a bowl of molasses-tobacco from half a piaster to five piasters so what used to buy you ten bowls now only got you one.

Hakeem's den thinned out until the only people left were a tiny, moneyed elite, who liked the ambiance of the place, and they drove the price of service up even more. Faruq al-Gamal, the poet, stopped coming. We tried to find out why and Rowdy Salih brought us a reliable report: at the Broadcasters' Club, the poet had met an actress of limited talents, who wasn't quite famous even though she'd been around for a while and was somewhat well known to the audience of the Ismail Yasin Company in which she'd had some supporting parts, but she did act in a lot of radio plays because she got along well with the keys. Someone asked, "What do you mean 'the keys,' Salih?" He said they were actors—actually talentless hacks—who were friends with directors who assigned them to go around collecting bribes from their fellow actors: an evening program costs this much, a radio play costs this much, and radio work provided an immediate and ample income. The actress invited the poet to a party at her apartment and he decided to cast his net on her. He could see she was on the verge of forty, suffering from loneliness and an emotional void so he volunteered to fill that void himself. He proposed and she agreed right away so he moved into her apartment in Hadayiq al-Qubba where she set up a little private hash den for him where he could entertain his closest friends. She, too, was a long-time stoner and spent more on hashish than she did on food and drink. She lavished the poet with a splendor Salih saw with his own eyes the day she came with Faruq to buy a whole quarter ounce of hash, bottles of arak, mezzes, meat, and fruit, which Salih carried for her to her made-in-Egypt Ramses car.

This news was soon buried along with its subject in the folds of forgetting as if it were something we chose not to remember, or perhaps because our attention had turned to something else. This was the relationship that had lately started to grow between Hayat al-Barri and the actor Zaki Hamid. When the only members of the old guard left were Zaki Hamid, Ibrahim al-Qammah, and me, we instinctively began to count Hakeem, Rowdy Salih, and Sabir al-Assal as members of the group if only because we'd known them for so long and that did away with the artificial barriers between people. Conversation flowed between us all on a humane plane of equality and it was during one such discussion that we all agreed that Zaki Hamid had used his strong eyes and their piercing, penetrating gaze on Hayat al-Barri and seduced her in an obvious— undeniably obvious—way. They started coming to the hash den together, and leaving together, too. She'd often wait for him to finish going over his lines for the radio play he was going to record in an hour so she could give him a lift to Maspero in her car. One evening I was sitting in the lounge on the fourth floor of the Maspero building waiting for the evening-shift staff of the petty cash office to arrive because I had to hand in a payslip that I'd got the day before, which could only be cashed by the evening-shift employees. I caught sight of a young woman as lithe and feminine as could be, walking haughtily and without the slightest affectation as if she were on her way to a Miss Universe competition and certain to win—no doubt about it. I twisted my neck to examine her backside after her frontside had turned my head and I almost fainted from the divine excess of unparalleled geometric symmetry in these two sides, like the two halves of a balanced scale. I almost lost my mind when the slender young woman began waving her soft, tender arm at me from afar. She walked back toward me from the corridor that led to Studio Thirty-eight. She came closer and reached out to shake my hand, and it was only then that I saw it was Hayat al-Barri. We sat in the lounge and she offered me a cigarette, then she called to the canteen waiter, who was passing by, and when he came over, she ordered us two coffees, medium sugar. Before I could translate my curiosity into words, she explained she was waiting for Zaki Hamid to finish recording in Studio Thirty-eight with the director Yousef al-Hattab on the *Best Stories Ever* program because they were meant to go to a work dinner together at some restaurant. Hayat told me she'd just signed a deal to translate the play *A View from the Bridge* by the contemporary American writer Arthur Miller for Radio Two; al-Hattab was going to direct and Zaki Hamid would play the lead. Then she answered the question I'd been wanting to ask: she said that she'd got the idea of translating that play in particular because of the striking resemblance between Zaki Hamid and the protagonist of the play and she'd soon discovered an even more striking resemblance in their life stories. She was taken by Miller's ability to capture the nature of these lost, noble characters who are ground up in the cruel gears of the industrial capitalist system. Personally, I was pleased to hear that Hayat al-Barri would be translating plays for Radio Two—and for theater troupes and publication, as well, for that matter—because to be honest she was far more talented than all those hacks who lacked her feel for the language and its various registers. But the dawning affection for Zaki Hamid that showed in her eyes hinted that there was something more than mere fondness there and that their relationship had entered the phase of manifest love. This made me take a personal interest in its course—the love, I mean—an interest matched only by my interest in understanding how and why it had irrupted so urgently so quickly; it didn't really match up with Hayat al-Barri's wisdom and intellect. What was it about Zaki Hamid that had seduced the headstrong, emotionally sophisticated Hayat al-Barri?

Sabir al-Assal had a cousin from a village in the Sharqiya province called Abd al-Wudud and it was a very apt name, to be sure, because he was the friendliest guy. He'd graduated from the Law School a few years ago and was working as a trainee lawyer at Abd al-Aziz al-Shurbagi's firm. He had a good heart, was humble, and he never waffled when Sabir introduced the gentleman as his cousin, never turned his nose up at exchanging affection and a special, intimate friendliness with Sabir like a real cousin. He was suave, never intrusive, never preyed on our sessions, and he only joined us every once in a while. One day he was surprised to find Zaki Hamid sitting there with us and both their faces lit up as they rushed toward each other, embracing, kissing cheeks, greeting each other warmly: "My, my, what a small world!" "How's it going?" "What are you up to?' etc. We learned that Abd al-Wudud and Zaki Hamid were childhood friends. They'd been born in the same house to the same midwife in the same neighborhood in their village and been nursed by each other's mothers. They'd been classmates from nursery through secondary—that is, high—school, but then they'd lost track of each other for many long years. Zaki was very happy to see Abd al-Wudud and they laughed hysterically together up from the font of their shared memories and all the way down to their spines. Abd al-Wudud remarked, laughing, that Zaki Hamid's face hadn't changed a bit since he was a child. When he got excited—happily or angrily—two prominent features, his eyes and his teeth, would gleam on his dark face. His eyes were like two windows with two panes of glass painted dark gray emitting a dusky light, dyeing his skin a brilliant red lead.

Zaki Hamid's childhood—according to Abd al-Wudud—had been unhappy and painful. His mother had been a girl of twelve when she got married to a handwoven-fabric merchant called Hamid Nabih al-Dahshan, who hailed from a family with Bedouin roots. He and his many brothers owned large fabric shops in the city of Zaqaziq and he ran a branch located in their village, San al-Hagar. He was in his forties, tall and broad, a hearty and generous man. He loved hanging out with friends and singing Mawawil songs and carving flutes of various sizes out of reeds: from the arghul with its double pipes and various sections to the maqruda with its one reed to the nayy to the sallamiya. When he came to ask for the hand of Hanim, the youngest daughter of al-Hagg Khalifa al-Farmawi, the head of the village watch, he was welcomed and no one said anything about the large age gap between him and the girl; after all he was offering a large dowry the likes of which would've suited the prettiest girl in the village. It was said that al-Hagg Khalifa al-Farmawi made certain that his daughter Hanim loved Hamid al-Dahshan and that she wanted nothing more than to be his wife till death did them part. It was true that she was still more or less a child, but she was mature and clever, and she understood that Hamid al-Dahshan wasn't like all the other men. One month later, she was pregnant with Zaki at whose birth his father rejoiced and cheered exuberantly, vowing to spend whatever it took for his son to get the highest degrees. But regrettably he died before his son's second birthday. He'd been struck by a pain in his right shoulder that made him scream all night long and as soon as it was morning, they hauled him over to al-Bandar Hospital where he breathed his last. He'd had an acute angina.

Hanim, Zaki's mother, was braver than any man even though she wasn't yet fifteen by then. She herself was still a child although she was already a mother, but she didn't even consider going with her child to another man's house after the loss of the man she'd loved. A year after his death, though, her family began pressuring her to strike while the iron was still hot—she wasn't getting any younger. After all it simply wasn't right for her to spend her entire life a widow when she was still in the prime of life. But she insisted that she was going to remain a widow so she could raise her son at a safe remove from stepfathers and uncles' wives. So long as her husband's brothers sent her money for the boy regularly, and generously, out of his father's share of the profits then what did she have to worry about? Unfortunately, though, she couldn't hold out for longer than four terribly strange years during which it was as if she were on the block in a public auction and all the market guys were fighting over her with ever-raising bids even though she shunned every last one of them. In the end, she had the luckiest stroke of all and a wealthy man from a neighboring village put some acres in her name and built her her own estate because to tell the truth she was still irresistibly attractive. Her family and her son's family pushed her to accept; both families were worried she'd give in to temptation despite her unimpeachable chastity and mental strength. She agreed to marry the man and traveled in an awesome procession to her own palace in the company of her new husband. Zaki was handed over to his family, entrusted to his grandmother—his father's mother—who, despite being in her eighties, was still strong and in control of all her faculties. She was more than capable of lavishing him with abundant maternal love. But now that his mother lived in another village far away, penned in a closed circle and a lifestyle far removed from his own, the connection between them was severed, all but for postal hellos and I-miss-yous and fleeting reunions at the rare get-together. His grandmother made up for the motherly affection Zaki lost, but still there was something missing in his life; something he couldn't exactly put a name to. This void in his life planted a mountain of depression and a fatal loneliness in his heart even though he was surrounded by a number of cousins around his age and they all lived together in the same house in the same village. Everyone except for his elderly grandfather, that is, who lived in Zaqaziq with two grown sons he'd had when he was younger with his previous wife, who'd passed away when she was young. Zaki would go to visit his maternal grandmother from time to time and occasionally he spent Thursday and Friday nights at her house, but he was always complaining to Abd al-Wudud about how lonely he felt. If he did well on his exams at school, there was no one to cheer him on. 'Well done' was just something cursory he heard, its echo dying out almost as soon as it left his uncle's lips, or his grandmother's, his aunt's, one of his cousins', and if he did poorly and had to retake an exam, there was no one there to console him. Months could pass without anyone bothering to find out whether he'd done well or failed or what grade he was in, or anyone asking him what was going on or what was on his mind. At home he was just one among many: he had as much food and drink and clothes and pocket money as he pleased, but he was alone, a stranger, and the embrace of his elderly, toothless grandmother only buried the depression deeper in his heart.

Deep down he knew his mother was right to remarry, he knew that it would've been cruel to make her devote her life only to him and that her suffering would've hurt him, too, but at the same time he resented her— not her personally—but her as a symbol of the utter lack of justice in the world, of surrender, of giving up, and of favoring one's self over one's own blood. Sometimes he cursed her and other times he issued poems of praise, fealty, and gratitude in her honor. He talked to Abd al-Wudud often when they'd study together in high school about the nature of women—to him an inexplicable mystery—and occasionally, in furtive moments, the discussion would bloom and branch out onto the topics of fickle fate, the dominion of money, and the untrammeled paths laid open for jerks and villains who controlled the destinies of the good and downtrodden.

Zaki inherited his mother's powerful good looks and her radiant eyes, which were simultaneously full of a deep sadness and an exuberant transparency, and her clear white skin that was mixed in with a little red— like fresh milk mixed with a spoonful of cinnamon that blooms beneath the surface and gives it the color of cocoa—so that you couldn't quite tell whether Zaki Hamid was pale or dark or tan or pewter. He'd also inherited his father's sharp, practical mind and his caring heart. From his Egyptian–Bedouin tribe, he'd inherited a thirst for justice and steely nerve in defense of tribal honor, which took the place of the fatherland, and an unhesitating, overwhelming generosity, which could sometimes verge on self-sacrifice. But that psychosocial makeup of his had also saddled him with a lot of puzzling contradictions. At one moment, you'd swear up and down that he was the epitome of a uniquely great man, and at other times, you'd say he was contemptible, backstabbing, and only cared about his own interests, nothing else. Opinions differed on the subject and there was a back and forth, but despite that everyone who knew him well loved him. His peers laid into him when he wasn't there, describing him in the most awful way and trying to get every last defect to stick, but as soon as they saw him, they couldn't help but smile and embrace him, and they didn't think twice about paying their last cent to make him happy; when he didn't turn up, they'd ask after him sincerely. Thus all throughout high school he was like a little star on a small stage. We saw him everywhere: every damned function, every wedding, every protest, every game, even in every student club—from debate to theater to journalism to scouts—where he always distinguished himself. He was always the axis, always the connector, he was the spokesman, he took the lead on everything even when it was something perilous that could endanger his future.

The kid—Abd al-Wudud told us—was an abnormally active little fireball, maybe it was because of all the anxiety and restlessness he carried within him. He preferred to spend his free time in hash dens rather than spend a single hour in one of his family's shops. Nothing made him happier than meeting new people, than seeing the gritty parts of a city. The search for new adventures was his constant preoccupation and so as soon as he finished high school, he got his application together and went to Cairo to enroll at the Institute of Performing Arts. The village eventually got wind of his acceptance at the Institute. It was true that his family were surprised by his decision, that they pooh-poohed it, that his grandfather had been hoping to rope him into the family business, but they accepted his decision and news of Zaki's growing success reached and delighted Abd al-Wudud. Then Zaki graduated to wider news circles and he began to read about him in the papers and hear his name on the radio; he was dying to see him again. The proverb had come true: "Families are always reunited even if it takes a lifetime."

The story of Zaki Hamid's life loomed greatly and we followed the development of his relationship with Hayat al-Barri with great interest, even acute anxiety. They'd started speaking for the other when one of them wasn't there. Despite our expectations of what might happen, despite—in fact—having already prepared ourselves, the news took us all by surprise. We were all shocked when one day we were invited to the Thousand and One Nights Ballroom at the Nile Hilton, which was just on the border of the Marouf Quarter. From their rooms on the top floors, tourists could see all of the Marouf Quarter laid out like a large wound in the belly of the indigestion-plagued city as it constantly vomited up residents, whether in the cemeteries packed full of the living or in the streets teeming with the walking dead, that tumultuous stifling mass: houses—some crumbling, others ancient and about to collapse—adorned with laundry basins, dogs, hens, workshops, hash dens, shacks, coops, and mountains of rotting, putrid garbage. We left these shacks like worms exuding from pus-filled sores and cut through Umm Yahya's narrow alley over to Antikkhana Street down to Abdel Muneim Riyad Square where we leapt like monkeys out in front of cars to cross the road to reach the Egyptian Museum, where we turned and walked along the walls so that we wouldn't have to suffer the trembling of disgust caused by the specter of the building of the Central Committee of the Arab Socialist Union. We started walking straight again as soon as we walked past its entrance on our way to the Hilton.

The invitation we'd received was for a wedding reception to celebrate the union of Hayat al-Barri and the actor Zaki Hamid along with a big crowd of hotshots the likes of which we hadn't been expecting. We felt positively pathetic in comparison: groups of Americans, British, French, Soviets, and Italians, a group of major artists from all fields, ministry chiefs-of-staff, radio station heads, TV presenters, journalists, writers, translators, raucous singers and dancers leaping up to sing and dance and clown about, but the bride and groom weren't looking at all themselves. We looked for Zaki Hamid and Hayat al-Barri's features in their faces but we couldn't find anything that linked them to the people we knew. The only way we could recognize them was by extrapolating from some unique gestures particular to them both.

On our way back from the party after midnight, it seemed that we weren't wholly satisfied with the whiskeys, beers, and steaks we'd had, so without even thinking we headed for the home of true highs in the Marouf Quarter. After the bright lights of the party, the gloom of the den was overwhelming and we had to feel our way to the seats in the darkness of the alley at the foot of the hill. We decided to take turns matching bowl by bowl and began to get stoned in a deep silence. Eventually Abd al-Wudud spoke, saying he'd discovered something very, very dangerous that night: the resemblance between Hayat al-Barri and Hanim, Zaki Hamid's mother. It was very strong indeed—if not identical—and he confessed that he was pessimistic about this discovery because the least it foretold was that the marriage wouldn't be a success. I asked Abd al-Wudud if he thought that Zaki would take his resentment against his mother out on Hayat or something like that and was that the unacknowledged reason for marrying her? Abd al-Wudud didn't think much of the question and answered: quite the contrary, he'd simply got her back! Zaki was as happy as he could be now because he'd got his mother back, his mother who'd been snatched away from him when he was a child, who'd snatched his childhood away from him. The question now was how long could this happy occasion last? And only God knew.

The truth was that Abd al-Wudud's analysis comforted me; I almost wanted to kiss him. Ibrahim al-Qammah seemed to have arrived at his own analysis of the situation, but—as if by some unspoken agreement— we never brought the issue up again whenever we got together. We spent long, serene hours interlaced with the gurgling rips of the bong, and then suddenly we raised our heads, locked eyes, and fell into a deep, stone-silent laughter as if we were forcefully emptying our bodies out onto the earth. Then we'd sigh meaningful sighs and each plunge down into his own private abyss. One afternoon I was surprised to find Zaki Hamid passing by the hash den after a decidedly long absence during which he'd turned into a page of den-lore that we occasionally liked to skim proudly and happily, and then we'd turn the page and say, "God help him." He'd broke into the ranks of stardom for real after he played the lead role in a TV series that audiences had taken to, and his path to other lead roles on stage and television seemed guaranteed. That afternoon he was on his way to Galal Studios to dub a Russian film—it may have been the Russian *Hamlet*; he'd been chosen by the Egyptian director to dub the lead role. I noticed he was wearing a short-sleeved, cotton, collarless shirt, just like the kind we wore under our clothes except that it was exceedingly elegant matched with light-gray, wool trousers. He'd put on weight since he'd got married, his features were fleshier, his hair thicker and he'd let it get a little shaggy. When he turned his head to reach for the stem beneath his full neck, I was overcome by a slight tremor because at that moment he looked to me exactly like Rowdy Salih. They were both sitting there right across from one another and I swear to God there was no difference between them but for slight superficial things like Salih's white hair and Zaki's clean clothes; aside from that they were—as it appeared to me—a single essence with the same voice, tone, lexicon. Zaki, who in the past had loved to imitate Rowdy Salih, was now even more convincing as Rowdy Salih than Rowdy Salih himself. This was only natural as Zaki had a wondrous and prodigious talent for mimicry and he could penetrate down to the essence of a character and wrap himself in their skin—it was if he were an exact copy, or rather that he'd become even more splendid and brilliant than the original. It was just like the sculpture of Saad Zaghloul, for example, which through the sculptor Mokhtar's chisel became even more glorious and charismatic than Saad Zaghloul himself. A cheeky smile flickered on my lips at the naughty thought that had begun to dance around in my mind: Hayat al-Barri had actually gone and married Rowdy Salih! But then Zaki Hamid started to come by the hash den from time to time once more, not only to catch a quick high before he had to act in a film or play, but also to have a good time and to give us a good time, what with the sight of all those children racing to surround him and shake his hand and with the excellent service we got on his account.

VOLCANO

Just as we'd been shocked by the ungodly defeat of '67, we were blown away—again taken completely unawares—by the news of our crushing victory over the Zionist enemy in '73. And just as we were surprised by the news of the enemy breaking through and encircling our Third Army and the ceasefire, we were also shocked—without the slightest premonition at all—by the news of President Sadat's trip to Jerusalem to show the Israeli leaders his good will and prove he was serious about wanting to pursue peace between the two peoples.

We were lulled into a sedate calm, convinced that President Sadat was merely trying to pull off the ultimate Egyptian joke, and it startled us when we began to feel like he was actually maneuvering behind the scenes, that there was no doubt that he would save us from our dilemma and break the siege of the army, which had fallen between the jaws of a vise, but we were absolutely shocked to discover that it was all unmistakably sincere. We could see it on television with our own eyes: there was President Sadat embracing and being embraced by our enemies, sitting with Begin, Sharon, Dayan, and Golda Meir at the same table in homes they'd seized from us with brute force.

Rowdy Salih pointed at some of the famous journalists there with him and shouted, laughing, but nothing at all like his usual happy, unadulterated, unbridled laughter; this laughter seemed more like the rhythms of a volcanic, violent anxiety: "Ha ha ha! Look! He took all the rowdies with him! Every last one of them's rowdy. Getting rowdy. 'Cause what they want is to get in on the rowdiness and they're going to pay the price of admission with our children's blood. Come on, you bums, you sons of bitches! You've been screwing us for twenty-five years talking about the Revolution, liberating our land, the Crisis in Palestine. Ha ha ha! Get in! They think we're going to buy it. Get in! How are we supposed to believe all that war that just happened? Get in! People's kids died for what? For nothing! Just so a few chair-crazies get to play musical chairs? Ha ha ha! Get in!"

As his emotions boiled over, he chucked the bowls and jumped up to leave. It was obvious that he was wigging out. After he walked out of the den, he came back in, prodded Hakeem's shoulder, and said, "Give me half a pound. Quick."

Hakeem didn't hesitate. He took a handful of ten-piaster notes from the pocket of his gallabiya, picked out five of them, and handed them to him. Salih grabbed the money and hurried out.

That night the whole crew got together—a strange happenstance after being scattered so long—but it seemed that the news of the actual visit and its broadcast live for all the world to see had raised the temperature of the public volcano, its peaceful explosions finding room to breathe on the supple ground: people percolated out of their houses into the streets and coffeehouses; the only people left at home were the few who owned televisions. The whole crew—except for Talat al-Imbabi and Mustafa Lami, who were abroad—was there: Qamar al-Mahruqi, Ibrahim al-Qammah, Faruq al-Gamal, Zaki Hamid, Abd al-Wudud, Mursi Khallaf, Wagdi al-Waki, and Walid Rashid. The TV we were watching, a seventeen-inch black and white, had been brought by Zaki Hamid in his car, a Fiat 132 he'd recently bought from a famous footballer for two thousand pounds. He said he'd been watching the reports live from Jerusalem at home, but had decided that he couldn't bear to watch the shameful scene without the companionship of his friends and lots of hash, hoping that might calm the raging volcano, which had begun roiling deep inside of him since the morning. Then, in a dangerous tone in which he criticized himself and us, he said, "Our entire destiny is changing at this exact moment and we're sitting here getting high."

Ibrahim al-Qammah threw his hands up exasperatedly and said that the whole thing—from the beginning of the revolution to right now—was all just one big smoke-up on a still evening that had lasted a quarter of a century. Hakeem added, "Exactly, Ibrahim! President Sadat was making everybody as happy as could be. Hash, hash everywhere! I can't understand why you guys are all mad at him. The proverb says, "If there's a hand you can't cut, kiss it." You know, he's not going there to kiss hands—God forbid!—this guy's the wily champ. He bit them a little and drew some blood and then he went to them, chest puffed up, and said, 'Here I am. You want to make peace? Be my guest. You don't want to? Well then, you're going to get more of that every day.' And anyway, we're Egyptians. Our blood's nasty, no one's going to drink it!" He dropped his head between his shoulders, choking back his smile; it looked like he was wringing it out in his throat. He seemed disappointed that what he'd said hadn't shifted the depression on our faces at all; it was as if we were at a fervid funeral. But then Hakeem suddenly sprung to his feet as if a hot coal had fallen in his lap and crouched down, pointing at the television and shouting in astonishment, "Look! Look! Do you remember that guy, Qamar? Ibrahim? It's that kid, Wagih Farhan! That bum, that poet who used to make our lives a living hell and Ibrahim used to have to cover his bill. Oh, you rotten little prick! People used to say he was from the same village as Yusuf Atris the journalist. The last time I had to kick him and the little floozy he was with out of here."

The camera lens had focused on President Sadat's procession as he was being welcomed and it caught Wagih Farhan's face as he called to his Egyptian friends in the president's entourage, embracing the broadcaster Ali Faik Zaghloul, warmly shaking hands with journalists and broadcasters in a way that bespoke a genuine intimacy. Our eyes froze in disbelief; they were hollowed out by our incomprehension and looked like little more than perforations from which darkness hissed out. We were probably all doing the exact same thing at that moment: rifling through our mental records to recall everything that had ever transpired between us and this Wagih Farhan, who was receiving the Egyptian delegation as a prominent

Israeli broadcaster. Our heads were spinning violently. I tried as hard as I could to remember the last time I'd seen him—many years ago—and I couldn't decide whether it was the one time in the broadcaster Ali Faik Zaghloul's office when he was making a deal to write some poetic segues to link the acts of *The Variety Show*, which was recorded in a theater in front of a live audience, or another time in the broadcaster Ihab al-Azhari's office, where he was trying to weasel a pound out of him with his fawning smile against the money he was going to earn the day after next when he recorded for Sudan Division Radio. Mamoun al-Naggar had been there and had nodded to Ihab as if to signal that he was telling the truth: that he was scheduled to record for them. I didn't know which of the two times had been the last, but I was absolutely shocked that I hadn't thought about him once over all those years—not once—and neither had any other member of the group because, well, we'd never heard about him again after he stopped coming to the den. I looked around me idiotically: "How do you all explain that?"

"If Talat was here, he'd say, 'There's only one explanation: the kid's Israeli and the Mossad planted him in Egypt to spy on the cultural-political scene from within the broadcasting service itself! He fooled us all and passed on the most dangerous intelligence,'" Faruq al-Gamal said.

Qamar al-Mahruqi laughed so hard his mouth looked like a crocodile's: "Wagih Farhan's Egyptian. I know his parents and his whole family in their village. I think he's got an uncle in Old Cairo who's a bus driver. I know people who were his friends at school."

Ibrahim al-Qammah threw his hands up in deep despair: "That makes it even shittier, man! As far as I'm concerned, I wish he'd turned out to be a Jew. That would've been better. That wouldn't make me so upset. But an Egyptian? A Muslim? Guys, does it get any worse than that? What the hell's happening to people?"

A flash of hellfire shone in Zaki Hamid's eyes: "Who knows? Maybe the Mossad planted the whole family in Egypt in the last century or something?"

Wagdi al-Wakil turned his whole body toward us and slid his glasses down to the tip of his nose, then he began wagging his finger at us insistently: "What would you all say if I told you I saw that guy at the airport in Libya when I went to work there? He came up to me and said hello and reminded me who he was. I remember there were people there with him who stopped and then started walking again when he walked off. I swear to God it was just like that. I also remember that for those few months I was there, customers would talk to me about Egypt and ask me about him and I'd tell them that he was there in Libya and that I'd seen him. I had to swear up-and-down to them that I didn't have his address."

He was interrupted by a child's shout, which was followed by Hakeem's little daughter running in and shouting, "Daddy, Daddy, come quick! The police are beating up Rowdy Salih!"

Hakeem shouted at her, "What do we care? Let 'em cut him into pieces. He's got it coming. He's been off getting rowdy and now he's going to get us all in trouble. Hey, I'll tell you what, Sabir, lock that door, and you guys move inside. Turn off that light and we'll turn on the kerosene lamp so whoever comes by sees we've closed up. I can tell tonight's not going to end well. We'll be lucky if the police don't come down on us on account of that crazy son-of-a-lunatic!"

"Why don't we all just leave?" said Zaki Hamid. "We've done pretty well here. Come on, everybody, let's go." With suave speed, he handed Hakeem a five-pound note with his right hand and raised his left hand to stop us putting our hands in our pockets. "It's all on me, Hakeem."

Qamar and his friends headed toward their cars, which were parked on Abd al-Khaliq Tharwat Street across from the Journalists Syndicate, right in front of the Church of the Sacred Heart. I followed Zaki Hamid to his car, which was parked on Antikkhana Street, and we saw the police dragging Rowdy Salih along, beating him on the neck with the butts of their rifles, kicking him on the ass. He'd been put through the wringer and he could barely straighten out his twisted tongue as he bellowed as loudly as he could, "Who told him to go make peace with Israel? He just does what he feels like? He just felt like it, like people say? Well, I just feel like telling him what's what! I mean, I mean if we're all just feeling like it, well so what? Anybody who just feels like doing something goes ahead and does it? What about those kids of ours who died? What about our planes that got blown up in Anshas before they could even fight? There are still kids out there who haven't come back from '67. Huh? What about the school at Bahr al-Baqar? Any of you cowards want to answer me?"

Kicks and smacks fell on him from every direction and it looked like a massacre in the true sense of the word. Zaki Hamid shivered and I went pale; it looked like we—him and me—were about to get ourselves involved in a catastrophe and maybe even find ourselves getting the same as Salih was getting. All of a sudden, Zaki Hamid snarled, shouting like he was addressing a large audience, "Uh uh! No! This is a bloodbath! You think you can get away with this? Where are we? I don't care what he said, he's an Egyptian citizen and he has the right to protest. This is just the way he is; he can't help it. Why are you treating him like this?"

I tried to pull him toward the car, to make him shut his rash mouth and get in, to get us as far away from that horrific scene as possible, but he yanked his arm from my grasp and charged over to one of the senior officers standing beside the police car. He started shouting at him, "Sir, I think what's happening here is shameful! This whole scene's a real disgrace for the police and for all of Egypt. I'm sure the press has already taken plenty of photos."

"What's that, asshole, you want some too?"

"My name's not asshole. It's Zaki Hamid. And I've got a fancy diploma just like you, and an Egyptian birth certificate just like you, too."

"Well I'm glad we know who you are now. Anyway, we're not going to put up with any of you all showboating at a time like this. You want to teach us how to do our job?"

"Officer, nobody's going to teach anybody else how to do their job, but this guy doesn't know what he's saying right now. He's just angry from the shock we've all had."

"He's a lunatic and we know all about him."

"Well, if you know he's a lunatic, just let him be."

"You want to give us the honor of gracing our lock-up tonight?"

A policeman brought Rowdy Salih over, looking like a corpse, his hands and feet shackled, his mouth muzzled, and they threw him in the police car. He opened his eyes and looked at us. Zaki Hamid called to him hoarsely, "Don't worry, Rowdy. We're going to get you a lawyer and get you out right away."

He went to his car; he was weeping. "I've got to go home right now to see if Hayat knows someone who's got pull with the police or something. We've got to get Rowdy out of there before they torture him to death. I shouldn't have opened my big mouth!" He started smacking himself viciously as he continued to growl, "I made a huge mistake that might cost

Salih his life. Now they're going to think that this Salih of ours is just a puppet. That he's got a secret opposition party behind him. Me and you made it seem like we're the guys behind him. Like we're in charge. We're the bosses and he does what we tell him. They're going to kill him to get him to tell them the names of his leaders. Of course, they're going to think this is all a huge conspiracy. You think I don't know how the Egyptian police think? There's three hundred officers out there desperate to find evidence of a scheme like that right now."

He opened the passenger-side door for me and I got in beside him. He took out a tissue and dried his tears. "He's braver than any one of us. Who else could do what he did?"

At that moment a pack of soldiers appeared, heading toward the car, carrying our friend the Marxist writer and translator, Ibrahim Mansour, and some other intellectuals, who only moments ago had been sitting in Café Riche. We could hear Ibrahim's enraged denunciations, which started out as dribbles at the café, but became clearer as he was brought closer until he appeared, handcuffed, shouting at the top of his voice, "Traitors! Crooks! Who are you all trying to sell this country to?" He was taller than the soldier; his long neck, narrow head, and long, pointy chin stood out above all the others, making him look like a whale leaping through the surface and taking a gulp of air. Zaki watched him and smiled bitterly: "He looks like he's going to need someone to save him too!" He drove off, dropped me at Bab al-Luq, and carried on toward Heliopolis.

None of our connections no matter what sector they worked in could help us get Rowdy Salih released; they couldn't even prove whether someone named Rowdy Salih even existed. One of our contacts was an amateur litterateur, who happened to be a police brigadier-general and the deputy minister of internal affairs for public relations. He was essentially the link between the minister and journalists of the written, seen, and heard varieties. Moreover, he was a mild-tempered man who wrote teleplays and attended the same salons and cultural soirées as we did. This dignified, decent man was apoplectic that he couldn't figure out all the twists and turns in the situation so he ended up taking us—Hayat al-Barri, Zaki Hamid, and me—in his car around to all the jails and the prison at the Citadel. He was given all the logbooks to look through, but still we couldn't find any prisoner named Rowdy Salih, not even Salih Abd al-Birr. Our friend Noor al-Din the brigadier-general was extremely embarrassed that we insisted that this person existed and was in police custody even though everyone else who'd been arrested for protesting against the peace initiative had been released—you can even ask your friend Ibrahim Mansour and his pals. Then we got it in our heads that we needed to go look in the police station lock-ups where they held suspects like him.

The operation was more like some awful joke when we went around in Zaki and Hayat's cars to all the lock-ups and tried to give the most detailed description we could: Salih Abd al-Birr Mahran, better known as Rowdy Salih. We went around to all the hospitals and looked through their logbooks; we even went down to the morgues and looked through all the corpses decomposing in the refrigerators, but that, too, was all in vain. We were at our wit's end; Hayat turned to some of her friends, journalists and certain writers who were allowed to tease the government a little. They included little summaries and inquiries at the end of their daily columns, and Hayat tried to find a photograph of Salih that could be published in the missing persons section of the newspapers in case he'd lost his memory and was out there somewhere lost in God's country, but we couldn't find any photos of him. Thus it fell to Hayat, who'd never once tried her hand at drawing—or knew the first thing about it—to lock herself in her house for twenty-four hours with paper, brush, and colors, killing herself to produce a blown-up likeness of Rowdy Salih's face from memory. Good Lord, it was extraordinary: we were all paralyzed by wonder as we passed the drawing around, examining every last feature, taken by the exactly identical resemblance between the drawing and the original. If anything, the drawing was even more authentic than the original because it gave off an aura that shouted, "Hey you! It's me, Rowdy Salih!" Hayat took the drawing to a friend of hers who was the editor of the back page of *al-Ahram* newspaper so that he could print it in that most popular section of the paper. That way anyone who'd seen him could call so-and-so at such-and-such a number. The editor at *al-Ahram* did indeed publish the drawing, in a nice border, in a prominent location, but beneath it he'd written: "Portrait by Hayat al-Barri."

Zaki Hamid wouldn't let it go and as the situation grew bleaker and bleaker it threatened to tear our lives apart. To him, it had become his own "To be or not to be" moment like his pal, Hamlet. It was obvious he wasn't going to forget about it, wasn't going to even consider giving up. Even wise, prudent Hayat couldn't calm him down; she may even have stoked his rage. He surprised me one day, barging into my room at the Imperial Hotel on Ramses Street. He was worried, anxious, chain-smoking; I figured he'd had a fight with Hayat—he was definitely capable of doing it—and flipped his lid and hit her with a sharp object and bashed in her skull, or maybe he'd grabbed her and thrown her out the window, or had at least sworn to divorce her and stormed out.

"Is everything all right, Zaki? What's wrong?"

"Get dressed and come with me. We've got an appointment. Hurry up."

"With who? Where?"

"With the Chief of Security!"

"The Chief of Security? Zaki, what for?"

"I'm not letting this case die. I filed a complaint with the public prosecutor accusing the Cairo Security Directorate of abducting and hiding Rowdy Salih. You and me are eyewitnesses: we saw the officers beat him up and throw him in the police car. I had words with the officer and I'm prepared to give them a complete description. The public prosecutor ordered an investigation into the disappearance of Rowdy Salih, seeing as the whole country's heard about him, and they want to know what's happened to their fellow citizen."

"Wait, so are we going to the prosecutor's office or the Security Directorate?"

"The Directorate. Our appointment's with the Security Chief. He asked to see me. He summoned me. I'd given them my number and address."

"Zaki, Are you nuts? We're no match for them."

"No, you're wrong there. We're plenty tough. I'm going to make them see that."

"Are you forgetting that they proved there's no birth certificate for anyone with that name?"

"And you believed them, you idiot?"

"Maybe they never registered him. Lots of people don't register their sons because they don't want them to get drafted."

"You're just as stupid as they are."

"Why do you say that?"

"I had a little divine inspiration, you see, and got my hands on a stamped, certified document that's going to make them shit themselves."

"Really?"

He whipped out a folded piece of copy paper from his pocket, unfolded it, and began waving it in my face. I took it from him and his brilliance swept me off my feet: it was a diploma from Marouf Elementary School proving that Salih Abd al-Birr Mahran had been a student there and that he'd received a diploma in such-and-such a year in a class that included so-and-so, so-and-so, and so-and-so; Zaki had underlined one of the names heavily with a marker. I asked him who that name was and, with a devilish glimmer in his eye, he explained that this was the grand surprise: that was the name of the public prosecutor himself. He'd got his elementary school diploma from the same school in the same class as Salih. Zaki said that he'd mentioned this interesting coincidence in his complaint to get the public prosecutor's attention and he was certain that the man remembered his childhood classmate.

The Chief of Security was rough, stern, and sweet all at once. He had coffee made for us from his own personal coffee stash, which he kept in a drawer in his desk. He drew out our welcome, examining us, considering every word we said, calmly and deliberately studying our characters. Finally he sat up and took on the guise of unyielding officialdom: "So Mr. Zaki, you claim that you spoke to the officer that arrested Mr. Rowdy Salih."

"And my friend here's an eyewitness!" Zaki said, pointing to me.

"Well then," the Chief of Security said, "if you saw the officer again, you'd be able to identify him, yes?"

"Of course, sir. I hated him right then and there because he was so rude to me for no reason at all. His face stuck in my mind because I hated him. I'd recognize him in the middle of the city."

"All right then. I'll show you all the officers and you can point him out to me."

"Now you're talking."

"Let's go. Bring your witness with you."

He picked up the phone as he stood up and said he was on his way down. Then he set the phone down and gestured to us to get up.

In the courtyard of the Security Directorate, no fewer than two hundred police officers dressed in their official uniforms were lined up. Starting at the first officer in line, Zaki and I started to examine and scrutinize every face: head-on, both profiles, from far away, from close up. The Honorable Chief of Security was exercising the greatest possible patience and a veteran, professional coolness as if to say, "Let's be done with the two of you once and for all." He was fairly grinning as we moved nearer the last of his officers, but a composed Zaki shook his head and said, "I'm sorry, sir. The officer I spoke to isn't here, but I'm certain he's one of your officers. I'm an actor, and I'm an educated guy, I've been around and I know how an officer acts. Even if he's naked and tries to completely change his appearance."

The Chief of Security looked like he was about to shout, "You speak the truth, my son!" but instead he just smiled. He seemed to blush a little and shook his head as if our honesty had impressed him. He explained that he'd just been testing us to see if we were there for the right reasons. It was true: none of these officers were on duty the night of President Sadat's visit to Jerusalem. His Honor had been trying to bore and pressure us that we might rush through and pick just anybody to get it over with and then the merciful logbook would show that the officer hadn't been working that night and we'd be humiliated in front of His Honor the public prosecutor. But now that he'd made certain we were telling the truth in our complaint and we could be trusted, he was going to take us to the real lineup made up of officers who'd been on duty that night from the Qasr al-Nil precinct all the way to the Khanka precinct. He took us to a conference hall that held more than ten immense conference tables populated by officers in civilian clothes; we figured they were all investigators. They all stood up when we came in, and the Chief of Security barked at Zaki officially, "Go see which one of these guys it was you talked to."

He walked alongside us and took part in the survey, but from the moment we'd entered, Zaki's attention had been drawn to a far corner where two guys sat, looking contemptuous of their colleagues who'd stood up. It was obvious they thought the whole situation was a joke because they'd stayed in their seats and disappeared behind the standing ranks. Zaki separated two officers and they made room for him to pass as he headed toward the far corner to examine the two seated guys. Zaki placed his hand on one of their shoulders and called out, "This is him, sir."

I also gave the man a thorough looking over and found myself crying out, "It is him! There's no question about it."

The officer turned to look arrogantly at Zaki Hamid, but Zaki fixed his strong gaze right on the guy and he wasn't able to fight off Zaki's burning gaze. He looked down for a moment, but then he shot his head up and started shouting hysterically, "You're lying! I don't know you! I've never seen you!"

Zaki Hamid didn't blink an eye, he just stared at him with a sardonic scowl and muttered, "Oh, give it up already!" Then he transformed himself into the officer that night: he leaned his arm on the chair and turned to me as if I were Zaki. It was a brilliant performance, a smashing success: his impression of how the officer sounded, how he talked, all his gestures and tics was spot-on. All the other officers broke out in laughter; some even forgot themselves and began applauding in amazement, looking pitifully at their colleague.

The Chief of Security, though, held his laughter back and regained his composure. Then he said, "Okay, Mr. Zaki. Your work here's done. This officer will be investigated." Then he turned to the officer: "Go wait for me in my office." The Chief walked us to the elevator, warmly shook our hands, and assured us that he'd carry out a thorough investigation in light of all the evidence and that the law would take its course—no need to worry—and that this officer would appear before the public prosecutor that evening.

We waited day after day and Hayat leaked new developments to the newspapers, who'd started calling it the "Case of the Missing Maniac." The next day, though, all the papers published a gag order from the public prosecutor prohibiting any reports about the case while it was still under investigation. But then something else happened; something out of that same old playbook burst in on our lives and further twisted the growing maze of our emotions. We could no longer tell delusion from truth and we got the unmistakable impression that the maze itself was the only truth and that everything else—even our existence—was nothing more than a delusion.

Begin—the Israeli prime minister and veteran terrorist, who had a long record of crimes and slaughters, the man who took great pride in himself for gallantly and heroically killing Arabs, disgracing Palestinians, and insulting Egyptians by announcing to the whole world, in the presence of the Egyptian president himself, that it was his Jewish ancestors who'd built the pyramids—this man was planning to visit Cairo, to return the gesture of Sadat's visit to Jerusalem, accompanied by an official delegation of the highest level in what was known as the exchange of good intentions and rebuilding ties between the two warring countries, Egypt and Israel; as if there'd even been any ties at all before the war!

I was at Maspero the morning of the visit. As usual I went to have coffee with my friend, Ali Faik Zaghloul the broadcaster, in his office. He was busy handing out parts to the actors who were going to take part in the upcoming episode of *The Variety Show*. Almost as soon as I'd sat down, the door opened and in walked Zaki Hamid; he, too, was going to participate in the episode that would be recorded the day after next in the city of Port Said the Fearless. Just as the three of us were beginning to enjoy ourselves, there was a knock at the door and it opened on to a face that was very well known to us all. It was just that he couldn't help but look decidedly unfamiliar on account of his new appearance, his clean, posh clothes: a coat of the most elegant and expensive wool over a silk shirt and a tie from some incomparably world-famous brand and black trousers and stylish shoes, which made the ground itself blush for its carpets. He exclaimed, grinning, as he came toward us: "This can't be! All my friends are here?"

We stood up, utterly astounded, and shouted in unison: "Wagih Farhan? What are you doing here?"

The surprise had bolted us down so we didn't notice that we'd managed to avoid embracing him, but I, for one, felt like I'd fallen into a quasi-coma for a split-second during which I imagined a hand patting me on the shoulder and a voice saying, "I swear I missed you." We sat back down, Zaki and I looking at him closely, perhaps trying to find some old thing we'd known once, more than ten years ago. It really was him: same face, same body even if he'd filled out and taken on the look of easy living and fine dining, that gushing quicksilver tongue you couldn't read any emotions on at all, the same narrow, shifty eyes like fleeting scenes in romantic movies that always end before the good part, those prominent, bronze cheeks. We scanned his features, but failed to detect any life in his eyes; even in his smile, which revealed his big teeth and had once given away the secret of his mysterious misery and toil; it was now like a dead corpse stretched out on the block of his face over a crimson sheet. This young Egyptian, who some ten years ago had been part of our group of friends and shared our love of country, who'd written poetry in Egyptian Arabic about the noble people, the revolution, the coming dawn, and the tragedy of the bad faith of certain higher-ups, who'd published a collection of poetry with an introduction by Salah Jahin, the leader of the vernacular-poetry movement, who'd got stoned with us at Hakeem's den, this same guy was now a diplomatic visitor in Egypt on an Israeli passport along with a high-ranking, official delegation. Was this a hallucination? Had he come to give his blessing? To take pleasure in our misfortune? Or to exact revenge? Or maybe, just maybe, he missed his family in the village of al-Beirum in the Sharqiya province.

It was scarily uncanny how Zaki Hamid and I were thinking the exact same thing—though perhaps it was only natural. Zaki immediately asked him, "Are your parents still alive, Wagih?"

He smiled and in that bursting, bellowing voice of his, said, "I'm hoping I can go see them tomorrow or the day after. It all depends on work, of course. I'm here with Prime Minister Begin's delegation after all."

His voice still retained a tinge of bitterness, a product of his taste for constant complaining and the feeling that he was always being persecuted. Zaki Hamid's face was turned all sorts of colors; it looked to me like he was trying to hold himself back from jumping on him and throttling him. My intuition was right because Ali Faik Zaghloul had also noticed Zaki Hamid's mood and offered him a cigarette, winking only at him and saying, "Smoke. Light up. Don't let it get you down."

Wagih Farhan took no notice of this remark because he—with his great sense of self—was in the middle of telling us a funny story that had happened at the airport when—as he put it—State Security officers tried to arrest him and the Israeli delegation made a huge fuss. It was about to turn into a diplomatic incident at the worst possible moment, but at the last minute Wagih Farhan nipped it in the bud by whipping out his Israeli diplomatic passport, which meant that the Egyptian police had no jurisdiction over him because an Israeli citizen couldn't be arrested during a diplomatic visit as part of a delegation headed by the prime minister himself. The police backed down, defeated and humiliated, and returned his passport with pathetic apologies, but still, Begin's chief of staff decided to berate them and give them a lesson in how to behave. Wagih took great pleasure in the story he recounted. I drifted out of consciousness for a moment and came to to hear him expressing his desire, or rather proclaiming his longing, to visit all the dear places where he'd once been poor and put-upon, especially Ihab al-Azhari's office and the petty cash office, then he looked at me and said he'd thought about coming by my office at the magazine to take me to Hakeem's den to smoke a couple of bowls even though nowadays he only drank whiskey and got high on fancy intoxicants; they looked down on hash in Israel, you know. Zaki Hamid replied that it was Israel who exported the hash and used the money they made to buy planes to bomb Arabs.

Up until that moment, Zaki Hamid had still been leaning toward Talat al-Imbabi's view that Wagih Farhan was an Israeli Jew, planted in Egypt by the Mossad and that after he'd carried out his mission, or they'd determined there was no point in him carrying on, he'd been called back to Israel before he could fall into the hands of Egyptian State Security. But right then, he leaned over to me and whispered that he was convinced it was precisely the opposite: that Egyptian Intelligence had planted Wagih Farhan in Israel to serve as their eyes and ears, but that he'd been discovered and apprehended, and that they'd kept him around to rub it in our faces and prove they were better than us. Likewise, he could tell them all they wanted to know about life in Egypt. That was the only way to explain why they'd brought him along to Egypt as part of an official Israeli delegation; it was a spiteful gesture intended to humiliate Egyptian Intelligence, one big fuck-you. That was the only way to explain Wagih Farhan's status and elevated sense of self. More actors came into Faik Zaghloul's office and had trouble finding places to sit, so Wagih Farhan stood up to say his goodbyes and told me that he might have a chance to see me again. I stood up as did Zaki Hamid, who placed a hand on Wagih's shoulder and pushed him affectionately toward the door as if he were being friendly: "You said you were dying to smoke a couple of bowls, well then, the sooner the better. Come on, let's go, let's go! There are so many friends who are dying to see you."

Wagih Farhan said he'd love to, but the only thing was that he had to go by his uncle's in Old Cairo to say hello and drop off some presents he'd brought for his cousins from Israel. If we didn't mind going along with him to his uncle's house, we could all go out again in the lovely afternoon, he said, and plus it would make him very happy to have some companions like us with him at his uncle's house for lunch. I thought that Zaki Hamid would be too disgusted and find a way to get out of the offer with some excuse or other, but he leapt at the invitation with a winning smile and pointed at him simply—*let's go!* At that point, it dawned on me that Zaki was planning to sift Wagih Farhan through a silken screen until he could find out every last thing about him, but what really surprised me was that Wagih had no qualms about anything. He didn't even feel like there was anything to be ashamed of. He never once gave any indication that he wanted to get away from us because he was afraid that we'd remind him of what he'd done; to the contrary, he stuck with us with a great deal of good feeling. I mean, who knew? Maybe deep down he thought of himself as some kind of hero. Maybe he wanted to regale us with funny stories from his annals of heroism. It was more likely, perhaps, that to him we were just sources of the intelligence he was hoping to gather. It was clear that he'd been assigned to mingle with intellectuals and find out just how much Egyptians believed in this unexpected sidestep and whether the talk of peace was just a Sadatian wish to get out of an embarrassing predicament or whether there was deep public support for his proclaimed initiative.

His uncle's building looked older than Old Cairo itself. It was located in a narrow alley beside the metro station behind the Old Cairo police precinct. We climbed up the still-solid, marble spiral staircase to the third floor. There was such an intimate magic to those old buildings and their apartments with double French doors. The glass pane had a little window that opened set within it and it was covered on the outside by an iron grate and on the inside draped with precious, frilly white curtains. Above the lintel, there was a small electric night-light, and beside the door, there was an electric doorbell. Immediately below the window pane, there was a rusted old oval nameplate made of copper engraved with the words:

Gamal Farhan
Director of Transportation
Egyptian National Railways

The door opened onto a short and narrow corridor; on the left, immediately past the entrance, were two adjacent doors opening onto the kitchen and the bathroom. There was barely enough room to turn around in the bathroom under the rusted showerhead, which was certainly all clogged up. In the kitchen, there was a table—brand: Ideal—covered in a ratty old oilcloth, burnt through here and there, surrounded by four plastic chairs. We carried on into the room at the end of the corridor. Through the open French door, we could see the dainty little balcony that overlooked the alley and whose iron railing was bowed like the skeleton of a duck. In this room, there was a bed, a wardrobe, and a modestly upholstered sofa. We sat on the sofa, but al-Hagg Gamal preferred to sit on a cushion on the ground. The resemblance between him and his brother's son was clear to see: same face, same features, same voice, same prominent teeth, but the man's Egyptian goodness was as clear as the Nile in the depths of a valley. He told us about Wagih's upbringing, made unhappy by his hobby of writing poems and song lyrics and reading books, which kept his mind off of all the jobs they tried to wrangle for him. Then he explained to us that his nephew didn't deserve to be blamed for what he'd done because Egyptian Intelligence had gone after him, harassed him when all he was doing was trying to earn a living. They breathed down his neck wherever he went. At first they'd thought he was a communist, but when it became clear that he was no more than a poor kid trying to make an honest living, they figured he was an easy mark and decided they'd make him work for them—for free, of course—as an informant against his colleagues working in radio, TV, and the press. Wagih was naive and didn't know how to play the game. The poor schmuck couldn't think of any way out except to escape to the one place where Egyptian Police didn't dare to tread: Israel.

Over a lunch of duck, mulukhiya, rice, and baked okra casserole at al-Hagg Gamal Farhan's apartment, Zaki Hamid asked Wagih Farhan to tell us the story—with all its boring details—of how he'd managed to escape Egypt and get to Israel. He broke out with that natural vigor of his. He told us that he'd sneaked away to Libya to look for work, but not forty-eight hours after he'd arrived, the Libyan authorities ordered him to leave the country. When they summoned him to the Security Directorate to inform him that he was being deported, they warned him that the Egyptian

231

authorities had put his name on a list of people who weren't allowed to travel and that they were going to extradite him from Libya sooner or later so the best thing was for him to leave the country now. They didn't want him to cause them any embarrassment with the authorities of their ally, Egypt. The first thing he'd done when he arrived in Libya was to record some stories and poems for Libyan Radio because a hot-shot Egyptian broadcaster friend of his worked there so he hurried off to collect his pay and also borrowed some money from his Egyptian friend. Then he took his wife and they got on the first ship going to Italy. Almost as soon as the ship had set off, he noticed there were some Egyptians on board and that they were keeping close to him and his wife: being imposingly friendly, trying to draw them into conversation, and when they got talking they hinted to them that a few of them knew how they could find decent work in Italy. When the ship docked in Naples, he wanted to get away from those hangers-on as quickly as he could, but his plan was severely compromised when he found he couldn't communicate at all with the staff at the port. Some of the hangers-on caught up with him and interceded with the staff, explaining that he was a tourist passing through town for a few hours. Then they told him to wait for them by the exit, but as soon as he got past the port gates, he and his wife jumped into the first taxi that rolled up to them. He hadn't even told the driver where he wanted to go when he looked back to see the hangers-on looking everywhere for him. They finally got into the cars that were waiting for them, which had obviously been sent by the Egyptian embassy, and that was when they spotted him in the taxi. He shouted at the driver in his deplorable English, "The Israeli consulate, please." The Egyptians in the car followed him the whole way there, but he quickly got out and slid through the door of the consulate leaving the taxi driver all the lire he'd changed on the ship.

He demanded to see the consul about an important matter, so after a thorough search and quasi-arrest he was taken into see him. Wagih laid out the situation as directly as he could and his candor proved effective. He told the consul that he was an Egyptian resistance poet and that he could no longer stand living in Egypt on account of this and that, and that he'd decided with all his heart to become an Israeli citizen so he could take advantage of Israel's open democratic government and live a life of dignity with the freedom to express himself, which he'd never had in his own country on account of Egypt's current dictatorship. He told them that he was prepared to undergo a whole battery of tests to prove his intentions were sincere. The truth of the matter was that it would've been impossible for him—or for anyone else for that matter—not to be arrested by the Israeli authorities after having barged into the consulate. Frantic phone calls went back and forth between the consulate and the embassy, and the embassy and the Foreign Affairs Ministry, and then eventually the Internal Affairs Ministry. Long story short: the sparrow had fallen into the cage and that was all there was to it. Wagih and his wife had to spend nearly a month living in a residence adjacent to the consulate, being examined, investigated, interrogated about anything and everything. He felt totally cut off from the world for a long time—he wasn't sure how long exactly—but when he came to, he and his wife were Egyptian refugees standing in the Israeli international airport and being granted political asylum. They helped him find a place to live, got him a job working for Israeli Radio's Arabic Service, and monitored him for a long time although they knew that no spy would ever try to infiltrate the country in such a hamfisted way. More and more sociologists, literary critics, historians, political analysts, and commentators came to ask him for help explaining some popular expressions, customs, and beliefs, and these people all vouched for him as a decent, untainted guy who was telling the truth about choosing freedom and democracy. They lobbied on his behalf and he was eventually granted Israeli citizenship while at the same time—Look at the Liberty and Progress!—they didn't demand he renounce his Egyptian citizenship.

The food had been stuck in our throats for a long time by then; we were so revolted we couldn't swallow or even spit up. Perhaps it started with the first bite and soon everything looked to us like the flesh of children's corpses—who knows, maybe the students from the Bahr al-Baqar Elementary School. We began to feel a painful loathing, and spasms of agony tore through our bowels. Zaki Hamid and I began tapping our feet violently beneath the table; we both wanted to run to the bathroom and vomit, but I was feeling very ill. I put my napkin down and said, "Thanks, Lord, for this meal," and then I stood up and asked where the bathroom was. Al-Hagg Gamal showed me the way, all the while complaining that we hadn't eaten enough. I shut the door of the bathroom and struggled not to make any disgusting noises, but in the end nothing came up except for some thin liquid and bitterness, febrile waves, and a sick stomach. I eventually washed my hands and face and went out to see Zaki standing there by the door. I waited a long while for Zaki to return, but Wagih Farhan was still eating as eagerly as ever. Never in my life had I seen anyone who could eat like that—literally stuffing his cheeks—and still be able to talk animatedly and clearly as if his teeth worked independently of his tongue.

We exchanged a look and then Zaki slapped his forehead and said, "Damn. I forgot I'm supposed to be at the studio right now." He stood up and I followed suit, saying that I was part of the same production, but that we could get together the next day at five in the evening at Groppi's on Suliman Street near Hakeem's den, which he knew so well. When he just carried on eating, I thanked God that I'd managed to get out of there without having to shake his hand. "Bye." I pushed Zaki ahead of me and we opened the front door for ourselves and left. We got into Zaki's car, which drove us itself to Hakeem's den where we plunged headlong into a deep, focused, deathly silent stoning binge that lasted for at least three hours. The whole time I was sitting there I felt that my mind was leaking down into my heart in hot, internal tears that flowed behind two inflexible masks, horrifying everyone around us. Even when we left the hash den, we could only wave to each other as we parted, each of us heading down his own distant alleyway leading to two different paths beneath the same screeching, cloudy sky of the same city that was so crowded it was beginning to feel like a graveyard.

REVIVAL

Two days after our breath-stifling encounter with Wagih Farhan, I went to Hakeem's den in the afternoon and found Zaki Hamid sitting there alone. He told me he'd just come back from Port Said, where they'd recorded Ali Faik Zaghloul's *The Variety Show*. He'd brought back some good hash from there, he said, and he thought he'd try it before he went back home. Then he showed it to me, and seeing I was mesmerized by the egg-sized clump in his hand, he cautioned me, "Just so you know, this is for me and Hayat."

"So are we going to try it or not?"

"Of course, you're going to try it." He cut off a couple of morsels the size of a jujube, balled them up, and placed them in my hand. "This is for you. You can smoke it all by yourself, just for you, and I'll pitch in for this whole session."

"You're the greatest, you know that?"

He said that Ibrahim al-Qammah had just been there and smoked ten bowls with him and left. Then he started telling me about Port Said and all the excruciating suffering he'd seen in the city and about the emergence of a new class of currency traders who'd managed to get their hands on the beach and Lake Manzala. I told him about a novel I'd just finished by a Jewish-Romanian author called *The 25th Hour*, which depicted the concentration camps where the Nazis sent the Jews and how the Jews were driven out of their homes with a cruelty the mind simply couldn't comprehend. After I'd summarized it for him, I told him how amazed I was at the Jew's ability to craft the story with such artistic talent that an ordinary reader couldn't help but be affected, couldn't help but pity the Jews, couldn't help but sympathize with them and feel guilty about what had happened. I said that if the novel had been translated into Arabic and printed in such a splendid edition by a Beirut publishing house then that meant that the Zionist propaganda we'd been fed since almost the beginning of the century had worked. Zaki Hamid said that if I were a real man, I would throw it right back in the Jewish-Romanian author's face: "Turn the tables on him."

"What do you mean, Zaki?"

He said that I should adapt it into a miniseries for television, but turn the Jewish hero into a Palestinian and make him suffer all the same indignities, torture, and dislodgment, but this time at the hands of the new Nazis: the Jewish Zionists who were at the root of Nazi ideology because the truth was that the myth of the superlative Germanic race was, in fact, only developed to confront the myth of God's chosen people, which Jews had used to vaunt themselves over everyone else. My imagination ran wild for a spell and I instantly began imagining the whole scope of the piece: all its drama, tension, and lessons. But then I suddenly realized that the atmosphere had become colored with a diaphanous veil of magical, amazing fantasy as if everything in front of me, both people and objects, was behind panes of colored glass, shimmering and sparkling, and I knew for sure that the hash we were smoking was very good indeed. I decided to take advantage of it and dive down to my deepest depths to search there for something that would help me really understand myself; that was what I always hoped to get out of every new variety of hash I smoked.

Life, then, seemed to me nothing more than a dream that dared you to watch, but then suddenly a scream rang down the alley and shook the walls of the den; our heads—still attached to our necks—crashed against a stone floor. There it was again, longer this time, and we began to come to, panting like frightened sparrows. There was as much excitement in the

236

scream as there was distress. It was soon translated into words, breaking in on us in the den in the shape of a woman who looked like a big basket of sweet potatoes. There was no question that this was Umm Yahya. The shock of the surprise stupefied us, we couldn't tell whether she was trilling in joy and delight or screaming and wailing in anguish. A long moment passed before we fully understood what she was saying: "Rowdy Salih's back, boys! Hakeem, Rowdy Salih's here! Hey you lot, wasn't he your friend? Look, he's back!"

Necks were craned, gazes fixed on the door in anticipation of Rowdy Salih's entrance. Hakeem stood up and started dusting off his gallabiya as if Salih were going to come in and go back to filling bowls straight away. Then he asked, "Umm Yahya, where is he? Why isn't he coming?"

"He's down there in the rubble where he sleeps getting rowdy."

Zaki cried out joyfully, "He deserves it, man. He's got it coming."

We all surged out, running, cutting through the courtyards of ostensibly occupied houses. We plunged through the ruins and came to the house where all that was left standing were the walls of the innermost room, which Salih had taken as his shelter. We stumbled over rocks, bricks, children's feces, until we got through to the ruined room. We saw Rowdy Salih, squatting there, resting his back against the wall, his head lying on his shoulder. He had a Coke bottle—cap ripped off, filled with a mixture of denatured alcohol and Coca-Cola—in his hand. On the ground beside him, there was another empty bottle and some leftover, rotten-looking pickles on a sheet of schoolbook paper. A gleeful Hakeem bellowed, "Hey, Salih!" It looked like he was smiling; the smile took up his entire face as usual, but his eyes were shut. Zaki went up to him. He held his head up and slapped his cheeks. He leaned him back against the wall, but his head slouched down.

A pale Hakeem went nearer and grabbed his wrist and at the same time Zaki put his hand over his heart. I crouched down in front of him, trembling; there was no life left in him. Hakeem let go of his arm and it fell. Zaki took his hand off and crouched down beside me, looking distressed and turned to me: "You know, I think he died only very recently. At most half an hour, otherwise he'd have gone stiff."

Hakeem cradled him in his arms and broke out wailing. Zaki was weeping, too, as he stood up, but he said, "There's no time for crying now, Hakeem. What are we going to do?"

"Help me carry him. We'll take him to my place until we can figure something out."

Zaki screamed at him, "No one touch him until the police come. They have to write a report and the prosecutor has to examine the body. He's been missing for a long time and the government said he didn't even exist. They have to investigate what happened. How else are we going to get a death certificate and permission to bury him? You and Umm Yahya and Sabir, go to the Qasr al-Nil precinct and report what you saw. Don't worry about a thing, me and Hayat'll take care of everything. We'll give him a respectable, twenty-four-carat burial like he deserves!" Hakeem nodded in agreement. "One of you guys stay with him," he said to the gathered crowd, then he turned to me and said, "You and me are party to the case so we should probably get the hell out of here right about now."

Zaki and I left. Cutting down Adli Street, we went to sit in the garden at Groppi. We cried hot, heavy tears, drank bitter coffee, chain smoked, and tried to get our heads around this mysterious turn of events, but we failed. Was there foul play here? Had he really been in police custody all this time? There was no question that if he'd been free, he wouldn't have stayed away from Hakeem's den for a single minute. Should we take the case to the courts to show that the government lied, and demand to see the autopsy? Or should we just disappear from the scene entirely and not get ourselves into the kind of trouble we simply couldn't handle? I mean we were both just at the beginning of ambitious careers and we knew full well that all the literary and artistic institutions in the country—the press, publishing, singing, acting, theater, cinema, radio, TV—were all the property of the government. In a country like ours, it wasn't unheard of that someone's future could be cut short because of a single innocent word that didn't please a certain someone; the future of Egypt itself was subject to the whims of just a single individual.

We left without coming to a definite decision, but we met at noon the next day at Hakeem's den. Umm Yahya had swept the alley and rinsed it with water mixed with fragrant soap. The neighborhood was shrouded in a dignified silence; it was so dignified it seemed slightly comic, just like Rowdy Salih himself, who combined a special balance of dignity and comedy that rarely succeeded in others. Ibrahim al-Qammah, his eyes swollen from crying, was sitting on the bench and there was a lot of noise coming from the house that was attached to the den. Ibrahim said that Hakeem had gone bright and early to the police station to get the burial permit and that the prosecutor had examined the body and allowed it to be taken to the house. He said Umm Yahya had brought someone to wash the body and he—Ibrahim—had brought the best fabric he could find from one of the shops whose displays he designed for a burial shroud. Zaki asked where we were going to bury him.

"At our family plot. We've got a plot near Imam al-Shafi'i and I called the gravedigger at dawn to tell him to prepare himself," Ibrahim said.

Hayat al-Barri showed up a little while later, looking genuinely breathtaking; it was the prettiest sorrow I've ever seen: plush black jeans, black blouse, her long, straight neck, her face full of meaning, secrets, and sophistication despite its pure, simple features. The Marlboro cigarette between her fingers was also sad, immolating slowly, its ashes left holding together, refusing to fall apart. "Is the body inside?" she asked. We nodded.

She went over to Hakeem's house and leaned in with her top half, surveying the darkness of the room inside. From behind, her long back looked like a spaceship orbiting twin planets. She disappeared inside and we soon heard sobbing and interrupted moans and Umm Yahya muttering soothing words. A few minutes later, Qamar al-Mahruqi and his three friends, Mursi Khallaf, Walid Rashid, and Wagdi al-Wakil, came in and we knew instantly that Ibrahim had called them the night before from the call office in Adli Street. Then Abd al-Wudud came, and Faruq al-Gamal came with his caricaturist friend who'd become his constant companion ever since they'd both been given jobs at a weekly satirical magazine. At around eight in the evening, Hakeem showed up with the burial permit. We started talking about how to move him to the cemeteries at Imam and we'd only just started disagreeing about the route we'd take, when an old man dressed in a somber suit came in led by one of the children of the alley. As soon as he walked in, he said, "I'm looking for Ms. Hayat al-Barri, please."

Zaki looked at him: "Who should we say is looking for her, sir?"

"I work for the undertaker she contacted."

"Yes, I'm Hayat. Did you bring the car?"

"It's waiting outside."

We all helped to carry the body down the long alley to the unmistakable hearse, which was parked prominently on Marouf Street.

Ibrahim al-Qammah and Hakeem got in beside the driver. I rode with Zaki in his car, and Umm Yahya and Hakeem's wife rode in Hayat's VW. Qamar rode with Mursi, al-Gamal rode with Walid, and the caricaturist rode with Wagdi. The procession of cars proceeded as if linked together by an invisible chain. We traveled through downtown: Ibrahim al-Qammah had insisted that the procession pass down Marouf Street to Antikkhana Street to Abd al-Muneim Riyad Square down Ramses Street and Abd al-Khaliq Tharwat Street and Suliman Street down to Tahrir Square and over to Lazoghli Square, crossing Mubtadayan and Zaynhum on its way to the Imam cemeteries. It was a lovely and solemn procession and it got everyone's attention; it attracted many cars on either side, curious heads sticking out through windows and asking with appropriately sad reverence in advance, "Excuse me, but who died?" With the same reverence and gravity, we answered, "Rowdy Salih. God grant you health."

People's smiles disappeared and some reacted as if they'd known him very well: "No, that can't be true! *We live unto God and unto Him we shall return.*"

At the cemetery, the workers took over and placed the body onto the bier. A blind sheikh the gravedigger had brought came over and stood in front of the bier, facing the Kaaba. We stood behind him in a single line, including Hayat al-Barri, Umm Yahya, and Hakeem's wife. We performed the prayer and stood there with genuine piety, and when the body began to slide down, disappearing into the hollow of the grave, we were all overcome by teary grief. Hayat al-Barri, though, crouched down, leaning against the tombstone, her head in her hands, fragile and pale. She was looking down at the ground and moving her lips as tears like dewdrops fell from her rose cheeks. It was plain to see that she—the former hardened Marxist—was muttering some Quranic verses; maybe the Kursi verse or the Ya-Sin chapter. We distributed a lot of pounds, most of which came out of Mursi and Walid's wallets, and then we went back to Hakeem's den with three kilos of kebab and kofta and a mountain of bread and containers of tahini and salad that Wagdi al-Wakil had bought, as none of us had eaten a thing since we'd heard news of the death. We sat on the bare floor, spread the food out, and ate hungrily. There were a lot of leftovers and Hakeem wrapped them up carefully and set them on the bench, saying out of habit, "Maybe Salih'll come later and want to eat." We broke down, weeping again, and he said, "I swear I meant to say Sabir."

He followed his wife into the house and came back out carrying a plastic radio—brand: The Voice of the Arabs—and set it down on the windowsill. He turned it on and tuned it to Holy Quran Radio. The pious, august voice of Sheikh Mahmud Khalil al-Hussari filled the air. We sat back, our heads lowered, and listened with a natural diffidence. Hakeem squatted down and started packing a set of bowls that would inevitably give strength to the wings of our imaginations so that we could soar the heights of the ascending verses and their irrefutable radiance, which gave the lie to all falsehood and untruth.

That was the last time we all got together. Very soon afterward the government sprang into action and shut down all the hash dens, even knocking down the market in al-Batiniya. It was easy to see that the move was only done in collaboration with the major, highly influential smugglers who were trying to get rid of hashish, which was both inconvenient and headache-causing when it came to trafficking and distribution. This was all in preparation for drowning the country in a flood of cocaine, heroin, pills, and Maxitone Forte syringes. These were light to transport, expensive, and their profits could easily satisfy the ambitions of everyone who participated in the trafficking, even if only by hurrying it past and pretending not to see. The only drug left for the toiling classes to get their fix was a type of Sudanese weed known as Bango; a five-pound bunch could get a whole party stoned.

Several difficult years passed and we lived through monumental events that completely changed the course of our lives. The best died down, while the worst rose up. Rowdiness reached the peak of absurdity. The Camp David peace agreement was sealed with the Israeli enemy and great writers started telling us to love our Israeli neighbors. The enemies of the July Revolution got their assets, positions, political parties, and newspapers back. Extremist Islamist groups assassinated Sadat. The public sector was sold off. Intellectuals and the elites in every field fled to the Oil Countries and Europe. Marxism–Leninism collapsed in uproarious scandal and the Soviet Union broke up and vanished in only a few minutes as if it had never been. The Arabs crawled over one another to make peace with Israel and the dreadful Gulf War was launched so the Americans could occupy the Gulf. Hayat al-Barri divorced Zaki Hamid and married a Dutch professor and moved with him to the States. Mahasin Asim divorced Qamar al-Mahruqi after having given him a son, who constantly defied him. The workshop failed and Qamar was left in pieces, going from failure to failure. Zaki Hamid, on the other hand, became a big star. The government's boys took control of all the newspapers and the Egyptian press was cut off from the rest of the world: it was no more than the diary of the ruling regime now. Investors and capitalists got their hands on every essential lifeline in the country. Noble values lost all meaning: freedom, dignity, morality, patriotism had all become mere words with bad reputations. More husbands killed their wives, more girls were abducted.

I got my own share of all this grand rowdiness. I'd just barely been able to get married and move into a modest apartment that still lacked running water. I bought a car—brand: Ramses—for five hundred pounds. For some strange reason, the lovely luxury cars that had recently flooded the country took a decidedly adversarial position vis-à-vis me and my car; apparently they looked at it as leftover scrap from the accursed July Revolution. That car actually was quite stupid and stubborn and wicked; its only pleasure in life was to break down at the most embarrassing moments. One day, it broke down on me in Mohandiseen, a few minutes before sunset, so I parked it on the shoulder and got in a taxi by the ramp to the Sixth of October Bridge to go pick up the mechanic at his workshop in Bulaq. As we headed toward Abd al-Muneim Riyad Square and the Maspero Building to our left and the Nile Hilton to our right came nearer, I was intrigued to see a big rowdy crowd of men, women, and children standing on the walkway at the side of the bridge. We slowed down to see if there'd been an accident involving one of the cars parked along the right-hand side, but what I saw took my breath away. Rowdy Salih was standing right there in the flesh. He had that same mulatto face, that same white hair, like a skullcap of snowflakes, that same towering stature beneath the dazzling spotlights. I got out of the taxi and ran toward Rowdy Salih with a manic longing born of the tempestuous disgrace of all those years gone past. We were still getting over the humiliation caused by the U.S.'s routing of our ally Iraq and forcing them out of Kuwait, which once and for all extinguished the last candle tended by my generation: Pan-Arabism. I was completely lost in a labyrinth of my own emotions and I really needed Rowdy Salih then to fill my head with that wise, primal logic of his and explain away my many despairs, which had piled up so high I'd forgotten what had caused them to begin with.

I pushed through the crowd; I wanted to throw myself in Rowdy Salih's arms. But then I was stopped by huge hands right at the moment when the truth hit me. Now that I was closer, I could see that the Rowdy Salih standing before me was actually Zaki Hamid the actor filming a scene for a movie. He was leaning against the iron railing of the bridge, sighing and looking out glumly over the Martyr Abd al-Muneim Riyad Square, which teemed with countless cars, an insane racket, and clouds of black smoke. His voice—that same cherished, familiar voice—began to unfurl with threats of looming disaster like Tiresias in a Greek tragedy: "God made the world a rowdy place and then he filled it with rowdy people. Everybody here's rowdy. They're all rowdy 'cause all they want to do is get rowdy and they either get to or they don't. And everybody here's run-down. But they're all run-down in their own way. And me, I'm the king of the run-down 'cause I'm run-down in every which way."

Suddenly all the lights went out and the city was plunged into a pitch-black darkness. Slowly we began bumping into one another like bodies turning in a grave even narrower than al-Hagg Gamal Farhan's bathroom.

Modern Arabic Literature

The American University in Cairo Press is the world's leading publisher of Arabic literature in translation.

For a full list of available titles, please go to:

mal.aucpress.com